PRAISE FOR *BEAUTIFUL SHINING PEOPLE*

'Cyberpunk meets *bildungsroman* – a real joy' Oscar de Muriel

'A fascinating exploration of what it means to be human in a world where everything can be faked, and an alarming projection into a not-too-distant and all-too-plausible future ... wonderful, insightful and thoughtful' James Oswald

'Totally engrossing from the start – the story, characters and settings will linger in your imagination long after you've finished ... truly wonderful' Jonathan Whitelaw

'Exquisite world-building, this book had me invested from the very first page. Vivid plot and irresistible characters and a real tug at the soul ... you'll drown in it' Lisa Bradley

'Set in a near-future Japan where technology has all but rendered human productivity redundant, *Beautiful Shining People* is a life-affirming book about what it is to be human: to live, to dream, to hope, to love. And at a time when we most need reminding of these things' David F. Ross

'Outstanding! Sci-fi showing how the past might impact on the future; part coming of age, part boy meets girl, with a strong sense of place and a glimpse into a terrifying and very plausible future' Michael J. Malone

'A striking and strange novel, about beautiful shining people in all their strangeness – and a searing statement about the dangerously thin lines between utopia and dystopia' B. S. Casey

'Masterful ... truly breathtaking, achingly beautiful passages of writing, from internal reflection to vivid descriptions of the surroundings. Grothaus's second novel moves for the most part relatively slowly, ebbing and flowing smoothly as it builds anticipation and suspense before coming together in a thrilling, captivating conclusion' *The Bookbag*

'This book was incredible ... I couldn't bear put it down'
Sophia Eck

'Devastatingly beautiful. It made me smile, it made me weep, it made me turn the pages faster and faster, holding my breath in suspense ... quite simply immense' From Belgium with Booklove

'The story is underpinned by mystery and suspense, but it is so wonderfully textured and nuanced that it is also so much more ... A truly beautiful story of friendship, trust and love, and it's most definitely highly recommended' Jen Med's Book Reviews

WHAT READERS ARE SAYING...

★★★★★

'Truly epic'

'I don't think I'll ever get this book out of my mind'

'The writing, the themes, are utterly beautiful'

'A modern classic'

'I am broken'

'A master storyteller'

'Extraordinary writing ... this book is very, very special'

'Thrilling ... thought-provoking and so powerful'

PRAISE FOR MICHAEL GROTHAUS

LONGLISTED for the CWA John Creasey NEW BLOOD Dagger

'Gloriously funny but dark as hell, you will laugh and recoil in equal measure' *Sunday Express*

'By turns comic and shocking, an extraordinary debut from a striking new voice' Michael Marshall Smith

'Complex, inventive and a genuine shocker, this is the very opposite of a comfort read' *Guardian*

'One of the twenty-five Most Irresistible Hollywood Novels' *Entertainment Weekly*

'Engrossing ... a captivating story that manages to be funny, sinister and surprising' *New York Daily News*

'A thrilling and highly original debut that cuts to the dark heart of celebrity and pornography. Michael Grothaus is one to watch' Eva Dolan

'Startling, inventive, funny and disturbing, compelling and oddly beautiful – *Epiphany Jones* is a novel that marks the arrival of a truly talented writer' Kevin Wignall

'The emotional range is astounding – Grothaus is an exceptional talent' J. M. Hewitt

'Grothaus writes with a delicate fluency that contrasts with the depravity of his subject matter. Humour and emotions: what more could you ask for in a thriller?' Maxim Jakubowski

'A real seat-of-the-pants read, and utterly uncompromising. It's graphic, visceral, mordantly funny, thought-provoking and at times profoundly moving' Raven Crime Reads

'This is gutsy, courageous, crazy crime writing ... A highly original debut that's disturbing, funny, grotesque and brilliant' Craig Sisterson

'Tragic, brutal, shocking – and magnificent' K. E. Coles

Beautiful Shining People

ABOUT THE AUTHOR

Michael Grothaus is a novelist, journalist and author of non-fiction. His writing has appeared in *Fast Company*, *VICE*, the *Guardian*, *Litro Magazine*, the *Irish Times*, *Screen*, *Quartz* and others. His debut novel, *Epiphany Jones*, a story about sex trafficking among the Hollywood elite, was longlisted for the CWA John Creasey (New Blood) Dagger and named one of the twenty-five 'Most Irresistible Hollywood Novels' by *Entertainment Weekly*. His first non-fiction book is *Trust No One: Inside the World of Deepfakes*, published by Hodder & Stoughton. The book examines the human impact that artificially generated video will have on individuals and society in the years to come. *Beautiful Shining People* is speculative literary fiction set in Tokyo.

Other titles by Michael Grothaus
available from Orenda Books:

Epiphany Jones

Beautiful Shining People

Michael Grothaus

**ORENDA
BOOKS**

Orenda Books
16 Carson Road
West Dulwich
London SE21 8HU
www.orendabooks.co.uk

First published in the United Kingdom by Orenda Books 2023
Copyright © Michael Grothaus 2023

A catalogue record for this book is available from the British Library.

ISBN 978-1-914585-64-7
eISBN 978-1-914585-65-4

Typeset in Garamond by typesetter.org.uk

Printed and bound by CPI Group (UK) Ltd, Croydon CR0 4YY

For sales and distribution, please contact
info@orendabooks.co.uk or visit www.orendabooks.co.uk.

For m.e. & k.n.

1 – The cusp of a new world.

Everything before me looks like another world, one normally hidden from the ordinary.

A patchwork of illuminated shapes stretches into the distance. The soft blinking of a thousand antennas. The drones silently gliding across the night. Behind them, glowing hues mist vast swaths of the landscape – a kaleidoscope of colours suggesting even stranger lands within this strange expanse.

Yet, as I look into the sky, I'm reminded that I'm solidly earth-bound. That this isn't some otherly world I've been transported to. My eyes adjust to the two artificial stations, the jagged silver crescents suspended between here and the natural moon. One American, the other Chinese. Both locked in their endless, paranoid orbital dance, neither yet finished, but each already suspicious of its incomplete neighbour.

The sound of a bell sinks my eyes back to the infinite city before me. On the narrow side-street below, a man rides his bicycle, its basket stuffed with groceries. He rings his bell again, warning the stray cat lounging outside a FamilyMart to get out of the path. At the corner, a woman watches a stream on her phone as she waits for the bus. On the next street over, a car ferries someone through the Tokyo night.

Yes, there's no mistake: this is the ordinary world with cats and convenience stores and a never-ending supply of content.

I glance at the time. Already quarter to eleven. Sleep seems futile, but I promised myself I'd try – so I at least have a shot of making the excursion I've missed the last three mornings. So yet again my lids don't close as dawn is breaking. I step back into the apartment and slide the balcony door shut. I strip to my boxers and take a piss. At the sink with its too-large mirror, I brush my teeth. As always, my eyes stay focused above my chest.

I crawl into bed and tell the apartment to turn out everything but the bedside lamp.

The clock says it's now an hour to midnight – but nothing, not a hint of tiredness.

This damn jet lag.

I pull my backpack from the floor and feel inside. My passport. The brochure. The paperback I've been reading. But it's too cerebral. It's the kind of novel that makes you think instead of making you sleepy. I need something dull. The magazine – the one the surgeon let me take this afternoon after his nurse noticed the person in the examination room was the person on the cover in the waiting room.

I'm not even sure what the publication is. Its language is set to Japanese. The cover shows the latest flagships from Samsung, Avance and Huawei, each rotating as Japanese script materialises and dotted lines grow and point out various features of the competing metalenses. But the cover scrolls, and it's now the picture of me taken my second day here. I'm standing next to a hive of quantum servers. I've worn that sweater every day for the last three. Mercifully, the cover scrolls again, now showing some kind of agrarian bot – then the sequence repeats.

I give up trying to find the language setting and toss the magazine back into my backpack. I think of calling Mom, but instead, I take out the brochure.

The models in its photos look so joyful – but I guess that's the point. On the inside flap, a good-looking man is frozen in a mid-air leap, about to spike a volleyball. And his smile ... well, I'd have that smile, too, if I were in his body. But the doc was honest. Even post-procedure, it won't look completely normal. Still ... just hearing what *could* be done, I felt like I was standing on the cusp of a new world.

The cusp of a new world. An odd phrase, I know. Almost old-fashioned, yet it's the one that popped into my head up in his office with its floor-to-ceiling windows overlooking Tokyo's expanse. I was on the cusp of a new world in which I could be as close to normal as possible, as close as I've ever been to all those millions of people working and living and strolling around with each other on the streets below.

The surgeon wrote his fee on the last page in yen and dollars and said to contact him if I decide to proceed. I read the brochure twice more, then fold it closed and set it on the nightstand.

Sixteen after eleven.

I turn out the light and shut my eyes.

When I next spy the time, it's eleven twenty-three.

Eleven thirty-nine.

At eleven forty-seven, red creeps across the room as silently as a shadow. Through the balcony's glass door, I catch the dim safety light of a window-washer drone as it glides by...

Screw it.

I dress and grab my backpack. I take the elevator to street level. The October air is chillier down here than on my heated balcony. The trio of vending machines give me my bearings, and I turn and follow the maze of narrow pavements and pedestrian alleyways until I spot the 7-Eleven on the corner, where I make a left onto a main artery full of darkened restaurants with their plastic foods displayed behind panes of glass.

The mist of multicoloured light ahead signals the right direction. Yet despite all its metascreens blaring bright, when I reach Shibuya and its famous scramble crossing, I find even this part of Tokyo makes time for sleep. Bots doing janitorial work behind department stores' locked glass or those doing street maintenance almost out-number the people still out. I cross intersection after intersection, but the only places open seem to be noisy pachinko parlours or smoky bars. I realise I've circled the entire scramble when I come back to a Starbucks that's been closed for an hour.

Terrific, I think, feeling like a batter who's turned up long after the game's ended.

Leaning against an empty bike rack, I pull my backpack's straps tight and fold my arms across my chest. My eyes drift from the cars moving in sync, to a bot polishing the floor inside a Uniqlo, to a glaring meta ad for Docomo looping four storeys up on a high-rise across the scramble. And as the surrounding hues go from blue-purple to pink-orange, someone shrieks. It's one of a pair of stragglers pressing their flapping coats against their bodies in response to a gust that's struck as they're crossing the scramble.

Are they out, fighting the wind, because of jet lag, too?

They make it to the other side as the streetlights go green and the cars waiting on the scramble's edges recommence their journeys in perfect synchronisation, indifferent to the night's conditions. All the while, the pink-orange glow of a gigantic cartoonish bunny creature advertising I don't know what washes over everything. Yet soon, even its light gives way. Now the harsh white of an NHK clip featuring the day's top story casts itself across all. The anchor mutely speaks as Japanese and English subtitles appear below him.

It's about a scandal that rocked China last week. A party leader has been cleared of wrongdoing after a viral video showed him beating a prostitute in a hotel room, duct tape balled into her mouth. The footage caused outrage across the country, the subtitled anchor says, but Chinese officials say their investigation proves it was a deep-fake created by 'a foreign adversary' to sow fury in Chinese society. The officials said a forensic deconstruction revealed the lighting on the man's earlobe in a few frames wasn't consistent with the air density in the room. It's not something you could tell with the naked eye, or even with commercial detection software, but given time – just days in this case – the power of China's AI allegedly cracked it. If it really was a deepfake created by a foreign state, the anchor says, it's believed to be the first that's broken into China's intranet in over a year.

'*Konbanwa*,' a voice says.

It's one of the few Japanese words I've memorised. It means, 'good evening'.

The greeting is from a tourist-information bot that's come to a stop at the end of the bike rack. They're common in high-trafficked areas of Tokyo. It's probably detected I'm sitting here looking a bit lost, so rolled on over.

I say hello, and it switches to English. It asks if I need help finding something or if it can call me a car.

'I'm just out for a walk. Can't sleep.'

'A nice night for one,' it says.

A nice night for one, I repeat in my head. It's funny, I always assumed America had the most advanced bots, but Japan's blow ours away. It's partly due to their form. Like this one's: its build is almost cartoony, like a mascot you'd see at a baseball game. Its domed digital face looks like an anthropomorphised cat with enormous eyes. In America, people-facing robots are plainer looking, appliance-like. Yet it's not just their appearance that makes eastern and western bots different. In America, bots' personalities are subservient; here, they're programmed to speak as if they're an easy-going acquaintance.

The tourist-information bot's domed head reflects a shade of blue as a new ad on one of the buildings mists the area in novel light. The bot's big cat eyes blink.

'Hey,' I say, looking down upon its arced face, 'are there any quiet places in the area where I could sit and kill some time?'

The info bot's big cat eyes blink again. 'There are fifteen clubs, thirteen restaurants, eleven hotel bars, six sports bars, three cigar bars, and one jazz bar currently open in Shibuya, all of which offer seating. Eight of those bars, six restaurants, and five clubs will close in the next hour.'

'But like somewhere quieter? Like a coffee shop or café where I could have some milk tea and read a magazine until I get tired?'

This is now the longest conversation I've had with anything but the surgeon in days.

'I'm sorry, I've checked, but there aren't. The last coffee shop closed forty-two minutes ago. But twenty-three coffee shops open at six a.m., followed by fifty-eight others at six-thirty a.m.'

'And there's not a single café open right now, either?'

'Unfortunately not. The average closing time for cafés in the Shibuya area on a weeknight is between ten and eleven-thirty p.m.'

I nod but don't say anything. Across the scramble, a gigantic girl blinks to life along the length of a glass skyscraper. She's soon joined by three other giants, all members of the same J-pop band. Their lips move, silently belting their latest hit, available for streaming now.

Two of the girls leap from the skyscraper's surface only to reappear on the surface of the department store opposite, where their gyrations continue.

'Can I help you with anything else?' the info bot says.

I shake my head. 'Not unless you know a trick for falling to sleep.'

'I'm sorry, I don't.' Its digital eyes blink. 'Sleep isn't something I'm acquainted with.'

'No, I suppose not.' I let out a breath. 'Well, it's getting colder. I guess I'll head back to my apartment,' I say as a way of goodbye to the robot.

'Of course. Stay warm and have a good night.' Its domed head shifts down, as if bowing.

I give it a little smile and rise from the rack. Yet I haven't taken more than a few steps when I hear it:

'You're on the cusp of a new world.'

The words stop me in my tracks.

You're on the cusp of a new world.

I turn back. The info bot hasn't moved.

Its short body glows a deep green, bathed in the light of a new ad. 'What's that…?'

But in that green glow, the bot remains silent. Its only reply, a blinking of its cat-like eyes.

I glance around. No one else is near.

'What did you just say?' I try again.

A cold gust whips over us, but for several moments there's only silence.

Finally, the bot replies.

'Stay warm and have a good night,' it says, its eyes blinking a few more times.

I stare for a moment longer as a shift in the light darkens the air another shade. In the eerie glow, the bot's cat-like eyes blink once more, yet it doesn't speak again.

My jet lag is making me hear things.

I cross the scramble and turn up a street parallel to the one I took here, leaving the gaseous glow of Shibuya behind. As the street curves, the last of the hues behind me fade, and with them, any illusion of warmth. I give a shiver and pull my backpack's straps tight across my shoulders, shoving my hands into my pockets.

A gust rustles the trees lining the darkened street. All the shops I pass are closed, their insides dim, and after a few moments I realise I'm the only one around.

Before me, a fallen leaf scratches along the sidewalk, blown by the October breeze. The tips of its dried body curl downward like brittle fingers attempting to stop its involuntary locomotion. It flips over, again and again. And just as I'm sure it's about to blow out of my sight, its crisp body smacks against something.

It's one of those sandwich board signs eateries put up outside – the kind with an embedded chalkboard where the day's special is written.

I'm not sure what the top portion says, as it's written in Japanese, but on the bottom there's an anime-ish drawing of a man's face laid sideways, an instrument inserted into his ear. His chalk face looks serene. Content even. Next to the drawing is the message: *Relaxing Ear Cleaning – Only ¥4900*.

The board's in front of a detached two-storey building. The banner above reads *MR. HAPPY CAFÉ* in white letters on a red background. A warm glow emanates from the door's glass pane, and I spot what looks to be the edge of a counter with someone behind it. I can't tell for sure, though, because a coat hangs on the rear of the door, blocking most of the view. There's another window to the door's left, yet a curtain's pulled across it.

I step back. Taking in the building as a whole, I can't help but feel it looks out of place. Its pinkish-peach colouring isn't tacky exactly, but it's nowhere close to mirroring the chic appearances of the better-kept establishments it neighbours. Still, from my new perspective, I can now tell someone's definitely behind the counter in the foyer. I can see an arm through the unobstructed slice of glass. And the window to the right reveals an additional dining area separate from the foyer. The dining area's empty, but its lights are on.

The thing is, I've walked this street a dozen times in the week I've been here, yet never recall noticing this place. Then again, I've never been out this late, and all the other times the street's been packed. It probably just never caught my eye through the crowds.

I look at the sandwich board again, the dried leaf still pushed against it in the now-howling breeze. The tourist-info bot definitely said all area cafés were closed – yet this one's lights are on, someone's inside, and their sign *is* still on the sidewalk.

A tiny bell clangs as I enter. As its resonance fades, a perfect stillness replaces it, as if someone's found the mute button for the room. But the foyer's stillness only amplifies the strangeness of what's before me. Behind the counter, the biggest Japanese man I've ever seen stares at me. Scratch that. The biggest man I've ever seen. His jet-black hair is tied up into a bun. Minimum he's six-four, yet it's his added width that makes him so massive. He's easily twice as wide as me, shoulder-to-shoulder. And he's gotta be four hundred pounds. At least. Yet it's an odd four hundred. Definitely a lot of fat, but the bulk of his shoulders and chest suggests he could bench press an ox without breaking a sweat.

But the big man isn't the oddest thing staring at me. That would be the tiny, white geometric dog sitting on the counter. At once adorable and surreal, the dog's hair has been styled in such a way that its head takes the shape of a perfect sphere two sizes too large for its body, the surface of which extends to the tips of its snout and ears, so much so that they no longer have any depth. The thin black lines of its mouth, its tiny coal-black eyes and its small, wet, black dot of a nose might as well have been drawn onto a snowball with a marker. Below its collar, the dog's midsection is cut short to better call attention to its head, which, really, is so perfectly spherical it looks like you could pop it off and roll it across the floor.

A pair of scissors hovers above the dog's head, suspended mid-air by the big man's meaty fingers. For several moments, both keep their gazes frozen on me like they've been paused by the same remote that's muted this room. Soon though, the dog cocks its head, trying to regain the big man's attention. And as if my novelty has worn off, the big man returns his scrutiny to the circumference of its head, inspecting individual hairs and deftly clipping any even a millimetre too long, just like an experienced gardener prunes uneven branches from a hedge.

'Ah, *konbanwa*,' I say, almost surprised sound does carry in here.

The big man stops clipping the dog's hairs and looks at me again. His expression is so flat I can't say he's 'studying' me. It might be better to say his expression is one of complete indifference – the way someone looks at a brick wall they're standing next to while having a smoke. After another moment, a sigh escapes his mouth.

He says something, but I don't know what.

'I'm sorry,' I say. 'Do you happen to speak English?'

He answers with silence. That flat expression isn't changing. On the counter, the dog gives a sharp yap, regaining his attention. He sets the scissors down and picks up a purple comb with just three long, thin teeth. He plunges the trio of teeth into the dog's cotton ball head and fluffs the hair outwards, then repeats. The dog seems to greatly enjoy this.

Without looking at me, the big man says something. It sounds like the same thing as before, but I can't be sure.

'I was wondering if I could do the ear cleaning?' I try, twisting my hand by my ear, miming a swabbing with a Q-tip.

This time the big man stares at me like an audience member thoroughly unimpressed with the show. As he recommences the dog's fluffing, he calls out unrecognisable words in a voice so deep it must be what a blue whale would sound like if it could speak.

He goes perfectly quiet again – all focus on the dog's sculpting.

In the muted awkwardness, my eyes flit around the foyer. Next to the door is a narrow ledge and stools. A chalkboard menu hangs over the counter. Behind it, an open partition exposes the kitchen. The foyer opens into the small dining area. Two booths sit next to the window overlooking the street. Across from them is a coffee table and couch. And between the couch and the foyer is an entrance to a hallway so void of light it's as if it's not even part of this world.

But nowhere is there anyone else he could have been speaking to.

'I guess you don't do it this late...' I say, now just feeling stupid.

But silence. Total silence from the big man as he continues teasing the dog's hair without giving me so much as another glance. The dog seems just as oblivious to me. It squints with such pleasure, the primping of its hair so relaxing, it may very well be on the verge of passing out. Lucky little guy.

'Well, *sayōnara*,' I say turning for the door, my fingers grasping its cold brass handle.

The voice that replies out of thin air is so soft I bet its algorithmically possible to demonstrate it's the exact opposite of the previous bellows. '*Konbanwa*,' it says.

But any thoughts of algorithms leave my head when I turn back. Inside my chest something contracts into a fist so tight, for a moment, I forget to breathe.

The girl's materialised in the invisible plane where the foyer and dining area meet. Her straight black hair flows to her shoulders, and her bangs barely conceal the dark brows resting above eyes so astonishingly clear, they're like the blue-grey of rain. The light pink of her lips rest in a perfectly neutral position, neither smiling nor frowning, neither agitated nor amused. But it's those eyes that hold all the power. They hold me for several soundless moments until I hear a distinct sigh.

I've become visible to the big man again, who now gives me a hard stare.

Shit. How long ago did the girl say '*Konbanwa*'?

I clear my suddenly dry throat. 'Ah, sorry, I don't Japanese. I was walking and then came here. I asked him, but we couldn't talk ... There's the ear-cleaning sign outside I saw, and I wanted to see if I could get it,' I say mostly those words in mostly that order to the girl.

It's the jet lag speaking. And nerves. I also threw in the universal gesture for Q-tips, which I now sorrily regret.

In the renewed silence, the girl studies me as if I'm some kind of still life. And then, though her lips remain perfectly neutral, I can't help but think I notice her smile. It's because of how her eyelids shift. Their edges curve downward ever so slightly, like tiny crescent moons.

'*Hai*,' she says with an abrupt nod.

I barely manage to stop myself from replying with an English 'hi'; and I think she notices – the edges of her lids curve again, and I feel my face warm.

She motions for me to take a seat on the couch in the dining area. As I make my way, I feel the big man's gaze stalk me across the room. The walls in here are covered in framed pictures. Most, old-timey travel ads. I sit and fluff my sweater out around my waist as the girl disappears into that hallway so void of light it might as well be a black hole. With the big man still eyeing me, I turn my attention towards a rack of unusual sweatshirts at the couch's far end. They're identical. All navy blue and all featuring a cartoony shark made of felt, launching itself from the wearer's torso. The sweatshirts' pockets hang outwards, like pectoral fins. A sign reads ¥7400.

From where I'm sat, the lighting turns the window by the booths into a mirror. I give my hair a tussle in its reflection and flare my sweater a bit more upon hearing the girl's returning footsteps. She exits the hallway's void, engrossed in the contents of a shoebox. A small pillow is wedged under a bare arm, her sleeveless denim dress following her slender body down to her ankles. She sets the pillow at the far end of the couch and kneels before me. At such proximity, I notice that a tiny trio of light, faint moles dot her face. It's as if they were put there because nature simply refuses to allow perfection to exist. Still, any way you look it, she's striking.

'It's my first ear cleaning,' I say just to say something.

The girl gives a sharp, affirmative nod, thankfully unable to tell I'm just blabbering.

How old is she? Older than me, but not by much.

She sets the shoebox on the floor and then gestures with both hands, running them in an up-and-down motion in front of her bare shoulders.

'Oh, right,' I say, realising I'm still wearing my backpack. She places it next to the rack of shark sweatshirts. As I lay down, I again fluff my sweater out around my waist. In the shoebox are instruments that look like long toothpicks, cotton swabs, and other items.

When I've settled, she says, '*Hai,*' as a way of asking if I'm ready. I return a little confirmatory nod.

Fishing into the shoebox, she retrieves a moist wipe and gently rubs my ear, pulling on the lobe before working deeper. At first, it feels weird, but soon it's actually pretty nice. But the problem is my eyes. I'm not sure where to set them. I'm staring straight ahead, yet because of where she's positioned, that happens to be at the swell of her breasts beneath her dress. I shift my gaze towards her face, but now I just feel like a Peeping Tom watching a beautiful girl carry out her work, which she's thankfully doing with such focus it's keeping her from noticing my predicament.

That's when a cold disquiet hits me: is this something only perverts do here? Getting a pretty girl to clean a part of your body? I don't think it is ... but what if I'm wrong? Then again, she's the one giving the cleaning, so she can't think it's too creepy.

As she readjusts and starts into my ear canal with a long toothpick-like instrument, I spy one of the framed pictures on the wall. It's a smaller one, and jagged around the edges, like it's been ripped from an old magazine. It's monochrome too, the digital ink long dried up. In it, a young, massive Japanese man with a beaming smile sits cross-legged as he holds a large fish up by its towel-wrapped tail. Next to him kneels a short, slightly stocky woman, who gazes in admiration as she claps joyfully. Behind the pair, others applaud.

But that's the final thing I see, because I can't help shutting my eyes as the girl works deeper into my ear. Her soft, careful touch and the tool's gentle scraping are so relaxing – within minutes I'm drowsy.

The last memory I have of my dad is from nine years ago – the night before he and Mom went to Angola. I was eight, and we were sitting on our front porch, legs swung over the concrete steps, watching the blazing pink Midwestern sunset. I'm not sure where Mom was – probably inside with Grandma, packing. Since he and Mom were going to be away for some time, Dad told me I'd need to be good and help my grandparents around the house. Every day I did my chores they were going to give me a quarter. 'By the time we're back, I know you'll have been so helpful this piggy bank will be full,' said Dad.

We called it a piggy bank even though it was just a big pickle jar. Already it had about an inch's worth of coins – previous rewards for doing my chores. Every month Dad stopped at the remaining bank in town to pick up some old physical money, for no other reason than this. I asked him how much was in the piggy bank now, so I'd know how much more I'd have earned by the time Mom and he returned. We dumped the jar onto the porch and spread the coins flat between us. Even now, I remember the way he observed my small hands arranging them. His gaze was full of such warmth – I haven't seen anything close to it in anyone's eyes since.

Dad slid one old coin at a time from the main pile into a new one as he counted the sum out loud. 'Five ... ten ... thirty-five...' Each coin slid across the porch's concrete made a pleasant scratching sound, which, when combined with Dad's deep voice, produced the oddest sensation in me: a warm, tingling feeling bubbled up and exploded inside my skull, as if my brain was floating in a container of heated seltzer water. That feeling extended down my spine and into my arms as Dad continued to slide and count the coins. Soon my entire body was cocooned in this tingling warmth, and I fell into a deep sleep. Dad had to carry me up to my bed, and it wasn't even dinner time yet.

It remains to this day the most euphoric sensation I've ever experienced.

In the time since, I've had similar instances where someone can make me feel warm and sleepy – even if it's in the middle of the day. Usually, it happens when someone is speaking or doing something gently very close to my head, like when I'm getting a haircut or going to the eye doctor for a check-up. It's why I came in here. I thought maybe an ear cleaning could have a similar effect. Maybe it could get me tired and help reset my internal clock – jet lag be damned.

And you know what? I was right. By the time the striking girl has me flip over to do my other ear, I'm so sleepy she could disrobe in front of me and it wouldn't even register. When she's finished the cleaning, she even needs to shake me a little.

My eyes open to find hers looking over me, the edges of their lids curved in that invisible amusement. I feel like I've awakened into another world, I'm so relaxed.

I pay the big man at the counter where the dog with the spherical head sits, neither seeming strange anymore. Even the short walk back to my apartment in the crisp October air doesn't rouse me.

And the last thing I see as my head hits my pillow is the infinite city's twinkling lights stretching beyond the balcony's glass door.

It's a city still shrouded in night, and it will continue to be for hours to come.

2 – Japan is good.

'I'm sorry,' I say to a maintenance bot carrying out minor curb work. I've bumped into it after glancing the time on my phone. It's just after eight p.m. and I'm headed back to my apartment, hoping my missing backpack is there. Hearing my apology in English, the bot replies, 'No worries,' and I turn the corner onto my apartment's street.

This morning, when I woke, it felt as if I'd been in a long, dense hibernation and for several moments I stayed motionless in bed. The fine particulates of atmosphere floating among the rays of light flooding the apartment were captivating, and as their microscopic bodies swayed overhead, I couldn't help thinking something was peculiar about the way they were illuminated – almost as if the photons adhered to some unknown physics that had developed in secret while I slept.

I rose, slid open the glass door and stepped onto the balcony.

It wasn't just the rays of light in my room – the whole world looked different.

Then I saw the time, and it hit me why: I'd never seen Tokyo in the nine-a.m. light.

Or the 9:09 a.m. light, to be precise.

I dressed and flew out the door. It was the first day I'd managed to wake in time; there was no way I was going to miss it again. I weaved so quickly through the crowded streets I reached Shibuya Station in half the time it should've taken. And despite the station being an endless tangle of paths and corridors, punctuated by indecipherable signs among a jungle of people, bots, stores, trains and buses, I caught the 9:45 tourist shuttle to Hakone.

My guide app listed Hakone as the best daytrip from Tokyo – just ninety minutes away. For the most part, the journey was unspectacular, but for the last thirty minutes, the shuttle skirted a bay and then the terrain became mountainous as we turned inland.

During this stretch, an elderly couple across the aisle struck up a conversation about how beautiful the water looked. They asked if I'd been in Japan long and where in America I was from. They were Canadians, and it was their first time in Asia. We chatted off and on, but when we reached the station at the mountain's base, we became separated as everyone formed into packed lines for the cable cars. The one I boarded was filled with Chinese tourists who had arrived via another shuttle.

The cable car took us over yellow pits bellowing sulfuric clouds. They're Hakone's most popular attraction – though one girl in my car almost fainted from their smell. She had to sit, and someone covered her nose and mouth with a damp cloth. The car dropped us at the mountain's summit, where we wandered the vast observation deck with good views of the yellow slopes. I took the obligatory pictures most everyone was taking, then rested my elbows on the safety railing and gazed at the plumes for a long time.

It occurred to me how clear-headed I felt. The fog of jet lag had finally lifted. I thought of the girl from the café. Her sleeveless denim dress and her clear, blue-grey eyes. I suppose I had her to thank for my slumber.

At one point, a priest from a Vietnamese tour group offered to take a photo of me overlooking the pits. I think he realised I was alone. I don't like to be in pictures but stood for one anyway and thanked him. I emailed it to Mom and told her I was having a blast, then rode a cable car to the opposite base of the mountain, where it met a massive lake, and I boarded a ferry for a cruise. It was all part of the package. Besides, it was something more to do, at least – to fill all the time I have. Out on the lake, I took in the views and spotted a striking orange gate in the waters just off the shoreline.

That's when it hit me: I didn't have my backpack. I couldn't remember where I would've taken it off on the observation deck. And then I realised I didn't even have it on the shuttle. Had I left it at the apartment in my rush out the door? Or did I leave it in the café after the ear cleaning? I was so sleepy when I left, and the girl had asked me to remove it. There was nothing valuable inside.

It had the novel I'd been reading and the magazine from the doctor's office. But my passport was in there, too.

It was almost four when the ferry reached the other end of the lake, right as rain clouds crept over the mountain. I followed the other tourists across the docks to the parking lot where we were to meet our rides; but once there an attendant announced an issue with some of the shuttles' nav systems and said we'd need to wait another hour for replacements. The ones that finally arrived were the old-school kind that required an actual driver – and it meant I didn't return to Shibuya Station until almost eight.

I enter my apartment. The morning's peculiar rays are long gone. Through the balcony's door, only the artificial lights of the infinite city can be seen, though their glow is muted by the moist air that's followed from Hakone. My backpack is nowhere to be seen.

I throw on a hoodie and head back out. The leaves rustle as the café's pinkish-peach exterior comes into view, but a weight hits my chest as I notice the sandwich board isn't on the pavement. Have they already closed? Some little establishments here keep irregular hours – staying open late some nights, while randomly shutting early on others.

Yet as I near, the weight on my chest lessens. A man steps from the café carrying a brown takeaway bag. He inspects the night sky for a moment as the stiff breeze hits him, then pulls his collar up. Through the window, I see a group of students in one of the booths. A couple of middle-aged women are on the couch where I had my ear cleaning – only they're chatting over coffee.

The door's bell clangs as I enter, and my eyes immediately go to the dog with the spherical head perched on the counter. Despite the eternal surrealness of the dog's geometry, the café has a distinctly different feel tonight. There's no stillness in the air and no muted silence. The world outside and the world in here are indistinguishable.

The dog's wet nose gives a sniff, and it greets me with a double yap that cuts through the chatter from the dining area. In response, the big man turns from the open partition that shows into the kitchen. He holds a plate in each hand, both bearing quartered sandwiches and small cups of soup. His eyes lock onto me but as always, his expression is flat. It's like he's chronically displeased.

He sets the plates on the counter mere inches from the dog, yet it doesn't so much as sniff the food, which is all the more surprising since, even from where I stand, it smells delicious. The big man eyes me for a moment more before his attention turns towards a small scratchpad on the counter. A second later, he bellows words I couldn't hope to understand in no particular direction at all.

'*Konbanwa* ... I was here last night,' I say, drawing his attention again. 'I did the ear cleaning.' And I mime a Q-tip in my ear. I bring my fists to my shoulders and move my hands as if I'm adjusting invisible straps. 'I think I might have left my backpack here?'

The big man's flat expression doesn't budge. Not one millimetre.

But as I drop my hands, something catches my eyes – a few flecks of brightness in that dark hallway that sits between the foyer and dining area. A sharp breath later, the girl materialises from its void like an apparition.

Unlike last night, every inch of her body is now concealed below the neck, from the ends of her ankle-length grey skirt to the collar of the black, long-sleeve T-shirt. Even her hands are covered by shiny, white gloves that run underneath the cuffs of her T-shirt all the way up to her elbows. I can see where their outlines end under her sleeves. They look almost theatrical; the kind you'd buy at a cheap costume shop if you were starring in a grade-school play set on the fashionable boulevards of nineteenth-century Paris. It's these shiny gloves that were the bright flecks in the hallway's darkness. And they bear my backpack by its straps.

'*Konbanwa*,' the girl says, smiling a soft, inviting smile that's replaced last night's neutral lips. And with that smile a fist again contracts inside my chest and I feel the air go just a little bit thin. She holds the backpack towards me like she's a curator presenting a delicate artifact.

'*Arigatō, arigatō*,' I say, taking it. 'Thank you so, so much. I was worried I'd lost it.'

And even though she can't understand what I'm saying, she smiles politely and occasionally nods as I ramble that I went to a mountain, and there was a boat, and that's where I realised I didn't have my backpack. I go on, telling her how on the way back, the weather started looking bad, and I thought it would be a good idea to check my apartment first, but the backpack wasn't there.

It's like that fist inside my chest is squeezing every last word from me like juice from an orange.

Regardless, I thank her again for keeping my backpack safe. Then I thank her for the ear cleaning. 'Japan is good,' I say for some reason. And as I'm running out of ramblings, the one thing I've thought most this entire time slips from my tongue before I can stop it:

'You make me wish I spoke Japanese.'

The edges of the girl's eyelids curve down into that invisible little smile.

Oh, God.

'It's OK,' she says. 'We can stick with English.'

That fist squeezes so tightly, my heart feels pulped.

Behind the counter, the big man seems to wonder, *How does this idiot get through the day?*

'I'm glad I could look after your backpack for you.' The girl gives that welcoming smile, ignoring the big man's gaze and, mercifully, whatever mortified look I'm wearing.

'I'm *so* sorry...' I breathe. 'I assumed ... last night, I was really jet-lagged. I just assumed you didn't speak English.'

I don't even want to know how red my face is.

'It's no problem,' she shakes her head. 'I'm just happy you came back. I hope you don't mind, but I looked inside after I found your backpack. I thought something in it might have the address of a hotel. When nothing did, and when I saw the passport, I hoped you'd return.'

Behind the counter, the big man lets out something between a sigh and a grumble, which the girl disregards, instead keeping her gaze on me.

'Would you like some food? Have you eaten?' she asks. The big man says something. He sounds annoyed. And from the counter, the dog yaps. She ignores them both, keeping that soft, inviting smile on me. 'I can bring you a menu.'

I manage a little smile, which goes a ways in helping me shrug off some embarrassment. 'Food would be great.' Truthfully, I'm not hungry, but I don't want to be rude. She saved my backpack, after all. Besides, what else do I have to do?

I slide into the empty booth by the window. At the counter, the big man speaks in short sentences, which the girl answers even more concisely. She grabs both plates from the counter and delivers them to the women sitting on the couch, then she brings me a menu. At the next booth, the group of students leaves, and another group takes the seats.

I order some scrambled eggs, toast and a coffee. It's easy to choose because the menu has pictures. It takes some time for my meal to arrive. Though the café's small, there's a lot of foot traffic, with more people coming in to order something to go than staying and sitting. It seems like it's just the two of them working here. The girl's obviously the waitress, but she also spends time in the open kitchen, preparing some of the orders. The big guy spends as much time preparing food as he does operating the register. As for the dog, he just sits on the counter. Almost everyone who comes in laughs at his haircut, and many take a photo.

Though it's busy, the girl stops by my table often and even seems to be giving me more attention than the other customers. Or maybe that's not really the case. When we find people attractive, we usually delude ourselves into thinking the attention they give us is beyond what others receive. She offers to refill my coffee and asks how my meal tastes. 'I like breakfast food at night, too,' she says.

When I next spot her, she's at the counter, packing an order. Her fingers seem to be having a problem with the small clasp on a take-away container's lid. She tugs at her gloves, pulling them on more snuggly, and tries again. It's something I've seen her do repeatedly tonight – fiddling with her gloves – especially when picking up thin utensils while clearing a table. They actually seem to be an annoyance to her. I don't know why she wouldn't just remove them. They're too fancy to be hygiene related. Besides, the big man isn't wearing any, and he makes most of the food.

Customers cycle in and out as I finish my meal. I sip my coffee, turning my attention to the weather outside, where Tokyoites scurry past with their transparent umbrellas. There's something oddly soothing about the way the rain forms a patchwork of small dots on the window, some of which break and merge with others to fashion a web of intricate streams.

It's now a quarter after nine. When the girl returns, I ask if it's OK to get some work done on my laptop – or if she needs the table?

'Stay as long as you like. I'll bring you more coffee. Do you want to try some dessert?'

'Sounds good. What do you have?'

'Goeido's specialty is an ice-cream dish. Want to try?'

That must be the big man's name. 'Yeah, why not?'

At the counter she gives him my order and he gives me a look before retreating into the kitchen. A few minutes later, the ice cream is in front of me. It's a big vanilla scoop with two smaller scoops set evenly apart at the base. A pair of round pieces of liquor-ice on the big scoop resemble eyes, and another bit resembles a small, black nose. Two lines of chocolate sauce form a mouth. When taken as a whole, the big vanilla scoop looks like the counter dog's spherical head, and the little scoops look like its tiny front paws.

'Brilliant, huh?'

'The similarity's remarkable,' I say.

She returns to the foyer to welcome more customers, their shoulders damp from the rain.

Ice cream consumed, I fold my phone out into a laptop. Mom hasn't replied to my earlier email, and there's another message from Sony's hospitality coordinator asking if I need anything to make the apartment more comfortable. After responding, I launch my dev tools, working at a leisurely pace. Occasionally, I'll pause to watch the rain, or whenever the girl returns to refill my coffee and give me that kind smile.

But at one point, that smile fades.

It happens at the next booth. The customers are middle-aged salarymen used to eating late. As she clears their dishes, one says, '*arigatō*', and she replies with a short word, pleasant smile and nod. But as she turns towards the foyer, two of the salarymen share smirks and a quiet laugh as the other whispers while gesturing like he's putting on an invisible glove.

His hands are suspended mid-air when the girl turns back. In an instant, that pleasant smile dissolves from her lips. Retrieving the forgotten chopstick, she casts her eyes down.

I pretend like I didn't notice any of it either.

A little after ten, the last customer besides me clears out, and when the girl comes to clean the table, I ask if they're closing.

'*Hai*, but it's OK. I'll be cleaning for a while, and it's pouring outside. Stay as long as you like – I'll bring you more coffee.'

So that's what I do. Besides, being in a cosy café on a rainy Tokyo night beats sitting in the apartment again. Once she's finished in the dining area, the girl mostly sticks to the kitchen, where I occasionally glimpse her and the big man through the open partition. Sometimes they'll say short things to each other. Sometimes it even sounds like they're bickering. But after just a few days in this country, I've realised that even the most benign conversations in Japanese can sound argumentative to an outsider.

After some time, the big man exits the kitchen. I feel his gaze as he approaches. It's like he suspects I've got the gold coins from his hidden safe no one should know about stuffed into my pockets. Thankfully, he turns, and that dark hallway swallows him whole.

The kitchen lights go out, and the girl wipes down the counter after placing the dog on the floor, where I notice a little bed below the register. The dog circles several times before settling into it. After locking the front door and shutting off the exterior lights, she squats to pet the dog, speaking softly to it. When she rises, she pours herself a coffee.

'I'll go now,' I say, about to fold my laptop down as she enters the dining area. 'Thanks for letting me stay so long.'

But she sits across from me.

'It's OK. It's still raining, and I'm not in a hurry. It's just good to get off my feet.' And she takes a sip from her mug.

I don't say anything, but right now I wouldn't leave this booth if it were on fire.

She takes another sip and looks out at the rain. Brushing her bangs with a gloved finger, she brings the mug back to her lips, where it hovers. Her eyes study me over its rim, but she doesn't say a word.

'I guess you close earlier tonight?' I say just to break the silence.

'We were closed when you came last night. Goeido just forgot to lock the door and bring the sign in.'

'Oh ... I'm sorry.'

She shakes her head. 'It wasn't a problem.' And she holds her eyes on me for a moment more before finally sipping from her hovering mug.

'Ah, I'm John,' I say. 'My name's John.'

'You don't go by—' and she says my first name.

'How'd you—?'

'Your passport, remember?'

'Oh, yeah. Of course. No. Only teachers called me by my first name. And Mom, when she got angry with me when I was younger. But I've preferred my middle name for years.'

'Why?'

I don't know how to answer that, so I just shrug. Mercifully she doesn't press me on it.

'I'm Neotnia.'

That's a pretty name, I want to say. Instead, I say, 'Well, it's nice to meet you.'

She nods then sets her mug down and peers over the top of my screen with an inquisitive grin.

'So, *John,* what have you been working on all night?'

'Oh ... ah, just a pet project I got the idea for after I arrived. A translation app.'

'Aren't there a lot of those already?'

'But this one isn't like any of the others. Well, if I get the code right.'

She doesn't reply. Clearly, she's expecting me to elaborate.

'Ah ... well, so most translation apps work by using a built-in bilingual dictionary, right? They recognise a spoken word and literally translate it into the selected language using that dictionary. But because they're coded using classical code – telling a computer the information via each bit that's either a one or a zero – those apps don't really have the versatility to adapt to the way people actually speak, especially in real time. The code's binary nature limits their capabilities – so they're not advanced enough to sense context, or things like sarcasm or the nuances of an individual's speech patterns. But you might be able to get around those limitations with quantum code...'

This is usually where even Mom's eyes would begin to glaze over, but Neotnia takes a sip from her mug without looking at it, her gaze locked on me like I'm revealing the meaning of life.

'Uh ... so with quantum coding, you're writing for qubits instead of bits. Whereas a bit can be either a one or a zero, a qubit can be a one and a zero at the *same time*, which greatly expands the computational power and ... Well, in short, with the right code, a quantum-based translation app could learn on the fly as you use it. It could detect how each individual is talking, identifying their tones and inflections and the context in which they're speaking. That could lead to it recognising things like sarcasm and such. Basically, it could result in quicker, more accurate translations, and allow two people who don't speak the same language to better understand each other.'

Neotnia's eyes remain bound to mine for several moments.

Outside, the rain makes new dots on the window.

'That sounds very cool,' she finally says.

'Thanks.' I give a shy smile. 'Honestly, I got the idea because I've been in Tokyo for about a week now and was relying on the usual translation apps to get by. But they work too slowly or are too inaccurate, so people get impatient or offended or don't understand what you're really trying to say. But anyway, who knows if my app will work? I'm just playing around.'

'So, that's really you on the cover then?' She nods towards my backpack. 'Sorry, I didn't mean to pry. I saw the magazine when I found your passport.'

'Ah ... yeah. That's me.'

'Woooow.' Neotnia draws out the word with a smile. 'And that's why you're here? Japan is full of computer scientists, but if Sony brought you all the way from America you must be really good.'

'I don't know. I only got into quantum coding a few years ago. Its duality – I just liked how something could be two things at once.'

'Well, the magazine seems to know.' She gives me a grin. 'It says you're a boy genius. How many people are called that? Not to mention, Japan's biggest company *is* buying your app...'

My face goes warm at the word 'boy'.

'I just don't think I've been doing it long enough for anyone to accurately label me as anything,' I shrug. 'And, you know, I was fortunate to even have an opportunity to learn to quantum code. Most people don't.'

'Oh? Why's that?'

'Well, it can't run on classical computers, like our phones – they just don't have the hardware capabilities. And many governments now restrict the technology anyway – an organisation needs to be licensed to even own quantum hardware. But my high school partnered with a big research university in the state to let us take a stab at using their quantum hive. So, the first thing I wrote was this app that could increase a phone's battery life by manipulating its classically coded power-management systems with my quantum code. The head of the university's quantum lab urged me to open-source it, which ended up getting me some attention from the tech blogs. But none of that would've even happened if I wasn't lucky enough to get the opportunity to access quantum hardware in the first place. Anyway, what I learned from coding that first app, I applied to writing what Sony is buying. But it's not actually an app – it's just a quantum algorithm.'

Neotnia scrunches up her mouth a bit. 'OK. So, what does a company do with this algorithm?'

'Whatever they want, kind of. It allows high-end quantum servers to find patterns in exabyte-sized data sets exponentially faster than contemporary algorithms. So, you can use that in any number of fields: AI, finance, e-commerce, gaming, social, meta, you name it – anything where you need to identify sequences or trends hidden in massive amounts of data.'

'And Sony wants it. That's really cool.'

'Yeah...' I feel my face blush. 'Well, a few companies actually approached me after I uploaded a proof of concept. It was kind of surreal, actually.'

'Surreal? How many wanted it?'

'Twenty-one.'

Another grin spreads across her lips. 'That's a little more than "a few".'

'Yeah. I don't know why I said that.' I clear my throat and give what's probably an awkward smile. 'Besides Avance, they were all foreign. ThaiX and LG were interested in it for search and meta. NEC and Samsung for communications and social. Avance too, until they dropped out. Lots of hedge funds were interested in it for trading. But, well, Sony actually hasn't bought it yet. I guess it takes the lawyers a long time to do their due diligence and get the international regulators to sign off. It'll be another three weeks or so before we sign the papers. I think their PR people are doing these cover stunts in the meantime so I don't back out. They know other companies are interested.'

'So successful at only seventeen,' Neotnia shakes her head. 'Sorry ... passport again. I might as well tell you, the only thing in your backpack I didn't read was the book, but that's because I've already read it.'

Her honesty makes me laugh. She smiles a big smile, and I want to say I'll be eighteen soon. Instead, I say, 'Your English is really good.'

She considers this. 'It's OK,' she decides.

'Did you learn it in school? Is it a requirement here?'

'They teach it in some schools. But I know it because of my father. He speaks it fluently.'

'Hey, hold on. How come you didn't speak English last night? You made me mime...'

'You do what you have to do to keep yourself entertained at work.' She gives a good-natured shrug. 'But also, Goeido says if you speak English, Americans will ask you for directions instead of buying something. So, I try not to, to keep him happy.'

'I guess he's not a big fan of us?'

'Oh, no, it's not that. He just doesn't mind separating them from their money, which is why he asked me to do your ear cleaning even though we were closed.'

Neotnia takes a sip from her mug, then rests her gaze on the rain tapping against the window. In the silence, I notice the projected shadows from the streams on the glass smoothen and arc across her nose and along the curves of her cheek as if they're trying to draw paths between her trio of faint moles. But as a stream splits into a new shadow, she turns as if reacting to its sudden presence on her skin, and she catches me taking in her features.

Her eyes dip for a moment.

'Ah, so, how old are you?' I say.

'Two.' But noting the look on my face, she shakes her head. 'Sorry. *Twenty*.' She blushes slightly. 'See – my English isn't as good as you thought.'

'It's still really good. Especially considering I know about four Japanese words.'

And now I'm wondering what kind of twenty she is. Has she just turned twenty, and there's only a little more than two years between us? Or is it an old twenty, and she's on the verge of twenty-one?

But I don't ask. Seeing her mug is now empty, I swallow the last of my coffee. Outside, the rain diverges into tiny new tributaries on the glass. I gauge the weather and peek at the time, yet as I draw in a breath to speak, Neotnia speaks up herself.

'Do you like hot chocolate? I love it, and ours is especially good. We've got some that's going down the drain if it's not drunk tonight...'

'Oh ... ah, sure,' I say, and notice the tension ease from her lips, allowing a little smile to cross them.

'Those shark sweatshirts are cute,' I nod towards the rack of them as she returns from the kitchen with a pot of hot chocolate and fills my mug at the table.

Her face brightens. 'Goeido makes those by hand. He cuts the fabric and sews them and everything.'

'Really? Those and the ice-cream dog heads?'

'*Hai*,' she hands me the mug, then pours one for herself.

'Wow. You wouldn't expect that.'

'What do you mean?'

'Well, he seems very ... serious.'

She eyes me, taking her seat. 'I think you mean scary.'

I let out a small laugh. 'Or that.'

She shakes her head. 'He's harmless.'

I blow on my hot chocolate in an attempt to make my next question sound casual. 'And is he your...' I want to say 'boyfriend', but my 'b' turns into 'boss?'

The edges of her eyelids curve just a bit.

'Not really. I mean, I work here, but I do it to help Goeido out. He owns the café and ran it by himself before I came. He lets me live in the spare room upstairs, so I return the favour by working down here. So, he's less like a boss and more like an overprotective big brother.'

'Cool,' I say before stupidly pointing out the obvious. 'He's a really big guy ... Not that there's anything wrong with that. I just mean he's bigger than most Japanese men.'

'He's sumo.'

'You're kidding?'

She gives her head a brief shake. 'Well, he was.' The way she doesn't elaborate makes me think I shouldn't ask what she means. She sips from her mug instead.

'Well,' I say, 'if he was a sumo, you and I have very different definitions of "harmless".'

Neotnia chokes mid-sip and cups a hand over her mouth, rushing her mug to the table. Swallowing, a depressurised laugh escapes her lips, an involuntary reaction that makes me laugh, too.

As we take a moment to catch our breaths, my eyes settle on her gloved hands, now resting on the table for support. A spot of hot chocolate has stained one of the fingers. Glimpsing my gaze, Neotnia shifts her hands almost instinctively, like she wants to withdraw them from view. Yet then she folds one over the other, as if forcing them to remain in place.

And I mean, yeah, the gloves do look a bit odd – but I guess that's just her style. You see all kinds of weird fashions in Tokyo, especially in Harajuku, which is not far from here. But I recall the smirking salarymen, and don't want her to feel self-conscious about her style again. I nod towards the dog, instead, snoozing quietly in its bed in the foyer. 'That's the best-trained dog I've ever seen.'

She looks over her shoulder and smiles. '*Hai*. He's a little sweetheart. His name's Inu.'

'Inu has a pretty crazy haircut.'

'That's Goeido's idea again. He gives him that cut and sits Inu on the counter because it pulls people inside. They see Inu as they walk by and just have to get a better look at the dog with the round head. And once they've given him a pat, they feel rude leaving if they don't at least order a coffee – especially if they've taken his picture. And coffee after coffee adds up to a lot.'

'That's pretty clever,' I say, the shadow from a particularly thick stream on the window suddenly growing across her lower lip. It breaks and curves around the underside of her chin, where it continues along the slenderness of her neck, and onto the shape of her breasts below. The thing is, when my gaze returns to Neotnia's eyes, it's apparent she's caught where mine have travelled from.

It's a beat before she replies.

'We sometimes try different things like that. Inu's haircut has worked well. And on some nights, we test other things to pull people inside. This week, we started the ear cleaning. But it hasn't worked too well ... and it mainly just brings in the perverts.'

And her lids narrow. On me.

A chill runs through my insides.

'*Is* it a perverted thing to do?'

'Totally,' says Neotnia. 'It's for sickos.'

She picks up her mug and leers at me over its rim, taking a sip.

My jaw drops.

'It's not like that...' I ramble about my jet lag and how, sometimes, when people work close to my face, it makes me sleepy. 'Like when an optometrist is fitting you for glasses.'

'It didn't look like you needed any glasses just now.'

'Yeah, I didn't,' I reply, now mortified. 'No, I mean, I don't need glasses. But I meant, like when you get an eye check-up. I don't know why it happens, but sometimes, depending on the person and their proximity and the sounds, I just get this tingling and it can help me sleep—'

'"Tingling"...' She eyes me intently. 'I'm sure that's one way to describe it.'

My throat goes dry.

I have no idea what to say.

'And...' I explain, uncertain of the words that come next, 'just now ... I was looking ... because there was a stream...'

'Mmhmm. A stream...?' She raises her eyebrows.

'On your ... shirt. From the rain...'

'On my *shirt*,' she parrots. 'From the rain ... outside?'

'A shadow from the window.'

'Ohhh, a shadow from the window ... I see...'

'I...'

Neotnia's hard look feels like the physical manifestation of eternity.

'I bet you're wishing I'd give you another ear cleaning right now.'

Her glare is unflinching.

'...' I respond.

It's only when the flush that's enveloped my face sears with the intensity of boiling tar that a big grin breaks Neotnia's lips.

'I'm sorry,' she shakes her head, smiling. 'I was just having some fun ... though I guess it never hurts to check. But the shadows from the streams are all over you, too.'

A relieved breath escapes me, her amusement lingering.

'So then an ear cleaning's *not* a perverted thing to do?'

'Well, I'm sure *some* people get turned on by it. But no, it's pretty normal here, though for some reason, many western tourists think it's a perverted thing. Maybe because so many maid cafés offer it. But Japanese women will go to parlours that specialise in ear cleanings all the time. Kind of like hair salons, but for the ear.'

'Oh, thank God.'

Neotnia laughs a little laugh. 'So, did it really help – my ear cleaning?'

'I slept like a baby for the first time since I've been here,' I admit.

'I'm glad,' she says, then looks into her mug, thinking. 'So, you've been here for almost a week, and now that you're sleeping better, you'll be able to enjoy your time more. How much longer are you here?'

'It's kind of open-ended. I need to stay at least until the papers are ready, but Sony's put me up in the apartment until the new year.'

'And do you like it here?'

'I do,' I nod. 'It's so different from America. I enjoy walking around the city. And the trip to Hakone was nice, too.'

'But...'

I give a little smile. 'But ... I get bored sometimes, I guess. I've spent most days by myself, except when I've met with Sony's people. But I'll have no more meetings for several weeks. And at night, I feel silly going to a restaurant by myself, so I usually just grab some food from a 7-Eleven or Lawson's and head back to the apartment to read or work on my app. But you know – that gets old.'

'Which is why you're sitting in a café talking to your waitress.'

I feel my face warm. 'Yeah.'

For a quiet moment, Neotnia seems to be considering me. But suddenly a voice booms from that dark hallway. It's the sumo, shouting from what sounds like upstairs. Neotnia turns, and shouts something back. The sumo replies, and Neotnia responds with an even shorter call back.

'He just wants to know if I need any help finishing up down here,' she explains.

I look out the window. 'I should let you go do your thing,' I say, though I really don't want to leave. 'The rain's mostly stopped, so I won't get soaked going home.'

Neotnia's body jerks faintly, like my words were unexpected, and for a moment her mouth opens before she seals it closed again into a smooth line. She nods.

I fold my laptop down into a phone and make sure I have my backpack this time. Neotnia walks me to the door and unlocks it.

'I need to pay,' I realise.

She shakes her head. 'The register's already off. It's on the house.'

'Oh ... well, thanks.'

She gives me a tiny smile. It looks like she has something on her mind.

'Are you staying far from here?'

I shake my head. 'I'm just up the street and to the right.'

And contemplating me with those clear, blue-grey eyes, she says that, if I have nothing to do, I'm welcome to meet her tomorrow morning. 'You can come with me on an errand, and after we can get lunch.'

'OK, sure,' I nod. 'Yeah ... that sounds good.'

She twists her mouth up and looks at me. 'But the errand might take me a while, and you might be bored...'

'I'm sure I'll love it,' I say.

She considers me for a long moment. 'OK,' she gives another little nod.

'So ... should I message you or call you or something?'

Neotnia shakes her head. 'I don't have a phone. I use Goeido's when I need one.'

'Oh, OK. So, should I ... call Goeido?'

This makes her smile – probably because she knows the prospect terrifies me.

'Just meet me here at ten, after the morning rush.'

3 – Maybe we'll be back to throwing sticks and rocks.

I wipe the condensation from the upper half of the bathroom's mirror. I comb my shower-damp hair and dab on some deodorant. I scan my reflection and, for a moment, can't help feeling a little satisfied. Yet, I know I'm only looking at half of myself. And that satisfaction? It would end with a wipe of the remaining condensation.

But I'm looking forward to today. I'm fine leaving the illusion in place.

Outside, it's a bright autumn morning – breezy, but not cold. As I approach the café, Neotnia's waiting. She's wearing white pants and button-up, short-sleeve shirt. A golden knit cardigan is tied around her waist, and in each hand is a takeaway cup. Her hands are gloves-free.

'*Konnichiwa*,' she smiles. Her straight bangs shift gently in the breeze.

'*Konnichiwa*,' I say. 'Hello.'

'Ten sharp. Right on time,' she hands me a coffee.

'I always try to be.'

Further down the sidewalk someone calls out. It's a man wheeling a dolly. Neotnia nods as he says something more, and then calls in through the café's propped-open door. A moment later, Goeido appears and slips through the frame.

'*Konnichiwa*,' I say, and he returns my greeting by saying nothing at all.

Goeido nods to the delivery man then proceeds to count the items on the dolly, pointing with his big finger: bags of flour, onions, several crates of vegetables, and finally six toasters, new in their boxes. Goeido authenticates the man's tablet then steps aside so he can wheel the dolly inside. He then turns his attention towards us. Looking at me, he presses his lips together.

'That's a lot of toasters,' I say, out of nervousness more than any-thing.

Neotnia touches my arm. 'We toast a lot of bread.'

Goeido says something to her, rolling his eyes slightly. For several seconds Neotnia doesn't blink, instead returning a cool gaze.

Finally, she replies in Japanese. Then to me she says, 'OK, we have a train to catch.'

I wave an awkward goodbye to Goeido. Next to me, a tiny breath of laughter escapes Neotnia's lips before she can catch it. The thing is, as we start down the sidewalk, my unease feels justified. Even without looking back, I can feel Goeido's eyes lingering on us.

We take a JR line train from Shibuya Station then transfer to a local train. Once on that, Neotnia points to a dot on one of the screens in the railcar.

'That's where we're headed.'

The railcar jostles. As another passenger moves past, I clench the pole more tightly and lean in towards the screen. The dot on the map reads 'Higashikurume.'

'And what's there?' I say, not even trying to pronounce the name.

Her lips tighten. 'I warned you you might be a little bored.'

'I won't be. I promise. Like I said, I've literally got no plans until I need to meet with Sony.'

She holds a suspect gaze for a moment before relenting. 'OK. It's a care home for the elderly.'

I nod as if that's exactly what I was expecting to hear.

'I told you – you're bored already!'

I laugh. 'I swear, I'm not.'

As the train comes to a stop in the next station, more passengers get off than on, so we take a seat. 'So, do you know someone there?'

'I know lots of people there,' Neotnia says. 'I volunteer there.'

'Really?'

'*Hai*. A few days a week. Whenever they need help. They're short-staffed. The residents outnumber the nurses by a lot. I normally don't volunteer today, but one of their regulars is away, so I'm helping with the lunch shift.'

'I think that's great.'

Her eyes dip a bit, and she nods so subtly I barely catch it.

'Ah, so will I be volunteering, too?'

'No, no, no,' Neotnia's face brightens. 'I didn't bring you to put you to work. There's someone there who I think would enjoy meeting you. I'll do my shift, and then, as your reward for bearing with me, I'm taking you to lunch.'

I can't think of who would enjoy meeting me, but don't ask. She would have said if she wanted me to know right now.

The crisp air feels good against my skin as we exit the railcar at Higashikurume. Neotnia says the care home is a ten-minute walk, during which we cut through the suburb's 'downtown' passing a FamilyMart and Denny's. We turn down a side street. Ahead on the corner is a boxy noodle shop and, opposite that, a park with a small shrine. Passing the noodle shop, we come to the rear of a two-storey motel, its back patio in mid-renovation. Through a half-finished fence, I spy a concrete mixer and two-by-fours scattered around the pool's deck. Fat, noisy hoses run across it. I guess the pool's heated like the one behind my building, or else they wouldn't be filling it in late October.

The care home lies across the street. The staffs' faces perk up when they see Neotnia. I follow her to a central station, where she speaks to a woman who I get the impression is the head nurse. Neotnia touches my arm as she says my name. I smile and try to look as friendly as I can. Neotnia repeats my name, then says, 'Joe.' Whatever she's talking about, the head nurse seems to agree. She says 'Joe' a few times, too, then smiles and bows to me, saying, '*Konnichiwa*.'

I return the greeting.

'This way,' Neotnia says. I follow her to a small locker room. She removes her cardigan and takes a white apron from the shelf, tying it around her waist. Outside, two large racks are waiting in the hall. Slotted into them are dozens of meal trays.

'This is Kiyoko,' Neotnia says of the woman who's delivered the racks. 'She volunteers here, too. Her grandmother is a resident.'

Neotnia says something to Kiyoko, who smiles at me. 'Welcome,' she says, struggling with the word. She wheels one of the racks down the hall towards someone identically dressed. It's apparent Neotnia's the youngest worker here by a long shot. Kiyoko appears to be in her mid-forties, and all the other volunteers and nurses look to be between their late thirties and early fifties.

Neotnia wheels the rack and I follow. Each ward has eight beds. Given no one has their own room, I get the feeling this is a home for people who are nearing the end of their lives and need constant watch.

'This way. He's over here.'

The ward we enter has a view of the motel and its pool. The beds contain people older than I've ever seen. The youngest must be in their nineties. Some look at me; some don't even see me though their eyes are open. Neotnia smiles at them all anyway.

The last bed is next to the window and its occupant immediately stands out from the rest. Like the others, he's thin, his skin wrinkled and blotchy. But unlike everyone else, he's Caucasian. Neotnia fixes her eyes on him, yet his attention is focused on something outside. Her face lights up as the old man finally turns his head. As soon as he notices her, his face brightens, too.

Neotnia takes an exaggerated bow, then excitedly speaks in Japanese. The old man replies in kind. By their tones, I can tell each seems to know what the other will say. Even with all the IVs, the old man's hands gesture enthusiastically towards the window. And the way he intones his last word makes me think he's ended on some punchline, to which Neotnia releases a laugh and gives a slight bow.

'Now, Joe,' she switches to English, 'I have someone I want to introduce, and I need you to take care of him while I work. This is my friend John, and, seeing as you're both American, I thought you should meet.'

Joe glances as if noticing me for the first time, then pulls his face back in exaggeration. Whatever he says to Neotnia causes her to dip her head and give a shy smile.

'Now, now, Joe. English from now on.'

Joe gives her a look and then scans me up and down.

Neotnia turns to me. 'One second...' and she walks back to the rack and returns with a tray. 'This is his,' she says loud enough for him to hear. 'Don't let him tell you it's missing some sugary dessert or talk you into stealing something from a sleeping resident's tray...'

She pauses and eyes Joe accusingly, who puts his hands up in a 'Who, me?' manner, making her laugh.

'OK, boys,' she gives a little smile. 'Take care of each other.'

My eyes follow Neotnia as she returns to the rack for another tray and delivers it to the first bed in the ward. Her interactions with the other residents are as effortless as with Joe. She greets each with a bright smile as she sets their meal before them. And their faces react in equal measure. To some, she'll bow and share an exchange of words; to others, she'll fold her hair behind an ear and bend close so she can hear their faint voices. Sometimes—

'You gonna give me that or what?'

I jump at Joe's voice.

'Sorry,' I say, realising I'm still holding his tray.

His gaze shifts from me to Neotnia delivering a tray at the other end of the ward, and back to me. A small grin crosses his lips.

I set his tray on his table then slide it over his lap. As I adjust the table, a juice carton tips over. I quickly right it before I notice its lid is still sealed.

He looks at me for several moments.

'Relax, kid. I don't bite.' He nods towards the juice. 'Any way you can open that? Grip isn't what it used to be.'

I do and retreat a step when it's done. Neotnia's now in the ward across the hall, conversing with a female resident who's rested her hand on her arm.

'So, how is America these days?' Joe says, snapping my attention back to him.

'Good,' I nod, perhaps a little too theatrically. 'I'll be going back soon. I'm just visiting.'

His eyes hold me. 'No shit, kid. Hey' – his hand beckons me closer – 'help an old man out.' He instructs me to push a button on the side of his bed, and the back raises, allowing him to sit up more readily in front of his meal. He scans the items, then deposits a spoonful of something that has the consistency of mashed potatoes into his mouth, savouring it.

'I know it doesn't look like much, but it's good,' he says without looking at me. 'When you get to be my age, you're just happy you can still taste.'

'So ... how long have you been here?' I say not knowing what to say.

'You mean here, or Japan?'

'Japan.'

'All my life. Was born here,' he dips the spoon back into the mashed something, swallows, then scoops something else.

'Really?'

'Yep.'

'You've never lived in America?' A gelatine smacks around his tongue as he tries to quickly swallow so he can answer. 'Sorry, I'll let you eat.'

'It's fine. Trust me, you're the best entertainment I'll get all day. Believe it or not, this place isn't exactly rocking. Now, what'd you ask? Have I ever lived in America? Nope. Been there a few times. Went for a summer when I was in my twenties. But never stayed longer than that.'

I nod. There's a brief silence. 'So, why were you born here?'

'Do you mind?' he points to the juice carton.

I pick it up and bring it to his mouth. After he takes a sip, I set it back on the tray.

'That was nice, but I was just gonna ask you to put the straw in it.'

I feel my cheeks flush. 'Sorry.'

I remove the straw from its paper sleeve and poke it into the juice.

'Anyhoo,' Joe continues, scooping more mashed onto his spoon, 'my pop was probably just over your age in 1945 and fighting at the Battle of Okinawa. My mom was his girlfriend from Iowa. After the war ended, he was stationed here for the reconstruction. Mom came over and married him. They had me.'

'Your dad must have really liked Japan if he stayed here.'

Joe's spoon comes to a mid-air stop. 'Jesus, kid. That much naivety will take years off your life.' He plants the spoon back in the mash like a flag. 'Pop despised the Japanese. Fucking hated them.'

'Oh...'

'Even when I was five, he'd tell me how the two bombs were morally righteous. How hordes of Japanese beasts mercilessly slaughtered his buddies on the shores of Okinawa. How every time he took the enemy's hand or head or leg off, he felt he was doing right by God.' Joe shakes his head. 'Even after we won, even after the Japanese disbanded their military, Pop thought they were just biding time, planning their revenge...'

Joe plucks the spoon from his mash and brings it to his mouth, sucking it as a thought rolls around his head. Then, as if coming to some conclusion, he plants it again, this time in purple puree.

'How ridiculous is that? Come on – tell me. I mean, Shidehara was the one who *willingly* disbanded Japan's military. America *wanted* them to keep it to help fend off the Communists in Southeast Asia. But they became pacifists by *choice*.' He scoops some purple puree, considering it, then shakes his head. 'They learned. We didn't.'

I'm not sure how to reply, so I remain silent.

After another batch of purple puree goes down his throat, Joe glances at me.

'But yeah,' he says, almost as if it's an afterthought, 'Pop was a racist son of a bitch – just like Truman. "Yellow Jap" this, "Nip" that. "Gook". For the first part of my life, I thought that's what Japanese people were actually called.'

I'm suddenly conscious of all the other residents.

'Relax, kid. The best of us are half deaf, and no one but me and you speak English. Anyway,' Joe lets out a long breath, 'then Pop fell in love with a Japanese woman and learned to shut the fuck up real quick. Left Mom real quick, too. Mom died, then he died, and his new wife raised me. She was at Nagasaki, you know?'

'Really?'

'I don't lie to impress people – I'm too old.'

I don't say anything.

'I tell ya, kid, it's crazy how much things change. Even when I was ten, you'd still think Japan was never going to recover. But look at it twenty years later, fifty years later, today. The world changes so much from when you're little. It becomes almost unrecognisable by the time you reach my age.'

He gives me a long look as if he's trying to interpret some detail on a painting.

'What are you? Sixteen? Seventeen?'

'I'll be eighteen in a few months.'

'So, the Chinese and American stations – you probably don't remember seeing a sky without them? When I was your age, something like that was pure science fiction. Just goes to show what's possible given enough time – and if your paranoia about your latest enemy is strong enough. But believe it or not, though we like to delude ourselves into thinking we can foretell what's coming next, there's not a person alive who can accurately predict what the world will be like by the time *you* reach my age. There's just too many unknowns that happen over the course of a life, kid – and each can send the world down an unforeseen path. Maybe we'll have fancier stuff, or maybe we'll be back to throwing sticks and rocks. The *only* guarantee is things will be radically different than they are today.'

I nod.

'You're wondering how old I am?'

'Yeah,' I say. No point denying it.

'A little younger than a hundred, a little older than a hundred. It doesn't really matter once you get past ninety.'

I'm about to reply when a moan rises out of nowhere. It grows into a cry, and I'm startled as it's followed by a clamorous crash. The contents of a tray have scattered across the floor in the ward opposite. Its owner wails as she violently rocks. It's as if she's trying to launch herself from the bed. Suddenly, the head nurse darts into the ward, followed by an orderly. Both attempt to restrain the woman as the nurse shouts in the direction from which she came. Seconds later Neotnia rushes in, handing a small red box to the nurse as the orderly places his palms on the wailing woman's shoulders and leans hard into her body. Neotnia draws the curtains shut, sealing off the spectacle.

Within a minute, the woman's wails are again reduced to moans, and, soon enough, to silence. When the curtains open, Neotnia is the first to exit. She carries away a bedpan and returns with towels, wipes the food from the floor, then collects the scattered utensils.

Joe shakes his head. 'Life breaks us all, eventually.'

I give him a small smile. I don't know how else to reply.

'It's OK, kid. Old folks' homes make people uncomfortable. You don't have to be embarrassed.'

'I'm not,' I say. 'I mean, I'm not uncomfortable. My parents are actually doctors, and sometimes they did consults from our house, so I grew up used to seeing people who are ... unwell. They also did fieldwork in places where people were really, well, broken, as you say, and they were always honest with me about what they saw.'

'Oh, yeah? Where's that?'

'Angola.'

Joe's jaw drops a little.

'The Stung?'

I nod.

Joe looks at me like he's waiting for me to go on.

'I know most Americans don't anymore, due to the keyword bans, but I heard all about the starvation and disease, first-hand and in detail – the disfigurements, too. What it did to them, not just physically, but psychologically.'

But at that, I stop and clear my throat, the past suddenly too near. All of it was caused by the biologics the UAVs released on the Angolan population, and it gave those impacted the name 'the Stung'. It's a topic taboo to most Americans, even before the bans, given it was our drones that did the stinging.

'Your parents were in the north the whole time?' says Joe.

'Yeah.'

'Wow, kid. They really must've seen the worst of it. The Americans and Chinese poured so much tech into the hands of their surrogate factions up there, it's a miracle there were any civilians left to be helped. It's been over a decade since the s'powers disavowed what happened in their little proxy war, but the north was so scarred they *still* can't grow their own crops. Japan's one of the nations that farm a genetically modified wheat to this day just to help feed them.'

Joe looks at me, but I don't say anything.

'You should get your mom and pop to record what they saw, for posterity's sake. Get them to write it down. Humanity has a convenient habit of forgetting our worst horrors.'

'Mom doesn't really talk about it anymore.'

'Well, your pop then.'

I hesitate for a moment.

'Only Mom came back.'

Joe's lips part.

'That's rough, kid. I'm sorry.'

I press my own lips together. 'Well, anyway ... my point was I'm not uncomfortable here. I know this place is heaven compared to how some have to live out their last days.'

I immediately feel stupid for saying that last part. But if Joe's taken offence, he doesn't show it.

'Well, let's hope places such as this stay like heaven, comparatively. But mark my words, kid: this cold war that's been going on since before you were born? It's not going to be cold forever – and its effects aren't going to be limited to far-off places like Africa forever, either. Small Sino-American proxy wars are always within a hair's breadth of spilling over into global ones. The planet's gotten too small for two superpowers with radically different worldviews – and they both know it.'

Joe takes a breath and looks down at his tray. It's as if he's suddenly worn out. He places the edges of his palms on the table.

'Hey, do you mind?'

I roll the table away from his bed.

'I'll save some food for later.' Then, adjusting the blanket over himself, he adds, 'A bit cold in here today.'

'Is there something I can do?'

'See the compartment down there? It should have an extra blanket.'

I open the compartment at the foot of his bed and find a thick blue cover. I help spread it across his body.

'Thanks, kid. It'd take forever for a nurse to come help me with this.'

'So, how long have you known Neotnia?' I say once he's settled, not wanting to return to our previous topic.

He thinks for a moment. 'About nine months. Ever since she started volunteering. We all adore her. We could use another thirty of her.'

'She mentioned they're short-staffed here.'

Joe nods. 'But it's not just here. It's been a problem in Japan since the twenties, at least. People stopped having so many kids. Soon there'll be more people over the age of sixty than under. That's what half of the news in Japan is about nowadays: "the elderly crisis". There's just not enough young people to care for the old.'

'What about bots?'

'We've got a couple here to help with the basic stuff – delivering meds, things like that. But beyond that, how can they help? We don't need them to build a highway in here or give us a tour of the place. I've seen construction bots lifting five hundred pounds of cement, no problem, but how could they help one of us get out of bed without breaking our frail bones?'

I nod.

'Not that it's just about helping us to the toilet. Neotnia's helped me to the toilet more times than I can count, but that's not why she's a treasure. A lot of us are lonely, and she gives us attention, genuine attention. A robot can't do that. And kid, let me tell you, that is re-markable – the attention she gives us. Most girls her age would be out in the clubs dancing, not here with us.'

As Joes says this, I glimpse Neotnia in the ward across the hall. She's now feeding the old woman who had the fit. She speaks gently to her as she refills the spoon with more puree from a fresh meal tray. When I turn back, Joe's eyeing me.

'How long have *you* known her?'

'Not long.'

'Well, I'm glad to know she has a friend,' he says after considering me for a moment longer. 'I honestly thought she might not – outside of my compatriots here, anyhow. She never mentions any. When any of us ask about her life, she says she spends her free time reading and going on walks. She's got a part-time café job, too. But soon enough, she changes the subject back to us, which tells you she really doesn't have one – a life, that is.'

I nod and glance back across the hall. Neotnia's now listening carefully to the old woman, who seems to have found a renewed vigour. Her head is thrust forward, immersed in whatever she's saying to Neotnia, who looks just as absorbed by her words.

'You never think it,' Joe says, watching Neotnia, too, 'but the prettiest are sometimes the loneliest.'

'Lonely?'

'Jesus, kid – look where you're standing. Young people with great social lives generally don't spend their free time hanging out with nonagenarians.'

A burst of laughter rings out across the hall but is cut short just as quickly. It's Neotnia – hand slapped over mouth. The old woman in the bed stifles a laugh of her own, her body jiggling.

'But surely she must have other outside interests. Her life can't just be working and walks and volunteering.'

Joe gives me a look. 'Is "outside interests" code for "boys she likes"?'

I feel my face warm, and Joe rolls his eyes when I don't respond.

'Sometimes I hear her chatting to some of the other residents about Shintoism. She seems to have an interest in it.'

'What's that?'

'I've been here all my life, and I still don't really get it. It's a religion but not a religion. Not like ours in the west, anyway. There's no book, or rules or guidelines, for starters. They believe in these things called kami, which may or may not be gods, depending on who you talk to. They give thanks to them at shrines.'

I nod. 'We walked past one coming here. In the park next door.'

'Nope, that's not a shrine,' Joe shakes his head. 'Do they still teach you about Nazis in school? The way America's gotten, you never know.'

'A little...' I say, uncertain how this relates to anything.

'OK – you know those religious buildings you go to here adorned in symbols that look like a backward swastika? Those are Buddhist temples. Hitler was so consumed with murdering people he deemed inferior, he couldn't spare an afternoon to create an original symbol for his fucked-up party. So, he hijacked the one that represents the Buddha's footstep, and just flipped it around.'

Joe looks at me to make sure I'm following. I nod.

'The places that look like a temple but have no swastikas and instead have a fancy gate with two crosspieces? That gate is a *torii*. If a structure has a torii, it's a shrine, which is Shinto. You see a swastika, it's a temple, which is Buddhist. The structure in the park next door is a temple, not a shrine.'

'I understand,' I say. 'So, she's likes to talk about Shintoism. Anything else?'

A grin spreads on Joe's lips. 'Of course. We don't only discuss theology over puree and bedpan changes every day. But like I said, she gives *us* attention. When we ask her about herself, she'll soon change the subject back to us. She asks a lot about our feelings, what we were like when we were younger, where we've been, what it felt like the first time I fell in love. That kind of stuff. And she makes it easy to talk about ourselves. She's a great listener – a genuine one.'

Across the hall, Neotnia now stands at the end of the old woman's bed. She brings her hands to her lips and presses her palms together. She bows, and the woman smiles and says something. Neotnia retrieves the empty tray and turns into the hall. She catches my gaze and responds with a little smile. I give a small one back.

'Christ, kid. Youth is wasted on the young. If you like her, go ask her out.'

Instinctively, I look towards the hall. 'Oh, no, we just met. I don't even—'

'Stop,' Joe holds the palm of his IV-stabbed hand up to me like he's directing traffic. He looks me straight in the eyes. 'When you get to be my age, you have no problem calling people out on their bullshit. Hell, I'm half blind in one eye yet can clearly see you're smitten with her.'

I begin to speak, but Joe cuts me off again.

'If you like her,' he says, 'do something about it. You'll be my age before you know it, kid. Now you're young. Good-looking. Besides, she's a good kid and deserves to have some fun. You seem like you are, too. And like I said, you're the first person I've ever heard her mention outside of here – much less bring with her.'

He keeps his gaze on me.

'But...'

'But what?'

'How?' I say.

'How what?'

'How do I ask her out?'

'Jesus, kid. It's not rocket science. Ask her to go do something. Take her to a movie. And I don't mean any of that meta shit where you watch it "together" virtually through fucking lenses. Take her to a real cinema. Have a real shared experience.'

'But, then what? I mean, how do you know if a girl's interested in you? What makes a girl like her interested in someone?'

Joe looks like he wants to roll his eyes, yet he finds the strength to restrain himself.

'Just treat her like she treats us,' he says, which I nod to. 'I'm not talking about changing her bedpan, kid. I mean, make her feel special – one of a kind. She takes an interest in *us*. She asks us questions about *ourselves*. She talks about *us*, not *herself*. If you want someone to find you interesting, find them interesting first.'

4 – A boy was dead, and people were angry.

'He likes you, you know? That's what he told me just now.'

That's what Neotnia says as we leave the care home. It's almost two, and the sky is a cloudless blue. She buttons her golden knit cardigan over her white work shirt, which is stained with a purple puree.

'I'm glad,' I say. 'I like him, too.'

She raises an eyebrow. 'And you weren't too bored?'

'No, not at all. Joe's an interesting guy. Seems like he's a bit of a history buff.'

'*Hai*, he is. He's taught me a lot about Japan's past. When you've been alive as long as him, I guess you see the world go through so much. Wars. The sea rises. Pandemics.'

We cross the street towards the motel, its pool still being filled by the fat hoses.

'So ... what does he have?'

Neotnia looks at me and scrunches up her mouth a bit. 'He's just sick,' she shrugs. 'That's all he's ever told me.'

'You wouldn't think it. He seems like one of the liveliest people there.'

'*Hai*, I agree. He's as sharp as a tack. But though he seems fine while in bed, his legs hardly work anymore. Once he's out of bed, he gets fatigued, really fast. Having only one foot doesn't help either.'

'What – he's only got one foot?'

My reaction causes a short laugh to escape Neotnia's mouth. 'I guess you missed that,' she smiles. 'To be fair, he was under a blanket. But yeah, he told me he had an artificial one for about five years, but his leg bones eventually became too weak to support it, so they had to remove it again.'

'Wow,' I say, thinking about that for a while. 'Well, it looks like you two have a good repertoire.'

'What do you mean?'

'Oh, when we first arrived, it seemed like you guys had a little banter going on – like a routine you go through. Or that's the impression I got, anyway.'

She stops and, for a moment, those wonderful eyes study mine. The breeze ruffles the straight bangs falling across her forehead.

'Well, I guess you *are* observant. We've got a running joke about this,' and she points to the motel's pool. 'They've been working on it for six months, and Joe's watched them from his window every day. He always says he's breaking out of the home and going for a swim as soon as it's done. Today he told me he can see they're filling it now, so it'll be ready for him soon, and he's not going to let anyone, even me, stop him from doing some laps. I always ask how he's going to do laps with only one foot, but he says his other foot is twice the size of a normal one, so it doesn't matter.'

A smile spreads across her face and stays there for several moments.

'He makes me laugh. I'm glad he's my friend.'

I think of what Joe said about her not having any friends – outside of the care home, anyway.

We continue down the street and Neotnia points to the boxy noodle shop. 'Is it OK if I take you here? It's small, but they have the best *yakisoba* in all of Japan.'

I tell her the place looks great. Inside, we sit on the stools by the window overlooking the park with Joe's temple.

'May I order for you?' Neotnia says.

'Please.'

She tells the waiter our order, and he returns a few minutes later with two ceramic cups and a pot of green tea. Neotnia pours for us. 'I think you'll like the *yakisoba*. It's a fried noodle dish with egg and vegetables, and I ordered ours with beef. It's my favourite.'

'It sounds good.' I take a sip of my tea and think of Joe's advice. 'So, how long have you volunteered at the care home?'

Neotnia twists her mouth a little. 'Since February.'

'What made you decide to?'

'It was winter, and freezing in Tokyo, and I was feeling down. I was in my room watching NHK on Goeido's laptop, and they had another report about the elderly crisis. They kept showing all these care home residents doing nothing but lying in bed for days at a time. Everyone they interviewed said it was one thing when the lack of staff made their meals or medicine late but what was worse was that they all felt so, so lonely. It just broke my heart.'

She pauses for a moment and gazes at the backs of her hands.

'It made me think of my father and how I would never want him to be so lonely. He'll be seventy next year, and I don't ever want him to be that sad. Joe's home was one of the ones featured in the report, so I went the next day.'

I do the math in my head. Neotnia is twenty, so her father didn't have her until quite late.

'Is your father in a home?'

Neotnia remains silent for a moment. 'No. But he does have a weak heart, and I worry about that.'

I take a sip of my tea. 'So, is he in Tokyo, too?'

She looks at her hands again. Her mouth tightens into a line. When she next speaks, her voice sounds so small.

'I don't know.'

'You don't know?' I say before I can stop myself.

She presses her lips together. 'He's been ... missing, for a while.'

And as soon as she says this, it's as if a dark shadow has descended across her face. She won't look at me, and the shine in her eyes has been blown away. Now, they're as cloudy as the sky before a storm. It's astonishing really, the change in her demeanour. If I was seeing her for the first time, I'd be sure I was looking at a girl who's never once laughed or smiled. Matter of fact, I'd be certain she wasn't capable of it.

'But ... what do you mean he's missing?'

But a voice cuts in. It's the waiter with our *yakisoba*. Neotnia nods and he sets the plates in front of us. She lifts her chopsticks and her clouded eyes gaze at her noodles, but I'm not sure she's actually seeing them. As I remove my chopsticks from their sleeve, I remember my grandpa and wonder if her father has Alzheimer's.

Could he have become confused and wandered away? He's almost seventy. Does it happen that early?

Neotnia's still silent, and I'm not sure she even heard my question before the waiter interrupted. That shadow hangs over her face like a curtain, and she thumbs her chopsticks like they're a new instrument to her.

'Um, what about your mom? Doesn't she know where he is?'

Neotnia gives a single shake of her head, but blink and you'd miss it. 'Father raised me by himself,' she says, still looking at her noodles. Finally, she pinches some between her chopsticks.

I think for a moment. 'I'm sorry, I've never asked ... do you have siblings or other family?'

'No, it's just Father and me.' And she puts a few noodles into her mouth.

And I feel horrible. 'Look, I'm sorry. I didn't mean to pry.' My chopsticks pinch some *yakisoba*, too. We both eat a mouthful in silence. But then, as if suddenly remembering I'm sitting beside her, Neotnia dabs her lips with a napkin and turns to me.

'You weren't prying,' she shakes her head. 'It's OK.'

I give her a little smile and take another bite of my *yakisoba*. Neotnia does the same.

After a few more bites, I say, 'Well, I've only got a mom. It's just me and her. No siblings, either.'

'Really?' She tilts her head up. 'No father?'

'Not anymore.'

She holds her gaze on me. There's a kind of sad desperation to it. And I really wish I had something to say that could scatter those clouds. Instead, I tell her the truth – an abbreviated version, anyway.

'My parents are – were – surgeons. They went to help in Angola when I was eight.' I prod my *yakisoba* with my chopsticks. 'I cried and cried when they told me they were going, but they explained that we had it better than the people in Angola, and it's the duty of those who are better off to help those less fortunate – especially for people with their skills. Besides, they promised it was only for six months. They'd be back before I knew it, and in the meantime my grandparents would look after me...' I shrug. 'Well, six months turned into twelve, and only Mom came back. Dad died over there helping the Stung.'

'That's horrible.' Neotnia's eyes look suddenly wet. 'I'm so sorry.'

'Thanks. It's OK, though. It's been a long time.' And I pop a big chunk of noodles into my mouth.

Neotnia pokes at her noodles for a few moments, lost in thought. 'So, your mom's a surgeon?'

'Um, not anymore. Not really,' I wipe some sauce from my lips. 'She was different after she came back. She's still a doctor, but she doesn't work much. She'll do consultations from time to time, but nothing that involves life-saving stuff.'

'I see.' For a moment, Neotnia absentmindedly toys with a noodle between her chopsticks before putting it into her mouth.

I decide to change the subject and tell her how delicious the *yaki-soba* is. She nods and tells me she thinks it's the tastiest of all the noodle dishes. We talk about noodles for the remainder of lunch. When we walk back to the station and board the local train, Neotnia's eyes are still full of clouds, and that dark shadow lingers on her face. We're both pretty quiet on the return journey, and I'm killing myself for making lunch such a downer – precisely the opposite of what Joe would have advised.

We're back in Shibuya by five-thirty, just as it's getting dark. The café's windows emit a golden glow. We stop in front of the door, but neither of us moves to open it. Inside, Inu's on the counter and Goeido's just taken an order into the dining area. Neotnia turns towards me as a gust blows past, sending autumn leaves scratching down the sidewalk. She looks up at me but doesn't speak. Her bangs flutter in the breeze.

'Hey, look,' I say, thinking of Joe's advice. 'I was in Akihabara the other day. A cinema is showing films in English. There's one I wanted to see and, well .... do you want to go with me tonight? My treat? I figure I owe you for two meals now.'

But Neotnia remains silent as the breeze caresses her bangs, her eyes taking their time on me as she mulls something inside herself.

Then, as if her eyes have found whatever they were seeking, the clouds in them lift and that dark shadow hanging over her face fades just a bit. For the first time since the noodle shop, a little smile crosses her lips.

'*Hai*,' she says, almost as if waking from a dream. 'OK.'

'Don't you want to know what movie?'

But she just shakes her head. 'Surprise me.'

Inside, Goeido's back behind the counter. 'And you don't need to help him here?'

Neotnia gives her head a few more gentle shakes, her eyes still on mine. 'Nope. This day of the week is always slow at night.'

'Well ... great,' I say with a smile I hope isn't too big and stupid-looking. 'Ah ... how about I meet you back here at seven-thirty?'

'*Hai*,' she nods, little dimples now making an appearance on her cheeks.

'Well, great,' I say again. And I really need to stop that. 'So ... I'll see you in a few hours?'

'OK.' Placing her palm on the café's door, she glances at me once more. And as the bell clangs, Goeido turns. Looking past Neotnia, he spots me outside.

I give him a wave, which he answers by squinting at me as the door closes shut.

*

I'm back at my apartment ten minutes later. I shower, avoiding the mirror until I slip into a crisp white T-shirt and my fancier blue sweater. Only then do I give a turn in front of it, thinking about what Joe said about me being young. Good-looking. I give another turn. The sweater's not too tight – it pretty much hangs straight down from my chest.

If only the surface we display for others could be the reality.

I push the thought from my mind. It's not something I have to worry about tonight. I grab a milk tea and sit on the balcony, taking in the patchwork of illuminated shapes, and the countless lights gliding across the sky. I spot the distant colourful haze at my two o'clock. Tonight Akihabara glows more brilliantly than it typically does.

Yet soon my thoughts return to Neotnia – to what she said about her father. If he was the only one who raised her, she probably never knew her mom. Could she have died during childbirth? Or maybe she walked out on them at a young age, and so her father had no choice but to raise Neotnia alone? There was a guy at my school that happened to.

But her father missing? How does an almost seventy-year-old man just disappear? Unless it *is* Alzheimer's. In Grandpa's final years, his often led to him becoming confused and wandering off. The sheriff once found him in a neighbour's cornfield nearly a dozen hours after he disappeared. Yet surely if the same thing happened to Neotnia's father, the police here could find a missing old man, too?

Unless he wanted to disappear. I bet someone could vanish into thin air in Tokyo – if they chose to. I bet it happens all the time in a city this size. Then again, why would a father abandon his grown daughter? Though, I do remember a metacast I once saw about foster parents who eventually discard their adopted children. It usually happens when one of the spouses passes away. The surviving partner loses that emotional attachment to the child, who didn't even come from the person they're bereaving. So, they wait out the years until they can legally remove themselves from their foster child's life.

I shake my head. I'm letting my imagination fill the gaps in the story. Neotnia didn't say a thing about being adopted. But whatever the reason was for his disappearance, I've never seen anyone look as despondent as she did when she mentioned her father. She became a completely different person. Even in the care home – dealing with all those sick people – she never once had any hint of those storm clouds in her eyes nor that dark shadow across her face.

I take a swig of my milk tea, finishing it. Looking into the sky, I find the moon and the two jagged, unfinished stations floating between here and it.

All I know is I'm not bringing her father up again tonight. Joe said she deserves to have some fun – and he's right.

*

The bell clangs as I enter the café, where I'm greeted by a few yaps from Inu. I pat his spherical head, and he smells my hand, giving it a lick with his tiny tongue. I peer into the dining area, where Goeido's clearing some plates. Besides a couple of people in the opposite booth, the place is quiet, as Neotnia said it would be.

I give Goeido a little nod. '*Konbanwa*,' I say.

His lips tightens as if he's holding in a sigh. But finally, he swallows it.

'*Konbanwa*,' he replies.

I move out of his way as he enters the foyer. When he passes, Neotnia has materialised from the dark hallway. She's changed, too, wearing a modest light-grey dress with blue floral patterns that goes down just past her knees. It's something you'd find congregants wearing to Sunday mass where I'm from. Still, she looks beautiful in it. It fits her slim form nicely.

'Hello,' she says. She grabs a light-green peacoat from behind the counter and says something to Goeido through the partition. They have a short back-and-forth that I can't understand, but a couple of times Goeido shoots his ambiguous glances at me. Passing the counter, Neotnia sinks her fingers into Inu's sphere and gives him a good scratch on the skull.

'Hold down the fort, and help Goeido out tonight,' she tells him.

As I get the door for her, I catch Goeido's ghostly image in the window's reflection.

He's staring, and he does not look happy. At all.

Outside, the car I order arrives quickly. We tell it to take us to the TOHO cinema in Akihabara. As it loops towards Shibuya and then heads north, I realise I'm quieter than usual. Neotnia's quiet, too, her hands folded in her lap over her blue floral dress. For some reason, I feel like the girl I'm sitting next to is different from the one I met two days ago.

Traffic slows to a virtual standstill as we near Akihabara, so we tell the car to drop us by the station. I've only been to the area twice, but even on a normal day Akihabara can feel overwhelming. Hell, it could be the poster boy for culture shock. Its streets are lined with maid cafés, idol clubs, bot dens, and twenty-storey shop after shop selling manga and anime and all things J-pop. And then there are the meta-arcades running the length of an entire block and the pachinko parlours that, when their doors slide open, roar with the sound of a hundred casinos. That's not to mention the random hostesses in their short skirts standing on curbs with a real owl on their shoulder or snake wrapped around their neck. They call out, tempting you into their animal café that's hidden among the glaring metascreens ten storeys up.

But tonight, Akihabara is acid-trip levels of insanity beyond anything I've seen before. If a cosplay convention had a baby with the world's largest street carnival, this would be the offspring. Throngs of people dressed as almost any character imaginable pack the roads. I see Batman. Ninja Bird. Harry Potter. Karate Rabbit. Epiphany Jones. An entire family of Wookies. There's Link, the Little Mermaid, Shrek. Mario. Peach. A quartet of Sailor Moon girls. And those are the ones I recognise. There's an entire subset of people dressed as characters I have no cultural reference point for. Still, their costumes are so intricate you'd think they just stepped from the set of the latest Chinese blockbuster. That's not to mention those dressed as your generic variety of sexy somethings. There're more sexy-cat and sexy-nurse and sexy-devil outfits than I can count. An entire horde of sexy zombies just walked past a meta-arcade. I even spot someone dressed as a sexy trash bag.

And it's not just down here. Above, the sky is lit with neon fire – and not only from the glow of the metascreens scaffolded onto the buildings all around. The air literally buzzes with hundreds of drone phones zipping and hovering overhead. Their safety lights flash while they metacast their owners to their followers in 256K SHVR.

Without warning I'm thrust backward with such force my feet almost lift from the ground. My heart pounds as a massive Titan-class agribot stomps past. It's been modded to look like a quadruple-tusked *kaiju*, and three cute Japanese girls dressed in hooded furry onesies sit astride it. One is a blue Cookie Monster; another, a red Elmo; and the third, a gold Pluto. Masses of cheering characters swarm as the girls throw chocolate-chip cookies into the crowd.

It's Neotnia who's pulled me to safety, and she bursts into a laugh at whatever stupefied expression I'm wearing. She leans in. 'I should have warned you Akihabara goes kind of crazy on the nights leading up to Halloween.' Though I can feel her warm breath on my ear and know she must be shouting, her words seem soft compared to the roar all around.

She grabs my hand, 'Come on.'

We weave across the packed road, then duck down a side street, away from the kaleidoscopic madness. Behind us, the crowds cheer at some new, unseen spectacle.

'That's insane,' I say when we're finally far enough from the clamour to hear each other.

Neotnia's hand slides from mine as a laugh escapes her mouth. '*Hai*,' she smiles. 'People go nuts.'

'But it's not even Halloween until tomorrow...'

Neotnia gives another little laugh. 'Are we still OK for the movie?'

I take out my phone as we pass a three-storey shop selling action figures and collectibles. 'Yeah, we've got twenty minutes. Avance Maps says it's just two blocks this way.'

We take a right at the corner, heading parallel to the packed main road. The hostess outside a maid café calls to us. Neotnia replies, giving her a wave. She holds on to a shy laugh until we're out of earshot.

'She asked if we wanted an ear cleaning.'

'Really?'

'*Hai*,' she grins. 'But I told her yours had just been done.'

We ride the TOHO building's elevator to the seventeenth floor and find our seats. I'm surprised the cinema's as packed as it is. Though it's subtitled in Japanese, the film's a musical, and I wouldn't think lyrics translate as well as dialogue. Then again, it features Hengdian's and Hollywood's biggest stars, though the Chinese leading lady is partially deepfaked to look fifteen years younger and the American leading man is entirely deepfaked because he's been dead for a decade. But I've seen both actors in ads over here, for coffee makers of all things, so clearly Japan loves them.

The movie's about an impoverished, world-travelling American writer in the early 1900s who falls in love with a circus owner's daughter in rural China. The twist is the daughter is a ghost – the spirit of the woman the writer's father killed while working as a hired gun during the Boxer Rebellion.

Every time I glance at Neotnia in the darkness, she seems to be enjoying the show. I am too – until about halfway through, when the song they highlighted in all the trailers is performed. The song itself is fantastic. Actually, it's utterly brilliant. But it's sung during a scene in which a poorly placed bucket of mop water spills over the writer, so he removes his shirt and finishes the number with his immaculate six-pack on display. I know his abs are deepfaked, but the way the girls in the audience react keenly reminds me of what's desirable to the opposite sex.

I don't look at Neotnia during the scene, though I feel her eyes on me several times.

It's near the end of the third act when I glance at Neotnia next. It comes when another big twist is revealed, and I instinctively look to her to share my surprise. The only thing is, I'm met with a sight so unexpected, for a moment, I'm stunned.

Neotnia's skin is so pale it looks as if it's lost all colouring, and her jaw hangs open. No, not hangs. More like it's frozen open. Matter of fact, her whole body appears frozen – except for one part. Her throat winces involuntarily in the screen's flickering light, as if she's desperately struggling to receive gasps of air through her gaping mouth.

I glance away as a cheer breaks over the crowd, yet when I look back Neotnia's completely fine, smiling with the rest of the audience as if what I saw never happened.

And maybe it didn't. The whole sight lasted mere seconds. Perhaps it was a trick of the flickering lights against her body. Indeed, she turns to me with a big, ordinary smile and raises her eyebrows, as if saying, *Can you believe that twist?*

When the movie ends, we get trapped up in the crowds as an usher bot directs everyone towards the packed elevators. It's not until we're outside that we have a chance to speak again. It's almost eleven, and the side streets have absorbed many of the Akihabaran characters celebrating Halloween a night early.

'Should we get something to eat?' I suggest.

'*Hai*. What do you feel like?'

'I'm up for anything.'

'Do you like burgers?'

I give her a look. 'I'm American.'

She laughs. 'OK. Let's head this way. There's a Freshness Burger by Ueno station. Have you had one yet?'

I tell her I haven't.

'They're *amazing*,' she beams, her eyes as clear as glass in the crisp air.

As we head down the street, I recall the trick my own eyes played in the cinema. And it had to be a trick. She's obviously fine. Though, for a moment, I do think about mentioning it. But no – I'd sound like a lunatic.

'Did you like the movie?' I say instead.

'I did,' she gives an earnest nod. 'Who doesn't like a ghostly love story? It's comforting.'

'How so?'

'That love can last even when there's no longer a physical body to contain it. Some of the residents have told me they've seen their loved ones after they passed. They say just knowing that their spirits are out there makes them feel less alone.'

I nod but don't say anything. In the silence I can feel Neotnia's eyes on me.

'What about you? Do you believe in ghosts?'

I shake my head. 'No, of course not.'

'Hmmm, I see. The brilliant genius doesn't believe in ghosts. "Of course not" – what a silly idea,' she teases.

But she holds her gaze on me. 'Still ... what would he do if they were real? If someone *proved* their existence?'

'How could they do that? What kind of data—'

'Doesn't matter. But say they can. Say they can prove it without a doubt.'

I give her a look. She's being serious.

'Without a doubt?'

She nods.

'Well,' I say, thinking about it, 'then I guess I'd have no choice but to change my beliefs. Data doesn't lie.'

Neotnia considers my reply. Suddenly, she grabs my arm. 'Look...' She points to an Akihabaran underneath a white sheet traipsing across the street. 'Data!'

'Fine.' I grin. 'I accept that as undeniable proof – but only until Halloween.'

She gives a satisfied nod. 'So, ghosts aside, did you like the movie?'

'I did,' I say. 'I'm glad I got to see it at all. Even though it's in English and features the world's two biggest stars, cinemas back home have refused to show it since it's mainly a Chinese production.'

'That's a shame. It was really sweet. And I liked the main song.'

'Me too. Actually, musicals are my favourite type of movie. I wish they'd make more of them.'

'Really?'

I nod. 'I know people our age are supposed to like pop or rap or whatever, but I love musicals. I can't help it. Did you know that when people hear a phrase sung to them, they remember what was said better than they would had the phrase simply been spoken?'

She shakes her head.

'It's true – I read it in one of Mom's medical journals. And did you know that for some reason, listening to musicals alters our neuro-chemistry? They reduce depression and can even alleviate pain. But – even better – if *you're* the one singing, the effects are more pro-nounced. Now, I can't sing to save my life, but these scientists found that you don't even need to sing for real. You can just *act* like you are, and your brain will go through the same neurochemical changes. It's crazy, really – like the human brain is happy to be duped. Sometimes, when I'm alone, I lip-sync to songs from musicals, and I *know* the scientists are right. Hell, sometimes, if I hear a great song, I can't even help it – I have to lip-sync to it right there.'

Neotnia gives me a look like she thinks I'm messing with her.

'No, really,' I protest. 'I know it all sounds stupid, but it *feels* amazing. Seriously, here...' I stop, pull out my phone and download the main song from the ghostly love story. Sticking one of my meta-buds behind my ear, I hold the other up. 'May I?'

Neotnia looks at the bud for a moment, then nods, folding her black hair behind an ear. As the bud makes contact with her flesh, her eyes shift towards her feet and the edges of her lips give a furtive curl.

'OK,' I say, tapping my foot on the sidewalk as the beats begin. 'Sounds good, right?'

'Right,' she smiles, taking in what I'm sure is my goofy expression.

'OK, wait for it...' I'm nodding along with the beats now. 'Here it comes...'

The star's baritone voice explodes into our heads.

'See,' I say, already feeling the energy. 'You're enjoying the song right now, right?'

'Right,' she says, an amused look on her face.

'Right,' I nod, tapping my foot. 'These lyrics make you want to dance, right? Makes you feel good, right?'

She laughs. '*Hai!*'

'OK, now wait...' My entire body sways in place to the music's beats. 'Wait for the next refrain ... wait for it. Here it comes!'

Stomping the ground with my foot, I grip an invisible microphone, my lips exaggerating wildly as I lip-sync to the refrain now exploding in our heads. Neotnia's eyes go wide at my gesticulations, clamping her hand over her mouth, but my lips continue their synchronization to the lyrics nonetheless. I don't care how goofy I look. The energy rushing through me has taken control. Besides, that astonished look on her face beats the shadow that hung there today. So, I continue until the final refrain, where I round my lips and belt out an audible 'AAOOHH-OOOOOHH' along with the last of the song.

A burst of noise erupts across the street. It's a horde of sexy zombie nurses, applauding. Their cheers make Neotnia laugh so hard her cheeks flush, and she hides her face against my chest. When her body finally stops shaking, she catches her breath and bends her head towards mine. Her bangs are dishevelled.

'Never do that again,' she smiles.

'But you felt the energy, right? Even watching me lip-sync felt so much better than just listening to the song, right?'

Behind us, Darth Vader squeezes by, his young kid dressed as RD-D2 in tow. Little R2 claps as he passes, too.

'Right,' she grins, handing me my metabud. 'Now, never again.'

A few of the sexy zombies whistle at me as we continue in the direction of the burger place. They wave and I wave back.

As Neotnia and I advance down the street, a breeze passes over us. That's when I notice how closely she's now walking by my side. Another breeze comes, but she seems not to notice. For several seconds more, she's quiet, thinking.

'So ... have you ever had a girlfriend?' She looks up at me.

For a moment I feel like I've lost the ability to speak.

I shake my head. 'Not really.'

'Not really?'

'Ah,' I twist up my mouth a bit, 'so, back when I was fifteen, during the middle of sophomore year, I hung out with this girl a lot. Mora. We had a coding class together, and the teacher made everyone partner up for the final project. She was one of the prettiest girls in school, and she chose me, so, you know, I was quite excited.'

I look at Neotnia, who raises her eyebrows, telling me to continue.

'Well, she'd often come to my house after school to work on the project. She seemed to really take a liking to me, and that felt good, especially since I didn't have many friends. Anyway, a week before the end of the trimester, I worked up the courage to ask her out. She said yes and suggested our first date be the night after we submitted our final project – to celebrate, you know?'

Neotnia nods, her eyes on me.

'Long story short: as soon as we uploaded our project, she stopped returning my messages. Even after we received the best grade in class, Mora never said another word to me. She wouldn't even look at me in the hallway.'

I keep my gaze on the pavement as we continue to walk but I can feel Neotnia's eyes lingering on me. 'Well,' she says after a few more steps, 'she must be regretting that now – after how successful you've become.'

I consider what she's said.

'Nah,' I shake my head. 'The thing about success – what little I've had, anyway – is it doesn't change how the people who knew you before see you now. They still think of you as the gullible person they went to school with. They still treat you the same. Success ... it only impresses the people you meet after you've accomplished something. Everyone who knew you previously just thinks, *There must be some mistake, how did* he *do* that?'

Neotnia remains silent for several moments. Then, she gives a little shrug. 'Well, I've never had a boyfriend, either.'

I almost stop in my tracks. The thing is, I don't think she's the type who lies to make someone feel better. But how on earth can that be true? Even in her Sunday-school dress, she's more attractive than any of the sexy zombies or sexy devils – or even the sexy trash bag girl – we've passed tonight.

But before I have a chance to reply, she stops. We've reached the Freshness Burger.

'I know it just looks like a bad fast-food chain,' she says, 'but be prepared to have all other hamburgers from here on out ruined for you.'

'OK.' I laugh a little. 'Let's do it.'

The place isn't too crowded, and we quickly find a booth in the back. Of the people here, about half are dressed in costumes. Of the ones who aren't, some leisurely sip a lone coffee or read a book. A few look like they're using the place as a study hall. We swipe through the menu mats. A few minutes later, one of the servers comes over.

'*Konbanwa*,' it says.

'Hello,' I say. 'How's your night?'

Immediately the server switches to English. 'Very well, thank you.'

'Good. Umm, I'm not sure what I'm going to get just yet...' I ask Neotnia if she knows what she's ordering and catch her staring a bit.

'I'm going to have the teriyaki burger meal with an iced tea,' she tells me.

I swipe the menu again. To the server, I say, 'OK, so one teriyaki burger meal with iced tea, and I guess I'll have the classic double cheeseburger meal with a Diet Coke.'

'Good choice,' the server says. 'Please verify the payment amount and tap below.'

Neotnia protests, but I tell her it's on me. I tap my phone to the glowing pad on the server's chest. It thanks me and begins to roll away.

'Oh, sorry!' I call out. 'Do you mind if I change my Diet Coke to an iced tea, too? Sorry about that.'

The server says it's not a problem.

'Great, thanks so much,' I give it a nod.

I watch it retreat towards the kitchen where trays of food wait to be delivered. When I turn back towards Neotnia, she's staring at me.

'What?' I say.

'I've never seen someone talk like that to a server bot before.'

'What do you mean?'

'You asked how its night was going, then you asked if it was OK for you to change your order, then apologised for doing so, and then you thanked it.'

'OK...'

'You talked to it like you would a human server – a person,' she says. 'Is it an American thing?'

'No...' I shake my head. 'I guess it's just the way I talk to robots.' But then I think about it a little more. 'OK, maybe it's a little weird. Most people just give them orders. But, I mean, they do people stuff, so I guess I interact with them no differently than I would a person. And, sure, over here, maybe I do it more than I do at home.'

'Why?'

'I guess I find them more approachable here.'

'Approachable?'

'Yeah. I mean ... like, their designs. You know, they have that Japan thing going on.'

'"Japan-thing"?' she grins.

'The cuteness ... What's it called? *Kawaii*?' I give a smile. 'The way they look and how they're programmed to be so polite to foreign tourists – sometimes you forget you're talking to a robot.'

'But its head is literally the shape of a giant cheeseburger...'

I laugh. 'I know *that* one's is, but they don't all have heads shaped like that. Most don't have heads at all.' I think about it. 'Look, I've just spent a lot of time over here by myself, and sometimes the only conversations I'll have all day are with a guide bot or a server bot, and I guess that makes me treat them, well, like I'd treat a person.'

Neotnia ponders this for a moment. The expression on her face, it's the same look she had when we talked about ghosts. 'But you don't really think of them the same as a person?'

'No, of course not.'

'Even though you interact with them like they are...'

'Yeah,' I admit. 'But at the end of the day, of course, I know they're different from us.'

'Because of their form?' she tilts her head. 'Because they're mechanical and a person is flesh and blood?'

'No. Not only that. Not even mainly that.'

'So, what then? What's the difference between them and people? Cheeseburger heads aside.'

'They have a purpose, and we don't,' I say, after considering the question for a while. 'And in that way, maybe they're the lucky ones.'

She waits for me to continue.

'If they could ever truly have awareness, they'd instantly know what the meaning of their life is. It's to serve burgers or to be a car and drive people around, or to build highways, or whatever task they were made for. They'd never have the agony of wondering why they're here. But people, we're always searching for meaning. You know, *Why was I put on this earth? What's my purpose?* But the truth is, we don't have one. I wasn't born for any particular reason any more than you were or that student over there was. No person was born meaning to fulfil a specific task. If we want to find meaning in our lives, we need to make our own. But not robots – they have meaning built right in.'

'You really don't think people have a purpose? That a person isn't born for a reason?'

'No, I don't,' I shake my head. 'When Mom came back from Angola – years after she came back and could finally talk about the things that happened there – she told me she was no longer religious. Believing in a god implied there was order and meaning and intent in the universe, and thus every one of us was born with a purpose. But Mom said no one could be meant to carry out those atrocities; there's no way an infant is born with the purpose of it growing up to slaughter people. No one was *meant* to do that. And she's right: we're all born blank slates. We exist before we have an essence. We choose what type of person we'll become. We can't blame it on a maker. At least bots can.'

As if on cue, Cheeseburger Head returns. Its gyroscopes are so precise each tray is perfectly balanced on the golf-ball-sized rubber protrusions at the end of its arms. I've read chains that adopt server bots instead of people will make the cost of each back in savings alone during the first three years. That's because bots never accidentally drop or damage things – not to mention they never get sick, or need days off, or give away free burgers to their friends.

Cheeseburger Head simultaneously places the trays on our table. I thank it and it tells us to enjoy our meal, then rolls away. I shoot Neotnia a side glance.

'I hope Cheeseburger Head didn't hear us talking. I'll have to run over and apologise if it did.'

She gives me a little laugh. She knows I'm being stupid.

We dig into our burgers and fries, and, for a while, just people watch. A group of friends dressed as Dragon Ball characters come in, followed by some sexy mummies. A guy enters with a guitar on his back, sits down and puts on his metalenses to chat with someone.

'So, what'd you think?' Neotnia says after I finish the last of my burger.

'You're right,' I wipe my mouth. 'All other burgers are totally ruined for me from now on.'

'I warned you,' she smiles, and she takes a sip of her iced tea. 'You know, Goeido introduced me to this place. I'd never been to one until I started working at the café.'

I want to ask how long ago she started working there and why she moved in, but I'm afraid the answer might have something to do with her father.

'So, what *is* with Goeido?' I say.

Neotnia puts her hands on the table and leaves them there. 'What do you mean?'

'I mean, what's a sumo doing running a café? I guess he retired from the sport?'

Neotnia gives me a little look. 'Not really.' I wait for more, and she says, 'Have you noticed the magazine clipping framed in the café?'

'The one with the guy holding up a massive fish by the tail? Yeah, is that Goeido? I wasn't sure. The person in the picture looks a lot younger – and, you know, he's smiling.'

'*Hai*, it's him,' she says, glancing at her hands for a moment. 'It was nine years ago when he was thirty. He'd just set another grand-sumo tournament record. When a sumo has a major win, it's common for them to hold up a fish in commemoration.' She knows I'm about to ask, so explains: 'The fish they hold up is a specific one called a *tai*. And in Japanese, "*tai*" is the last syllable in "*omedetai*", the word we use when a celebration's in order. So, the fish is a pun.'

'So, Goeido was really good?'

'He wasn't just good. He was a grand champion: a *yokozuna*. By his nineteenth birthday, he had won virtually every lower match possible. He first became a *yokozuna* at twenty, right after his father died, making him the youngest *yokozuna* ever. Then he won nearly all grand-sumo tournaments the next year and the next and the next. At twenty-six he married, and he won all six tournaments in a single year – that's only the second time in the sport's history that's happened. The next year his mother died, but he achieved the all-time consecutive win record – even the match right after her death. And when he turned thirty, his daughter was born, and the week after, he broke the record for all-time championship wins.'

'Wow,' I say, genuinely impressed.

'You see,' Neotnia says, 'no matter what life threw at him – deaths, love, a child – nothing slowed him down. By the age of thirty, he was the most decorated *yokozuna* of any century – and to this day, he remains so.'

'I didn't know he had a wife and kid,' I say. But the look on Neotnia's face tells me he doesn't – at least not anymore.

'During the match where he broke the record for all-time championship wins, he felt something go in his knee, yet fought on. He managed to ground his opponent first, but his knee was badly injured,' Neotnia says, then pauses. She looks at me. 'I don't want you to think I'm telling you something Goeido wouldn't want me to. He keeps that magazine clipping in the café so everyone knows: Yep, he's *that yokozuna* and he doesn't give a damn what people think.'

I see how serious she is. 'I understand.'

She holds her eyes on me for a moment more, then goes on. 'So, after the match, Goeido found out about his knee. He could have come back from the injury. He could have dedicated the next year to rehabilitation. But that would have taken him away from his family even more than regular training does. He saw all the fame he had on the one side, and the wife and new child he had on the other, and he knew he had had a good life in the ring already and decided now it was his job to make sure his family had a good life at home, with a husband and father who was around. So, Goeido retired from competition, but not the sport – and at thirty, he became the youngest sumo ever to open their own stable.'

'Stable?'

'It's a facility where sumo wrestlers live and are trained from an early age. Think of it like a dormitory for young sumos.'

I'm trying to picture what that looks like. All I see are multiple Goeidos sharing bunk beds. 'OK, but then what?'

Neotnia presses her lips together. 'Two years after his stable opened ... a young sumo died there.'

'What?'

'The young sumo died under the hazing of another sumo in training. Goeido had no idea the hazing was occurring – he would have kicked out the ringleader the instant he knew. Even the police investigation found he didn't do a thing wrong. But because of his stature in the sumo world, some in the press came at him with their knives out – not to mention those in the industry bitter about his successes. But that wasn't the worst of it.'

I look at her, afraid to ask what the worst of it was.

'A boy was dead, and people were angry. The young sumo who hazed the dead boy – he was too young to have his name revealed to the public. So, people needed a different target – someone they could identify, someone they could vent their rage on. The mobs on social media – they were the worst. And they turned themselves on Goeido – even though the police already publicly stated he didn't do a thing wrong.'

She shakes her head and looks at me for a moment.

'Then someone created a deepfake of him. It spread online like a flame on an oil slick. The deepfake showed Goeido beating the boy – the one who died. The Goeido in the video, he kept striking the boy as he cried, telling him he was nothing. The deepfake wasn't amazingly good or anything, and anyone who wanted to take the time to see the truth could pretty easily tell it was faked. Even the police publicly discredited it. But it didn't matter. It was the excuse people needed to manifest their anger. Five days after the police discredited the deepfake ... someone burnt Goeido's stable down.'

'What?'

Neotnia's lips form a little frown. 'Then, the stable's investors pulled their money out. Goeido's reputation was ruined. In the year that followed, his wife took their young daughter and left, just like that. You can still find the deepfake online.'

'Jesus,' I sit back in my seat.

'*Hai*,' Neotnia gives a glum nod.

I stare at my iced tea for a while, thinking of everything she's told me. 'So, then he opened the café?'

Neotnia hesitates for a moment. '*Hai.*'

Three friends wearing bunny ears and holding stuffed animals enter and grab seats by the window. Cheeseburger Head rolls over and takes their order, then comes to us and clears our trays.

'Thanks,' I say, 'it was great.' And from the corner of my eye, I see Neotnia giving me a little smile.

'You're welcome,' Cheeseburger Head says. 'It's now after midnight and Freshness Burger has a Halloween sale on our amazing pumpkin shakes. Would you like to try one?'

I give Neotnia a glance. 'He asked so nicely...'

'We'll have one to share,' she tells Cheeseburger Head.

A few minutes later, there's a sizeable orange milkshake before us. It has a mound of whipped cream, topped with a sugar cookie shaped like a witch's hat.

I plop my spoon into the shake and take a mouthful as Neotnia skims some whipped cream with her finger and licks it clean. I'm silent as I watch a flock of demons exit.

'Hey,' Neotnia says. 'What are you thinking about?'

'Goeido, actually. He's a conundrum. I mean, he's this big, strong guy who's survived a lot of horrible stuff. And you'd think that'd make him even more hard, more tough. But at the same time, he makes all those cutesy things at the café: the shark sweatshirts, the ice-cream dog dessert, Inu's haircut ... yet I've never once seen him crack a smile.'

'I know he looks tough, but he's a big sweetheart on the inside.'

'I don't think he likes me.' I plunge my spoon into the shake again.

'Why would you say that?'

'Um, past experience.'

Neotnia laughs.

'I'm just saying he always, at best, looks annoyed when I show up.'

'He's just like that with new people. But once you get to know him, he's a big softy.'

She holds her gaze on me.

'Look, tomorrow, the café's going to be busy all day because we're doing Halloween-themed stuff, which should pull a lot of customers in. But we're closing for the night around ten. Why don't you come over then, and you, Goeido and me can hang out? We'll have a late meal and eat leftover Halloween treats, and you'll see how friendly he really is.'

I shoot her a look, but she deflects it with her big, bright, genuine smile. A smile that was completely absent during lunch today.

'OK,' I nod.

'Great.' She snaps part of the witch's hat cookie off and slips it into her mouth. 'Trust me, you'll see Goeido is completely harmless.'

5 – Sakeee!

For the past ten minutes, a young mother in business attire has walked a dozen feet ahead of me. The whole time she's been bent to the side, grasping her daughter's hand so she doesn't stumble. The daughter's head barely reaches her mother's hips. She wears a bright-pink kimono and white sandals, the right of which flops loosely on her small foot. The Halloween sun shines through the gaps in the leaves, casting splotches of swaying light on the gravelled path between us. Not a sound from the city penetrates our surroundings.

After Neotnia and I left Freshness Burger last night, we strolled through Ueno, watching the costumed stragglers, then took a car back to Shibuya. It dropped us in front of the café, which was dark inside. I walked her to the door, but instead of opening it she turned and looked at me. I was glad to see her eyes ending the day as they had begun – with no hint of clouds.

'I had fun tonight,' she said, her hands linked by her waist.

I said I did, too. I added that I liked her dress. She gave a little smile and replied that she liked my sweater. Then came another quiet moment and, just as when I first laid eyes on her two nights earlier, I felt a fist contract so tightly inside my chest, it was suddenly harder to breathe. At that point any normal person would have acted, yet I didn't move.

After a brief moment more, she gave a small nod. 'Well ... I'll see you tomorrow night?' she said. I waited to make sure she got in OK. After locking the door, she waved goodnight through the glass.

I sat on my balcony for a long time after, thinking of how Neotnia had looked at me as we'd stood there, the corners of her eyelids narrowed ever so slightly, and I recalled how it felt earlier when she had leaned into my chest, her flushed face tilted up towards mine. Inside, I picked up the surgeon's brochure and got into bed.

I called his office this morning. It's why I'm on this gravelled path now, headed towards the Meiji Shrine. His office is in a skyscraper on the other side of the forested grounds, and I've got a few hours to kill before I need to be there.

I sit on a bench at the shrine's main complex. The mother and daughter proceed to a small pavilion where the mother lifts a ladle from a basin and pours its water over one hand then the other. Then she pours water into her cupped left hand, drinks, and spits it onto the ground. She crouches at her daughter's side, showing her how to do the same.

The mother grasps her daughter's hand tightly as she insists on climbing the shrine's steps herself, a white sandal still loose on her small foot. Reaching the top, the mother smooths her daughter's kimono then tosses something into a wooden box under the awning. From the sound it makes, it must be an old coin. She bows deeply twice, claps her hands loudly twice, and bows deeply again, staying that way for almost a minute. She guides her daughter through identical steps.

Others perform the same actions. By the looks of them, they're from wildly differing walks of life. Some wear kimonos. Some are in school uniforms. Some look like they're on their break from the boardroom. One has a white chef's hat wedged under his arm. Yet they all perform the same ritual.

'*Konnichiwa*,' a voice says.

It's a tourist information bot similar to the one I spoke with in Shibuya a few nights ago. But this model's lower half is different. It's Japan's version of an Atlas Class-2 bot. It's bipedal, likely because it needs to navigate all the steps and uneven gravelled paths in the shrine's complex.

'Hello,' I nod.

'Hello, and welcome to Meiji Shrine.' Its enormous cat-like eyes blink. 'Would you like to know the shrine's history?'

I shake my head. 'I'm just relaxing. Thanks, though.'

'Of course.' Its domed head rotates downward, nodding. 'It's a beautiful day to relax. Please enjoy your stay, and if you would like any information on the shrine or related activities in the area, please let me know.'

'Will do,' I say and watch as the bot's digital face flips to the other side of its domed head. My eyes drift back towards the shrine. 'Actually, excuse me...' I call after the bot, and it returns. 'What are they doing?' Together we watch fresh visitors bow twice, clap loudly twice, and bow again. 'What's with the clapping?'

The bot's large feline eyes blink. 'Every shrine is the home of one or more kami. Followers of Shinto come to shrines to give thanks to these kami, or in times of need or trouble, to ask for their help. The clapping is an attempt to attract the kami's attention so they will notice the respect the visitor is paying them, with the hope that the kami will pay attention to their prayer in return.'

I think back to my conversation with Joe. 'And these kami are the gods of Shinto?'

'Not in the western sense,' the bot replies. 'Kami are not inherently holy. They are simply another type of creature that exists in our world, yet they are usually invisible to our eyes until they inhabit something, and thus cross into our perception.'

'Inhabit what sorts of things?'

The bot's digital face blinks out, and images of mountains, rivers and sunsets cycle across its domed head. 'They can inhabit almost anything: a rock, a flower, a seashell, the snow – even a tool. A kami can also be inside a remarkable animal or person. It's often said that if something rouses awe in an individual, that individual is looking upon a kami.'

'And they help people?'

'They can, and it is believed they usually do.' Its cat eyes reappear. 'But nothing in nature is perfect, including kami. They can err, just like a person. They can even misbehave. And while they often attempt to influence events for the benefit of those who pray to them, they may influence events for their own ends, too.'

I watch another visitor do the bow-bow-clap-clap-bow.

'So, this place is basically a pilgrimage site for those seeking help from kami?'

'For some,' it nods. 'But while the Meiji Shrine is one of the largest and most impressive in Japan, shrines can be any size and need not be opulent. If there is a shrine, no matter how small or plain, a kami will find it.'

I understand what the bot means. I've stumbled across rudimentary, homemade shrines tucked away in random Tokyo neighbourhoods. I found one behind a thrift store the other day, and another down an alleyway next to a 7-Eleven. My guide app even has a section about the best 'hidden' shrines in the city.

I recall Joe saying Neotnia has an interest in Shintoism. 'Are most Japanese people Shintoists?'

The bot's cat-like eyes blink out again, replaced with a projection of a pie chart. 'As of the last national survey, seventy-six point three percent of the Japanese population identified as having no religion, though most still partake in Shinto rituals. This is because the Shinto religion goes back millennia, and so its rites have infused with Japanese culture. Take Japan's national sport, for example. Sumo wrestling originally took place at shrines to venerate kami, hoping doing so would result in an abundance of crops—'

'Oh, sorry, no – I don't need the whole presentation.' I wave my hand as the info bot's domed head begins projecting images of old woodblock prints featuring sumos. 'Thanks, though.'

I stay sat on the bench a while longer, watching the steady flow of visitors offering prayers to the kami inside. On my way out I spot the mother in the business attire again, her daughter in her arms, fast asleep; her chubby face slumped against her mother's shoulder. A sandal-less foot dangles below her pink kimono, like a pear from a branch.

*

I meet with the surgeon at the appointed time and tell him I've decided to proceed. He asks if I understand that, even after the procedure, I won't look completely normal. I tell him I do. After some additional questions, he says he'll see me in January and asks that I wait in the examination room for his office manager. As I do, I stare upon Tokyo's expanse. From this height, even Meiji Shrine's sprawling grounds appear no larger than a baseball diamond; the metros ferrying untold numbers look like toy trains; the people on the streets, no bigger than granules of pepper. And gazing over a city teeming with tens of millions of people living tens of millions of different lives, that odd phrase pops back into my head: I feel like I'm standing on *the cusp of a new world*. A world in which I can finally belong.

The office manager recaps everything: the chance of infection; the risk of embolism; the unavoidable, permanent, loss of sensation that will occur across a large swath of my body even if I manage to avoid the other complications. In other words: the trade-offs for being normal – or, as normal as possible, anyway. She shows me the final cost on her tablet. There's no way I could afford it if not for the Sony deal, but that will close in a few weeks, and they don't need my deposit until a month before the operation.

When I return to the apartment, I notice I've missed a call. It's from Mom even though it's well past midnight back home. I immediately call her, fearing she's had another setback, but she says she was just up late thinking about me and wanted to know how I was doing. We talk for some time, and she tells me she's glad I'm enjoying myself. Despite saying everything's OK, she sounds distant.

The call ends without me telling her about the procedure. By the time I need to pay the deposit, I'll be eighteen, so won't need her permission. Besides, when she was a surgeon, she performed operations on people out of necessity – do it or die. I don't know if she could understand why I'm electing to go through something like this. I think it's hard for anyone who's been normal their whole life to understand. And I know she won't like that I'm having it done here, but I don't want her to have to take care of me afterward. I don't want her seeing me struggle through the recovery. I'm not even sure she could handle it.

But most of all, I don't want her trying to talk me out of it.

I decide to force Mom and the surgery from my mind and work on my translation app until it's time to get ready. A little before ten, I stop into a FamilyMart to pick up a cake. A ghoulish marzipan hand pries its way from a casket of grey icing. The more popular pumpkin shape is sold out.

It's an ideal Halloween night: crisp, breezy and with skies just the right amount of cloudy. They obstruct the view of the stations while still letting the moon's natural form bleed through. Outside the café, they've strung up an inflatable skeleton, and Jack o' Lanterns guard either side of the door. The *closed* sign is up, and the foyer's lights are dimmed, but Neotnia said to come at this time, so I let myself in.

Instead of the bell's familiar clang, there's a crack of thunder and a grotesque scream. I see where they've wired the motion sensor to the door. But they didn't stop there. Fake cobwebs dot the foyer's surfaces. An old-fashioned devil's mask with shifting eyes hangs below the register. A faded poster of a creepy cemetery is tacked up near the dining area's entrance. Occasionally, a ghoul will crawl from one of its graves, or a ghostly apparition will appear in its distance. A witch streaks across its purple-grey sky, but her journey is always cut short as the poster's top corner is torn away.

And then there's Inu. He's at his customary spot on the counter but he's even more spherical than usual. His doggy costume makes his midsection look like a plump pumpkin. I set the cake on the counter and sink my fingers into his spherical head, giving him a good scratch on the skull. 'Oh, buddy, look at what they've done to you...'

That's when I flinch. Goeido lumbers around the kitchen's partition. He's dressed in a kimono and tucked under one arm is a boxed toaster. But tucked under the other: a severed head. A head that's instantly familiar despite its swollen tongue and disgorged eyeball. It looks exactly like the salaryman who mocked Neotnia's gloves the other night.

My throat tightens as Goeido looks at me flatly.

'*Konbanwa*,' he sighs and sets the head on the counter without slowing his march. He rolls his eyes as he passes and makes a sharp left into the dark hallway – the toaster still tucked under his arm. I watch that black space until the clomps of his feet cease.

I pick up the head and inspect it. A whistle escapes it as I squeeze.

'Hey...'

The voice comes out of nowhere. It's Neotnia. She's materialised from the dark hallway.

'Goeido said you'd arrived.'

I set down the head. 'Yeah,' I clear my throat.

Neotnia's nose is topped with a dark smudge, and whiskers line the curves of her cheeks. Cat ears sprout from her black hair as if they've grown there organically since I last saw her, and her long black gloves are embossed with skeleton bones that run to her elbows. Her sleeveless dress ends halfway down her thighs, exposing the tights underneath, also black, and also featuring embossed bones all the way down to the toes of her shoeless feet.

Bones aside, she's got fantastic legs.

'So, you're a cat,' I say. 'And a skeleton.'

A subtle amusement crosses her face. 'I'm a cat whose run out of all nine lives. And you ... didn't dress up.'

She's right. But I tell her I did.

'Oh?' She gives my sweater and jeans a once-over. 'What are you supposed to be?'

'An American tourist.'

Heavy footsteps signal Goeido's return, and he emerges from the darkness carrying a wooden chair, which he sets next to the hallway's entrance. Behind Neotnia's slim form, he looks colossal. You could fit three of her shoulder-to-shoulder within Goeido's frame and she'd need to grow almost another foot to surpass his height.

As Goeido makes his way towards the kitchen, Neotnia says they're just finishing preparing dinner and asks me to make room for everyone at the far booth. 'OK, little pumpkin,' she picks up Inu, the whiskers on her cheeks bending as she gives him a smile. 'Go with John and his non-costume.'

I follow Inu into the dining area, where he hops onto the couch. As in the foyer, fake cobwebs drape the surfaces. Strung pumpkin-shaped fairy lights spread an orange glow across the room, and a tall plastic tombstone embossed with skull and crossbones stands beside the coffee table, adding to the atmosphere.

I assume Neotnia meant make room for Goeido at the booth, so I push its bench back several inches. Then several more. Neotnia returns with the chair and cake box and then with dishware. As I set the table, I spy that old magazine clipping of Goeido on the wall. The one Neotnia talked about last night. The one with him and his wife looking so full of joy they could burst. It occurs to me that the kimono Goeido's wearing tonight matches the kimono he's wearing in the photo.

Neotnia sets a platter of sushi on the table, and I instantly know who made them. There's salmon nigiri cut to look like Jack o' Lanterns, octopus sashimi to look like ghosts, and tuna sashimi with spread avocado that look like Frankenstein heads. Even the dried seaweed on the triangular onigiri are cut to make them look like black cat faces with white whiskers.

'See?' She arches an eyebrow. 'Big softy.'

Goeido places a large iron crock on the table, and we take our seats – Goeido across from me, Neotnia on the chair at the end of the booth. She gives us both a little smile.

After glancing at me, Goeido says something to Neotnia.

She replies without making eye contact.

He holds his gaze on her as if she should say more, but instead she ignores him and picks up the pot of tea, serving us.

'Ah, sorry. I don't know...' I address Goeido. 'Do you speak any English?'

But he just stares at me.

Neotnia shakes her head and places a hand on Goeido's arm, speaking to him. 'He knows basic words like "yes" and "no", but he doesn't speak the language. But it's OK,' she puts on a bright face. 'I'll just be the translator tonight.'

And for the first time, the logistics of how this dinner needs to work occurs to me.

'Well, the food looks good.' I make sure to address them both as I speak.

Neotnia translates this to Goeido, who nods, '*Hai*.'

Realizing he's not going to expand on that, she presses her mouth tight as if holding in a little sigh. Then she points to the main dish.

'It's a stew called *chankonabe*,' she says. 'It's a common dish sumo eat. Goeido's version is made of dashi, chicken, halibut, and the vegetables are daikon, carrot, cabbage, green onion, and enoki.'

His gaze still on me, Goeido motions towards the ladle. I'm not sure if he wants me to sample it, or if I should serve everyone, so I do the latter to be safe.

'It's fantastic,' I say after tasting it, and I mean it.

Neotnia translates this for Goeido, who stares at me like I've said nothing at all.

Soon, the only things in the room making noise are our chopsticks.

'So, how were your days?' I say after the silence becomes undeniably awkward.

Neotnia looks like I've thrown a life preserver. She says her day was busy as a lot of customers came for the Halloween-themed foods Goeido prepared. 'They all sold really well. People seemed to especially like the black-cat onigiri and the Frankenstein sashimi,' she says, and then translates for Goeido. And by the frosty look she holds on him, I get the feeling she's prodding him to reply with more than a word.

And this time, he does. Looking at me with that flat expression, he says ... something. Something ... short.

'It was Halloween. We had many customers,' Neotnia translates with a glum look.

And that's how dinner continues: stilted translated conversation interspaced by awkward silences. Whenever I glance at Neotnia, she puts on a good-hearted smile. But inevitably, she returns to probing her chopsticks through the stew's broth, searching for any stray vegetables left behind. Even her drawn-on whiskers look crestfallen. And whenever I glance at Goeido, most of the time I find his eyes already fixed on me – almost like he's sizing me up.

By the time we finish our dinner, not thirty minutes later, it feels like we've been at the table for hours. With no food left to fidget with, Neotnia looks at Goeido and then me. I give her a polite smile, hoping it doesn't betray how awkward this is.

'Well, the dessert you brought looks good,' she says, rising.

She stretches across the table and pulls the box towards her. As she lifts the coffin cake from it, its form suddenly feels apt as this dinner has all the energy of a funeral.

'I'll grab us some fresh plates,' she says.

As she pads away, my eyes can't help but fall on the shape of her legs in the black tights. But just as quickly, I feel eyes on me.

And indeed, Goeido's staring.

He calls out, stopping Neotnia in her tracks, and speaks at length for the first time tonight, his eyes still on me. As he continues, Neotnia's eyes narrow and stay so for several beats. She replies with a shake of her head. Yet that only causes Goeido to speak at length again, which she responds to in equal measure. Throughout their back and forth, I begin to catch a repeated word I think I recognise.

'Uh, what's up?' I say after they seem to have reached an impasse.

Neotnia's lips are drawn tight as if she's displeased. But Goeido simply raises his eyebrows and motions towards me with his big hand.

'Goeido was suggesting we open a special bottle of sake he has in the kitchen,' she explains. 'But it's OK – I told him we have the tea. And tea goes better with cake.'

Goeido's holds his eyes on mine. He grins.

'*Sakeee*,' he draws the word out, almost like it's a challenge.

Look, I've never had a drop of alcohol in my life, but if this *is* some kind of challenge, I don't want to look like a coward in front of Neotnia. And if it's not? Well, I don't want to offend Goeido by rejecting his offer. So, I say, 'Sake sounds great.'

Neotnia shakes her head. 'You really don't have to...'

'No, I want to,' I nod. 'I love sake. Let's do it.'

And I look at Goeido, who's looking at me.

'*Sake*,' I say.

'*Sake*,' he nods, that confident grin returning as if we've entered into some kind of Faustian bargain, the terms of which only he knows. He slides from the booth, giving Neotnia a look, which causes her to roll her eyes.

'Well,' she says, a little breath escaping her. 'I guess we should clear the table first.'

Neotnia hands the empty crock to Goeido, holding a cold look on him, which he ignores. As he heads towards the kitchen, I help stack our used dishes. I ask if I can take them for her, but she shakes her head and tells me it's OK.

Left alone in the orange glow of the dining area, I spy Inu on the couch. He tilts his head inquisitively at me, and I'm reminded of how well-trained he is. The chicken in the stew smelled incredible, but not once did he come begging for a piece.

Shortly, muffled words drift into the dining area. It almost sounds like Goeido and Neotnia are arguing in the kitchen. And though I can't understand them, I feel bad that I'm privy to a private conversation, so I leave the booth and squat behind the tall tombstone by the coffee table so I'm eye to eye with Inu, and I let him distract my attention. He gives my hand a sniff and a few licks, and I sink my fingers into his spherical head, giving him a good scratch on the skull.

But as I'm toying with him, a clatter draws my attention. I peek over the tombstone. It's Neotnia. She's rounded the kitchen's partition with a stack of plates and utensils. Yet in the next instant, something so unexpected happens, it feels as if the air has evaporated. The colour fades from her skin, and in just a few more steps her face turns so pale in the foyer's dim light it's as if she's become an apparition. And, as if fearing she's about to lose the ability to hold physical objects, she rushes the stack to the countertop.

Gripping the counter's edge, her jaw drops and her entire body freezes – except for her throat. It winces as if there's a ghostly hand wrapped around it, barring her lungs from receiving oxygen.

Yet before I have a chance to move – the wincing, the suffocation, it all stops, and the colour returns to her skin. She takes a deep breath and removes her hands from the counter. She picks up the stack, and crosses in front of the dark hallway, entering the dining area wholly composed. That composure only breaks for an instant when she notices I'm no longer in the booth, yet it returns as she finds me crouched by Inu behind the tall tombstone.

'Isn't his costume adorable?' she says, giving me an utterly ordinary smile. 'It was either that or a vampire outfit, but I think a pumpkin suits him more.'

I'm at a loss for words until I realise that, by my being behind the tombstone, she assumes I haven't seen a thing. But I did, and it was exactly as what happened to her at the cinema – only then I dismissed it as a trick of the light.

'Good choice,' I nod, perhaps a beat too late, because her eyes shift, then she turns her back to me and sets the plates on the table, where she begins slicing the cake.

Within moments, Goeido returns and sets the bottle of sake on the table. It's so large the accompanying shot glasses might as well be thimbles. And despite her previous objections, Neotnia now seems relieved to have him back in the room.

Goeido speaks.

'He says this bottle is from the mid-thirties. He's been wanting to open it for a while,' Neotnia explains as I slide back into the booth. She distributes the cake, then takes her seat.

In the glow of the fairy lights, Goeido's massive frame is a devilish orange. He breaks the seal on the bottle and removes its stopper. '*Sake*,' he grins, like an enormous Jack o' Lantern.

Neotnia twists her mouth up, then takes a bite of her coffin cake. Goeido fills the shot glasses to the brim and pushes the first to Neotnia and the second to me. He slides back into the booth and picks up the third between his giant thumb and index finger, holding his gaze on me. I lift mine, meeting his stare, and we hold our glasses up for some time, looking at each other. From the corner of my vision, Neotnia's eyes flit between us like she's a bored spectator waiting for one cowboy to draw first. After a moment, she lets out a little sigh and picks up her glass, too.

'*Kanpai!*' Goeido says and downs his shot.

'*Kanpai!*' I repeat. I down my shot so fast the liquid barely touches my tongue.

Neotnia looks from me to Goeido to me again and shakes her head, a small, resigned laugh escaping her lips.

'*Kanpai!*' She downs hers, too.

Goeido seems to be considering the way I took my shot. He nods, apparently impressed. But then he picks up his empty glass and arches a heavy eyebrow.

'*Sake?*' he challenges.

I meet his gaze and hold up my glass.

'*Sake*,' I accept.

Neotnia eyes us both, raising her empty glass.

Goeido refills them all.

'*Kanpai!*' his deep voice booms, and he downs this shot as quickly as he did the first.

I do the same, but this time the sake strikes my tongue and I feel its crisp dryness saturate my buds. It's a pleasing flavour. Sweet – but a bit too strong. I cough as it hits my throat.

'*Kanpai!*' Neotnia follows us.

We do this a third time. And a fourth. It's only after Neotnia sees Goeido going for a fifth round that she protests.

'No,' she shakes her head. 'Not until both of you finish your cake. Neither of you have even had a bite.' She says this in English and then Japanese.

Goeido purses his lips and gives a sideways nod. He spoons a big chunk of his coffin cake into his mouth. I start on mine, too.

Neotnia looks over her shoulder and calls out to Inu, who hops off the couch and jumps into her lap. The dog's spherical head pops above the table's edge, his coal-black eyes trying to discern what spectacle is playing out.

It's after I take the last bite of my cake and reach to give Inu a pat that I realise how fuzzy my hand feels. It's heavier and warmer than usual, too, and I quickly spread it flat on the table, as if I didn't it would somehow fall there anyway. I guess I stare at it a bit too long because Neotnia says, 'Everything OK?'

My focus shifts to her, holding Inu. Her gloved skeleton hands folded around his breast. The cat ears sprouting from her black hair. That trio of faint stars on her face. Below her dark lashes, I see those eyes gazing at me in the orange light.

'Everything's amazing,' I nod. And I turn towards Goeido, who's got a big grin on his face.

'*Sake?*' He arches an eyebrow.

'*Sake,*' I volley back.

'Ohmygod,' Neotnia mumbles.

Goeido pours another shot for me and then himself. But Neotnia stops him from pouring a shot for her. 'Time out for me,' she says, placing her palm over her glass. 'You two might want to think about a little time out, too.'

I shake my head. 'I feel ... I'm totally fine.'

Neotnia sighs and says something to Goeido who replies and puts forward both his hands as if saying, *He said he's totally fine.*

She rolls her eyes, but Goeido ignores this and holds up his glass, signalling our next match is about to begin. '*Sake.*'

It's as if an entire language is in that one warm word. But as I lift my glass, I bypass the customary '*kanpai!*' and down my shot before he has a chance to down his, and I sit staring at my opponent with a big, warm, satisfied grin on my face.

Laughter spurts from Neotnia, and even Goeido lets out a laugh before downing his shot, too. But when he sets his glass back on the table, he doesn't move to fill it again. Still eyeing me, he says something to Neotnia, and as I look to her for the translation, I realise my head is now as fuzzy as my hands.

She studies me for a quiet moment, thinking.

The corners of her eyes narrow just a bit.

'He says he wants to get to know you better,' she finally says.

'Me?' I say. 'That's ... great. Me and Goeido.' I look at him and nod. 'Good.'

He grins, his eyes reflecting the orange of the lights like embers in a fire. And looking right at me, he speaks.

I look to Neotnia. She tightens her mouth for a long moment. 'Is this your first time in Japan?' she translates.

I look at Goeido. 'Yeah,' I nod.

To Goeido, she says, '*Hai.*'

He nods, then says something back.

'Why did you come into our café that first night?' she translates.

I shake my head, and when I do, it feels like warm particles are scattering inside my skull.

I remember walking down to the Shibuya crossing. I remember talking to the bot. I remember its short body glowing a deep green in the light of a new ad. I remember ... *You're on the cusp of a new world.*

You're on the cusp of a new world.

'It was, well ... it was because I saw the ear-cleaning sign,' I say.

She tells Goeido my answer. When he replies, a little grin crosses her face, and she shakes her head, but Goeido tilts his and gives a look, prodding her.

She lets out a sigh.

'Is it a fetish thing?' she translates.

I feel my face go red. 'No...' I shake my head, mortified. I look at Goeido. 'No. I told her – like I told her – it was to help me sleep. It's *relaxing.*'

Neotnia stifles a laugh and relays my answer. But Goeido just purses his lips and arches an eyebrow like he really doesn't believe me. And I guess I've got some kind of horrified expression on my face, because Neotnia shakes her head. 'He's kidding,' she says. 'He knows.'

Goeido laughs, and, as if to show he was just having a bit of fun, he says, '*Sake?*'

'*Sake.*'

He fills my glass and I drink it down as he watches, contemplating something. And as if he somehow knows when the liquid's stopped warming my throat, he says something short to Neotnia. She hesitates for several moments before translating, almost like the question annoys her.

'Do you like attention?' she finally says.

My mouth gapes. I'm not sure what that even means.

But with his critical eyes still locked on me, Goeido continues.

'You were on the cover of a popular magazine,' Neotnia translates begrudgingly. Goeido says something more, and Neotnia adds, 'They called you a "boy genius".'

I cringe inside at the beautiful twenty-year-old associating me with the term 'boy'. Yet given the look on Goeido's face, I think he knows it bugs me, which is probably why he added it.

I guess it only makes sense that she would have shown him the magazine when she found my backpack. I explain that it was a PR stunt orchestrated by Sony.

'Big companies sometimes arrange things like that to try to impress the people who have code they want – so they won't take it anywhere else; or, if you're cynical, to railroad them. Either way, they asked me to do some interviews, but I told them my code should speak for itself – it's what's important, not me.' I notice how closely Goeido's inspecting me as I answer. 'And, well, I don't know if you read it, but I finally did. The article was mainly about the code. The little personal information about me came from what Sony's PR team told the magazine. I never gave an interview. So no, generally, I don't like attention. I mean, I'm not even on social media. I've never seen the point.'

Neotnia translates all this and, judging from the glare she gives Goeido, I get the impression she's a bit annoyed with him. He tightens his lips and seems to consider her for a moment, yet then he simply shrugs and says something else.

'Did you think I was holding a real head when you arrived tonight?' Neotnia translates, trying not to smile.

This question, on top of the last … I shake my head.

'I'm not sure if you realise, but you can be … intimidating,' I say, looking Goeido in the eyes. 'So yeah, it crossed my mind for a few seconds.'

Neotnia lets out a big laugh. Then, having heard the translation, Goeido lets out a laugh, too. He nods toward my glass.

'Sake,' I say, and he fills it.

It's only when I've set the glass back on the table and I meet his eyes again that he asks me another question.

'Are you a trustworthy person?'

But from the way Neotnia translates and holds her eyes on me, it seems she's very interested in my answer, too.

'I like to believe I am.'

Neotnia tells Goeido what I've said, and he replies with a single word. She translates it without shifting her gaze from me, as if the question is her own.

'Why?'

I contemplate the question for several moments.

'For the same reason I never laughed along with everyone else when a jock slapped the tray from some freshman's hands in the school cafeteria,' I shrug and look down at my empty plate, remembering. 'I've had my trust broken before. Once you've experienced a certain type of suffering, it makes you want to never have any part in propagating that hurt upon someone else. Well, it makes me never want to, anyway.'

Neotnia's clear eyes remain on me for a long moment. It's as if she's reading something on my face only she can see. Finally, she translates my answer.

Hearing it, Goeido nods almost imperceptibly and drinks a glass of sake, as if the liquor will help him digest my reply. For what seems like minutes, his eyes remain on me. Then as if conveying some conclusion to Neotnia purely by sight alone, he turns back and fills his glass again. He nods to mine and I raise it to be refilled. He then nods to Neotnia, and she removes a gloved skeleton hand from Inu's breast and extends her own shot glass. Our outstretched hands hover the clear liquid in our glasses, and instead of '*kanpai!*' we all shout, '*sake!*'

The stillness that follows is the first comfortable silence the three of us have ever shared.

Outside, two girls in dalmatian dresses and floppy ears pass by the window, followed by someone dressed head to toe in some kind of seaweed monster outfit. A bot rolls past. A possessed nun. A ghost. A trio of avenging angels. Another bot. Pikachu.

Goeido cuts another slice of cake for himself and motions to Neotnia, who pinches her fingers together. He sets a thin slice on her plate, and I can't help but notice that, though it sits mere inches from him, Inu resists going for even a simple sniff.

Holding the knife above the cake, Goeido motions towards me. But as I shake my head I experience what feels like trillions of warm particles penetrating every inch of my body.

As they work on their slices, my eyes drift towards the framed magazine clipping, the one with Goeido and the fish. What did Neotnia call it? Yeah, the *tai*.

'Hey,' I say, the warm particles suddenly making me feel bold. 'I have some questions for you, too. This is a two-way street, right?' And I look at Neotnia. In a quieter voice, even though I know Goeido can't understand anyway, I add, 'It's nothing about what you told me last night.'

She gives a little smile. 'I know.'

I tell them I went to the Meiji Shine and a bot explained how sumo wrestling was originally connected to worshipping kami. Neotnia translates all I've said and Goeido nods, amused, and gestures towards me, telling me to proceed. Yet as I'm about to ask my first question, it suddenly slips my mind.

It's the sake's doing.

'OK, wait...' I say, taking out my phone.

While I was waiting at the surgeon's office, I'd thought about what Neotnia said about Goeido last night, and what the bot had said about sumo ritual. I read up on sumos and saved some notes, wondering how many of the more wild factoids I'd found were true.

'OK,' I say, squinting at my screen. 'Do sumo referees really carry knives with them for the purpose of committing *seppuku* if they make a bad call?'

Neotnia translates, and Goeido replies.

'Some do.'

'Wow, that's hardcore,' I say. Neotnia lets out a little laugh, I think more at how I slurred the phrase than at my actual reply.

'Alright, next: when people used to drive cars, were sumos really not allowed to drive?'

Goeido says a single word and fills his sake glass. Neotnia says, 'True.'

I take a shot after Goeido fills my glass, too.

'Is a sumo's hairstyle really made to act as a kind of cushion in case they fall on their head?'

'Some say it is, but the style actually harks back to the Edo period and the days of the samurai.'

'OK...' I nod. 'The loincloths you guys wear ... is it true they're never washed?'

Neotnia laughs as she translates this, and Goeido smiles as he gives his answer.

'It's true,' Neotnia says. 'They're never washed, even though they wear the same one all the time. It's mainly a good-luck thing. But washing may also deteriorate its threads. Sumos are disqualified if their loincloth comes undone in a match.'

'Wow,' I say, and eye his kimono. If it's not the same one as in the photo, it's identical. 'You're not wearing it under there, are you?'

Neotnia laughs and translates and laughs again when Goeido gives his answer. 'No comment.'

'OK, this one I really want to know: can sumos really hit with up to fifteen G's of force?'

'*Hai*. Yes.'

'Jeez. Any way you want to come and beat up some of my old high-school bullies?'

Neotnia laughs, and Goeido lets out an even louder roar when she translates my reply. And I know it's because I'm drunk, but still, seeing Goeido's reaction, with his deep voice rumbling throughout the room, I feel like I'm watching a gigantic, happy baby laughing in slow motion – one that's fully aware it could kill you with ease.

'OK, OK – last one. Do sumos really eat *ten thousand* calories per day?'

Neotnia translates, '*Hai*. Yes. With all their training, they would easily lose several kilograms a day if they didn't consume so many.'

'That's insane,' I say. But I do the math in my head. 'Though I guess if the average sumo is about four hundred pounds, maintaining that mass, even if the body is completely at rest, would require at least four times the average adult's daily caloric intake. And as you said, the training requires even more energy.'

Goeido pours me another as Neotnia translates this. I hear a couple '*hai*'s' from him as he offers sake to Neotnia. He fills his glass, too, and we all drink, the sake warming our bellies once again. For several moments after, we sit in another comfortable silence under the orange glow of the lights. Goeido glances at the framed magazine clipping, looking as if he's reminiscing about his sumo days. Neotnia cuddles Inu in her lap, who looks up at her attentively as she whispers something in Japanese. And it occurs to me that, sitting here, with these two, sharing drinks – this is the closest thing I've ever had to a night out with friends. And it feels good.

I've lost count of how many shots we've had. I think Goeido and I have had the same amount – and I can feel how affected I am. I probably wouldn't be able to walk straight right now. Goeido looks a bit tipsy, too. Not drunk but unwound. It makes sense he's less affected, given he's got to weigh almost two and a half times what I now do.

Yet when I look at Neotnia I realise she doesn't seem affected at all. She's had to have at least six or seven shots, and she can't weigh more than one-ten or one-fifteen, yet she shows no sign of even the slightest buzz. It's like every shot has phased right through her.

'*Sake?*'

It's Goeido. He's offering to pour me another.

I accept, Neotnia passes, and he pours one more for himself. We drink, and as he places his empty glass back on the table, he sits back with a big warm grin on his big face. I imagine the cold sake gliding down his throat like a raft on a waterslide, making its short journey into his toasty belly. And as I look at that big belly, it reminds me of, well ... me.

'You know...' I nod towards the sake bottle and pour myself another '...I used to be a pretty big guy, too. Not as big as you, but much bigger than I am now. But I was all fat, where you're a lot of muscle underneath.'

Neotnia considers me for a moment. And truthfully, for a second it slipped my mind that Goeido can't understand me outright. She translates my words as he takes the bottle and pours himself a shot, too. As he does, I glimpse the framed magazine photo. The one where a younger him beams with pride as he holds up that fish, his wife and the audience behind him clapping in adulation.

'I know here they respect you for that – your size. And that's got to feel great, being big and on top of the world like that...' Neotnia continues to translate as I speak, and Goeido nods, listening respectfully. But even as I go on, the reason I'm saying any of this has slipped my mind. It was ... Was it because I mentioned the school cafeteria earlier? '*Now* everyone thinks I'm a "genius". But if I was still overweight, no way would anyone back home call me that. Where I'm from, they judge you based on your appearance. They see it and decide your trustworthiness. Your intelligence. Your intentions. Your worth. And they don't decide them kindly. Where I'm from, being big makes you an outsider, and as long as you're like that, you'll never belong.'

Neotnia finishes translating just after I pause, and I can feel her eyes settle on me. Goeido remains quiet, attentive. But why am I saying all this? There was a point ... Am I getting off track? I shake my head and the warm particles scatter around my skull. I glance at the magazine clipping on the wall again. Yes, it's got something to do with that. It's because ... I want him to like me. When I arrived tonight, I was certain he didn't. But now I want him to. Because this *is* the closest I've ever had to a night out with friends – and it feels good. But what is it with that photo? I see it, and it makes me want him to know ... Yes, to know we're the same in some way. But how?

'When I was twelve – and by that time, I had gotten really big – one day I was waiting in the cafeteria for my mom to pick me up after school. The door opens and my homeroom teacher comes steaming in and demands to see my backpack. She searches it and says, "*So you've already eaten it then?*" and storms away as quickly as she came...'

And now ... I know. Yes. It's because of what Neotnia told me happened to him. I want him to know I can relate. Because people you can relate to, you like.

'I had no idea what my teacher was talking about, but the next day when I arrived for school, I was met by her and the principal. She said the day before a box of anniversary chocolates her husband had given her had disappeared from her desk. Other students, including the class prez, told her I'd stolen it.'

I pause, remembering feelings I've not felt in a long time.

'You'd think such a lie might work if kids were simply telling it to other kids. But the fact this lie worked on an adult, the fact she so readily believed my bullies based on no data but my size – it taught me a lot about how individuals, when they're angry, are willing to blame anyone served up to them – especially if that scapegoat is already an outsider. And it taught me how that blame – that quiet judgment – is so infectious among groups, regardless of an individual member's intelligence or reasoning capacity. Data just doesn't matter when emotion's involved. By the end of the day, not only was there not a single student, there wasn't a single teacher who didn't believe the school's one fat kid stole the chocolates.'

I glance at Neotnia, and my heart stops upon realising a hint of those clouds from yesterday have returned to her eyes. Yet she continues to translate, albeit with a certain quiet now in her voice.

'And, well, that was the worst thing about it...' I say to Goeido, regretting I ever opened my mouth. 'Worse than getting detention for something I didn't do. Worse than realising the way I looked was why I was being blamed. Having a lie told about you, and everyone believing it – you can't understand how horrible that feels until it happens to you...'

I trail off, and once Neotnia finishes translating, such a stillness fills the room it's unbearable. I want to bang my head against the table as hard as I can, but I know I'd throw up. So, I'm *that* kind of drunk – no filter; real downer.

After what feels like eons, Goeido's voice breaks the silence. An instant later, Neotnia's joins his. And at her voice, my heart sinks. Though she's translating his words, she's doing it in a tone that I know is pitying.

'Don't listen to those who can't look past the external. Even in sumo, the audience misjudged me because of my size. They thought my size *was* my strength – that it was the reason I was a champion. But my true strength came from here: inside. I couldn't have succeeded in the *dohyō* through size alone. That is impossible.'

Neotnia pauses. I can feel her eyes on me, but I can't bear to look at her.

'Let people misjudge you – condemn you, even,' she says for Goeido as he speaks again. 'Smile at them, then carry on with your life. Their faults weaken only them.'

I take a breath and finally raise my eyes. I nod, hoping he knows I appreciate his words. But when I look at Neotnia it feels like someone's placed a heavy stone on my chest. She's wearing a smile that's meant to cover up the fact she's clearly feeling sorry for me. And I mean, *fuck*. Terrific fucking job getting precisely what you never want: the beautiful older girl to pity you.

I take the sake and fill my glass, then Goeido's.

'Wow, this sake...' I shake my head, 'it's great, but it really messes with your mind.' I raise my glass. '*Sake?*'

And Goeido knows I want to move on. '*Sake*,' he nods, and that happy, gigantic-baby grin appears on his face again.

We down our glasses and I refill them, glancing at Neotnia. I'd give anything not to see that expression on her face. At least Inu looks his normal happy self.

'I swear,' I say, the particles swelling into a storm inside my skull, 'that's the best-behaved dog I've seen in my life. He hasn't begged for food once tonight. You guys have trained him so well.'

Neotnia gives me another pity-hiding smile and translates what I've said. But as she does, there's something new in her voice. Her tone, her translation: it's slower – almost like she's been asked to translate something she knows isn't really true.

Or maybe I'm just drunk for the first time in my life, feeling tremendously foolish, and everything in the world is distorted right now. I've made a colossal fool of myself. But hey, thank God for sake. I'd hate to know how stupid I'd feel without it.

And as I raise my glass the particles inside my skull now fizz like they're inside a shaken soda bottle.

'*Sakeee!*'
And everything goes black.

*

Hundreds of fireflies float above me. I move my head, and they sway in the same direction. I move my head back, and the fireflies sway back, little trails of light fading behind them.

My vision focuses. No – not fireflies. Fairy lights.

I push myself up. My head feels heavier than the rest of my body. My elbows feel like they could buckle under my weight. I'm on the couch I had my ear cleaning on. A pillow has been placed behind my head, and the blanket draped over me has crumpled to my lap.

I look across the room.

Hello?

But my voice won't carry beyond my lips. The orange atmosphere is so still it's like someone has pushed the mute button on this world. Or maybe I'm the last person in it.

My eyes catch the flicker of a shadow. A tall, slender figure passes on the opposite side of the window. An antlered head and red, leathery skin.

I jump upright, unleashing a pounding in my chest and skull.

Deep breath.

I wait for the pain to subside.

OK ... it's still Halloween. How long have I been passed out?

I reach into my pocket, but my phone's not there. I spot it at the booth. The now-empty sake bottle is there, too, as are the shot glasses and the pumpkin outfit Inu wore.

I take a step, but it feels like my centre of gravity is off. My stomach churns.

I freeze.

I need to throw up.

I turn towards the foyer, its lights now wholly dimmed. Inu is sitting up in the doggy bed, his distinctive spherical head instantly recognisable even in shadow.

'Inu, buddy ... I guess you're not so well-trained you can show me to the bathroom?'

But Inu doesn't move an inch. His silhouette is frozen solid.

'Inu?'

I take another step, but as I come to the dark hallway separating the foyer and dining area, my insides turn again. And again. And I don't move another muscle until I'm sure they're not going to turn another time.

OK ... I've never seen a bathroom down here.

I peer at the hallway. It's so void of light that it seems reasonable to conclude it may very well be nothing more than a black rectangle painted onto a wall. But my stomach churns again so I step into it, and as I do, an inky darkness envelops me. Even if I had the strength to turn around, I sense that I'd find there was no longer any café behind me. It would just be an endless black nothingness with no way back to the world that was.

I reach out until my palm hits a smooth plain and I advance forward – or what feels like forward. Soon my toes hit something solid, and steps rise to meet me. Or maybe I've fallen to meet them. Regardless, once I'm sure I'm not going to throw up on the spot, I kind of do this monkey-crawl until I reach a plateau where a thin, bright sliver shows itself.

They must have left the bathroom light on for me.

I slide against the wall so I won't stumble in the darkness, and inch towards the sliver as quietly as a mouse.

Then I push.

And it is the bathroom.

The thing is, Neotnia's in the bathtub.

She's in a white T-shirt and panties, and the tub is filled almost to the brim. She's sunk down, so the waterline submerges everything below her collarbones. The ends of her black, shoulder-length hair skim the water's surface. The painted cat nose and whiskers from earlier have been wiped from her face.

Goeido, meanwhile, stands beside the tub. He's still in his kimono, but in one big hand he's holding a toaster that's plugged into a thick extension cord. The toaster's inner coils glow an electric orange.

And he's holding it directly over the bathwater enveloping Neotnia.

And I feel like the three of us are staring at each other with the same stunned expression, but for entirely different reasons. As I look from Neotnia's face to Goeido's, Goeido looks from me to Neotnia and back to me again. Then he turns his gaze once more to Neotnia. A beat later she shifts her eyes from me to Goeido and gives him a quick, sharp nod.

Raising his free, non-toaster hand, Goeido spreads his beefy fingers apart like he's about to choke something.

And as he lunges at me, the whole world goes as dark as the hallway below.

6 – It made the world look like it was simply black and white.

It's dark.

I'm floating in a void, sinking deeper a step at a time.

Then I'm deposited somewhere. Someone takes my hand.

'I wish I were like everyone else, because I like you.'

There's a prolonged silence.

It's a while longer before the hand holding mine slips away.

And I'm left alone in the darkness.

*

There's a loud yap, and my eyes spring open.

I'm flat on my back. Above me, the pumpkin fairy lights are off.

My head throbs.

I press my eyes shut as I sit up on the couch, only opening them after the pain recedes.

The booths are bathed in morning light.

I feel for my phone. It's in my pocket. It's just before eight.

Another yap. Inu's at his usual place on the counter, his tongue flopping happily from his mouth as someone pats his spherical head. Goeido's at the register with a customer. Neotnia exits the kitchen and hands him a paper bag. The customer leaves, and she sees me.

'He's alive,' she grins, entering the dining area.

She hands me a coffee. It's in a takeaway cup.

'*Arigatō*,' I say taking a sip, then set the cup down. For a long moment I look at Neotnia as if it's the first time I've laid eyes on her.

'God, I had a messed-up dream.'

'I bet. You were pretty out of it last night. A few hours ago, Goeido found you on the floor and had to put you back on the couch.'

'I'm sorry.' I shake my head, which amplifies the throbbing in my skull.

She smiles. A little polite smile.

'Are you hungry?'

I look towards the foyer. Now three customers wait to order.

'No,' I try not to shake my head again, and rise despite a new pulse of pain behind my brow. 'A drunk in the dining area probably isn't great for business. I should go home and get some proper rest.'

'*Hai*,' she nods.

'But I had a good time last night,' I add. 'Are you free later?'

She hesitates before answering. 'It looks like we'll be swamped today, and then I'll need to help take down the Halloween decorations.'

As with her smile, there's a certain politeness to her voice. And I can't help noticing she didn't say she had a good time, too.

'That's OK. Tomorrow, maybe?'

Neotnia looks at her feet. 'I don't know what my schedule is yet.'

The bell clangs, and she looks over her shoulder. Another customer has entered.

'Well ... I should get going. It's getting busy.'

'*Hai*. It's going to be one of those days. Oh – don't forget this.' And she hands me the takeaway cup.

Inu gives me a yap as I pass the counter, and Neotnia begins on the logjam of orders.

I catch Goeido's eye. '*Sayōnara*,' he says.

It's the first time he's ever told me goodbye.

As I exit, I give a final glance over my shoulder, but Neotnia's back is still to me. Stepping onto the sidewalk, Shibuya's crawling with people just starting their day. But I make my way through the crowds to my apartment, and my bed.

When I wake, my headache's gone and the golden afternoon glow of a November Tokyo shines through the balcony. I shower before heading out for a late lunch, ending up at a cafeteria chain in Shinjuku that only sells different varieties of udon.

I can't help but think of Neotnia. The way she was this morning

– did I do something wrong last night? I vaguely remember becoming a depressed drunk. But before that, I know we were having a good time. Everyone was laughing. Yet this morning it was as if she were keeping her distance. Treating me differently. It's the way she treated me the night I came in for the ear cleaning. Politely – like just another customer.

I swirl the udon with my chopsticks and slurp a noodle into my mouth.

Did I humiliate myself? I wouldn't have spoken about the school stuff if I weren't drunk. I mean, no one's ever been impressed by a pathetic-fat-kid story. I remember we talked about trust at one point, too. And then ... sumos. Did I let slip the specifics of what she told me about Goeido's past? I can't see myself doing that – but I've never been drunk before either. And, God, that messed-up dream – as if she'd asked Goeido for his help in ending her life and he was more than willing to comply.

A heavy feeling comes over me. You don't need to be a Freudian scholar to interpret a guy's dream featuring the half-naked older girl he's attracted to and her intimidating friend who seems like he never wants the guy around. Goeido lunged to choke the life out of me, and I fell into that black void where someone took my hand. And the person who took it ... I told them I liked them.

Please tell me I didn't actually tell her that last night.

Yet if I did, it'd explain her behaviour this morning. That is, it would explain it if the feeling isn't mutual. And why would it be? How often do beautiful twenty-year-olds fall for even normal-looking younger guys? It's such a cliché: the teen boy head over heels for the older girl. It probably happens to her all the time. And if her intention has only been friendship, and she now thinks I've misread everything, how uncomfortable would that make anyone feel?

I give the udon another stir, watching a sliver of scallion swirl helplessly. There are so many ways I could have messed up last night, I can't even be sure which is the most likely. But if I keep thinking about it, I'll just end up chasing my tail.

I go for a long walk and by eight, I'm back in Shibuya. I pass the café on the other side of the street. The pumpkins are gone and the sandwich board is back, but ear cleaning is no longer on the menu. Through the glow of the window, the booths are packed, but I don't look long enough to make out Goeido or Neotnia. I stop in a Lawson's to grab a light snack for later, then head to the apartment. For the remainder of the night I sit on my balcony, working on my translation app, the infinite city stretching before me.

*

It's not until three days later that I see Neotnia again. It's just after four in the afternoon, and dusk is coming. I'm headed to the 109 department store to kill some time, and as I'm approaching the café, Neotnia is just leaving it. It's the coldest day in Tokyo yet, and she's wearing a red winter coat and seems to be having trouble with the zipper.

I stop on the sidewalk, but she's so focused on the zipper she doesn't even notice.

'Ah, hey,' I say.

She looks up and for a moment considers me with an expression that suggests her mind was in another world and she's only this instant realised her body's in this one.

'Hello,' she presses her mouth tight, turning back towards her struggle. And she gives the zipper an aggressive yank, unsticking it.

'How have you been? I stopped by a few days ago and saw Goeido, but you weren't in.'

'*Hai*, he told me,' she says, finally zipping her coat. The battle over, her eyes settle on mine. The cold breeze flutters her bangs, which she brushes straight with the tips of her fingers. 'I was out. I'm sorry I missed you.'

And there it is again, in her voice: the polite Neotnia from the morning after Halloween.

'Yeah. Hey, look...' I say before I can stop myself. 'Did I do or say something that I shouldn't have on Halloween—'

'No,' she shakes her head. 'No.'

'Because if I did, I'm sorry. I know I got pretty drunk, and I'm sorry you two had to babysit me.'

'There was no babysitting,' she insists, giving her head another shake. 'That's what's sake is supposed to do – especially when Goeido is plying you with it.' She considers me for several beats, composing herself. 'I've just had some things I needed to take care of.'

And that composure – I'm reminded of something I'd forgotten until now: her gripping the counter on Halloween, pale as a ghost, desperate for air, then walking into the dining area moments later, similarly composed as if nothing had happened.

Another breeze blows past, and Neotnia folds some hair behind her ear. It's obvious she's not going to elaborate on whatever it was that needed taking care of.

'Where were you headed just now?' she says after a second.

'Nowhere in particular. I was just going to browse some shops; go on a walk maybe. You?'

'I'm going to the care home to help with the dinner shift. It's the first time I've been able to in a few days.'

I notice she's wearing her white work pants.

'Do you want company?' I shrug. 'I wouldn't mind saying hi to Joe.'

For a moment Neotnia doesn't answer. The way she looks at me, it's as if she's inspecting a set of scales on which she's balanced on one side me, on the other some unknown variable.

'*Hai*,' she finally says. 'OK.'

The JR line from Shibuya is packed, and it's not until we transfer to a local train for Higashikurume that the crowds thin and we can sit. We're both quiet, gazing out the window opposite us, watching the sunset. Whenever we make eye contact, Neotnia gives me a courteous smile but is soon lost in thought again, the air humming all around us as the carriage jostles. Yet just past Nerimatakanodai Station, we finally manage some small talk. I tell her I've heard Tokyo might get a light snowfall overnight. She tells me she heard the same.

'What have you been up to the past few days?' she says after the next station has passed.

'Not too much,' I answer. 'The day after Halloween I just recovered. I explored the Roppongi district the next day. Then yesterday morning, I received an email from a company called Kanō. Have you heard of them?'

She shakes her head.

'I hadn't either. It's a biotech firm in Tokyo. A really tiny one, apparently. They specialise in treatments for rare conditions – so rare only a few hundred people in the world have them. Conditions the big biotechs would never dream of tackling because the pool of customers is so small.'

Neotnia's eyes shift. 'What did they want?'

'To meet with me. They found out from the magazine that I'm in Tokyo, so invited me to their lab that afternoon.'

'Are they interested in your code, too?'

I nod.

'For what?'

'For formulating new molecular structures for drugs faster than they can with classical computer models.'

'Your code can do that?'

I shrug. 'They think it can.'

Neotnia considers this for a moment. 'So, they want to buy your code, too?'

'Well ... no. Not exactly.'

'Not exactly?'

I shake my head. 'It's funny, I expected their lab to be all high-tech and everyone to be walking around in white coats with metalenses glued to their eyes and stuff. But I met with the president in her office, and it looked like it was originally decorated in the twenties and hasn't changed since. Honestly, it looked like the old den at my grandparents' house. There wasn't even a single bot in the building.'

She waits for me to go on.

'What I mean to say is, they don't have the money. They're nonprofit. Funded entirely by public grants. They don't have the massive cash stockpiles the big biotechs do to splash out on quantum code simply because they're trying to treat conditions hardly anyone has.'

Neotnia glances at her hands for a long moment. '*Hai*, I see.'

'They knew Sony is already buying the code but ... well, they wanted to know if they could have permission to use it, too. They gave me the pitch: They wouldn't make a commercial product from any molecular models my code helps formulate. Any eventual treatment generated would be provided free to those who need it. But they said even that wouldn't happen for five or ten years, since they'd need to do clinical trials first. And though they don't have the money to pay for my code, they offered me a consultant's fee – though it's literally less than one percent of what Sony's paying me.'

Neotnia's face brightens a shade. 'But that's wonderful they think your code can help people who truly need it. It must feel great to know it can do that. You should be really proud of yourself.'

'The thing is ... I know Sony won't allow it,' I say. 'Even though Kanō's application of the algorithm wouldn't compete with theirs, no tech giant is going to let another company use its most-prized code. Sony wouldn't, Baidu wouldn't, Avance wouldn't – Tencent, Apple, ThaiX, you name it, no one would. The reason they offer the sums they do for these algorithms is, in part, to protect the intellectual property of the products the code helps create. When a tech giant's patent on a product is challenged, the company supports the patent's defence with costs showing how much they paid for any base code. They do this to show that not just the final product, but all its individual components have an intrinsic value. Sony would be less able to successfully defend their patents and block competitors from using similar code if theirs has been freely given to a non-profit to use as they wish. Even part of the contract I'll sign with them will be an agreement not to create any code that's remotely similar – that could compete with the code they're buying, in any way – for twenty years.'

I rub my palms on my thighs, my eyes linger on the backs of my hands for a long moment.

'So, if I tell Sony I want to let Kanō use my code, too, my deal with them is dead.'

Neotnia gives a nod so slight I barely catch it.

'I see,' she says, her own gaze shifting to the hands folded in her lap.

We're both silent for some time, the carriage's muffled hum serving as a natural cocoon for everything going through my mind.

'I'm thinking about my mom,' I finally say, still staring into my lap. I feel Neotnia's gaze return to me, though I can't lift my eyes. 'She ... doesn't work much anymore. Sometimes ... she can't. Mentally, she just can't. And I can never be sure when the next little break she needs to take will be her final, permanent break. And this Sony deal, it'll ensure I've got enough to take care of her for the rest of my life in case things get worse.'

The carriage's hum envelops me again. For how long, I don't know. But then, from the corner of my vision, Neotnia's hand inches into view. After a moment's pause, it bridges the gap between our thighs, and her pinkie finger lifts before hesitating, as if the digit itself is debating something. Only after a moment does it give my hand a few furtive, cautious taps, like it's the paw of a cat testing whether a patch of thinly frozen pond is sturdy enough to traverse.

'Your mom is lucky to have you,' she says in a tiny voice.

After another moment's hesitation, her hand retreats to safer grounds.

For the remainder of the ride, the only sounds are from the carriage's dull rumble.

At Higashikurume, we walk the short distance to the care home. We're both quiet, moving at no great speed, each lost in our own thoughts. Yet as we turn onto the small side street, a smile breaks across Neotnia's face. She points towards the back of the motel.

'They've filled the pool completely. Look at all the steam! Joe must be so excited...' But pausing, she sets a finger on her lips. Soon a quizzical expression appears. 'You know ... we might *really* need to make sure he doesn't make a mad dash for it. I wouldn't put it past him. He can be really tricky...'

Her newfound playfulness is contagious. It's the first time today she's seemed genuinely carefree.

'A mad dash with only one foot?'

'But remember, it's twice the normal size,' she arches an eyebrow.

'Ah, good point...' I grin, thinking of us as co-conspirators. 'OK, deal: I won't let him past me.'

*

But Joe died earlier that afternoon.

He passed away a few hours before we arrived.

As we approached the central nursing station, Neotnia still had that playful look about her. But I watched it drain away over a few brief moments as one of the head nurses told her something. Neotnia didn't reply with many words. I heard some soft '*hai*'s' and a few longer sentences. Then she came back to me and told me what had happened. She didn't show much emotion beyond displaying a distant look in her eyes.

I followed her and the nurse down a hallway to a room with a closed door. Through the small window, I saw a covered body on a stretcher. The nurse said something, and Neotnia told me I could come in with her if I liked. I did, and the nurse waited outside. Though we were still in our coats, the room was cold. The thin sheet over the stretcher contoured Joe's body underneath: his narrow torso and his long arms and legs. On one side, a foot was outlined and on the other the cliff edge of the outline ended earlier.

We didn't remove the sheet to look at his face, and neither of us spoke. I simply stood at Neotnia's side as she gazed at Joe. Or, gazed through Joe, would be more accurate. She looked in his direction, yet her mind seemed far away. It was during this time I saw those unfocused eyes cloud over and that dark shadow return. After some moments, I took her hand. It felt so warm in the cold room, and I gently squeezed it. That seemed to bring her back, and I gave her a look asking if she was OK. She nodded and rubbed my palm with her thumb. She cast one final look over Joe's body and then bowed deeply, arms at her sides, and remained in that position for some time. I bowed too, as best I could.

We exited the room. Neotnia removed her coat and put it in the small storage area, then tied a white apron around herself and pushed a waiting meal rack in the direction of Joe's old ward. Around seven-thirty, she said one of the nurses wondered if I could help some residents in the upstairs wards eat their meals, so I did. But unlike with Joe, the language barrier meant there was nothing I could do but smile politely when they spoke, waiting for me to bring a spoon-ful of puree to their lips.

It was shortly before nine when I saw Neotnia next. Descending the stairwell from the upper wards, I opened the door to find her exiting a ward further down the hall, retrieved tray in hand. But before she reached the meal rack her body shuddered and she lurched for a bench. She trembled and, at first, I thought she'd begun to cry, holding so much in about Joe. Yet I soon realised her body wasn't trembling at all – it was seizing; wincing like it did on Hal-loween. And, as on Halloween and at the cinema before it, it seemed as if Neotnia was fighting a ghostly grip around her throat.

The whole episode lasted only seconds, though, and when she rose, she glanced around as if to see if anyone had noticed. But the hall was empty, and she didn't spot me in the stairwell in the distance.

Thirty minutes later I was sat in a row of seats close to the central nursing station. Neotnia approached wearing her red coat and said her shift was over. She looked once more towards the room where Joe's body rested and then said we could go.

*

We're now back in the *yakisoba* shop down the street. Besides placing our order, Neotnia hasn't said a thing since we sat. When the food arrives, the server makes a point of glancing at the clock on the wall. It's nine thirty-five, and the sign on the door says they close at ten.

Neotnia takes a few miniature bites of her *yakisoba*. That horrible dark shadow still casts a pall across her face.

I finish a bite of my own *yakisoba* and clear my throat. 'Did Joe have family?'

But Neotnia doesn't answer. She picks up a few strands of noodles with her chopsticks and puts them into her mouth, almost mechanically. Whatever her eyes are looking at, I can't tell. Maybe even she can't.

'Did Joe have family?' I try again.

Her head makes a small movement, and it's as if she's only now realised she's at dinner. She places her chopsticks on the table and dabs her mouth with a napkin.

'He had a wife, but she passed away decades ago. They never had children.'

'I see,' I say. But I sense she's going back to that place in the shadow, so quickly, I add, 'I really liked him. I only met him the one time, but I could tell how much he adored you.'

She gives a slight nod. When she speaks again, her voice is quiet.

'Do you think he was scared when he died? Do you think he felt alone?'

I give her questions some thought. 'I don't know. I mean, he seemed like he was a pretty tough guy.'

'He was tough. But I know he was lonely, lying in that bed all day. Even before he became a resident, he'd been alone for years and years since his wife died. And, some days, I think that really made him sad.'

I don't know what to say, so I remain quiet. For several moments Neotnia stares into her *yakisoba*, her eyes unfocused, as if weighing something deep in the recesses of her mind.

'Is it wrong that someone's death makes you think of yourself?' she says, not really looking at me. 'Of those living that you love?'

'No,' I shake my head, looking at those cloudy eyes for a long moment. They have a thin film over them. 'No. Quite the contrary, I think that's the most natural reaction in the world. Death makes us think about a lot. Ourselves. Others. Not just those who've passed.'

And I hold my eyes on hers until she focuses on me.

'My father ... sometimes I'm worried I'll always be alone if he never returns. That I'll go through this world by myself. I keep telling myself he's missing ...' She hesitates as if afraid to let the next words flow. 'But what if ... what if he abandoned me? What if I'm always going to be alone?'

As the clouds in her eyes tumble, she stares at me with such a horrible sadness, it's nearly unbearable. It's a crushing, desperate look.

And, yeah, when Neotnia first mentioned her father was missing, everything from abandonment to Alzheimer's ran through my head. But getting to know her as I have in the last several days, the former seems impossible. Neotnia seems like a 'good egg', as my grandpa used to say. Her laugh and smile are infectious, she's considerate of others, she spends her free time helping the elderly, and her affection for a friend like Goeido is evident. I don't see how someone could ask for a better daughter, and I can't think of any reason her father would voluntarily disappear from her life.

Yet I don't think listing her attributes would be of any help right now. Across from me, her lips are held tight as if she's afraid opening them again will unleash emotions better stayed dammed up.

'I don't know much about your father,' I say, placing my chopsticks on the table. 'But I can't imagine anyone would willingly abandon you. And I don't think there's any chance you'll ever go through this world alone. I truly don't. But I do understand how overwhelming that fear can be...'

I hesitate, afraid to share what I'm thinking, and Neotnia gives a vague nod and looks back down at her food, the clouds in her eyes tumbling once more. But I can't stand that look any longer. I saw it on Mom's face after she came back. The desperation, the futile wish that someone somewhere has some wisdom or insight they can speak that will magic your anxieties away. Yet I have no such wisdom. I have no magical insight.

So, I work with the only thing I do have.

'I, well ... My body isn't ... totally normal.'

Neotnia's face raises at my words, and her gaze holds mine.

'I'm not like a burn victim or anything.' My voice breaks a little. 'But I'm ... Part of me...' I draw my mouth tight. 'I look different than other people.' And even as I'm fumbling this, I notice Neotnia doesn't glance down to search out what part of my body is abnormal. She just keeps her eyes on mine. 'What I'm trying to say is ... that fear that comes from being different from everyone else? Well, it makes me fear I'll always be separate from everyone else, too – and because of that, I'll always be alone.'

The way she's looking at me, it's the first time since we sat that I feel she's fully present.

'So,' I continue, 'I understand that fear and believing you're destined for it. But I also think that everyone – even supermodels or movie stars or people who still have both parents – has that fear from time to time. It's normal, I mean – no matter our circumstances. But fearing something and having it come to pass are two different things. And I'm willing to bet most of what we fear will never happen, or we can take steps to change it. But even if we do find ourselves alone, it probably won't last. I mean, if there's one thing the underlying principles of quantum coding has taught me, it's that nothing in this universe is fixed, so why should being alone be any different?'

I don't know if any of that made sense, or helped at all, or if I just embarrassed myself, but Neotnia holds her eyes on mine long after I've stopped speaking. Yet before either of us can say another word, a hand slices the silent space between us, depositing the cheque onto the table. I glance at the clock as the server looks on. It's five to ten. But that's fine. Neither of us has the appetite to finish our meal.

Outside, I look up to see thick clouds obscuring a partial moon. The lights from the unfinished stations are too weak to break the cloud cover, and it occurs to me this is how the sky must have looked every night when Mom and Dad were my age.

Neotnia looks towards the care home.

'Do you mind ... before we go to the station, can we walk past Joe's window one more time? By tomorrow, a new resident will be in his bed.' The temperature has dropped, and her breath is frosted.

The street is deserted, so we walk down its middle until we're directly between the care home and the motel. The area's so dark I bet we could see hundreds of stars shining bright if not for the clouds. There are hardly any lights left on in the wards, and from the other side of the street the only real illumination comes from the dim glow of the pool's underwater lamps, diffused by the steam rising from the water's surface.

Neotnia gazes at Joe's window for a long moment, then gives it a little bow and a final glance before turning towards me.

'I hope Joe got to see it all ready for swimmers,' she says, looking over my shoulder.

I turn to look at the pool, too. Its fence is still unfinished, but the concrete mixer and hoses from the other day are gone. The deck is draped in shadow, silhouettes of stacked patio chairs and pallets of planks needed for the fence's completion add even more darkness.

'I'm sure he did,' I say, peering at the hazy glow above the water.

'And I really wish he could have used it.'

'Even with his one foot?'

And for the first time since we left the care home, that infectious smile crosses her face, which seems to diminish its shadow.

'Even with his one foot,' she says. After a moment of contemplation, she adds, 'I want to do something for him.'

'OK,' I nod.

'I want to have a swim for him – since he can't do it himself.'

'OK...'

'Will you do it with me?'

'Wait – what? You mean, right now?'

'*Hai.*'

'But it's ... November. I thought you meant, like, during the day, and when it gets warmer.'

'"If you want to have a life, have a real good life, don't keep putting things off. You never know how long you have – and even if you have decades, they'll pass more quickly than you can imagine." That's what Joe said once. Tonight the pool's fence isn't complete. Tomorrow it could be.'

And without saying another word, she takes my hand. Her palm is soft against mine as she guides me through the gap in the fence, where the deck's shadows envelop us. Peering at the water's glow, her fingers slip from mine, forever taking part of me with them. And that look on her face ... I know she needs this. I know this is her way of honouring their friendship, but...

'Won't we get in trouble?' I hear my voice break as she unzips her coat.

'Who's going to see us?' She places it atop a plastic-wrapped pallet.

I look out over the fence. The darkened street is deserted. There isn't a living being in sight.

'The people in the motel?'

Neotnia motions towards all the objects providing us cover.

'No one can see us from the motel. And it's always empty, anyway. Look, there's not a single room with any lights on. Besides, the reception is on the other side of the building.'

'What about security bots?'

She slips off her shoes. 'It's a motel in Higashikurume, not the Imperial in Ginza.'

'But isn't it too cold?' My frosted breath provides supporting evidence.

'The pool's heated.' She pulls off her socks.

'We don't have swimsuits...'

'We have our underwear.' And she turns around, loops her thumbs into her waistband, and slides her white work pants down her toned legs, revealing the curve of her hips under black panties.

My mind screams at my mouth to shut up. But...

'We don't have towels.'

Neotnia places her folded pants next to her shoes on the pallet, then tears the plastic wrap enclosing it as easily as if it were tissue.

'Deck towels.' She pulls one from the opening. She unbuttons her work shirt and slips it from her shoulders. The white undershirt that remains is thin enough to see the outline of her bra. It's tight enough to see the swell of her breasts beneath and the softness of her belly.

'Get undressed,' she orders as her fingers lift the bottom of the undershirt, revealing the tight indentation of her navel and pale flesh goose-bumped from the cold. Yet despite its undeniable allure, I also know that, well ... it's a stomach whose contours are not rare. As a matter of fact, it's a stomach any normal person has.

'Wait...' My voice cracks as her ribs expose and the bottom of her bra comes into view, her undershirt halfway lifted. Neotnia's eyes hold on me in the shadows, examining some expression on my face that I cannot know. 'I think we should leave our shirts on,' I say, my chest pounding for two different reasons. 'Just in case someone sees us through the windows. Just so they know nothing ... funny is going on.'

And as my chest pounds, something about the way Neotnia looks at me makes me think she can hear it. Her eyes flicker like she's come to a particular realisation – a secret understanding my shame prevents us from speaking.

And she nods.

'*Hai*. Good idea,' she says. 'We should leave our shirts on ... so no one thinks something funny is going on.' And she pulls her undershirt back down around her belly. For a moment more, she gazes up at me in a way I've never seen her look at anyone before. Then without another word, she turns and pads towards the pool's edge. She puts one foot into the water, then the other. Her black panties cling around her bottom as they draw moisture in. Her undershirt is next, soaking and sticking to the small of her back on up, until only the tops of her shoulders are above the surface. And in one motion, she submerges herself entirely.

When she next breaks the surface, she's in the pool's centre. Whether she can still see me among the shadows, I don't know. Just like I don't know if what she does next is purposeful or not. She rotates 180 degrees, as if suddenly taking an interest in the pool's far end.

I drop my pants and throw my sweater to my feet, and I'm at the water before I can count to three. By four my boxers are submerged and by six I'm crouched low, up to my neck. The water's warmer than I expected, and with each step I take, the more my legs can lengthen. It's only when I'm within a couple feet of Neotnia that she rotates back around. Instinctively, I suck in my stomach, yet when I glance down I'm relieved to find my T-shirt bellows from my abdomen like a jellyfish swaying in the sea.

Neotnia's bangs are plastered against her forehead. A clear drop sits on an eyelash like dew on a petal until she blinks, sending it back into the water. And I can't help feeling that, by entering these waters, we've somehow entered another world, one shrouded by a fog of steam, which the ordinary world's components are incapable of penetrating.

Indeed, the only sound I hear is a gentle lapping. The only light I see comes from beneath the surface. Even our breath is no longer frosted.

Neotnia studies my face as if she's never looked upon me before. The clouds in her eyes have cleared, revealing their brilliant blues and greys once more. She seems completely at ease now, as if she's been here many times before. To this world, that is. Me, on the other hand – my throat's dry, and I'm treading my hands slowly back and forth even though my feet are flat on the floor.

A bead of water glides down the slender length of her neck.

'I was born in Kamakura,' says Neotnia, holding that gaze on me. 'Do you know it?'

I shake my head. I'm not sure I'm capable of speech right now.

'It's a seaside town south of Tokyo,' she says, gently swaying. 'Father and I lived in a small house there. It was nothing special. Barely big enough for the two of us, but it was home. At twilight we'd often go for walks on the black-sand beaches. One of my earliest memories is staring at the foam crests of the waves as they reached shore. It made the world look like it was simply black and white.'

She pauses and glances at the water, lingering on some thought.

'During one of those walks, I found a shell sticking from the sand,' she continues. 'It was the first I'd ever seen, and I asked Father where it came from. He pointed to the sea, and said, "Out there." I asked if there were more shells in the sea, and he said there were more than you could ever count, as well as all kinds of marvellous creatures.'

Polygonal ripples project a web of lamplight across her face.

'I told Father that I'd like to see all those marvellous creatures one day. But he grew stern and said I must never go into the sea because the waters around Japan are dangerous, and I could drown. Or worse – be eaten.' Her lips form a little smile, and she shakes her head. 'It was a father being overprotective of his daughter. But the next day, he took me to a pool, and I went swimming for the first time. Tonight is the first time I've been swimming since he disappeared.'

She falls silent again, lost in a thought. As she gently sways, my eyes drift towards her white undershirt, plastered wet against her collarbones, and the image from my dream pops into my mind as clearly as if it were happening now: her in the bathtub in a white T-shirt and panties; Goeido looming, toaster in hand – its inner coils glowing orange.

But the recollection is pushed from my mind. Neotnia is now several feet from me, propelling herself backward. Yet her eyes are still focused on mine. With each stroke, the water beats against me like a tide. Reaching the pool's far end, she grasps its ledge and bows her head, as if praying. When she returns, she stops inches from my chest, and from the way she's swaying, I can tell she's on her tiptoes.

'That's for Joe.'

Her black bangs stick damp against her forehead, the wetness drawing from her face. Below, the thin column of water separating us grows warmer.

'He really liked you, you know,' she says, and a small smile breaks her lips as she raises an eyebrow. 'He said you were shy, of course. And kind of awkward. And he seemed to think you wished you were just a bit older...' But then her face loses its teasing expression, and she settles an earnest gaze on me. 'But he called you a "good kid". It's the nicest thing I ever heard him say about anyone other than his wife.'

Even through the steam, her breath moistens my skin. Like my tongue, my insides feel all twisted, conflicted. I suck in my stomach, her body dangerously close to my shame. I can feel her warmth and want to be nearer to and farther from it at the same time.

Yet as that column of water between us narrows further, the shirt hiding my deformity brushes against me, causing my insides to rattle like windowpanes in a storm. In a blink, white spots explode across my vision – and they halt Neotnia's advance.

She sways backward, looking into the sky.

'Snow!'

The flakes fall by the millions. Some dissolve mid-air when they meet the pool's steam. Others make it to the surface, where they become one with the water. But the largest touch down in Neotnia's wet, black hair, shining briefly like brilliant stars in the cosmos before burning out.

For several moments we stare at the snow cascading into the

steamy waters. It's as if its presence is the bridge between the two worlds. The ordinary we left in the shadows with our clothes, and this world of lamplight and vapour.

But having found that bridge, Neotnia's gaze soon shifts from the flakes falling from above to the care home across the street. And gazing for some time, I know she's sought out Joe's window.

'What will happen to his body now that he's gone?' she asks without looking at me.

I suck the steam's warmth through my nostrils, moistening my throat.

'I'm not sure.'

She turns back and considers my face for several moments. The melting flakes form streams on her cheeks.

'Do you think he's with his wife now?'

I swallow. 'I don't know...'

'Did he tell you about her?'

I shake my head.

The ends of her lips curl. 'I thought maybe, because you both are boys, he might have.'

'He didn't say anything.'

Her lids shift almost imperceptibly, their edges curving ever so slightly. 'He told me about *everything*,' she says, that shy curl on her lips turning into a smile at a memory. 'Anything I wanted to know about him, he would tell me: early loves, his fears, the wrongs he'd done. Yet the only thing he ever told me about her is that she died years and years ago and that, to this day, she was the prettiest thing he'd ever seen. But that's all he'd say. I don't know how they met or even her name. Whenever I'd ask, he'd just say that some memories are too special to share.'

Neotnia's fingers break the surface to fold damp strands of black hair behind her ear. The movement causes her undershirt to cling to her collarbones like a thin film of wax, and it tightens even more against the swell of her breasts below.

When I look back up, her eyes are fixed on mine.

'When you returned for your backpack, you said I made you wish you spoke Japanese.' Her gaze doesn't waver. 'Was it because you thought I was pretty?'

I'm once again aware of how dry my throat is.

'Yeah...' my voice breaks. 'Yes, I do.'

Her mouth parts just a little, and that watery column between us narrows once more as her eyelashes dip. Under the surface, her palms follow her new line of sight and come to rest where my chest thuds through my T-shirt. For a moment, it's as if she's measuring its beats. But then her palms shift, and they press hard, the force sending her back several inches. Yet her gaze doesn't drift.

'Where do you think people go when they die?' she says, her fingers walking out towards my shoulders, their tips pressing into my flesh.

'I don't know.'

Her fingertips slide my skin over the balls of my collarbones, then run across my neckline like they're inspecting a priceless vase for minute cracks. My throat tightens against her touch and my heart pounds so heavily it must be creating ripples on the water's surface.

Yet her examination continues upward to my jaw, my chin, my mouth. She tilts her head, and her eyes look into mine. But they don't blink. Not once. Not even as the white flakes fall onto her damp, dark lashes. Her gaze only breaks from mine when she places her palms against my chest again and says, almost absentmindedly, 'A body is so delicate.'

And those palms, they trace their way down my chest onto the upper part of my abdomen, where her fingers prod the soft spot below my sternum.

I swallow, ordinary breathing now impossible. And once again, Neotnia tilts her head and I watch her striking face taking in my trembling one. The flakes' remains wet her skin. Her eyelashes. Her lips. And as her fingers begin their descent, her clear eyes keep me in place as if they were ropes binding me. Her fingertips run along the bellowing T-shirt that hides my shame, her eyes never leaving mine.

'My...'

Her fingers pause.

My mouth is dry. 'Like I said...' My heart, pounding. 'My body ... It's not like other people's.'

Neotnia studies me for so long I couldn't even begin to guess the number of flakes that have melted onto the curves of her cheeks.

'Neither is mine,' she replies.

So, I was wrong. She does lie to make people feel better.

But that lie and her unfaltering gaze are enough for me to permit her fingers to proceed with their exploration. They press my billowing T-shirt into my flesh and cross the bump of my boxer's waistband. I wouldn't think it's possible to be petrified and aroused at the same time, yet my body proves otherwise. And maybe she notices, too, because the edges of her lids curve just a little.

I suck in my stomach even more as her fingers reach the end of my T-shirt and crawl inside. They travel away from my erection and continue higher. Then, they make landfall on the flesh of my abdomen.

They delicately explore in one direction, then the next. Up and then down. Right and then left. The whole time Neotnia's face is tilted up, gazing into mine, her fingertips working by touch alone.

I taste saltiness at the edge of my mouth. It's not just melting flakes that stream across my cheeks now. 'I can get it fixed...'

Those clear eyes hold mine.

'Why do you need to?'

And her fingertips, they continue their delicate exploration, traversing my abdomen like a curator's fingers skimming the keys of the world's oldest, most valuable piano. But my ruined body, it's trembling now. And in an instant my entire vision goes white this time. It's so blinding, I can't even see Neotnia any longer.

Immediately, I know I'm passing out.

The only thing is ... I don't.

Instead, a booming voice shatters the border between our two worlds. It's yelling something I don't understand.

It's getting closer.

And as my eyes adjust through the steam and falling flakes, I realise all the lights on the deck are shining bright.

'It's the owner!'

We're out of the pool and at the pallets so quickly it's like we leapt there. We pile our clothes between us and bolt through the gap in the unfinished fence, dashing down the deserted street, drenched and half naked, under the falling snow.

7 – Isn't it nice, the way it comes down?

It's remarkable how the world can change in only a few days.

The apartment seems to burst with colour compared to the grey outside. Rain hails down like ten-thousand pencil scratches so heavy it's impossible to see more than a few buildings into the distance. Not one drone has glided by since I woke – yet perhaps they're still grounded due to what happened yesterday, and not because of the weather.

It's ten to eleven. Neotnia should be here soon. It'll be the first significant amount of time we've spent together since the pool three nights ago. After making our escape through the fence, we hid in the park with the Buddhist temple. In the safety of its darkness my chest pounded as we pulled our dry clothes over our soaked undergarments. When a car finally arrived, we had to share it with existing passengers. None spoke on the drive, though they cast glances at our damp hair from time to time.

The snow had stopped midway back to the city. In Shibuya, everything was cold but dry. The car dropped us outside my apartment.

'So, this is your building?'

I nodded. 'I'm in 1402.'

It was the first we'd spoken since leaving the park.

We shared a brief silence, then Neotnia said she'd better be getting back. It was after midnight, and I said I could walk her, but she said it was OK. 'It's only around the corner, and Tokyo is the safest city on the planet.' After the shock of Joe, I was glad to see she seemed a little more herself.

The next afternoon I stopped by the café to gauge her interest in joining me for some touristy stuff, yet when I laid eyes on her I was immediately struck.

She looked ... 'tired' isn't even the right word. 'Weak' is more accurate – the way someone looks when they're recovering from some horrible infection. She walked slower than usual, and the plates she'd cleared looked as if they were almost too heavy for her. She wore one of Goeido's shark sweatshirts with a turtleneck underneath, and her white gloves again hid her hands. It was a getup you'd wear if you had the severe chills.

When I asked if she was feeling OK, she said she was just tired because the morning rush had been non-stop. She added that she was busy that day and the next, but I could tell she didn't want me to take it personally. She asked if we could go to the Imperial Palace the day after the next, so we made plans to meet at my apartment.

But it was the next morning that the world changed. It happened as I was at the Sony Design Museum in Ginza. I'd gone to see an exhibition on their robotic innovations over the last century, from their first toy robots to the bots we have all around us today. As I exited the museum it felt as if the whole world had glitched. Everyone on the street stood frozen, staring into their screens.

Many were calling it the most destructive offensive on the west since the Pearl Harbor incident more than a hundred years ago. Yet since civilians were the primary target, others argued it was more akin to that attack in New York at the turn of the century.

Regardless of the comparison, it was the most devastating cyber-rattack to ever hit a developed nation. Just twenty minutes earlier, at around six a.m. local time, Paris's AI was taken out. The city went dark in an instant, severed from the regional Euronet like it never existed. Anything meta went down, vehicles stopped, locks failed to open – even water wouldn't flow from taps. Over in the Fourteenth Arrondissement, two arriving office workers were crushed when an Octo-class construction bot slammed into the pavement. It had been replacing a window twelve storeys up when it lost signal and its safety line snapped. In the Seventh Arrondissement, courier drones rained from the sky like hail.

One of the most frequent scenes shown during that first hour was of the Eiffel Tower. Instead of its sparkling lights, all you saw were shadows on rusting iron as a grey morning broke. First-responder drones zoomed about, revealing dozens of renovation bots clinging to the iron structure like spiders that had frozen to their web in an early-morning frost.

As the hours went on, the news only worsened. The attackers had not only targeted Paris's primary AI, they also injected a trojan into the city's backup metro systems. It tricked rush-hour trains into thinking they were the only ones on the tracks. One collision alone saw 173 passengers killed. By nine a.m. local time, confirmed collisions reached thirty-two.

As the day progressed, more news trickled out, though it was getting harder to know what was real and what wasn't. Official media reports said that a stateless dark-web hacking collective had claimed credit. But within hours deepfakes spread like wildfire across regional intranets. They purported to show everything from Chinese people living in France cheering the attacks, to the American president giving a streamed address to all forty-nine states admitting the incident was a joint U.S.-French cyberwar exercise gone horribly wrong. The deepfakes claiming to show Chinese or American involvement were the most technically convincing but, though there was little doubt about where those had originated, there hadn't yet been enough time to analyse and officially discredit them.

By nightfall, an eerie quiet had fallen across Tokyo, which I wouldn't think was even possible. Drones were grounded, and half of the cars were taken off the roads. Those still allowed were limited to three-quarters their usual speed. The Tokyo metro doubled the length of time between trains. On the streets, parents draped their arms around their children and hurriedly scuttled past whenever they came across construction bots working overhead. Anytime you went into a Lawsons or 7-Eleven, flashlights and powercells were picked over.

I called Mom to check in. She told me cities back home were taking similar precautions. I could hear the anxiety in her voice even though home is half a world away from Paris. But she's been like that ever since Angola. No matter which distant place cyberattacks have hit, it always throws her off for days. This time, the deepfakes really weren't helping either. Mom said one's been going around showing the governor warning that similar attacks on rural towns were imminent. Another claimed to show a popular Asian American actor famous for his superhero roles demanding reprisals against the U.S. for its cyberwar exercise going off the rails. I told Mom to ignore them all – they're just fakes. She said she knew, 'but still … it makes you wonder: what if some *are* true?'

The rain continues to pour in heavy grey streaks. When there's a gust, the lines curve and lash the window as if the apartment is the bridge of a fishing trawler caught out during a typhoon. I glance at the clock before turning back towards the charcoal world outside. It's ten past eleven and with the weather I wonder if Neotnia's even coming anymore.

Everything that's occurred in the past day has distracted me from what happened between us. Before the attack, so many questions ran through my head my mind felt like a spinning top. The morning after Halloween I was sure she didn't like me, and when I saw her leaving the café and asked if I could accompany her to see Joe, I was certain I was correct. Truthfully, I felt terrible coming. I felt like she only said yes because I put her on the spot. Even on the train, she seemed so reserved – almost withdrawn – from me.

But everything changed when we learned about Joe.

I know everyone handles loss differently, but at the *yakisoba* place such a dark demeanour fell over her, it was surreal – almost as if she were momentarily devoid of life. And the pool … The way she gazed at me as she explored my body, inch by inch. The questions she asked. Was that shock over Joe's death, too, and she simply needed attention right then? When Mom first started becoming the way she is now, I watched plenty of metavids about loss. Many said the grieving process compels some people to seek out physical contact – *sexual* contact. It's an attempt to feel pleasure – the one thing that can, however temporarily, extinguish the emptiness death leaves us with.

There's a faint knocking. It repeats as I enter the hall, passing the kitchen and bathroom.

My jaw drops as I open the front door. 'Jesus…'

It's Neotnia, soaked to the bone. Her hair is plastered to her face, and her clothes are leaking water. She looked drier in the pool.

'*Hai*,' she says. Her expression is so flat and sad I can't help but release a sympathetic laugh. But her eyes narrow on me, and I quickly wipe the smile from my face.

'Come in, come in,' I motion with my hands. She slips her shoes off outside the door, then steps onto the hallway's doormat in her sopping socks. 'One sec,' I say, and I reach into the bathroom, grabbing a towel.

'*Arigatō*,' she replies in a defeated voice and runs it through her drenched hair.

'Ah, so you didn't think you'd need an umbrella?'

Neotnia pulls the towel from her face and shoots me a cold glare. 'It blew away.'

Seeing that pathetic expression, I'm almost successful at stifling another sympathetic laugh. Almost. Thankfully, my little laugh makes her laugh a sad little laugh, too.

'OK, OK,' I nod. 'Here, give me your coat.'

It weighs twenty pounds from all the water it's absorbed. I hang it over the showerhead. Back in the hallway, I give Neotnia a look head to toe. The rest of her clothes are just as soaked, and there's a puddle slowly growing on the doormat. From over my shoulder, a flash brightens the main room. It's followed a few beats later by an echoing boom, then, a softer crack.

Looking like a drowned sailor, Neotnia says, 'I think our trip to the Imperial Palace might be off.'

I nod. 'I think so, too.'

'So,' she raises her eyebrows, 'can I borrow some clothes?'

I'm gazing at the torrential rain when Neotnia enters, ruffling her hair with my bath towel. My sweater hangs halfway to her knees, making it look like she's wearing a potato sack.

'I'm surprised everything fits as well as it does,' I say.

She finishes pressing a section of damp hair through the towel. 'The drawstrings on the pajama bottoms are a lifesaver,' she smiles, then pads across the floor in her bare feet, joining me at the balcony's door. '*Woooow*,' she draws the word out, looking at the downpour. 'It's so thick you could swim through it.'

She turns and scans my apartment. Ninety percent of the place is this room with the bed on one side and the sofa and coffee table on the other.

'It's nice.' She spies something peeking from under the bed. 'Mind if I wear those? My feet are cold.' She scoops up a pair of already worn socks, sits on the sofa and slips them on. Just like the rest of my clothes, they're twice the size she needs. She slides a comb from the pajama bottoms' pocket. 'It was on the sink. I hope you don't mind?'

I shake my head, and she runs it through her damp hair.

We decide to watch a movie. 'Do you have a preference?'

'Anything Japanese. Anything I wouldn't normally see in America.'

'Hmm…' she says, scrolling through the listings. 'But then you have to read subtitles.'

'I don't mind.'

As she searches, I check what's hidden in the kitchen's cabinets. I return with two bowls of microwaved convenience-store ramen. Neotnia scoots over to make room for me on the sofa. It's a small leather two-seater whose armrests are as high as its backrest, making it feel more like you're sitting in a catcher's mitt than on a couch. You can't help but slide into the other person on it. But besides the bed, it's the only place to sit.

'So, how is it?' I say after Neotnia deposits some ramen into her mouth.

'Mmmm…' she gives a satisfied grin. 'It's warm and amazing.'

I take a mouthful of mine. My face twists in revulsion. 'It's horrible!'

'I know,' she pinches more ramen between her chopsticks. 'That was for the umbrella comment. But hey, beggars can't be choosers. Look at it outside. We might be stuck in here forever. I just hope there's more horrible ramen to sustain us.' She looks up at me with a little smile, swallowing a mouthful.

Being stuck in here forever with her doesn't sound bad at all.

'Well, there're no musicals, but how about this?' She's chosen the original *Godzilla* from the mid-1900s. 'Is that lame?'

'No. I like old black-and-white movies, and I've never seen it.'

'Me neither.'

And so, as the torrents continue outside, inside, we slurp our horrible ramen and watch a man in a shoddy rubber monster suit invade the Japan of almost a hundred years ago. Yet it's when we finish our ramen that I sense an awkwardness between us. It's because of our hands. Now that they're not holding bowls and chopsticks, we both seem uncertain where to rest them. Finally, we settle them awkwardly in our laps, folded, like we're in church.

When Neotnia shifts, she gives a shy smile and my awareness of her thigh's warmth against mine amplifies, which in turn causes a warmth to rise in me. Sometimes we'll crack a joke about the bad effects in *Godzilla* but mostly we remain frozen, packed like sardines on the little sofa, staring at the black-and-white world in front of us. But as Godzilla unleashes his atomic breath on Tokyo's suburbs, a breaking-news alert appears.

We switch to NHK English, assuming it's about the storm.

We're wrong.

It's another cyberattack. It hasn't even been twenty-four hours.

This one's in Zambia. It hit around midnight local time. The anchor says the attack targeted the AI that runs the north of the country, instantly severing it from the African Union's intranet. NHK's stream cuts between scenes of blackouts – buildings dark, traffic stalled – but then the stream changes. Spotlights from emergency drones shine down on white-water rapids. It's only when the shot zooms out that it becomes evident the rapids aren't natural at all.

The anchor explains that the dam's emergency backup AI was intentionally crippled once the north's primary AI was down. That crippling is why the dam was unable to adjust its hydraulics. Pressure built, fracturing its barrier. The resulting overflow doubled the volume of water that's typically released into the river below, causing a mudslide five kilometres away.

When the stream cuts again, Neotnia brings her hand to her mouth.

'At least eighty percent of the village's estimated population of five hundred are missing,' the anchor says over the scene of a wailing woman holding her soiled, unmoving child in the darkness. Spotlights from first-responder drones reveal roofs sticking from the muddy ground. 'As news of the incident spread, videos featuring the American and Chinese presidents claiming credit for the attack quickly circulated across social media inside the African Union. The videos have been determined by NHK to be deepfakes, yet that hasn't stopped them from inciting both anti-Chinese and anti-American sentiment in the region—'

A blast of thunder shatters the air outside. But Neotnia doesn't even hear it. She's glued to the stream of the village, the survivors frantically digging into the black mud as the body of another child is extracted.

'At first, U.S. officials would not comment on the cyberattack,' the anchor continues, 'but as reports of the mudslide circulated, the White House moved quickly to say it was not involved. Still, experts believe the attack could be swift retaliation for Paris, which American officials have privately attributed to stateless actors working under the direction of Chinese authorities. France is a close U.S. military ally in Africa, and Zambia is the largest recipient of Chinese investment on the continent. The dam was China's largest infrastructure project in the region, worth the equivalent of ninety billion dollars.'

And as the anchor explains that Chinese state media is claiming that the country's AI has already prevented hundreds of deepfakes alleging Chinese involvement from infiltrating the Sinonet, which its officials say is proof foreign adversaries are attempting to mislead their citizens about the incident, we watch as NHK streams more scenes of the devastation. We see villagers digging futilely into the wet earth with their bare hands. We see the legs of cattle sticking from the muddied ground like grotesque trees. We see a father covered in mire, screaming for his children.

'American and Chinese technology giants have already announced plans to send aid to the region, with America's Avance saying it is sending its top AI engineers to help get northern Zambia running again, while China's Baidu has promised to deploy fifty of its Atlas Class-4 search-and-rescue bots to the village by—'

I've taken the remote and shut off the TV.

Next to me, Neotnia's eyes are glassy, staring at the blank screen.

'It's horrible...' she says as if still seeing that muddied child. A hint of that dark shadow falls across her face as her gaze falls to the hands in her lap. 'I don't ... I don't understand how people can be so terrible to one another.'

I consider her face for a long moment, watching that shadow trying to take hold. Outside, thunder rings in the distance.

'Does it scare you?' She looks at me.

'The attacks?'

Neotnia shakes her head. 'Everything. The superpowers. This never-ending digital cold war. Joe talked all about it.'

'Sometimes. If I think about it,' I admit. 'But then again, sometimes I guess it's just kind of like the sky for me, too.'

Neotnia looks at me but doesn't say anything. I take a moment, thinking about how to explain it.

'You're twenty,' I say. 'So, when you were born, and up until you were eight, the stations weren't yet being constructed. That means, even though you were young, you probably still have memories of gazing into the night sky and only ever seeing a natural, lone moon – right? That was the ordinary world for you.'

Neotnia's nod is so slight you could miss it. But she doesn't say anything.

'Well, for me, I was only five the year America and China started building their stations, so I only ever remember seeing a night sky with a moon and the fragments already in it. I was simply born too late to remember a sky without them. And if there's anything that represents this cold war and its proxy battles, this paranoia and the unending streams of disinformation, it's them, right? So, these digital battles – like the stations – they're just an ordinary part of the world, from my perspective. It's what's always been – it's the norm. And normal things, I think, for better or for worse, tend to have less of a pull over us.'

Neotnia gives another barely perceptible nod. But still, she stays quiet.

'I will say, though, that the scale of the attack in Paris, the scale of this attack today – yeah, it's unnerving. Even for cyberattacks, their size and targets are outside the norm. What's happened to those people is horrible, and I think anyone is right to find that scary.'

Neotnia looks at me as if weighing something in her mind. Outside, the sky rumbles.

'Yesterday, when I heard about Paris, it scared me *so* much,' she finally says. 'My first instinct ... Well, my first instinct was to talk to you, actually. You ... you're kind of like Father, in a way. He knows about coding, too. But he always spoke about how code can change the world for the better. Yet all it ever seems to do is hurt people. That deepfake of Goeido. The Paris metro. This dam...' She shakes her head, a sad, pensive look stretched across her face. 'Even that American superhero actor – you know the one? He's in the hospital today, fighting for his life. I heard it on the news this morning. His parents were from Japan, but he was born in your country. Has lived there all his life. But last night, three Americans bashed his head in with a brick because someone's code made it look like he said something he didn't.'

We're both quiet for a long moment. Outside, the rain pelts the windows as if a thousand gloved knuckles are tapping on the glass.

'I think I'd mostly agree with your father,' I say, after giving it some thought. 'I think he's right. Code can ... *does* do a lot of good. But you're right, too, about it being used to hurt people. Like this dam – I don't think I'll ever get used to the fact that code can turn almost anything into a weapon. Mom—'

I stop. Somewhere deep inside, an uncomfortable feeling I've not experienced in a long time rises like a cork released from the depths of the ocean. Neotnia notices whatever expression it is that's come over my face, but she doesn't say a word. Her glossy eyes wait on me.

'Mom ... she told me, well ... it's when she and Dad were in Angola. They were monitoring a group of about three hundred Stung, making their way from the north to the south. Since they were victims of the biologics, most aid agencies shunned them. Their deformities were so bad they needed almost constant medical attention, even amputation. But they had no choice but to move because two opposing factions were converging, and their camp was right in the middle. So, Mom and Dad were in the caravan that day. It was made up of these old, self-driving, open-top trucks built for moving grain, not people. Each held about thirty or forty Stung. No one in that caravan could have made the journey on foot. Some didn't have feet left.'

I pause for a moment and clear my throat, that cork inside me bobbing around in choppy waters.

'So, the caravan starts crossing this long bridge, and it's acting as a kind of bottleneck, making the trucks proceed single file at a crawl because it's so dilapidated. They don't know how stable it is – if it can support two trucks side-by-side, you know?'

Neotnia nods.

'Well, Mom's in the last truck in the caravan, and Dad's in the second to last. Those trucks had the most badly injured, so it's why a doctor was in each. But as the last truck, the one Mom's in, gets onto the bridge, the truck that's leading the way, about eight trucks ahead of hers, turns and accelerates through the bridge's railing, careening over the side into the gorge.'

Neotnia's lips part. And looking at her, seeing that shadow spread, I think I should stop. For her sake, if not my own. But the memories of what Mom told me now rise inside like a flood.

'The next truck in line does the same – plummeting over the side, taking all its occupants with it,' I go on. 'That's when Dad orders everyone to jump from the truck he's in and yells at Mom's truck behind him to do the same. As soon as his feet hit the bridge, he sprints towards the remaining trucks at the front of the caravan, waving his hands and screaming for everyone to get out, to jump for their lives. A second later, another truck at the front of the line accelerates and goes off the bridge. And, well, as Dad's helping people from the back of the next truck, it also accelerates – and so does the truck behind him. And as that one shoots past the railing, it knocks Dad off with it...'

And right then, I feel a familiar touch. Neotnia's fingertips have found the top of my hand, the way her pinkie did on the train. Her gaze is frozen on me, and her eyes shimmer with a terrible little sadness. I'm not even sure she's aware her hand has moved.

'Anyway,' I clear my throat and nod, though I don't know why I'm nodding. 'Dad went over the bridge along with all but sixty-three of the Stung. His actions managed to save most of the people in the last two trucks, including Mom. But, well, the reason I'm telling you this is it turned out that one of the warring factions had hacked the caravan's systems. They thought the trucks were hiding the other side's soldiers. So, you're right. My dad. Goeido. Paris. This superhero actor. Zambia. Code can cause some scary, horrible things if we choose to use it that way. It can have awful consequences.'

Across the room, the rain rapping against the balcony's glass provides a sombre soundtrack. And Neotnia, her fingertips still on my hand, the way she's gazing at me with that tragic little look in her eyes? It's the same way anyone looks at a kid when they learn how his parent died. And I know the next words from her mouth will be 'I'm so sorry' – because, well, what else can you say?

Thankfully, a crack shatters the air so loudly it's as if a bomb has gone off. I go to the balcony's door. Though it's barely afternoon, it looks like it's almost evening outside. The rain now falls in such packed, dense lines I can't make out the next building over.

I watch for a long moment as the world blurs into one big charcoal sheet. As it does, my focus shifts to the glass's reflection, and I glimpse Neotnia staring at me. It's the way someone stares when they've come to some realisation. A realisation of what, exactly, I don't know.

Another crack in the distance pulls my eyes to the outside world once again.

'This weather's crazy.' I shake my head, glad to have an excuse to change the subject. 'Three days ago, we had flurries – now this storm. Just imagine how many feet of snow we'd have right now if it were as cold as when we were in the pool.'

And when I look back towards Neotnia, that focused gaze has been completely wiped from her face, along with any hint of lingering shadow. Now, well ... I've never seen her blush so much. The longer I look at her, expecting her to reply, the more at a loss for words she seems. As she casts her eyes furtively into her lap, I realise I've inadvertently brought up the elephant in the room. And when she glances at me again, I'm suddenly at a loss for words, too.

But another crack rings across the sky, followed by a bone-rattling boom so loud we jump with such fright it's comical. Indeed, we break into a relieved laugh once our limbs have settled under our control again.

Catching my breath, I walk back to the sofa and pick up the empty ramen bowls.

'Hey,' I say, putting one bowl into the other, 'you know what I found at FamilyMart the other night? Microwavable hot chocolate with those little freeze-dried marshmallows. It reminds me of back home. You want a cup?'

Neotnia hesitates as if she was expecting me to say something else.

'*Hai*,' she nods, 'OK.'

I take the bowls to the kitchen and return a few minutes later with two mugs. Neotnia's still on the sofa, yet she seems more on her toes than when I left the room. Her eyes follow me as I sit, steadying both mugs as our hips slide together once more. I hand her a mug.

'*Arigatō*,' she says and tucks a lock of hair behind her ear, exposing the slenderness of her neck. When she looks at me again, I feel a shy warmth spread across my skin.

We sip our drinks and then just kind of sit there as if we're mirror images of the other. We're each wearing my clothes, holding our mugs in our farthest hands while our thighs press together thanks to the catcher's mitt we're in.

'They have hot chocolate like this where you live, too?' Neotnia finally says. 'It's my favourite drink.'

'Convenience-store, microwavable hot chocolate is your favourite drink?' I raise my eyebrows, as if the topic is the most interesting in the world.

'Well ... I prefer the kind we make at the café best,' she nods. 'But I like all hot chocolate, generally speaking.'

'Me too,' I say, noticing something at my thigh. It's increased pressure from hers. 'Ah, but yeah ... where I live, there's a little coffee shop, and, during the winter, they serve *white* hot chocolate.'

'Mmm,' she nods, her eyes on mine. 'Where is that exactly?'

In the corner of my vision, Neotnia's mug-free hand drifts closer, like an autumn leaf riding a stream.

'Ah, Grahams' Bakery on Seventh Avenue.'

The mug in Neotnia's hand has apparently become too heavy to bring to her mouth again. It hovers by the gentle swell of her chest. The same forces affecting it seems to be exerting a pull on her eyes, which are now looking at my mouth.

'No ... where do you live?'

My throat tightens. 'Oh ... it's just a little town in the Midwest...'

'Do you like it?' I see her lips say. 'I've never been outside Japan.'

'I like Tokyo,' I say.

And by our thighs, our fingertips meet.

Then her hand is on my leg, and my hand is touching her face, and I don't even know what we've done with the hot chocolates. I feel her lower lip between mine. We draw each other close. Through my sweaters, her breasts crush against my chest.

But one of us kicks the coffee table. The hot chocolate no one cares about has spilled.

We stare at each other, our faces flushed, our breath shallow. The way Neotnia looks at me – it's how she gazed at me in the pool. Like she's considering something about me deep inside herself.

Outside, the sky trembles.

She takes my hand. It leads us to my bed. She lifts its sheets, and I get in. I feel the weight of her body as she joins me under the covers and spreads her thigh across my torso. She's so warm. Her eyes find mine. Her mouth finds mine again, too. My hand slides down her spine and onto the curve of her hips. Yet as our bodies warm even more, her lips pull back.

Her shimmering blue-grey eyes linger on me for some time, her face flushed, her breathing heavy. Then, without a word, she rests her cheek against my chest. The way her breathing changes, it's as if she's trying to steady it, and it's a while before she shows her face again. When she does, her eyes look moist.

I fold her black hair behind an ear and place my palm on her cheek.

'Is everything OK?' My voice sounds alien to me.

But she doesn't answer. She's not even looking at me. Looking in my direction, yes. But it's like how she looked at Joe in that cold room. She's looking right through me – and I feel as if she's about to cry.

My thumb caresses the spot under the first in her trio of faint moles.

'Are you OK?' I try again.

Her mouth twists up a little bit, and I see her eyes focus. She sets them on mine for a moment more before returning her cheek to my chest.

'I just want you to hold me,' she says in a small voice. 'Is that OK?'

I pull her close. Her body is so soft, I could hold her forever.

Outside, a rumble reverberates across charcoal skies.

'I just don't know how to interpret these feelings,' her tiny voice says. 'They're new to me.'

'Me too,' I say, holding her tight.

*

The room is dark. It's evening now. The rain still comes, but not as heavily. I let my eyes adjust as I listen to the taps at the glass. The clock says it's just after six. Neotnia's in my arms, her head resting on my chest. After several moments, her body shifts, and she tilts her face towards mine. The room's blueish shadows fall across her.

'I was listening to your heartbeat,' she whispers. 'I could tell when you woke by the way it changed.'

She inches up and finds my mouth, kissing it, and returns her head to my chest. I pull her tight. In the darkness, I fold a lock of her hair behind an exposed ear, then repeat the motion, slowly, rhythmically. Her arm, draped across my body, wraps more tightly around it.

'I feel safe with you,' she says. 'It's the first time in a year I've felt safe.'

She's quiet for several moments as I continue to stroke behind her ear, exposing her pale neck to the blue shadows. I watch as its sinew tightens.

'What was it like when you found out your father died?'

Maybe my body's reacted in some way I'm not aware of, because her fingers curl into my shoulder, gripping me as if she's afraid I might drift off.

I consider her question for some time, recalling what I told her earlier.

'A relief,' I answer. She adjusts her head on my chest and waits for me to go on. 'When Mom came back from Angola ... she was a different person. She went there with a life in her but left it somewhere over there. I was nine when she returned. At the time she told me that Dad had stayed there and wasn't ever coming back – just like that.

'And for a while, I believed her. I thought Dad simply decided to stay. But as time passed, I began to understand that he was gone for good – and I think Mom knew I did, too. Still, it was only when I was twelve that she finally spoke about what happened. I don't know why she decided to then and not earlier. Maybe it was because by then both my grandparents had passed. Or maybe she saw all the changes in me and hoped addressing the past could reverse them. Regardless, when Mom finally told me he'd died, she told me everything. Everything about the horrors she saw, and all about the caravan, too...'

I let out a breath, thinking.

'You know what's funny about that? I really don't think about it much. It's been so long. But when I do ... my thoughts always turn to the code. I wish I could have seen the code that turned those trucks into weapons. Back then, it would have been gibberish to me, of course. But now, if I saw it ... Well, code leaves footprints. Now I could easily tell which faction did it. Hell, I might even be able to identify the individual who did.'

As my words linger in the darkness, Neotnia's body seems to take on more weight against mine. I rake her hair with my fingers, watching her black locks slip through them.

'Anyway, like I said, when Mom told me he was dead, it *was* a relief. It gave me hope that maybe if she could address the past head on, she might be able to get back some of that life she left over there.'

Neotnia rubs my chest, then squeezes me tighter. We're silent for several moments, and I know she's listening to my heartbeat.

'What did you mean that, by telling you the truth, your mom might have been trying to reverse all the changes in you?' Her voice is as soft as the rain.

I run my fingers through her hair again and watch the black strands drizzle free. I inhale a deep breath through my nostrils. Her head rises and falls with my chest.

'When I was around ten, I started gaining weight. That's when I happened to start doing poorly in school, too. By the time I was twelve, I was easily the heaviest kid in school – and known as one of the dumbest. And I think, by then, Mom worried those changes had happened because Dad was missing from my life. But you know, who knows if that was the case? Regardless, I was heavier than ever, and I didn't have friends. Most lunch periods I'd sit alone in the computer lab. Messing around with them was one of the few things that took my mind off the bullying.'

Under Neotnia's cheek, the beats of my heart have broadened into slow lubs. I wind a lock of her hair around my finger and let it drop.

'But things only got worse. By fourteen, I was in danger of flunking my freshman year of high school. No matter how hard I studied, I could never remember anything when I sat to take a test. Being the fat, dumb classmate was bad enough, but what was worse were my teachers thinking I was simply lazy.

'One day Mom met with my principal. He told her I needed to

study or I'd be held back for a year. But Mom ... I'd never seen her react in such a way before. She was nearly screaming at him, trying to get him to believe I *did* study every night at home, with her, and that I knew the materials inside out – she'd seen it with her own eyes. But my principal simply countered that, if that were the case, then why was I flunking almost every class? The thing is, I think if it were any other parent, they would've been believed. But by that time, word had gotten around town that Mom was a bit off.'

I go quiet for a few moments, my fingers still playing with Neotnia's hair in the darkness. I gently lift their black strands, then let them fall. It's as if they're attached to my memories – as I raise one, a memory rises with it.

'But Mom knew the truth. Matter of fact, that was the last time I really saw her fight hard for something. Like it was the last part of her old self left. She convinced an old colleague to meet with me. He diagnosed me with a learning disability – a significant one – and put me on medication.' I shake my head, remembering. 'It was amazing. Life-changing – literally. Suddenly I could recollect what I'd studied. But algebra, man ... I'd flunked algebra for years, but now it was my *best* subject. Its logic just clicked. After only a few months, I was actually getting bored because the teacher was going *too* slow. A few months later, I didn't need him at all. And with my new understanding of algebra, combined with my lunches in the comp lab, that's when I got into quantum coding. Its duality was reassuring, in a way – this empirical proof that the world isn't only black or only white, which is how most in my town seem to view everything. And by fifteen, I may have still been the fat kid of the school, but I was also its smartest. Well, in some things, anyway.'

I let Neotnia's hair drop and gently fold it behind her exposed ear. Her other ear to my chest, I feel like she's considering my heartbeat the way a mother considers a sleeping newborn. She lingers on it for some time to make sure it's OK, laying there in the darkness, before feeling comfortable enough to move on. And as if my heart has passed her inspection, her hand moves from my chest to my abdomen, skimming my sweater. It reaches the overlap by my khakis and then, as in the pool, changes direction and turns upward, sliding under my sweater and the T-shirt beneath. I tense at the sense of her fingertips.

'And this?' she says, tilting her face. Though her eyes try to hold mine, I release a quiet breath and turn my gaze towards the ceiling.

'Earlier this year ... I just ... I wanted to be normal. So, I did the math and lost a lot of weight, quickly. Over a hundred and ten pounds in six months.' I know Neotnia's eyes are still on me, yet I can't bring myself to look at her. Her fingertips knead into me as tenderly as a kitten's paw. 'I hate it,' I say, and pull her hand from under my sweater.

The mattress shifts as Neotnia props herself on her elbow and hovers her face over mine so I can't ignore her gaze. Her hair skims my cheek like the edge of a feather.

'That doesn't mean I have to,' she says, and kisses me.

I force a smile. 'Thanks...'

Neotnia raises her brows.

'But...' I answer her expression, 'I wish I could be like other people.'

'Hmmm. No father. No friends. Judged for the way you used to look. And *clearly* too smart for your own good.' She shakes her head, feigning disappointment. 'You're definitely not like other people. An outsider, even – a regular Meursault, from the book in your backpack...' The edges of her lids curve down ever so slightly. 'But I *like* that you're different. I've always felt like an outsider, too.'

And for a long time, she holds a look on me like she's studying me while simultaneously arranging the pieces of some convoluted, invisible three-dimensional puzzle into the perfect order.

'I want you to do something for me,' she says. 'I want you to take off your shirt.' A dread runs through me, and as if sensing I'm about to protest, Neotnia says, 'I said just because *you* hate your body doesn't mean *I* have to.' And her face retreats from mine as she sits up on the mattress, the balcony's dim light casting a faint blue glow over her. 'And I want you to take off your pants,' she continues. 'And I'm going to take off my clothes, but I want your promise you can control yourself, OK?' She looks at me with a most severe expression. 'I want your *promise* this isn't going to go further. My – well, I guess they're *your* boxers – they stay on me, got it? I just want to feel your skin against mine.'

'...OK...' I barely manage a nod.

'You *promise*?' She gives me a hard stare.

'I promise.'

'OK.'

Neotnia rises from the bed and lifts my potato sack of a sweater from her body, dropping it at her side. Then, holding her gaze on me, she raises my red T-shirt over herself. Like a curtain on opening night, it reveals her soft, pale belly, the tight indentation of her navel, the round firmness of her small breasts, and then, their dark nipples. She inspects her naked chest in the blue light, and the edges of her lips curl in reaction to whatever look is plastered on my face. Next, her pajama bottoms drop out of sight, too. Below her belly, the elastic band of my boxers is folded tight around her waist. As she removes her socks, I see the white firmness of her calves.

She returns to the bed, kneeling at my side, as if presenting herself. I take in her naked form for a long time, examining its pale curves and dips, its slopes and angles. Neotnia blushes, noticing how long my eyes spend on her breasts.

'OK,' she finally says, 'your turn.'

I sit up as she slips my sweater over my head. She unbuckles my belt and undoes my fly. I kick off my pants and they come to rest somewhere near the bed's edge, where she drops them to the floor with my socks. And then, looking at me with the softest smile, Neotnia pulls my T-shirt from my body. She gazes at my abdomen, yet that soft smile doesn't change. But even in the darkness, I'm unable to follow her gaze. Thankfully, placing a hand on my shoulder, she guides me back towards the mattress, then slides beside me and pulls the sheet across us. I take her in my arms. Her bare breasts press against my torso; her soft thigh is smooth against my own.

I've never felt anything so wonderful.

'Not so bad, huh?' She kisses me as the rain sounds behind us.

Settling her head on my chest, I trace the features of her face. Her dark lashes. The slope of her nose and the shape of her mouth. I run my fingers through her hair again, and I know that she's listening to my heartbeat once more.

The thing is, it's pounding, and I cringe as I realise my erection is jabbing against the flesh of her thigh.

'That feels weird,' she giggles. 'But it's OK.' And she props herself up on her elbow. Under the sheet, her hand moves down my stomach then slips past my boxers' waistband, where her fingers grasp me. 'Remember,' she says with that most severe expression. 'You *promised* you'll control yourself.'

I can only nod, and when I do, a little grin crosses her lips.

'You can do it into this,' she says, scooping the red T-shirt from the floor, then her fingers grasp my penis again. She gives it a few tight squeezes, which makes me harden so much it feels as if its skin might well burst like an overstretched balloon. With another squeeze, she gives a firm gaze and says, 'Remember – watch those hands.'

And she begins moving her fist. It feels so incredible I could die. Her palm's flesh is so soft against my hardness; the strength of her grip modulating from firm to unbelievably tight – the pleasure's nearly unbearable. More so when I see that satisfied, almost wicked, look in her eyes, realising the power she has handling me. My gaze flits from her face to her jiggling breasts to her fingers wound around me. I never want this to end.

But even after it does, Neotnia continues to grip my limpness for some time, inspecting it like one might an unknown sea creature just pulled from a net. She gives it a few squeezes and flops it back and forth, scrutinising it with narrowed eyes. Some of me got onto her fingers, but when she finally lets go she just wipes them on the T-shirt, too, then gives a little satisfied grin, returning to my side.

After a brief moment, a laugh escapes her. 'Your heart is beating much slower now,' she says, and I squeeze her tight.

We lie quiet for a long time after, neither of us speaking. My fingertip tracing a route along her slender neck over and over as the rain falls across a soaked Tokyo.

I finally break the silence. 'So, you've never been outside of Japan?'

It's a moment before Neotnia answers, as if her mind was somewhere far away and it needed time to return.

'No.' She readjusts her head on my chest. 'But one day I'd like to see the world. Maybe start with America. Father knows English, too, and after I find him, I hope we can go there together. Then maybe travel down to Mexico, and through South America – and maybe even take a boat back to Japan across the Pacific.' I can feel her smile in the darkness. 'Wouldn't that be nice? A proper adventure.'

'It would,' I say, stroking her hair. It's smooth and, when it drizzles against my chest, cool against my skin.

'You said he's good with code, like me,' I say. 'Does he know a lot about programming?'

Neotnia's fingertips press into the flesh of my shoulder, holding on to me. It's a moment before she replies. 'He knows lots about all kinds of things.'

I consider my next question for some time.

'How old were you when he … disappeared?'

There's a prolonged silence.

Neotnia's fingers loosen their grip on my shoulder. Her head trembles on my chest. Slowly, her whole body follows suit, shuddering against mine.

I pull her tightly, letting her cry.

It's only after several moments that I notice how cold she's become.

I push her hair aside and glance at her slim neck, her bare shoulder blades. I'm startled by what I see. It's as if her skin has lost all colouring. That's when I realise she's not trembling at all. Her body is wincing in my arms in short, sharp bursts.

I pull back and call out her name, but she's powerless to turn towards me. I roll her flat on the mattress. Her face is as white as a ghost, and her lips are parted, frozen as if caught in a wail. From them a horrible rasping escapes, like her windpipe is being crushed by some invisible hand.

A panic seizes me. I grip her shoulders. I yell her name. But her eyes remain unfocused as her body jolts like tiny firecrackers are exploding along her spine. She's now so pale it's as if she's fading right from this world. Yet that horrible rasping only grows...

I slip a finger past her lips, feeling for what could be blocking her airway. I press her tongue flat. My knuckles hit her teeth. I squeeze her jaw to pry it further apart, but it's as if her muscles are petrified. I scream her name again. I shake her shoulders. 'Neotnia!'

Her ribcage inflates like a balloon. Her breasts pool back on her chest. Her mouth grows wide, emitting an otherworldly moan like she's a banshee sucking all the air from the room. Then, as if some invisible stopper has been ejected from her throat, her ribcage deflates. Her wincing ceases. She presses her eyes tight, inhaling another breath. And another. That ghostly whiteness fades as if she's once again re-joined this world. My heart pounds between my ears as her eyes regain focus. She blinks, her lashes fluttering, her gaze finally settling on me.

Only then do I realise I'm drenched in sweat.

I open my mouth to speak, but I'm unable to utter a word.

'I'm OK...' Her voice is feeble.

I stare in stunned silence.

'I'm fine,' she gives me a weak smile, the movement of her chest now normalising. 'Really, I am...'

'Neotnia—'

'Please...' she sits up slowly. I place my palm between her shoulder blades, afraid she'll fall back at any moment, she looks so weak. Her eyes pierce mine. 'It's OK,' she says.

She gazes at me for a moment more, her breasts exposed in blue shadow, the lungs underneath them replenished. Placing a palm on my pounding chest, she guides me back to the mattress, then joins me. I feel the weight of her body against mine, her head resting against my heart.

She's soft and warm once more.

'I'm OK, really,' she whispers. 'I promise.'

'I—'

'Hold me,' she says. 'Please, just hold me.'

I fold my arms around her. Her thin fingers dig into my opposite shoulder. I feel her soft rhythmic breath against my chest, her lungs rising and falling. We lay like that for a long time as the rain continues outside, my fingers stroking her hair and the back of her neck, soothing her. Or maybe me.

I think back to our conversation about ghosts. It's only after some time that I speak again.

'Neotnia ... are you sick?'

It's a while before she answers. 'No.'

'I've just ... I've seen this happen to you before...'

She lifts her head. For a moment, her eyes gaze at me in the darkness. Then she draws close and kisses me. Outside, thunder rumbles far away.

'Let's just listen to the rain,' she says, returning her head to its resting place on me. 'Isn't it nice, the way it comes down?' And, as she squeezes me tight, I feel a warm drip hit my chest as if a single drop of that rain has found its way inside.

'Let's just hold each other and listen to the rain.'

*

When I wake, Neotnia is still in my arms. The clock on the wall says it's past midnight.

And my heart – it's throbbing.

Neotnia's squeezing her body against mine with such force, it's like a snake wrapping around a thing for warmth. In one horrible instant, I realise it's another seizure. But then her face tilts up towards mine. She's awake and moving of her own volition. Yet her eyes look at me with an intensity I've never seen before, almost like this is a different Neotnia. And under the sheet that drapes us, I realise I've got the hardest erection I've ever had. It's jamming into the softness of her thigh.

Silently, Neotnia props herself up, letting gravity pull the sheet away from her body. Her breasts jiggle in the shadows enveloping us. Their nipples dark and tight. And that intense stare of hers shifts. She brings her mouth to my neck. She drags her tongue across my throat, drawing a line on it, and I feel like, if she had stronger jaws, she'd bite into my jugular this instant. But her tongue changes direction and travels onto my chest, where she laps at a nipple as her fingers trickle up my thigh.

I place my hand on her cheek, my thumb pushing between her lips. Like a fish on a hook, I bring her mouth back to mine. I sit up and gravitate towards her. Her tongue. Her throat. Her breasts. I taste every part. Below, her delicate fingers are around me again.

When our eyes do meet next, it's as if we're two ravenous animals in the shadows, both desiring the same prey. Her fist squeezes me so tightly my penis feels like it will burst. I kick off my boxers and her hair falls across my belly as she takes me into her mouth. It's so wet and warm, it's unbelievable. But I need her. I need to taste her. I pull her away and bring her to my lips. I taste her tongue. I bite her nose. I nurse her tiny earlobes. Our tongues intertwine again. Below, she's stroking me so hard her palm feels like it's on fire.

My hand finds her belly. It slips under the waistband of her boxers. I reach around and feel the smooth curve of her hips and the warmth of her crack. She presses her hips into mine, her tongue penetrating my mouth as deeply as it can.

And my blind hand reaches between her pale thighs. My fingers search. And search.

And search.

'Ah ... where's your vagina?'

8 – Does the dog speak fucking English or something?

'Neotnia?' I say before the bell's clang even fades.

Inu's on his customary perch and when he sees me, he gives a yap. Goeido, however, gives me a look I've not seen before – one that suggests a particular understanding. Of what, I don't know. He holds my gaze for a moment before his attention returns to a waiting customer.

Last night Neotnia ... When I felt between her thighs, at first I thought I was touching the wrong spot. It was dark and disorienting, and, well, it was my first time exploring a girl's body. But there really was no opening between her legs. It was solid flesh. And as soon as those words – 'Where's your vagina?' – escaped my lips, that frenzy of hers, that gnawing hunger that felt like she was trying to devour me whole, ceased in an instant and her eyes refocused on mine with such terror it was as if she only then became aware we were in bed together. She pushed me so hard I'd have fallen off the mattress had it not been against the wall.

A new horror grew on her face as I held the back of my throbbing skull, and she inched away and fled naked from the room. A snapping noise and short commotion followed before a cold draft flooded the apartment. For several moments I was too stunned to move. When I finally pulled myself up I found the front door swaying open in the night. In the bathroom, the shower curtain rod was twisted, one side snapped clean from the wall. The clothes she'd hung to dry were gone.

I grabbed the first clothes I could find, but by the time I reached the street, Neotnia had vanished. The earlier rain had turned into a cold mist that stung my lungs. The few people I passed as I sprinted across Shibuya's wet pavements gaped at me like I was a madman. I wore undersized guest slippers, and my red T-shirt was stained with my semen.

The café's door was bolted shut. I pressed my face against its window. Shadows covered everything. I backed away to see if I could spy light from the second floor, but none showed there either. I tried the door again and rapped the glass, shouting Neotnia's name. A couple passed behind me, the girl held tightly by the man, both looking at me as if I were a dangerous escapee. I stumbled backward, my lungs heaving. It felt like I was drowning. I scanned the street, yet the only person in the cold mist was a man on the next corner, half shrouded in shadow, gazing at me through his metalenses.

Back at my apartment, I replayed the night over and over: our conversations, her hand around me, our bodies on each other, her gasping for air – and then, the space between her thighs; that horror on her face.

I searched online. There's a condition called Mayer-Rokitansky-Küster-Hauser syndrome where the vagina doesn't fully develop. It happens to about one in five thousand women. But Neotnia's ... there was *nothing* there. That's when found literature about *complete* vaginal agenesis – the lack of any vagina at all. It's so rare, fewer than a dozen cases have been reported in medical journals. My body shook as I recalled Neotnia's interest when I told her my mom was a surgeon. I thought back to our train ride to Higashikurume the night Joe died, too, and remembered her demeanour when I spoke about Kanō and its search for treatments for exceptionally rare conditions.

I fell to sleep on the sofa as it grew light outside and woke just after nine this morning, my laptop slumped across me. I came straight here.

Goeido hands a brown sack to the customer and turns towards the kitchen, where several orders wait on the partition. As he grasps them, he shoots me another look.

'E-ya Neotnia,' he says as he lumbers into the dining area.

'E-ya?' I repeat as much to him as myself.

He delivers the food to one of the booths. 'E-ya Neotnia,' he says again as he goes to the kitchen. After several moments, he looks at me through the partition, and that expression on his face – now it seems like he's thankful we don't speak the same language.

'E-ya?' I shake my head.

He presses his lips together, looking at me. 'Neotnia no,' he shakes his head. 'Neotnia no café.'

And look, I don't know if he's being honest. For all I know, Neotnia ran upstairs or is crouched just behind the partition. But given that customers aren't sitting around with stupefied expressions suggesting their waitress suddenly high-tailed it out of sight, he's most likely telling the truth.

'OK. *Hai*,' I nod.

His eyes still on me, Goeido doesn't reply.

I exit the café and walk in no particular direction, my stomach tied in knots. That look on Neotnia's face, my hand between her thighs, is burned into my mind.

It wasn't just terror. It was shame. Pure shame.

I sit on the marbled steps of some department store overlooking the scramble and suck in a deep breath, letting the chill November air flood my lungs. It's a beautiful, sunny day, but I know Neotnia's world is draped in that horrible shadow this very moment.

I linger on the scramble for a long time with that thought in my head, watching thousands of people crisscross each other's paths like blades of mowed grass blown by a storm. After the cars' turn, the blades of people swirl once again in this infinite city of tens of millions. My shoulders sink.

Should I even try to find her? Maybe she doesn't want me to? But no. If that's the case, she'll have to tell me herself. I'd rather hear those words than have her out there thinking *she's* the outsider – that whatever condition she has makes me not want to see her.

I tell a car to take me to Higashikurume. It drops me in front the care home. For a moment I look at Joe's former window. What I wouldn't give for his advice now. Inside, I recognise one of the nurses. '*Konnichiwa*,' I say, and looking at my phone's screen, read the phonetic translation of 'My name is John, and I am friends with Neotnia. I was wondering if she is volunteering. I was in the area and wanted to say hi.'

The nurse considers me for some time. It seems as if she's trying to translate my translation. After a few moments, she gives a curious but kind smile. Her reply contains Neotnia's name, but also what sounds like 'e-ya'. She shakes her head, and I feel my chest go tight.

Outside, I look across the street. The motel owner wasted no time completing the fence after our little escapade. Still, I stare at the pool as if Neotnia will suddenly break its surface and recall something from that night. As she put her hands up my T-shirt I warned her my body wasn't normal. *Neither is mine*, she replied.

From the care home, I check the park we took cover in. I even stop at the noodle shop before heading back to Higashikurume Station, replaying last night in my mind. Her smell. Her hand around me. Then the wincing – it must have something to do with her condition, too. If she was born with missing sex organs, surely she could have additional internal deformities. One making it hard to breathe – something with her lungs or nervous system.

Then it hits me: is this why her father disappeared? Mom told me about parents who can't cope when they discover their child has a significant abnormality or terminal condition. They shut down emotionally, unable to deal with the lifelong consequences or inevitable loss. Some simply desert their child. And that child, they're left feeling it's futile even hoping for a normal life or relations because of their body. Some even welcome a terminal diagnosis.

I feel such a coldness in my bones. Is this why that shadow takes hold of her?

Even if her condition isn't terminal, now I understand why she's never had a boyfriend. My body's kept me from taking chances with others, so I get the logic. Yet at least I have all the working parts. What must it feel like to be *missing* a part of her body? Especially one so important in romantic relationships, and one essential for what most people eventually pursue? And what Joe said about her not having any friends – I can see how, with a condition like hers, a young, beautiful girl like Neotnia would shut herself away from others. Other girls would have experiences with boys that Neotnia would have no reference point for. They'd also have dreams for children that, to Neotnia, would seem pointless to ever hope for.

By the time I reach the station, my eyes are wet. I feel sick knowing she's somewhere out there, alone, a movie of me disgusted by her body playing through her mind.

It's early evening when I arrive back in Shibuya. I go straight to the café. In the dining area a few schoolgirls sit in one booth and a man in metalenses is in the next. Clearing some dishes from the coffee table, Goeido turns – but this time he doesn't give me a chance to speak.

'Neotnia no,' he says. And he places himself right in front of the dark hallway.

I twist my eyes up at his massive frame. 'Goeido, please ... *is* Neotnia here?'

But he stands in place like a big stubborn elephant. His girth blocks all but a sliver of that dark void.

'Goeido, please.' I look up at him. 'I just want to know if she's OK.' I know he can't understand my words, but maybe my tone can sway him.

He replies with a firm shake of the head. 'Neotnia no.'

And I feel the breath drain from me.

As Goeido continues to imitate a brick wall, I glance at that sliver of darkness again, then look at the dishes keeping his hands occupied. Noticing where my gaze has settled, he stacks everything into his left hand, freeing his right.

'Goeido—'

'No,' he gives his head a single, slow shake. 'E-ya.'

And I know his 'e-ya' no longer relates to claiming Neotnia isn't here. It's him saying, *No, please don't make me have to stop you.*

And the only reason I abide is the obvious one: he's a fucking sumo, and even with one hand tied up he could toss me across the room without breaking a sweat.

He opens his mouth again to speak, but I cut him off with a breath.

'Yeah, yeah, I get it.' I shake my head. 'Neotnia e-ya.'

Only when I head for the door does he advance from his position, like he's a big boulder that's suddenly grown legs. As I exit, I give him a final glance. And the look Goeido returns – it's as if he feels bad for me, like he's just following orders.

I half hope Neotnia will be waiting outside my apartment, but no. Inside, I fix the shower rod as best I can, then sit on the balcony for the longest time. Tokyo's night sky is still absent of drones. It makes the entire world feel different. Yet I find some normality when I look towards the moon, at least. As always, the two unfinished stations persist in their paranoid orbital dance above us all.

Shortly before midnight, I return to the café only to find shadows once again casting their pall across everything inside. A breeze sends fallen leaves scratching across the pavement. With nowhere else to go, I head towards Shibuya's multicoloured mists. Most everything's already shut for the night, though I reach the Starbucks overlooking the scramble just before they lock up. The barista lets me order a drink to go.

I lean against the bike rack, slowly sipping my coffee, watching the metascreens' lights paint the autumn air. Occasionally my heart stops as I spot Neotnia crossing the scramble – yet it's never truly her. Still, I remain against the bike rack for a long time, allowing the glaring media to glow across my skin. The atmosphere changes with each new piece of content.

White. Yellow. Grey. And there's a gigantic Totoro as tall as the twenty-storey department store across the street.

Blue. Purple. Orange. And a multi-building ad featuring a beautiful Japanese girl shows off Avance's latest foldable.

Red. Grey. White. And there's an NHK update about Paris.

When I finally take my eyes away from the metascreens, the Starbucks is draped in shadow, and I realise I'm one of the few people left in the area. It's well after midnight and my coffee has long gone cold. I finish it anyway, tossing the empty cup into the trash as the air takes on a dim green glow.

'You're on the cusp of a new world.'

I freeze as soon as I hear the words.

It's the tourist information bot, resting at the end of the bike rack. Its enormous cat-like eyes blink on its domed head; its short body absorbing the deep green of the surrounding atmosphere. My mouth opens, but for a moment, I'm unable to speak.

The bot wasn't there a second ago – I'm sure of it.

In the green air, we stare at each other.

'What did you say?' I finally ask.

The bot doesn't make a sound. Its cat eyes simply blink.

I look over my shoulder. There's no one near us. On the distant corner, someone tells a car where to take them.

I look back at the bot.

'What did you just say?' I demand.

'*Konbanwa.*' The bot's reply is immediate. Its eyes blink.

And they blink again, staring at me with a digital lifelessness.

I quickly scan the area again. Across the street, a janitorial bot stands behind the department store's glass doors. On the sidewalk out front, a man appears from around the corner but turns the next just as quickly, out of sight.

I stare at my bot before stepping closer. But my body freezes as I catch my reflection in its domed head, the air going thin in a snap. I'm so struck by what I see, I actually gasp.

The reflected face is mine, yet its details are so lacking it's almost formless – as if it's just an approximation of me. An empty one with no shadow or depth. And the longer I gaze upon my morbid reflection, the more intense a sense of sorrow, fear and hurt washes over me. In a moment, the world feels so unbearable the only thing I can do is look away.

Yet when I glance back, my reflection is ordinary again.

My heart pounds in my chest.

'Where did you come from?' I finally say.

The bot's eyes blink. 'Factory of origin queries can be directed to the Tokyo Tourism Office by messaging them at—'

'No.' I shake my head. 'Just now – where did you come from? You weren't there a moment ago.' A shift in the green light darkens the air another shade, yet the bot remains silent as a breeze whips around us. Its lifeless eyes blink as if synchronised with the beating in my chest. 'I said, where—'

'*Konbanwa*. Welcome to Tokyo! How may I help you?'

My mouth gapes, at a loss for words.

'What is the first thing you said to me tonight?'

But even after a dozen thuds in my chest, only the breeze replies.

My blood rises. 'What's the first thing—'

'*Konbanwa*,' the bot's eyes blink.

'Fuck it.' I shake my head. I must be going crazy. I jam my hands into my pockets and turn away. 'Leave me alone.' I wait for the pedestrian light to turn so I can cross the scramble. As the breeze blows, the thuds have moved between my ears.

'You're on the cusp of a new world—'

'There!' I spin and jab my finger at the bot. 'Why do you keep saying that?' The beating between my ears grows heavier. 'I said, why do you keep—'

'*Konbanwa*.'

I let out an exasperated breath. 'Are you malfunctioning?'

'No, I've just checked. All my systems are normal. And the Tokyo Tourism Office would like visitors to know recent events in Paris should not cause concern here. Japan's AI is more advanced than those found in Europe and—'

'I don't give a shit. If you aren't malfunctioning, why do you keep saying "you're on the cusp of a new world"? Where did you get the phrase from? Why do you keep repeating it to me?'

The bot's eyes blink.

'*Konba*—'

'My ass you're not malfunctioning,' I snap, my hands clenching into fists. 'Show me your serial number.'

The bot's eyes blink out of existence.

In the dim glow, its curved face is blank. Like it's lost all power.

But then ... a single glyph appears.

神

The glyph itself glows a deep green.

'No. Not kanji. Show me your serial number in Roman alphanumerics.'

神神

'No. Roman alpha—'

神神神

神神神神

'No—'

神神神神神

'Stop.'

神神神神神神

神神神神神神神

神神神神神神神神

'Stop...'

神神神神神神神神神神神神神神神神神神神神神神

神神神神神神神神神神神神神神神神神神神神神神神神

神神神神神神神神神神神神神神神神神神神神神神神神

神神神神神神神神神神神神神神神神神神神神神神神神

神神神神神神神神神

'Stop!'

In a blink, all kanji disappear.

My heart pounds.

But the bot's eyes don't return. It seems completely bricked now.

I stare at my ordinary reflection in its blank domed head, and re-calling the horrible one, I reach for the bot as if to confirm it's really in front of me. With my touch, its eyes instantly spark to life and the atmosphere around us changes from a deep green to a bright pink. For several moments we stare at each other like it's the first time we've crossed paths. But then it merely turns and rolls away, going around the corner, out of sight, leaving my outstretched fingers lingering in the air.

I pass the café on my way back, its insides still draped in shadows, and continue towards my apartment. Though my thoughts turn to Neotnia, the info bot slips into my mind. Its idiosyncratic manner-isms. That phrase. For a moment, my thoughts linger on the kanji it displayed, already forgetting the specifics of its form.

I wonder what it said. If only I could read Japanese—

I stop in my tracks.

I turn back and find a Lawson's. I haven't eaten all day. I pick up a sandwich and several canned drinks that look like they're brimming with caffeine. Even though it's already late, my night is far from over.

When I finally do sleep, I'm with Neotnia again. I feel her softness in my arms. I stroke her smooth legs. Her cool hair.

I see her body go pale and wince in sharp jolts.

Who doesn't like a ghostly love story?

*

I wake early, having slept only three hours, and finish my work. Just before noon, I take a car to the care home. Again, I ask if Neotnia's around. Then, again, I check the park and the noodle shop and even the pool. By half past three, I'm back in Shibuya and go right to the café. As I pass its windows I see no customers inside, which is why I waited until now to come.

The bell clangs and Inu gives me a yap as Goeido comes from the kitchen. But before he can say anything, I fold my phone out into a laptop and set it on the counter. His eyes go from me to the laptop to me again, like he's watching a ping pong match. I open what I spent all night working on and jack up the volume.

'Please, Goeido, please,' I say, and as I do, I watch my quantum code run in the app's window.

'*Kudasai*, Goeido, *kudasai*,' my app says in a Japanese voice.

Goeido's eyes widen, and Inu's ears perk up.

It's not perfect. There's about a second's delay between my speaking and my app translating because my app's quantum code can't run natively on the classical machine that is my phone. Instead, my code is running remotely on a quantum cloud hive Sony's given me access to. But simple words are one thing; now, it's time to see if my quantum app really is better than all the classical ones populating the Avance and Baidu app stores.

'I don't know if she's told you what's happened, but I need to see her,' I begin.

My app speaks my words in Japanese. It's like I've got a flesh-and-blood person doing a near-real-time translation right next to me.

More importantly, from the look on Goeido's face, the translation seems flawless.

'I can't stand not knowing how she is.' I stare him straight in the eyes. 'If she doesn't want to see me anymore – fine. But I need to let her know that whatever's going on with her, it's OK with me. So please, Goeido ... I'm so worried about her. I need to see her, just once.'

Goeido looks genuinely conflicted. Or at least he realises he doesn't have the protection of a language barrier anymore. He contemplates me for what feels like forever.

'Neotnia no,' he finally speaks that same familiar phrase, shaking his head. Because he said it in English, my app doesn't translate it.

'Goeido, please—'

But all he does is shake his head again.

And my heart sinks inside my chest like a heavy stone dropped into a deep lake. I release a loud breath, squeezing my fists in the air. '*Pleeease.*' I clench my teeth so tightly it feels like they'll crack. 'If she's not here, just tell me *where* she is. Please, Goeido. *Please.* I care about her so much...'

I feel like I could collapse, and my eyes are moist – and that appears to catch him off guard. For what seems like forever, he stands there considering my face while simultaneously looking like he's debating something inside himself. Then his gaze shifts towards Inu, and he holds a thought on the dog before looking at me again.

'Aight...' my app says. And I jump a bit, realising Goeido's speaking to me. 'Aight ... I don't know where she's at or when she'll be back.'

The thing is, his translated words come from my app in Australian English, making it sound like Goeido's being dubbed live by a guy who's been raised in the outback. It was four in the morning, and I was tired, so took a shortcut by borrowing an open-source neural voice developed by some grad students at the University of Melbourne.

'OK,' I nod, thrilled he's saying anything other than 'Neotnia no'.

'I don't know where she's at or when she'll be back,' he repeats. 'But ... the dog will tell you.'

I screw my face up. That's got to be a mistranslation. I specifically heard Goeido say Inu's name, but the app doesn't know his name is Inu, so it wouldn't insert 'the dog' for it. Besides, 'But the dog will tell you' makes no sense.

'"The dog"?' I repeat, wondering where I could've messed up in the quantum code. And my app translates: 'Inu?'

Goeido nods, '*Hai.*' And his '*hai*' correctly translates to a very Aussie-sounding 'yep.'

I let out a sigh. 'The dog's name is "Dog"?'

'*Hai*,' Goeido shrugs.

I roll my eyes.

'It's funny,' the app translates for Goeido.

'But wait ... then you really meant Inu will tell me where Neotnia is?'

Goeido gives a sharp nod that seems to be trying to compensate for the fact that what he's said makes no sense.

'I don't understand.' I shake my head, getting frustrated. 'Does the dog speak fucking English or something? How can Inu tell me where Neotnia is?'

Goeido answers by saying nothing at all. His gaze shifts to Inu, and his expression suggests he understands that, if he does whatever he's considering, there's no going back. He looks at me once more then touches Inu's collar. Instantly, some of its fibres light up red, and that red begins spiralling around the black collar in waves as Inu stands on all fours.

Goeido places Inu on the floor, then plods to the door and opens it. Inu exits and waits on the sidewalk, looking back at me. 'Go with dog,' he says.

I eye him one last time.

He gives a sharp nod like this is the most normal thing in the world.

Outside, watching Inu trot along makes me suddenly cognisant of his full ridiculousness. The volume of his head makes it look much heavier than it actually is, which makes it seem like Inu could tip forward at any moment. And the spiralling red visibility collar is pointless. Even without it everyone would notice the dog who appears to be assembled from cotton balls. Indeed, nearly everyone on the street points or laughs when they spot him. Yet Inu keeps trotting along, ignoring pleas to come hither for a pat from adults and schoolgirls alike. It's as if he's the one dog in the world with the indifference of a cat.

He keeps about ten feet in front of me, and whenever I think I've lost him in the crowd, I find he's always just ahead, waiting. As soon as I catch up, Inu continues on his stubby little legs. He even pauses at crosswalks without me telling him to stop, like he understands the concept of pedestrian traffic – his tiny coal-black eyes peering up at me like he's the best 'good boy' ever.

After five minutes, we're out of Shibuya's busy district. Ten minutes after that, we've turned down our third or fourth side street and are now in one of those quiet residential areas with mid-rise apartment buildings all around. Inu still leads with such focus it's as if he's on a mission from God, his black collar spiralling even more rapidly in waves of red. He takes a sharp right onto one of the pedestrian walkways between the backs of apartment buildings that locals use to cut through a neighbourhood. Not thirty feet ahead the walkway dead-ends against a concrete wall, yet still, Inu trots at full pace. At the speed he's going, he'll ram into it within seconds.

But a few feet from the dead end, Inu makes a sharp left. I increase my pace, closing the distance between me and where he turned on a dime. It's a passage only wide enough for one person. I enter just as Inu exits the far end.

After about twenty feet, the passage breaks into a small courtyard wholly enclosed by the walls of the surrounding buildings. In the centre, a timber torii stands in front of a small shrine surrounded by four stone pedestals. Paper lanterns and faded red banners adorn its awnings. In the middle is a water basin, and behind that stands a statue of something even larger than Goeido. Maybe it's a kami, whatever they look like. This one gives no hints. It's covered head to toe in thick green moss, obscuring all details. The moss creeps over the basin, too, as well as the large, round stones beneath it.

And to the basin's left is a stone bench. On that bench sits Neotnia. She wears a woolly orange sweater and a simple blue skirt that runs to her ankles. And on her lap is Inu, sitting contently as she strokes him. His once spiralling red-and-black collar is now a solid red. She delivers a few more stokes to Inu's back then turns her head and gives me a sad little half-smile, like she's not all that surprised to see me here.

'Neotnia...' I feel like someone has removed one of those large moss-covered stones from my chest.

'I guess Goeido likes you more than you thought, huh?'

And in reply, I begin, well ... saying everything. I tell her I'm sorry about the other night, how things got away from us, and that I've been worried sick about her. I tell her how I went to the café after she ran from the apartment. How the next day, I went to the care home and the park and back to the café. I tell her I'm not mad if she told Goeido not to let me see her. And I tell her that if she's got some kind of ... deformity ... well, join the club. I don't care. 'I've just been so worried about you, and I need to know if you're OK.'

And Neotnia, on the bench, her eyes still on me, she's still got that sad little half-smile that suggests she knows some game is up.

'I mean, you're OK, right?' I say, swallowing. 'I didn't tell Goeido anything, just so you know. I didn't know if I could. And I want you to know you don't need to hide from me. You don't need to be ashamed of anything.'

Neotnia looks down at Inu. His tiny tongue rests happily outside his small mouth as her hand runs soothingly down his spine. His solid red collar glows bright.

And that collar, it makes me shake my head, as if doing so can somehow help organise all the thoughts tumbling through my mind. And watching her stroke Inu on her lap – the guide who led me right to her – one thought, one question, springs forward.

'How did Inu know where you were?' I tilt my head.

And then, 'And how's he so well trained that he can navigate Tokyo so precisely? It's ... unbelievable.'

Neotnia's clear blue-grey eyes turn towards me one more time. She looks at me like I'm on the deck of an ocean liner that's moments from departing on a one-way voyage, but I just don't realise it yet.

Her eyes fall towards Inu. Her hands stop stroking him, and she seems to consider something for a few seconds. Then, her fingers run up under his bright-red collar and around the front of his throat like she's going to give him a good, deep neck massage.

But as she does this, Inu growls a little annoyed '*grrr*'.

Like a cork from a champagne bottle, there's a muffled pop, and Neotnia's jaw tightens.

Then she bends Inu's head straight back as if it's on a hinge.

And standing here in this little backwater shrine, I stare at the girl without a vagina holding the dog with the decapitated head, a mass of red flesh packed inside the exposed cross-section of his neck.

His stomach still rises and falls with each breath.

His stubby legs still shift to maintain balance on Neotnia's soft lap.

And his upside-down spherical head folded back onto his body – it still *grrr*s in irritation.

9 – So, you like the Mossman?

This is the first time I've seen something and felt it's literally impossible to look away. A lunar shuttle could thunder through and slam into me right now, but even as I flew across this courtyard my eyes would remain locked on Inu's little body with its severed head bent back as if on a hinge.

In the cross-section of Inu's neck is a black structure that looks something like the vertebra of a spine. It's surrounded by those masses of flesh that resemble biological tissues – but the colours are off. What looks like muscle tissue is bright red – the colour you'd see saturating the ice of a strawberry snow cone. The tissues that look like ligaments are as glistening as polished ivory. Real muscles and ligaments are darker – I've messed around with my parents' old meta surgical training apps enough to know this.

Yet it's not only Inu's tissues that are off. Where a dog should have arteries and veins, Inu has translucent cords that pulsate with a silvery-blue gel. The cords glow faintly, like the tendrils of bioluminescent jellyfish. And despite his head being folded back onto his body, his belly still rises and falls. His nose still sniffs. His eyes still shift. And his tongue, though now flopped over the top of his jaw, still occasionally licks his chops between bursts of short growls, as if he's annoyed at the state he's in.

My stomach goes hollow. Not only is Inu not a real dog, he's not even some kind of advanced bot. A robot would look just like that inside: a titanium skeleton, hydraulic joints, gyroscopes, sensors, circuitry and wiring. Yet Inu's internal appearance isn't even the craziest part. I've been around him for almost two weeks now. He *acts* just like a real dog – he's indistinguishable.

Over the years, synthetic skin or fur has occasionally been applied to bots – most often the entertainment types you find in amusement parks and haunted houses. But while adding synthetic skin may make a bot look like a biological creature at first glance, you can tell it's not organic quickly enough by the way it holds itself. A robot doesn't fidget like we do. Its legs and arms don't get cramped and need to continually adjust like ours. It doesn't need to stretch; it's always comfortable in any position it sustains itself in. Robots lack the nuanced involuntary micro-movements every living creature makes every second of every day. And even if you wanted to code those movements into a bot, it's currently an impossible task. The code would be trillions of lines long.

Yet Inu has those involuntary micro-movements, just like a real dog.

I look at Neotnia, still sitting on the bench, holding Inu in her lap. His upside-down snout still pointed at her chest. Neotnia studies me as intently as I'm studying Inu.

My jaw goes slack. 'This is an android, isn't it?'

And Inu's upside-down head gives a few happy yaps.

Neotnia remains silent, though her eyes, they answer, 'Yes.'

'But how is this possible? The code alone ... who would have the ability – the knowledge – to create something so lifelike? Code that can mimic biological creatures so perfectly, it's a century off. Maybe two – and that's even if the silicon can handle it by then.'

I feel Neotnia's eyes lingering on me as I continue to gape at Inu's body, his white belly puffing up and down, question after question entering my mind like embers bursting in a crackling fire. Yet, as Inu's stubby legs adjust on her soft lap, one simple question floats above the rest.

'What's an android dog doing in a Shibuya café?'

The way Neotnia looks at me, with those clear eyes that are now moist, it's as if she's trying to convey something her mouth won't allow her to speak.

And another ember bursts.

I look around this small, backwater shrine. At its faded banners and its paper lanterns and at a statue so old moss covers it entirely, as if it's been forgotten by time itself. I gaze at the passage's narrow opening. A passage that takes so many twists and turns to get to, it would be hard to find without a map. And I turn back towards Inu, still on Neotnia's lap. His collar glowing a solid red.

'How...' I say, 'how did Inu know where you were?'

The sinew of Neotnia's slender neck tightens and her gaze breaks from mine.

A sinking feeling grows inside me.

'Neotnia... How did Inu know *exactly* where you were?'

When she looks at me again her eyes are trembling pools.

And I think of her body.

I think of her missing vagina.

My chest goes so tight.

'Neotnia...' For what feels like eons, I'm unable to continue, gazing upon the pitiful, anxious face staring up at me. But then my words slip: '...Are you an android, too?'

A pair of tears slide down her cheeks.

Her nod is sharp.

'*Hai.*'

And all the air is sucked from the world.

'Holy shit,' I hear myself say. Or think.

Holy shit.

Holy—

'*Nah, brah, Mossman is through here...*'

My body jolts – the words so unnatural, so abhorrent, to the vacuum this courtyard has become.

'No, brah, through *here*...' they continue.

'Bro, it's not!' These sound different.

'Brah, fold your phone the other way. No, the *other way*,' the original voice says. 'Avance Maps says it's right through here.'

I turn to find a tall man exiting the narrow passage. He's mid-twenties and dressed in cargo pants and a North Face jacket, his long hair up in a bun. A scarf and sunglasses and at least three pendants dangle from his neck. And as his eyes land on us, he freezes. Behind him, a second man emerges. He too stops dead when he spots us. They look at each other in utter bewilderment, as if to confirm they're seeing the same thing. The click of a photo follows, and when the lead man lowers his phone again, that dumbstruck astonishment is still plastered all over his face. To be fair, though, it's the same expression I must have had when I first saw the headless dog on the android's lap, too.

'Brah ... That's the most *adorable* dog *ever*!'

My eyes widen. I look over my shoulder. Inu's still on Neotnia's lap, but his head's folded back into place; his collar black again. His tails wags at the two strangers as he gives a friendly yap like he's just a plain old, ordinary, real dog with a stupid haircut.

'Your pooch is *amazing*,' the second man proclaims as they invite themselves closer. 'That head. That haircut. *Bro*!' Yet their fascination with Inu immediately takes a back seat when they register how pretty the girl holding the pooch is. No trace of those tears from a moment ago remain. Then one of the men gives me a perplexed once-over, like he's pondering what a boy like me is doing with a beauty like Neotnia. As if concluding the riddle is unsolvable, he looks at Neotnia again and gives his best alpha-male nod. 'Sup,' he says, like that's supposed to slay her or something.

And I swear I don't need any other shit thrown into the mix today, but I'm forced to stand on the sideline as Brobrah explain to Neotnia how they're 'social explorers' interested in meeting as many new people as possible on their round-the-world trip 'because we're all human and we all have to live on this little rock together, so we should all get to know each other more intimately, ya know?' One says that of all the countries they've been to on their 'expedition,' Japan is their favourite. 'It's wild. We really dig you people. *Arigatō*, yeah?' Then the other, or maybe it's the same one, he adds, 'In our culture, we honour the locals we meet by taking them for a drink.'

For fuck's sake, I think. Or maybe say – not that they'd notice anyway; their focus on Neotnia is absolute. She, on the other hand, gazes at them with that same polite smile she gives most of the café's customers.

'So, you like the Mossman?' they're saying. 'We obviously dig it. Been going to all the obscure Japanese chapels like this one to capture content for our followers, matter of fact. Three million plus and growing, by the way. These mystical dives really drive the likes. I mean, who woulda thought spirituality is good for the soul *and* engagement, am I right? But seriously, we're just trying to show our followers what's real. It's about the Buddha, not us. What about you? How long have you been into the Buddha?'

Neotnia's eyes shift between the pair as they finally shut up. She considers them for a long moment. Finally, her lips part, and Brobrah lean in with an assured confidence.

'English ... no.' She shakes her head with a shy, apologetic smile.

She sets Inu down and rises from the bench as Brobrah's faces deflate. Her fingertips touch my hand, and she leans into my ear. 'Let's go back to the café.' Her breath is warm against my skin. 'Please?'

Inu takes the lead as Neotnia guides me towards the courtyard's exit. 'Nice one, dumbass,' bro says to brah, behind us. 'Way to blow that. I told you Japs are Hindus, not Buddhists...' And as Neotnia steps into the narrow passage, I let my hand slip from hers.

We retrace the route Inu used to bring me here. He's always in the lead, followed by Neotnia. I trail several steps behind, though I feel like I'm not so much trailing as being pulled by an invisible leash, without which I'd simply stand still, stunned by the weight of things. The only times I manage to take my eyes off Neotnia are when she casts furtive glances at me. Before this afternoon, I'd have embraced those glances, but now ... I'm numb. I'm walking through a world that's not the one I knew.

When she's not looking at me, I stare. I stare at the way she walks and the way her arms sway by her sides. I stare at the way her fingers curl up into her palms. I stare at the way her black shoulder-length hair tickles the top of her sweater. I stare at how that sweater hugs her torso. How that skirt sways by her ankles. I stare at the way she stubs her foot on a curb. At how she squints and shields her eyes as we pass a blazing yellow metascreen. And when I stand at her side as we wait for traffic to pass, I stare at the way she presses her lips tight, lost in a thought.

Every movement she makes is impossible.

'Please don't look at me like that.'

She's glanced at me before I can avert my eyes. Her voice sounds small.

'Like what?' I try too hard to sound innocent.

'Like I'm different than I was two days ago.'

We reach the café as dusk settles. The bell clangs when Neotnia opens the door and lets Inu prance inside. She holds her eyes on me as if she's not sure I'll follow. But I do.

Goeido's in the dining area, collecting the empty dishes from a group of four in one of the booths. They're the only customers. He pauses when he sees us, but then enters the foyer where he considers Neotnia for a long moment, as if wanting to give her the chance to express her anger over his actions. But she simply yields an understanding look.

The four diners enter the foyer to pay. They're hipsters, dressed retro like it's the 2020s all over again. Goeido follows them to the door and locks it behind them, shooing someone about to enter away, too, and he flips the closed sign. Even though I can't understand the words that follow, I can tell from his expression he's asking Neotnia if she's OK. She nods, but for several moments, he lingers on her the way a parent does when judging if their child really is fine, despite what they've professed. When he finally looks at me again his eyes simply acknowledge I now have an understanding I didn't possess before.

Goeido calls Inu and points towards the hallway. Its darkness swallows them both.

For the first time, I detect the dull hum of a refrigerator in the kitchen. That's how quiet Neotnia and I are. I glance at her, but when she looks at me, I can't help but look away. I walk into the dining area for no clear reason. I put my eyes on anything that isn't her: the shark sweatshirts, the booth we drank sake at, the couch I had my ear cleaning on.

'Please say something.'

I hear the anxiety in her voice, the worry. But I ... I just don't know what to say. Inu is one thing ... but *her*?

I spy that framed magazine clipping of Goeido on the wall. The one with the fish.

'My God...' My voice sounds almost alien. 'Is Goeido—'

'No,' Neotnia shakes her head. 'No. He's like you.'

I nod but go quiet again, though she waits on me to say something – anything – more. She holds one hand atop the other against her stomach, as if it's in knots.

'So ... you're really an android?' I say, then shake my head. Just vocalising it...

'*Hai...*'

The confirmation escapes her lips and I recall the warmth of her breath as her cheek rested on my naked chest. Her soft body. How blushed her face got from our...

'Does anyone else know?'

'Just you and Goeido and Father.'

I give a half-nod, falling back into my thoughts. I begin pacing. Not quickly, and not far – just from the edge of the sweatshirt rack to the first booth. Moving, the rhythm, it helps me process. I feel Neotnia's eyes following me, but it's several moments before I say anything.

'So ... when you said your father is missing...' I shrug and look at her. 'Did you mean ... your creator?'

The corners of Neotnia's eyes narrow. 'I mean my father.'

'But ... he's the one who made you, right?'

Her mouth forms a firm line. 'Yes.'

'OK...' I pace a few steps, my mind whirling. 'So, your creator is missing...'

'My *father* is missing,' her jaw tightens.

'But ... I mean, you were made—'

'Weren't you made by your mother and father?' There's an edge to her voice. 'Do you refer to them as your "creators"?'

I don't know how to reply. But it doesn't matter. Another thought has taken hold.

'When we first spoke – the night I returned for my backpack – I asked how old you were, and you said two. But then you said you misspoke, that your English wasn't *that* good, and you meant to say you're twenty. The thing is, ever since then ... well, I've never once heard you speak anything but perfect English...'

Neotnia's eyes shift, and she lets out a little breath. 'I was born two years ago.'

'"Born"...'

'Yes. *Born.*'

'Looking like you do now?'

Her throat tightens. 'Yes.'

I glance at her head to toe. So many thoughts – so many memories – flood my mind. They intertwine and mix as if in a blender.

'But ... you like hot chocolate...'

Neotnia returns a perplexed look. 'Yes...'

'And you liked the main song from the musical we saw...'

'*Hai.*' Her eyes taper.

'And Freshness teriyaki burgers...'

'*Hai...*' She draws the word out, her gaze turning steely as if I'm about to accuse her of some crime.

'Do you sleep?'

Her mouth parts in disbelief. 'You know I do.'

I nod, absentmindedly.

'I know you eat, but I mean ... do you get hungry?'

Neotnia clenches her jaw. '*Hai...*'

'What about ... Do you dream?'

She screws her face up. 'Don't we all?'

I freeze. 'Are there more like you?'

'Not that I know of—'

'But why "we"?'

'What?'

'You said, "Don't *we* all?"'

'We ... *us*,' she exhales. '*People.*'

'People...' I say to myself.

Her lips draw tight as a breath seeps from her nostrils. 'I was person enough for you two nights ago, wasn't I?' Her searing glare stays locked on me for so long it feels like time has stopped.

From the kitchen, the refrigerator hums.

'And do you feel—?'

'*Hai*,' Neotnia bangs a fist against her thigh. '*Hai! Hai! Hai!* Yes, I feel everything. Pain, fear, desire, anxiety, hope, and whatever else you were going to ask. *Hai. Hai.* Yes – to all of them!' Her chest heaves and her cheeks flush as her lips compress to contain the flood of anger. Still, that lingering glare could light me on fire.

And I want to say I'm sorry. I do. I just can't quell all the questions swirling through my mind long enough to do that.

'What?' Neotnia says the word with bite.

I let out a breath.

'Why do you do the things you do?' I shrug.

'What is *that* supposed to mean?'

'Why do you volunteer at the care home?' And I want to stop myself there, but... 'I found you at a shrine today. Why did you go there? Were you seeking – what: Help? Comfort? Why did you feel the need for that? And, you know – you *kissed* me. Why?' I shake my head. 'Why do you do the things you do? What tells you to do those things?'

And that glare of hers – its incandescence reaches an intensity previously reserved for the sun's rays channelled through a magnifying glass onto an ant.

'Why do *you* do the things *you* do?' she snaps. 'Why did you choose that outfit today over a different outfit? Why do you like musicals? Why do you lip-sync to songs when you're all alone? Why do you like to drink hot chocolate? What tells *you* to do those things?'

She draws her mouth so tightly her nostrils flare. You couldn't thread a single hair between her lips.

In the room's renewed stillness, the refrigerator's distant hum intermingles with the rising and falling of Neotnia's chest. I hear the pounding in mine, too, and take a long moment to quiet all the thoughts scrambling my mind. Yet every time I lay eyes on her...

Neotnia's teeth clench. 'I said stop looking at me like that.'

'I'm not looking at you any particular way.'

'Yes, you are.' Her eyes moist over in an instant. 'You're looking at me like I'm different from how I was – and you can't even see it.'

Out of nowhere a rattling fills the foyer. It's the front door. Yet we remain unmoved, our eyes fixed only on the other. Her distraught face on mine – I don't want to know what my face looks like to her. After some loud raps on the glass, the customer finally gives up.

Something hits me.

'What?' Neotnia says without me saying a word.

'The night we had sake, on Halloween. I was drunk, and I had a really messed-up dream. Goeido, he ... he was trying to electrocute you with a toaster in the bathtub—'

Neotnia's gaze breaks from mine.

'My God – that wasn't a dream? Why in the world would you let him do that to you?'

But she doesn't speak, her eyes on the floor. And I see the beginnings of that horrible shadow descend across her face.

'OK, look...' I run my hand through my hair, taking a breath. 'I'm sorry for how blunt I'm being. But you gotta understand – this ... you ... what you've told me: it's the *last* thing I expected when I went looking for you. I'm trying my best here, I swear I am. But you gotta help me. You gotta tell me what all this is. I can't process it on my own.'

And at first, I don't think she's heard a word I've said. She just keeps gazing at the floor, that shadow growing darker. But then her face turns up, and her eyes find mine.

'Will you sit with me?'

I nod without saying a word.

'OK,' she nods, too. 'I'll make hot chocolate.'

A few clangs and a beep from the kitchen later, she returns with two mugs. She hands me one. 'They're just the microwave kind, too. We're out of the good stuff.'

I take a sip. We sit on opposite ends of the couch – our knees pointed towards each other, and I'm reminded of when we shared hot chocolate in my apartment. Right before we...

I set the cup down.

'I was born in October just over two years ago,' Neotnia finally begins. 'The first image I ever had was of a man standing in front of me, smiling a warm, gentle smile. He was elderly, but kind-looking, with grey hair and a grey beard. Inu was behind him on a workbench, sitting there looking at the two of us – though back then, he obviously didn't have the haircut he has now.'

She stares into her mug for a moment, the softest smile appearing on her mouth.

'The man told me my name, and he told me I was his daughter. We were in our garage in our house in Kamakura. It was a small, simple house. It didn't have many belongings or furnishings, but we had each other, and that was enough. During my first few months of life, Father and I spent every minute of every day together. We talked about the world and watched movies and played board games, and, around twilight, we'd often go for walks along the beach. The walks would make him tired, though, and when I asked why, he told me it was because he had a weak heart.'

Setting the mug down, Neotnia glances at her hands. She strokes the middle finger of one as if she's lost in a memory.

'When he first told me, I was so scared for him. But he said it was OK, and he explained what a pacemaker was and how he had one inside of him. Still, I worried about him. I knew he was a good man, and though he was a positive person, I could tell he hid a sadness deep, deep inside. Yet whenever I asked about it he just smiled and patted my hand and said, "I'm never sad with you around."'

A furtive smile crosses her lips but disappears as quickly.

'After those first few months I began to realise I was different than other people. I was only a few months old, yet I looked like a young adult. Other people my age were small babies. There was also my language. Some of the movies Father and I watched were in English, and I understood them all. Father and I also spoke in English sometimes, and I could even read English. Yet when I tried to speak English to other people who looked like me – the attendant at a grocery store, for example – most didn't have that ability.

'And then there was my strength. One night I walked to the market to buy some vegetables for a stew we were preparing. There was a young woman my size who was struggling to load a thirty-kilo sack of rice onto her bicycle. I went to help, and when I picked up the sack I realised that what she found heavy, I considered light.

'Shortly after, I asked Father why I seemed to be the same as other people in some respects, but also seemed to be different. I told him I knew I wasn't human, but I didn't know what I was. I knew he could see the worry and confusion in my eyes when I asked, "What am I?" He could tell how badly I wanted to know, yet at the same time, I think he understood I was also afraid to know.' Neotnia looks at me.

'But then, he took my hands in his and he looked at me with warm eyes and said I was special. I was unique. I was an android – the most advanced being on the planet. And that's when he called Inu and opened him up and showed me his insides, just like you saw them. And Father explained that my insides look similar to Inu's, and that they're different insides than the rest of the people I meet have.

'So I asked, if Inu and I are the same inside, does that make me more like him than like other people? But Father shook his head. He said our similarities end with our internal structures – just like how a chimpanzee's and a human's similarities end with their internal structures: a stomach, a heart, bones. And looking right into my eyes, he smiled and said, "In here" – he tapped my forehead – "and in here" – and he tapped my heart – "you are just like the rest of us." After all, he said, just because he had a pacemaker inside him, it didn't make him any less of a person than other people who had a completely biological heart. I was no less of a person than anyone else, either.'

A little flutter crosses Neotnia's face as a shy smile shows on her lips. 'I remember how happy that made me. And I could tell how glad it made him that I was happy. And then he said, "But to answer your questions more succinctly: you are my daughter, and you have the potential to be anything you choose to be – you can do anything another person can."

'Of course, I had so many other questions, but Father said he would answer them in time. "For now, let's just enjoy *our* time together." And we did. Even on days Father would be more tired than usual and I'd need to help him, we treasured our time together. I'd spend those days reading to him when he had to rest and ask him about things in the books I didn't understand. I've never been so happy as I was then.'

She pauses for a moment, and her eyes dim.

'But on my first birthday, we were celebrating at home, just like any father and daughter would. We had a cake with a candle, and he even hung streamers in the house and made me wear a birthday hat. It was warm for an October night, especially one by the sea. So, after cake, we went for a walk on the beach and then went for ice cream in town—'

Neotnia abruptly stops, like she's trying to keep something inside herself from coming out. After several moments, her eyes shift.

'That would be the last night we spent under the same roof. The next day, he woke me early and said we were going to see a friend of his in Tokyo, and Inu was coming with us. Before then, I didn't know Father had any friends. We always kept to ourselves in town, and though Father would be polite to shopkeepers and café owners, he never stayed long to chat. And despite being on our way to see his friend, as we left for the train station that morning, even though he was putting on a good face, I knew he was sad inside.'

Neotnia pauses, and I see a sadness rise up in her, too.

'It wasn't until we were on the train that Father said Inu and I would be staying with his friend for a few weeks. I was so confused, but he said it was nothing to worry about. He would be back in a fortnight and would explain everything then. But I *was* worried. I asked if, when he returned, we would go back home, and if we'd continue living our lives as normal. And he rested his hand over mine and placed his other on my cheek and promised we'd go back to the exact same life we had – nothing would change. I thought about what he said for a long time. He had never lied to me before, so, though I was scared, I decided I had no reason to worry. And so, he dropped us off here, with Goeido, and said he'd be back for us in two weeks.' Neotnia pauses. 'That was over a year ago.'

I remain quiet for some time, Neotnia's clear eyes watching me. Occasionally they'll dip towards her lap, but they always find mine again.

'So, Goeido is friends with your father?' I say after I've had time to think. 'But ... Isn't there like a thirty-year age gap?'

'*Hai*,' she nods. 'Goeido is the son of two of my father's middle-school friends. When Goeido married, his father had already passed away, and his mother invited my father to the wedding in memory of Goeido's, as they were best friends in school. Father and Goeido are both fans of Shintoist tales, and at the reception they bonded over that.'

Neotnia goes quiet for a few seconds, and a gentle smile crosses her lips.

'Well, they bonded over that and sumo wrestling. Father *loves* sumo wrestling. He told me that when he was young, he wanted to become sumo. But he's not much bigger than me, and even after eating all the food he wanted for a month, he only gained two kilos.'

For a moment, that gentle smile lingers on Neotnia's lips, but soon enough it dissipates like smoke.

'After what happened to Goeido – with the boy that died at his stable – Goeido's mother was no longer alive when that occurred. And Goeido's wife ... she had abandoned him. So, he was all alone, and the world was blaming him, as he himself was. He felt such dishonour and shame and pain and regret over the boy's death – so much so, he planned to take his own life. But then he received a letter from Father. Can you believe that? A letter. Father has always liked physical things, though. On our walks in town, we'd often visit the library for the physical books. We had stacks of them.'

Neotnia presses her mouth into a line, thinking.

'We don't know where Father was living at that time – this would have been six years ago, so four years before I was born – but he heard about what happened from the news. And in the letter, Father told Goeido that even when the world is condemning you and those who claim to love you are abandoning you, you cannot abandon yourself, not so long as there is another person out there who believes in you and knows the kind of person you truly are. And Father said that person was him.'

She gives a proud little smile.

'People, especially when they band together, he told Goeido, can be cruel and judgmental and condemn a person without knowing them, simply because they are scared and angry and looking for someone to blame for the unfairness of life. But those people are to be pitied, he said, not have their outrage acted upon. And then Father told Goeido that his parents were good people and, though he had only met Goeido in person once, he knew that Goeido's parents' goodness had passed to their son – as did their inner strength. It was that inner strength, Father said, that was the reason he knew Goeido could persevere. Father ended the letter by saying, "All of this is a long way of explaining why I'm not worried about you in the slightest."'

Neotnia holds her eyes on me for a moment.

'That letter stopped Goeido from taking his own life,' she says and looks around the café. 'It's why this place exists. It's why Goeido is still here.'

I glance around the room, too, my eyes settling on the magazine clipping. I consider it for a moment. 'So, did Goeido know about you before your father dropped you off?'

Neotnia shakes her head. 'He didn't know anything about me – not until Father told him that morning.'

'You mean he told Goeido you were an android?'

'*Hai*.'

'But did your father tell him how to contact him? Where he was going? Did he tell Goeido anything else?'

'No,' she shakes her head. 'Ever since they met at the wedding, Father and Goeido would keep in contact periodically through letters – two a year, maybe three. But Father's letters always came from a post-office box. Goeido didn't even know Father had been living so close to Tokyo until we showed up at the café that morning. All he told Goeido was that he must watch out for me until he returns.'

I give her a look. 'And that's it? I mean, his parents' old school friend literally shows up, unannounced, and drops a pair of androids off at his café and asks him to let you and the dog stay – and that's it? Goeido doesn't ask any questions?'

Neotnia begins to speak but stops herself.

'What?' I say.

'Goeido's never told me this, but because Father told him to watch out for me, well ... I think he sees me as a way to redeem himself for his pupil's death. He couldn't protect the boy, but he can protect me.'

She pauses again, looking hesitant. Then she lets out a little breath.

'When Goeido saw me for the first time – even before Father told him anything – Goeido says he knew, instantly, I was something ... more than other people. The very *second* he saw me he said he knew it – right then. He thinks—'

But Neotnia stops herself again.

'Thinks what?'

In a small voice, she says, 'He thinks I'm kami.'

My eyebrows arch. 'He thinks you're a *god*?' I shake my head. 'Of course he does. Because this needs to be any stranger.'

'He thinks I'm special,' Neotnia shoots back. And I can tell from her tone she feels I'm being disrespectful to Goeido. 'We all account for things that are out of the ordinary in our own ways, don't we?'

We both go quiet for some time. In the stillness, Neotnia takes a sip of her hot chocolate then returns it to the table.

'Hold on,' I shake my head. 'If Goeido thinks he's your ... protector, if keeping you safe can redeem him, why was he trying to electrocute you?'

Neotnia's eyes sink to the hands in her lap. For a moment, she looks lost in thought.

'By last December, I'd been here for almost two months. By then it was clear to both of us Father wasn't coming back. I started wondering why. Was I abandoned? Or had something happened to him? Soon it felt like I was drowning. Like I was sinking into this void, and it was taking me more and more each day, deeper and deeper. Even sleep wasn't an escape.'

And as she's saying this, that horrible dark shadow lengthens across her face. She shakes her head as if wrestling with a memory.

'By February, it had been four months since Father left. And it was such a horridly cold month – the sun never showed once. Or at least for me it didn't. But then one day I saw the news report about the shortage of carers in homes for the elderly. The residents they showed all looked so frail and lonely. They reminded me of Father, of his weak heart, and how tired it made him sometimes. And right then, I just felt like ... like I needed to do *something*, or else that void, it was going to swallow me up and eat me whole. So, I began volunteering. And soon ... well, that void started getting a little shallower.'

A brief smile crosses her lips.

'And then I met Joe and got to know all the other residents, and I learned so much from them. Just listening to their stories about the lives they'd led ... Well, they were all remarkable. Every single one of them had faced challenge after challenge in their lives – and they all came through it. The void didn't get them. And when I asked how they had made it, they almost always said the same thing: they had other people to be strong for them when they were weak. Or, sometimes, they needed to be the strong one for someone else even when times were tough for them – and that kept them going. Many times, the people were their spouses or lovers. Sometimes these people were their children or their friends, or even their work colleagues. But the point was, they got through it because of their relationships.'

Neotnia tilts her head, and her lips form a pensive little smile.

'And for the first time I started feeling like I could be part of the world. That I could belong, even without Father. For the first time, I thought that maybe I could make friends and have relationships just like other people do.'

But then her little pensive smile fades away.

'But one day I was asked to change the pads of some residents who'd gone to the bathroom in their beds. It was the first time I'd been asked to do this, and the nurses said the process was simple: pull out the tear-away pad between their legs and put a clean, dry one in its place. But when I lifted their covers so I could reach between their legs and replace the pads ... it was the first time I realised men and women had genitals – different ones.'

Neotnia turns away for a moment. When her eyes return to mine, they're tinged with shame.

'But I had neither,' she says. 'I went back to the café that night and borrowed Goeido's phone. I told him I was going to look for a movie to watch, but instead I searched online about people's bodies. I watched videos of sex and I learned that's how people express their romantic love to each other—'

Neotnia abruptly stops, her gaze falling to her lap. Memories of us in bed flood my mind. She'd made me promise my boxers would stay on her, yet when I woke after the rain it was as if she'd lost herself in natural urges, and we both let our guards down.

When I look at her again, her eyes are already on mine.

She knows what I've recalled.

'Yet I lacked what they had,' she shrugs. And lingering on some thought, her shadow deepens. 'But more than that: Father, for some reason, he *lied* to me. When he said I was no less of a person than anyone else, he was *lying*. When he said I could do anything a person could, it was a *lie*. And that hope I'd gotten? That, even if Father never returned, I could at least connect with others, have relationships with them, find happiness with them, feel like I belong with them – it went away in an instant. My body will forever separate me from others.' She looks at me with pitiful eyes.

'And that horrible void came back worse than ever. Most of the time I'm OK at hiding it. It helps when I'm in the café with Goeido, waiting on customers or playing with Inu. Or when I go to the care home. Those times I can keep it at bay – mostly. But it's always there, waiting for me just offshore. And sometimes it just washes right over me, and everything around me disappears.'

It's a few moments before Neotnia speaks again. She makes a little noise, as if clearing her throat.

'But three weeks ago,' she says, 'I was having a particularly bad day. I couldn't concentrate on anything. After closing, I filled the kitchen sink and began washing the dishes. Goeido was at the booth in here, inputting orders for supplies on his laptop. He was annoyed because the wireless had been going on and off all day. Back in the kitchen, my arms were up to their elbows in suds. When I reached for another stack of dishes, I knocked the toaster off the counter and into the sink. It was still plugged in. I plunged my hand into the water to retrieve it, but as I did, I hit the lever that turns it on.'

She shrugs.

'At first, I didn't think much had happened. The fuse blew, and one of the lights in the kitchen went out, and I felt a small sting on my hand, but that was it. Yet when I took my hand from the water, my skin from my fingertips to my wrist was blackened. The skin itself wasn't charred – instead, it was as if someone had taken ashes and rubbed them over my hand, covering every inch, and those ashes had seeped into my flesh. Yet besides the initial sting, my hand didn't hurt, and I could move it just fine.'

Neotnia wiggles the fingers of her left hand, inspecting their motion.

'While all this was going on in the kitchen, Goeido was out here fiddling with his laptop, trying to get the wireless to work. And as he messed around with the networks, he suddenly saw a device appear in the list called, well ... me. My name appeared in all caps for about twenty seconds, and then disappeared like it never existed.'

I guess I've reacted a certain way because Neotnia gives me a little look. Yet I remain silent.

'When he came into the kitchen to tell me what he'd seen, he found me with my blackened hand over the sink,' she continues. 'Neither of us knew what to think when we told the other what happened, but at that moment Goeido was more concerned about my hand. He wanted to take me to the hospital, but we both knew we couldn't do that. So, we decided to wait, and over the next several hours, my skin began to lose its blackness. By morning, it looked normal again.'

Neotnia presses the thumb of her right hand into the palm of her left and stares at it for a second.

'The thing is, I didn't tell Goeido everything...' She looks at me.

'A few hours after I pulled my hand from the water, I felt something else – something off – within me. The only way I can describe it is it's like a big mental splinter stuck deep inside me that's expanding against my insides. I never felt it before I was electrocuted, but now there it was – this feeling like something's deep inside me that doesn't belong. And it doesn't feel like it's in any one part of my body. It feels like it's everywhere at once. I feel it every second of every day. Most of the time, it's just uncomfortable. But, sometimes, it makes me so sick I want to pass out. The worst is when it becomes so bad it feels like someone's choking me from the inside, and I can't move.'

A chill comes over me. I see us in bed. Her pale body jerking. I feel that horror again as it dawns on me that she's suffocating, like there's a ghostly hand around throat.

'By the end of that first week, the feeling was driving me crazy. And I couldn't get it out of my mind that not only was this mental splinter connected to the electrocution, but that the electrocution was connected to me showing up on Goeido's laptop. So, when Goeido was sleeping, I took his laptop and set it by the sink and opened the network settings. I filled the sink and plugged in the re-placement toaster, then put my left arm into the water, all the way up to my elbow. I turned on the toaster with my other hand and dropped it in.'

My lips part, yet no words escape them.

Neotnia raises her eyebrows. 'And the same thing happened. I felt a more painful sting and when I took my arm from the water, my skin, all the way from my fingertips to my elbow, was ashen black.'

Her finger traces an invisible line on her forearm.

'But this time,' she continues, 'as soon as I dropped the toaster in, I kept my eye on Goeido's laptop. And sure enough, my name ap-peared in the network settings. Only this time it showed for a little more than thirty seconds – close to *twice* as long as Goeido said he'd seen it. And something else happened too. That mental splinter I'd been feeling? I could still feel it inside me, but during the time I showed up on the network, I didn't feel the extreme pressure. It was as if a window had opened and, for thirty seconds anyway, that mental splinter had more room to breathe – it wasn't rubbing against my insides.'

Neotnia looks at me for a long moment, considering something.

'Look, if I'm an android it only makes sense that there's some kind of code running through me – code Father made me with, right?'

'It would make sense,' I say without needing to consider it.

'Right,' she nods. 'And so, if I have code, couldn't part of it be corrupt? Couldn't that be what this mental splinter is?'

'I guess it could. I don't know,' I shake my head. 'Maybe.'

'And if someone could see my code, wouldn't they be able to confirm it and extract the bad part? Take it out, like a novelist deletes a bad sentence in a manuscript?'

I shrug and let out a breath. 'Maybe.'

'Well, that's what I asked Goeido to help me do,' Neotnia says. 'In Japan most kids are taught to code at a young age, so everyone knows the basics – same as with reading and writing. It's no different in America, right?'

I nod.

'Well, I don't have that ability. Father never taught me. But Goeido, he knows the basics just like most everyone born in the last forty years.' She shakes her head. 'Of course, he was furious when I showed him my blackened arm the next day, even though by that time the worst of it had faded. But then I told him about the splinter and the pain. And, well, I'm stubborn. He knew if he didn't help me, I'd try to do it myself.'

Neotnia studies my face for a moment like I've suddenly written something on it. But then, as if whatever it was has faded, she continues.

'So, we decided to wait a few days and try again. If my hand made me show up on his laptop for almost twenty seconds, and my arm made me show for over thirty seconds, I reasoned both arms would make me show for twice as long, which could give him enough time to connect to me and pull me up on his laptop. And so that's what we tried the night you first came into the café. When you left after your ear cleaning, we locked up and went into the kitchen. I put both arms in the sink, and we dropped another toaster in.'

Neotnia clenches her jaw and shakes her head.

'This time, the pain was *much* worse. It just gets that way. The more of me electrocuted, the more it hurts. But Goeido *was* able to connect to me, just not for long enough. The length I showed up didn't exactly double this time. Just as he opened a terminal and pulled me up, I disappeared from his screen. So that night, all I had was two black arms with nothing to show for it,' she shrugs.

Something occurs to me. 'When I returned the next night for my backpack, I noticed you were wearing gloves.'

Neotnia gives a little embarrassed smile. 'My arms were still blackened the next day. It seems the larger the surface area electrocuted, the longer my skin takes to heal. When I woke that morning still with two black arms, Goeido went to a thrift store in Harajuku to buy me gloves. I told him I wanted to work, even though he insisted I rest. But working is better for me. It helps me ignore the pain from the splinter.'

I nod but don't say anything.

'After that, well, two full arms didn't give us enough time. I wasn't going to do this piecemeal any longer. So, I made up my mind to go all in.'

'The bathtub,' I say.

Neotnia nods.

'We filled it all the way, and I got in up to my neck. Goeido put his laptop on the sink and plugged in the toaster. Even after he pushed the lever there was a moment where I thought I was literally going to have to punch him to get him to drop it into the water. But then ... he did.' Neotnia hugs her sides and gives her head a shake. 'This time it hurt *soooo much,* like my skin was on fire, and pressure expanded through my body so rapidly I thought my insides were going to burst. Then the fuse blew, and the only thing left illuminated was Goeido's face. I tried to stifle my cry because I wanted his eyes on the laptop, but I could barely focus as he banged at the keys. Yet this time, he was able to connect to me – and he even had time to look at my code...' She raises her eyebrows. 'Except, the only thing that showed was code like he'd never seen. It constantly changed and shifted, and chunks of it seemed to teleport from one place to the next. "It's as if it's alive," is what Goeido said. And then, just two minutes after the toaster hit the water, I completely disappeared from his screen. My code blinked out like it never existed.'

Neotnia shakes her head.

'When I tried to get out of the tub, I could hardly move. I guess it only makes sense that the more of me that gets electrocuted, the more it takes out of me. Still, it felt like I'd been hit by a *Shinkansen*. Goeido had to scoop me up and carry me to my room in the dark. He put me in bed then went into the hall to change the fuse. When he returned, the way he looked at me, I thought his eyes were going to fall from their sockets. But I guess it does look quite the sight. My body was ashen black all over, from my neck to my toes. I slept for *such* a long time that night. Honestly, the toaster probably took the beating better than I did, and it was wrecked.'

Something suddenly occurs to me. 'The day we first went to the care home, I met you outside the café, and a delivery arrived. There were half a dozen toasters with it.'

Neotnia looks at me but doesn't say anything.

My jaw drops. 'How many times has he electrocuted you?'

'I'm desperate.' She gives a crestfallen shrug. 'This thing inside me, this splinter, I need to get it out. I need it gone. It's driving me mad, and the attacks it brings, they're only getting worse. Besides, what if...'

Her eyes quiver in the dining room's light. It's as if she's too afraid to finish the sentence.

'What if, what?' I say.

'We've now got a way to look inside me, right? To see my code?'

She waits for me to nod or speak or something, but I don't move.

'And you yourself said that code leaves footprints,' she goes on. 'So, if we keep exploring mine, couldn't it give a clue as to something about Father? At least where he was when he made me, or maybe even a way to contact him?'

The way she's looking at me, I know she aches for my next words.

'But it could also reveal absolutely nothing,' I shrug, so many thoughts swirling through my mind. 'Besides, who knows if the same rules apply to you? I'm not even really sure what you are.'

After some silent beat, Neotnia's eyes drop to the hands in her lap. She nods so subtly you could miss it. It's several moments before she speaks again.

'Well anyway, we got two minutes last time,' she says without looking at me. 'I've made Goeido promise we'll try again, this time with my head submerged, too.'

'Neotnia—'

'I'm desperate.' An exasperated half-smile breaks on her lips. 'And maybe it'll give us more time to look around inside. More surface area, more time.'

My eyes widen as I recall a story Mom told me about a patient. 'Or it could destroy you. Just because these electrocutions haven't destroyed you yet...' I let out a breath. 'Look, you don't know what submerging yourself entirely will do. Maybe it'll give you more time, or maybe it just ends you. It's electricity, Neotnia. Nothing's invincible. It's easy to think we are, but then one day we do something we've done multiple times before and that's it – it's the straw that breaks the camel's back.'

Neotnia nods a little, as if she's heard me, yet she gazes into the space before her for some time, her eyes unfocused, looking at something only she can see.

'What if ... there is one other way?' she says, a thread of desperation crossing her face. 'Goeido can see my code, he just can't make sense of it – not in so little time, anyway. But maybe ... maybe he just doesn't have the skills? Maybe not many people do? Father does, obviously, but he's not an option. But you...'

'No.'

Neotnia freezes. 'Please...'

I shake my head. 'No.'

She springs after me as I rise from the couch.

'But when it comes to coding, you're a genius. You know you are.

The magazine even said so. Maybe you'll see something Goeido hasn't in the time we have? And my code – couldn't it be quantum-based? Couldn't that be why Goeido can't read it? Couldn't it ... Please, couldn't it...?'

Her lips tremble as she holds that pleading, anguished gaze on me. But all of this ... It's too much. I think of everything that's happened over the last two weeks. Everything that's happened over the last two days. And it's just too much.

'If you do run on quantum code, you're lucky Goeido hasn't destroyed you already,' I answer. 'Quantum code is *incredibly* unstable. It needs to be written and maintained precisely or the entire system that relies on it can shut down – for good. I mean, you don't understand how lucky you are that Goeido hasn't accidentally struck a single key while viewing your code...'

And with each word I speak, I know any remaining hope Neotnia had only slips further away. I see that anguish drowning her pupils, and I want to stop, but she needs to hear this.

'Just one wrong keystroke – injecting just one random character into a quantum codebase – can destroy *everything*. And who knows, maybe this "splinter" you're feeling? Maybe some of your code did get messed up when you electrocuted yourself. If that's the case, it's Russian roulette, Neotnia, and you're not going to keep winning.'

The way her jaw drops, it's like I've suddenly punched her in the gut. It's a moment before she recovers.

'*Winning?*' she grits in a single, coarse burst. Her chest rises and falls with such exertion it's like someone's laid a heavy block across it. Two tiny streams break down her cheeks. 'I haven't won at *anything* in over a year.'

Her wet gaze bores into me for what feels like eternity.

And of all things, looking at those streams running down her cheeks, I think of Dad. One of the final conversations we had was about his role as a field surgeon. He explained what a responsibility it was to operate on someone whose life depended on you. If you choose to do it, he said, you must be sure you can live with the consequences if things go wrong – because they often do.

I look at Neotnia, her inconsolable eyes refusing to blink in an effort to stem even more tears. But all this ... I just can't.

And from whatever look I have on my face, Neotnia can tell where this is going. 'No, no, please help me.' Her face breaks, its streams thickening. 'You don't know what it's like. I need this out of me. And I need to find my father. My differences from others are even greater than he led me to believe, and I need to know why...'

Her shimmering eyes rattle around my face as if she'll find the reply she wants there. But I have no idea what to say.

'Look at me,' she pleads, holding her hand up, fingers spread wide. 'Outwardly, I'm indistinguishable from a person. I'm indistinguishable in all but one area. That was intentional, it *had* to be. And I need to know why. Why did he lie and tell me I'm no less of a person and can do anything a person can when my body clearly proves otherwise? I need to find him; I need answers, and this, being able to see my code – it's the only lead I've *ever* had.'

Her throat tightens as her jaw trembles. But I'm shaking my head.

'Please...'

I'm not my father. I'm just a seventeen-year-old kid who's in way over his head. 'I'm sorry...'

'No. *Chōdai!* Please...'

I open my mouth to speak, but I'm unable to utter another word. I see her tears merging into the tub's bathwater where she's being electrocuted. I see her sinking below the surface, unmoving.

I see her in my bed, our bodies intertwined.

'*Chōdai!*'

And the bell, it clangs as I exit the café into the Tokyo night.

10 – It's a bullet in the brain.

I've been all over Tokyo in the last twenty-four hours – running from something. An inescapable presence. A thing wanting to devour me whole.

As soon as the café's bell clanged, I felt the air go thin and a terrible disorientation washed over me. The atmosphere all around turned blue then pink then green, as if I were stumbling through multiple worlds. A cacophony of indecipherable symbols and sounds blared from every direction. Wherever I looked, people and machines moved in tangled synchronised waves like a single organism painted in neon light. Even the sky brought no clarity. For there was no moon nor stations, only a kaleidoscopic haze floating in a thick mist between forty-storey department stores, drones zipping across their aerial alleyways like strange sparrows.

'*Konbanwa*,' something said, its voice amplified tenfold like everything else that vented a sound. It was the info bot. I'd turned right from the café instead of left and wandered to the scramble. '*Konbanwa*,' its eyes blinked again; its domed head reflected a green glow. 'How may I help you?'

All I could do was retreat before it uttered another word. I knew if I glanced at it again, if I peered into its dome for an instant, I'd see that morbid, formless approximation of me reflected back, and the unbearable essence of this world would wash over me. I wanted solitude. Somewhere to hide from a reality that suddenly felt so unreal. I passed my apartment and kept going. Even when I reached Shinjuku, I didn't stop. By ten I was somewhere in the far north of Tokyo, where small wooden houses still line mazes of spaghetti streets – peaceful, comforting remnants of a quieter, long-gone era. At the meeting of two intersecting strands, I rested for some time under the dim light of an old vending machine gently buzzing in the night.

That's when I first felt it. That presence. Ghostly. Formless. Waiting for me just out of sight. Its hunger was palpable. I knew I needed to move again. It took me hours to retrace my steps, and when I reached my apartment, I left the lights off and cried in the darkness.

I woke to the fleeting feeling that what happened yesterday had been a dream. Yet any relief vanished as reality took hold. Sitting up in the new day's light, I soon felt that presence again. I needed to move, to put distance between me and it. I grabbed my backpack and headed in a direction that would take me farthest from the café.

At midday, I passed under a large outdoor metascreen in a JR station plaza. It relayed an NHK update about Paris and Zambia. But I watched the people staring at the screen. Everyone sought the most recent information about events they feared could radically transform the world they knew. Yet the world they knew was already gone. Every person gazing at that screen was indistinguishable from Neotnia, and she from them. Yet each still believed they knew a person looks like 'me', and an artificial being looks like that receptionist bot in the lobby or that construction bot across the road.

They had no idea the world's no longer like that.

And what if they did know? Would they be amazed? Or afraid? And if they got to know Neotnia like I have, and then discovered the truth – would they feel like I'm feeling now? Or would they know how to process this better than me?

At a bookstore with a small café, I ordered a coffee and sat for a long time, that presence lurking somewhere near. As the girl placed the saucer before me, the tendon on the underside of her slender wrist popped up, just as the tendon on Neotnia's wrist does when she sets a coffee on a table. Their wrists were indistinguishable. But how? Neotnia said her father made her, but how could one man do that? Synthetic muscles have existed since the early 2030s to help smart prosthetics merge with amputees' limbs – but building a being from scratch with them? How could one man do that, especially considering Neotnia said she was 'born' in a small house by the sea and not in some R&D lab? And her skin: the biosynthetic skin used to treat burn patients, you can tell its synthetic; yet Neotnia's looks and feels perfectly natural. How could her 'father' have achieved that?

And just as with Inu, Neotnia makes all the involuntary micro-movements a biological being does: the blinks, the fidgeting, the twitch of a nose, the bending of the mouth in reaction to some thought. Yet how could any person code those abilities to such a degree that they appear natural? While achieving such a thing with Inu is incredible, with Neotnia, it's unbelievable. Yet clearly, he succeeded. So why abandon her? Why not go public with his creation? He'd be the most famous person on the planet – maybe in all human history. He'd be awarded the Nobel Prize in Computing and the Turing Award and garner every other recognition out there. And he'd be rich beyond belief.

So why give all that up and disappear?

My mind only got relief from its tsunami of thoughts as I wandered into the grounds of the Imperial Palace. The canopy of the surrounding trees was a fiery orange, and their beauty in the late-afternoon light seemed to form a protective cocoon in which only natural things were allowed to be considered. Yet that same beauty begged to be shared and, as that realisation dawned, I sensed the closeness of the presence again; its hunger for me.

'*Konbanwa.*'

I've only now arrived here. It's past eight, and I've missed the dinner rush. It's not the same Freshness Burger as before, but the servers are identical. I sit at a booth and as I wait for a cheeseburger head, my eyes settle on a couple by the window. Their burgers are untouched. The man is maybe twenty-five or twenty-six and the girl maybe a few years younger. He looks at her as she quietly sobs over her French fries. Her lips move, yet she speaks so softly I wonder if even he can hear her words. His gaze is cold, even annoyed.

I give a cheeseburger head my order, then look at the couple again.

The girl has stopped weeping, and both now eat their burgers in silence. After a moment, each opens a packet of mayo, squeezing identical globs onto their wrappers. Each then dips a fry into their glob and consumes it. Neither seems to realise their actions mirror the other's.

The longer I stare, the stronger that presence feels.

I thank Cheeseburger Head for my order and recall a conversation Neotnia and I had after the movie. She was startled to see me talking to the cheeseburger head like it was a person and wanted to know what I thought the differences between a bot and a person were. I told her a bot never has the agony of wondering why it's here. Every bot is made with a purpose, I said, while people aren't. Only now do I realise that conversation wasn't about bots at all.

What are they doing right now? Is she sitting in the bathtub this instant with Goeido holding a toaster over her? Or would she have told him what I said, and would he refuse to help again? Refuse to take the action that might allow her to quench that agony of wondering? Would it be fair of him to do that? Then again, was it fair of her to ask me to help, considering what could happen? Was it fair to let me believe we were alike?

I take my time walking home. The breeze is warm for a November night. As I arrive, Mom calls. She thanks me for the photos of the palace trees and asks if I'm enjoying myself. I tell her everything's fantastic. It's the first conversation in forever where she hasn't sounded distant or anxious, and I don't want to ruin that. Yet as I lie, I sense that formlessness stronger than ever. It's so close now, it might as well be painted to my skin.

I sit on the balcony for a long time after the call, letting the warm night air waft over me. Sometimes I see Neotnia in my arms, her head on my chest, listening to my heartbeat. Sometimes I see myself at her side, terrified as that horrible rasp escapes her lips. Sometimes I see her sobbing, tears streaming as she begs for my help. *Chōdai!*

It's some time before I can force the carousel of scenes from my mind.

On the streets below, it looks as if the normal volume of cars is permitted once again. Across the horizon, the expected quantity of lights blink red as drones glide along their chosen paths. And above it all, the unfinished stations shine down like shattered celestial crowns, providing the illusion that this is still the ordinary world – if only for tonight.

*

Neotnia looks at me with a sly grin.

'Vaginal agenesis?' She laughs. 'No. I'm *synthetic*.'

I wake with a start – my heart pounding.

It's here. Right on top of me.

I feel it as clearly as a summer day's humidity on my skin.

Yet ... no matter how long I inspect the room, the presence doesn't make itself visible.

I check the clock. It's late morning. There's a notification on my phone.

I throw on a T-shirt and khakis. I microwave a cup of instant coffee and sit on the balcony. I set the coffee to cool on the ledge. The notification is for an email from Sony, and I read it with increasing alarm. They say there's a problem with the regulators, and I should contact them.

But as I hurry my reply, a violent gust cuts across the balcony and in an instant my chest is on fire. I jump, knocking the now-empty coffee cup from my lap as a blistering pain sets in. I dart to the bathroom, peeling the scalding T-shirt from my flesh, and fling it over the shower rod. Yet as I turn towards the sink a new alarm takes hold.

Alarm?

No. *Horror*.

In the too-large mirror I glance my naked abdomen for the first time in months, my gaze now frozen on the thing I've tried so hard to avoid. My stomach's skin droops like deflated dough taken too soon from the oven. Its weight pulls around my navel, bending my belly button into an unnatural curve, as if my abdomen's frowning at the pink marks rutted into it like they're the aftermath of a vicious attack by some mythical beast. The marks run all the way to my waist, where my skin hangs in a thick, deformed fold – an apron of human flesh.

I gaze at that apron the way one gazes in curious disgust at some unknown thing that's washed to shore. My mirror fingers prod its baggy tissue. They spread it taut in one direction, then the other, flattening it against my abdomen. They do this again and again, offering the brief illusion that I'm normal, that this can't possibly be me. Yet the moment they release my skin, it droops back down, like a pug's face; like I'm more mongrel than man.

A burning more searing than the scalding coffee rises in me.

This is the body I've been dealt in addition to everything else I've had to endure. *This* is the cherry on top of the great unfairness of my life. *This*—

A web of splinters appears over the freakish figure before me as my mirror fist connects with my real one. And like that – that formless presence that's been lurking near for so long finally shows itself. I see it clear as day when I catch my face's reflection above my splintered body. It's my own terrible shadow – like Neotnia's, yet tailor-made by my unique fears and pain. It's ready to devour me. And I want to let it.

Its ingredients span my life: Dad's death. How Mom's become. How I always need to lie and act like everything's OK around her – all in the blind hope that one day she'll get back that life she used to have in her. That life I *need* her to have. Because I'm not OK, and I shouldn't need to hide how I always feel. I want to scream at her, *I'm the child, and you're the parent. You're supposed to take care of me!* Yet I never do because that could be what breaks her completely.

But those fears and pains aren't limited to my parents. My shadow is deep, and its ingredients are many. It's rich in loneliness. Isolation. Alienation. Loathing. I don't know what it's like to have friends because my size ostracised me. I've never been on a spring break or to a party or a prom. The only people who give me attention are executives three times my age who want my code because they can't grasp how to do it themselves. All the while, blogs and magazines throw around the label 'genius' like it's a good thing. Like it's not merely another term for 'outsider'.

Even after I've toiled to change myself physically so I can look like other people – so I can have just the *chance* of fitting in – it doesn't work. Because my shadow's final ingredient is its most awful. Its cruellest. It's this fucking organic prison I'm wrapped in. I can't even wear regular clothes in public because my skin folds up underneath, giving me the contour of a melted candle. Instead of T-shirts, it's always thick hoodies. Instead of dress shirts, it's always bulky sweaters. I want nothing more than to make this grotesque apron vanish. I *need* it gone. But now, Sony's email … if the regulators won't approve the transfer, there's no sale. And if there's no sale, there's no money. There's no *surgery*.

I can't keep living with this. I won't.

My shadow, it's the only thing that knows how I feel.

It's the only thing that has the answers.

I work a splintered shard free, mirror-me gripping it like a dagger. *Amputate yourself*, it says.

A globule of blood erupts like oil from a well as the shard's tip punctures the rubbery bundle of flesh pinched between my fingers. The shard penetrates deeper, widening the laceration as red fluid mixes with yellow fat and tears cascade over my cheeks.

I slice, that dark shadow enveloping all.

I need this off me. Now. I won't keep living with this.

No one knows what it's like. Unless you have a body that's abnormal, you can't possibly understand what you'd do to be freed from the alienation it wraps you in—

And as the tears run down my face, I stare at the splintered reflection of my violent act.

I stare at it with that realisation in my mind for a long, long time.

*

It's mid-afternoon when I hear the clang of the bell again. Inu's at his perch on the counter, and he gives me a little yap.

'*Irasshaimase*,' Goeido says reflexively from the kitchen, his eyes cast down, concentrating on something in front of him.

'*Konnichiwa* … Goeido.'

When he looks up, it's the first time I've ever seen surprise on his face. '*Konnichiwa*…' he says, gaping at me. Yet his line of sight soon drifts.

Neotnia's entered the foyer. She wears a long denim skirt with a white T-shirt that exposes her bare arms. And I'm relieved to see nothing about those arms looks ashen.

She stares at me with such a stunned expression I worry the dishes she's collected might slip from her grasp.

Beneath my hoodie, my bandaged wound stings.

'I'll try,' I say. 'If you still want me to, I'll try.'

She blinks as she processes my words. And right there, those clear blue-grey eyes, they break my fucking heart. They stare upon me for several silent moments more as if contemplating whether she's heard right. Then the edges of her mouth curl into a smile so slight most people would miss it.

'OK...' she nods. 'Yes.'

And as if suddenly remembering he's here, too, she looks at Goeido who's gazing at us like he's watching a foreign soap opera. She nods to him. '*Hai*,' she says, that slight smile growing brighter.

For a moment, Goeido considers the word as if it's hanging from Neotnia's lips, still waiting to be read. But then a big grin breaks his face. '*Hai!*' he shouts, slapping a kitchen towel across the partition. He grabs the dish he was preparing and delivers it to the dining area, repeating '*hai*' as he passes.

Neotnia follows his trajectory with her eyes, then turns to me. Their clearness scans my face.

'Could we talk in private for a second?'

For perhaps a beat too long, I say nothing.

'I think it's best to focus on the issue at hand,' I finally reply, lost for other words. 'I ... we don't know much about what we're dealing with, and if any of this has a hope of working, it's going to need every ounce of our attention.'

Neotnia's gaze breaks from mine. '*Hai*,' she gives a stiff nod. 'Of course.'

Goeido returns from the dining area, and it's decided they'll shut early, in an hour. They ask if I want some food in the meantime, but I tell them I'll come back.

When I return the closed sign is up. I fold my phone out into a laptop and set it on the counter by Inu and launch my translation app.

'We're all alone now?' I say, and the app overlays a Japanese voice on my own.

'*Hai*,' Goeido nods, and his Aussie English voice says, 'Yep.'

'OK, good,' I say, suddenly feeling like I'm a high-school football coach giving the team the play before they retake the field. 'Well, look, there's so much I don't know. I don't know if we'll even be successful, to be honest,' I shrug, and Neotnia casts her eyes down, giving a nod so slight I barely catch it. 'But I'm gonna try. However, if we're doing this, we need to do it right. I'm going to need to know *everything*. And I'm going to need him, too.'

And realizing the three of us are suddenly staring at him in some unexpected way, a low '*grrr*' escapes Inu's mouth.

'It's OK,' Neotnia whispers in his ear as she lifts him from his perch. We head back into the kitchen, placing Inu on the stainless-steel counter next to the big sink.

'We're not going to electrocute him, right?' Goeido says in Aussie English.

'What?' I give him a look. 'No. *Jesus*.'

Goeido shrugs.

I roll my eyes. 'Look, Neotnia's father said she and Inu have a somewhat similar makeup – physiologically anyway. So, before we resort to electrocuting *anyone*, I want to know as much about *everyone* as possible – because maybe there's another way to access her systems. Makes sense?'

They both nod. Neotnia reaches under Inu's collar, and I again hear that soft pop right before she bends his head backward, exposing the cross-section of his neck. Over the next several hours, I examine Inu with Neotnia at my side. Occasionally, she'll stroke his upside-down head, calming his little growls of annoyance. Sometimes Goeido stays in the kitchen with us, observing. Sometimes he goes to the foyer to get some cleaning done, or to shoo away a customer who's banging on the door.

Here's what I know so far: Inu's bones appear to be made from graphene. It's why they have that dull blackness about them. An elephant could literally step on him and wouldn't break a single bone in his body. His skin is synthetic, obviously. It's more advanced than ordinary synthetic skin, but not as advanced as Neotnia's. But, thanks to his fur, that's hard to tell. This makes me think Inu may have been an early attempt at trying to create the technologies that eventually went into Neotnia. Like he was a first step, and once that was done, her father moved on to something more advanced.

The silvery-blue cords that course through his synthetic muscles appear to be a combination of artificial veins and nerves that transport some type of biovoltaic gel. I assume they carry electrical signals to give Inu's muscles movement. Further down, a dull grey structure lies behind a knot of synthetic muscles. It looks to be made from some type of quantum material, but I don't know which. Perhaps it's a power source, but I can't imagine what it could be converting energy from. Then again, it could be something else entirely.

What's interesting is there's a universal input next to the exposed graphene vertebra. You have to push a bundle of cords out of the way to see it, but it's there. And it means I can literally plug my laptop into Inu using the same cable I'd plug into a server or any other terminal, which is precisely what I do. And like that, 'I001' appears as a connected device on my screen.

I open my terminal app to have a look at the device's – Inu's – code. It's definitely quantum. It's complex, but readable – if you know a lot about quantum coding, anyway. It's entirely local, too. That is, Inu's not running the quantum code from a remote hive somewhere, which is incredible. It now makes me think that dull grey structure deep inside him is some kind of tiny, self-contained quantum computer – an astounding breakthrough in itself.

Quantum processors require specific quantum materials and architecture to run inside devices, like hives, and those components are both delicate and relatively large – not to mention extremely costly. So far that's ruled out shrinking a quantum computer into something small enough to fit the form-factor of a phone or laptop. And even though you could probably stuff a weak quantum computer into some types of bots – if they're big enough – the quantum computer could be too easily damaged by the bot's movement. Besides, a quantum computer inside a bot simply isn't needed since standard AI can run directly on it using far cheaper and more practical classical components, which is all a bot needs to carry out its tasks.

All this has been true … until Inu, it seems. And, if it's true for Inu, it's likely the same for Neotnia.

I show Goeido Inu's code and ask if it's what Neotnia's code looked like, but he shakes his head. He tells me what Neotnia said he'd seen: her code shifted around on the screen, and chunks of it seemed to teleport from one place to the next. Regardless, I sift through Inu's code for some time. There's an insane amount of it, but the more I examine it, the more I glean a few reasonable assumptions.

First, Inu's quantum codebase is tens of millions of lines long. But the quantum nature of the code, the quantity of it, and the fact he seems to have a quantum computer inside him probably explains why Inu can produce micro-movements like a biological dog can. Accomplishing that with AI on classical computers would require trillions of lines of binary code, which would take hundreds of years to write and debug – and even then, there'd still be no guarantee the AI would be able to produce realistic micro-movements.

Second, since Neotnia revealed they were both androids, I've wondered if Inu was like her. By that I mean she clearly seems to have awareness – of herself, of the world, of everything. Does Inu possess the same awareness, or is he just mimicking the awareness and independence a biological canine has? From his code, I can now see it's likely Inu is just a mimic of a real-life dog. He'll fetch the ball for you and look like he's enjoying it, but not because of any separate internal essence or desire to play. In other words, he's doing it because his code tells him that a person who looks at him with a ball, and then throws it, wants him to retrieve it and look happy doing it.

On the stainless-steel counter, Inu's nails make tiny little taps as his feet shift. Neotnia gives him a scratch on the top of his upside-down skull, which calms him. Yet soon enough, he releases another annoyed '*grrr*'.

'Sorry, little buddy,' I say as I continue scrolling through his codebase. 'Almost done. I just want to try one more thing...'

The day I came looking for Neotnia, Goeido told me to follow Inu because he'd take me to her. The spiralling red waves on Inu's visibility collar sped up as we neared and turned solid red when Inu found her. I ask if he knows how that tracking process works, but he says he only knows how to activate it – by touching Inu's collar, which Neotnia's father obviously modded with a DNA authenticator. Indeed, Goeido says her father had him register his biometrics on the collar when he dropped them at the café.

But I've discovered that Inu's collar is physically part of him, too. A thin cord runs underside the back of it and into his body, which suggests the collar is merely the access point that allows an authorised person to activate Inu to find Neotnia, and it serves as visual feedback for whoever is following him. In other words, the collar isn't itself the tracking device that locates Neotnia – Inu is. And that suggests there's some unseen connection between them.

'Did your father explain how Inu can do this?' I ask.

Neotnia shakes her head. 'He just said he's a way to find me should I ever get lost.'

I return Inu's head onto his neck but don't press down to seal it in place – I still allow the cable to run from the input by his vertebra to my laptop so I can monitor his code in action. I touch Inu's collar, but as expected, the collar stays black. Yet when I ask Goeido to touch it, the collar spirals in waves of red and Inu rises on all fours, turns around, and faces Neotnia. When he sees her, his collar turns a solid red.

I search my terminal for any changes in Inu's code while he's in this tracker mode, but nothing stands out. Then I remember something. After Brobrah showed at the Mossman shrine, when I looked back to Neotnia and Inu on the bench, his collar had stopped glowing red and turned black again.

'Was that automatic?'

Neotnia shakes her head. 'No. When I touch his collar, if he's been activated, it deactivates him.'

I have her do just that, and Inu's collar goes back to black. Yet I still don't see any change in his code. 'And I guess you can activate Inu in this way, too?'

'Not by touching his collar.'

'I don't understand. You can activate him another way?'

'*Hai.*'

'How?'

Neotnia twists her mouth up a little. 'By thinking it.'

'Sorry?'

'I think it, and it activates him. It tells him to come find me.'

'I don't—'

'Here,' she cuts me off. She picks Inu up and turns him away from herself. Then she retreats a few paces down the counter. And next she simply closes her eyes and, a moment later, Inu's black collar spirals in waves of red. He turns and walks to her, dragging my laptop as the cable goes taut. His collar turns solid red as he stands in front of Neotnia at the steel counter's edge.

'Jesus.'

I look at the terminal, yet there's still no sign of any code triggering this tracking protocol. No GPS. No Wi-Fi triangulation. No UWB. Nothing.

'But how does that work?'

'I don't know,' Neotnia shrugs. 'Father just said it's for if I ever get lost, I'll have a way of letting whoever Inu is with know.'

'How far does it work?'

'I don't know,' she says. Then she stifles a little grin. 'I've only ever done it in the café. It comes in handy at night when Inu's down here and I'm in bed upstairs and want him to come cuddle. I don't have to get my feet cold walking downstairs to get him.'

My mind reels thinking how this is even possible. Best guess: the particles from some quantum structure inside her and the particles from some quantum structure inside Inu are engaging in quantum entanglement. It would allow them to 'talk' to each other, no matter the distance. Regardless, I'd hoped the fact that Inu could locate Neotnia remotely might reveal some means of accessing her systems without electrocuting her, but it's a dead end.

From the way Neotnia's looking at me, I think she can sense my disappointment.

It's now dark outside, and we decide to take a break. As Neotnia and Goeido fix some dinner in the kitchen, I ask to use the bathroom. Cutting through the foyer, the hallway's inky blackness envelopes me. I run my hand along the wall until my feet stub the steps. The upstairs is small, and the bathroom itself is tiny and seashell pink. The tub brings back memories of Halloween night.

Instead of using the toilet, I lift my hoodie and peel the blood-crusted gauze aside. My laceration is long, red and I don't know how deep. It burns and, in the mirror, my shadow lingers across my face.

Back in the foyer, Neotnia's placing three beef *donburi* at the booth. Goeido enters carrying a salad bowl.

'You know, a light in the hall really wouldn't hurt,' I say.

'I'll clean up a customer's mess after they eat their tucker, but I draw the line at wiping their slash,' Goeido cuts in in his Aussie voice. 'The darkness keeps blokes and Sheilas from looking for the dunnie.'

Neotnia gives me a look that conveys she and Goeido have been through this before, and it's a no-win situation.

We eat and discuss where things stand. I go through everything I can think of. I ask anything that may give me some idea of another way to access her systems. My bluntness catches Neotnia off guard, but she confirms her body is whole – it's not like Inu's, where you can take a head off. There's no jack or flaps or anything I could plug my laptop into – but that's something I knew already.

I ask them to explain again how she appears as a device on Goeido's laptop after she's electrocuted. But they both say the same things Neotnia's already told me. Now there's no doubt in my mind there's some kind of quantum firewall around her, acting as a sort of encrypted 'force field' that keeps her invisible to networks. It's likely her father's the only one who knows how to temporarily shut the field down without electrocuting her.

I ask how she's powered. She doesn't know. She eats and drinks and goes to the bathroom. Obviously, only number two. She may convert food into energy like we do. Maybe. Regardless, how she acquires energy doesn't appear to be a vector we can exploit. Besides being able to trigger Inu remotely to come find her, it doesn't appear Neotnia is connected to anything else. She says she's not connected to any intranets. She can't download data on the fly. She can't suck up information from an online encyclopaedia and know its entire knowledgebase in an instant. She was 'born' knowing how to speak Japanese and English, but besides that, she seems to acquire information and understanding like the rest of us do – through experience and study.

In short, it appears there really is no way to access her systems other than by electrocution. So, after finishing the mochi-ball dessert Goeido's made, we take our plates to the kitchen and then, like some kind of ultra-dysfunctional, sadistic family, we decide to electrocute Neotnia's arm so I can see what happens.

Neotnia shuts off the tap as the water approaches the rim of the big sink. Across the kitchen, Goeido unboxes one of the new toasters, which sit on a shelf by a freezer. Neotnia pushes her right T-shirt sleeve above her shoulder and Goeido plugs the toaster into the socket near the sink.

I can't help but shake my head.

'It's OK,' Neotnia says. 'When it's just my arm, it doesn't hurt much. Besides, it's nothing compared to what I'm constantly feeling inside.'

Goeido asks if she's ready. She gives a firm nod, then submerges her arm all the way to her elbow. I unfold my phone into a tablet and open the network settings. Goeido moves his hand in a swatting motion, telling me to take a few steps back, then presses the lever on the toaster. Seconds later, its coils glow red hot. He looks at Neotnia once more, and she nods. And like that, he drops the toaster into the sink.

There's an almighty pop and the kitchen's rear lights flash out. But even in the shadows, I can see Neotnia clench her jaw in pain. It's only when her eyes find mine that I realise I need to be looking at my screen. And indeed, 'NEOTNIA' has appeared as a device. I tap it and it begins establishing a connection, but before anything more shows, 'NEOTNIA' blinks from existence.

'That's it,' she says from the shadows the moment her name vanishes. I look at the elapsed time. Barely thirty seconds.

'How'd you know exactly when the connection was lost?'

She pulls her arm from the sink as Goeido walks between us, headed towards the kitchen's fuse box.

'Like I said, when I'm connected, I don't feel that pressure inside. It's as if the splinter has room to breathe – like a window is open. When the connection breaks, I feel the window close.'

As the kitchen lights blink back to life, the breath goes out of me.

Her electrocuted arm is exactly as she described: its skin blackened from fingertips to elbow, like ashes have seeped into her flesh and stained it. She fishes the now-dead toaster from the sink and places it on the counter. I consider its scorched body and her ashen arm for the same long moment. Neotnia just gives a little shrug as if to say, *It is what it is*.

I look at my screen where 'NEOTNIA' showed moments ago and release a resigned breath.

'The more of your body surface that's electrocuted, the longer you appear visible on the network, right?'

'*Hai*.'

'OK,' I shake my head. 'The bathtub it is.'

*

After Neotnia sinks into the tub, we decide I'll stay in the bathroom as it isn't big enough for Goeido and me at the same time. I sit sideways on the toilet, using the sink as a desk for my laptop. Goeido stands outside the door, an oven-mitted hand holding the toaster, which is plugged in via a long extension cord. In Goeido's other hand are a flashlight and extra fuse for when the toaster blows the current one.

I adjust the countdown timer on my screen. 'It'll be OK,' Neotnia says from the tub. And that's when I realise my hand's trembling just a bit.

'I know it will,' I lie.

As on Halloween, she's stretched out in the tub, her back slouched along its rear. Everything below her neck is submerged, the ends of her straight black hair floating on the water's surface. Beneath it, she wears a white T-shirt and panties. It feels like her arm's ashen blackness should diffuse in the water the way soot would, yet it remains ingrained in her skin.

I look over my shoulder at Goeido. The toaster's coils are red hot.

'You ready?' I say to Neotnia.

Her nod is decisive.

'Alright.' I let out a breath. 'You tell him when. I'm as ready as can be.'

I look at the timer on my screen. It's set for two minutes.

Neotnia takes a deep breath and looks Goeido in the eyes.

'*Iku!*' she shouts, and my finger jabs the timer as Goeido releases the toaster at her feet.

A split second after the splash, there's the almighty pop and Neotnia's head snaps back, her body seizing, its rigid limbs churning the surface. And just as the light blinks out, I catch her mouth stretch wide.

Her scream shatters the darkness.

My heart pounds. My instincts howl to pull her from the tub, but then I hear it—

'Go...' her tiny voice sounds into the blackness.

And there, 'NEOTNIA' is on my screen like it was in the kitchen. Only now I have enough time to display her code in my terminal. It's precisely as Goeido described: surreal, shifting, even teleporting around. But I catch something – a pattern. I scroll and type and scroll and type as the timer counts down. And in the dim blue glow of my screen, my eyes widen as I realise *why* her code looks the way it does.

My fingers work feverishly and in an instant, I feel like I've crossed from the bathroom to some void that exists separately from our

world. Goeido and Neotnia might as well be a million miles away –
the only things that are real are her code and me.

And in this void, I search and search. And then I see it.

The splinter.

And now I understand.

*

Goeido went to bed an hour ago. We've been taking shifts watching
over Neotnia since we carried her here from the tub. This room used
to be his office before she came to live with him. The desk is pushed
against the wall, making space for the small bed. In the darkness I
notice a shelf bearing at least a dozen sumo trophies. More are piled
in the corner.

I'm in a wooden swivel chair I've rolled next to the bed. Neotnia
sleeps on her side, one arm bent up under the pillow, the other resting
on top of the blanket drizzled over her. Even in the darkness I can
make out how blackened her skin is. On her neck, it's as if I'm gazing
at the equator separating the moon's light side from its dark. Her
face looks unnaturally pale when compared to everything below.

My eyes run from the curve of her naked shoulder, across the
length of her arm, to the ends of her fingers with their blackened
tips, and I recall the story Mom told me about treating someone who
was electrocuted. A man was in a puddle when a powerline came
down. The electricity ripped through his body with such force his
fingertips shot off like little rockets. He lived thanks to the speed at
which a defibrillator drone arrived to restart his heart, but even after
his surgeries his hands were never the same.

My gaze travels back to the equator on Neotnia's neck. When I
glance upon her pale face, her eyes are staring at me in the darkness.

'Thank God for turtlenecks, huh?' she says in a small voice.

'How are you feeling?'

She brings her blackened hand before her, inspecting it in the
darkness. 'I'm OK.' Then, after a moment, 'What time is it?'

'Almost three in the morning.'

She bunches the pillow behind her so she can sit up a little. When she looks at me again, I can tell she's afraid to ask, but does anyway. 'How did it go?'

'It went ... well, I guess.'

Her eyes remain on mine, but she doesn't say a word.

I think how to best explain it.

'Goeido was right about the way your code appears. When I first pulled it up it looked, well, surreal. It constantly moved and altered, and some parts literally appeared to be teleporting around at will. At first, I thought there was no way to understand any of it, but then I noticed what seemed to be repeating markers. And these markers, they looked like what I'd call a type of pattern-recognition key.'

I go silent for a second.

'Long story short: the way your code displays itself – it's like a giant jigsaw puzzle. But you can solve that puzzle if you can match the pattern-recognition keys to each other and then do a bit of quick quantum coding on the fly. So, that's what I did. And, well, now I know your codebase at first seems like it's teleporting around because it's being viewed all flattened together – scrambled – which prevents anyone from messing with it. But once you run the pattern-recognition keys through a compiler, it displays your code how it should be viewed, and only then does it stop looking like it teleports around, and you can read it. It's brilliant, really. There are probably only a handful of people who'd have the knowledge to even recognise the pattern-recognition keys hidden among the gibberish, much less understand how to align and unlock them. It's a clever security protocol. If your father did this all by himself, he's got to be one of the smartest people on the planet.'

Neotnia waits for me to go on.

'The thing is, when you look at your unscrambled codebase, it's evident you don't have just one layer of code, you have three. Three layers of quantum code, all distinct from one another, yet all reliant on one another, too. And two of your layers of code, they look like normal quantum code. But the third layer? Well, there's no discernible syntax, algorithms, or structure. It's clearly quantum, but it's not any quantum code I've ever seen. But that's not even the most unusual thing about it...'

Neotnia's clear eyes gaze at me.

'This third layer of your code is massive. And I mean *massive*,' I say. 'Look, Inu's codebase is immense. Basically, his code is probably equivalent in size to all the books in an old library. But the size of your third layer of code alone? It's insanely larger – maybe even to the extent that it's equivalent to the size of every printed word in human history.' I shake my head. 'But I don't see how someone could have coded all that. Logically, it's impossible. Yet there it is – and it's written in an indecipherable quantum language.'

I press my mouth shut. But I can see she knows I've got something to add.

'Except for one part,' I say. 'There's a single strand of data in this third layer that stands out. It stands out because it's written in standard quantum code – floating there among the indecipherable quantum language. To put it another way: it stands out because its normality is abnormal to that third layer of code – like it's a drop of saltwater in a freshwater lake or a maggot in a raw steak. And this strand of data? I think it's the splinter you feel.'

Neotnia's lips part, but she doesn't utter a word.

'At the ends of it,' I continue, 'on either side, there's standard quantum anchoring code that looks corrupted. Anchor code is usually used when someone tries to keep a file deep in a system – to lock it in place down where it can't be found or manipulated. And this corruption of the anchor code, it could have happened when you first got electrocuted. A stray electron passing through code can change it. It's something satellites have to worry about all the time with solar flares. It's possible that since this splinter isn't like the rest of the code in your third layer, its anchors could have snapped when a massive flow of electrons shot through your body – just like they did when the first toaster fell into the sink. My guess is this strand of data – this splinter – broke off from one of your two other layers of regular quantum code and is now randomly floating around this third layer, like a foreign object in that part of your body. It would be as if a screw from a metal plate in a hip implant broke off in a human's body and it was now floating freely around, say, the large intestine. Just as a person's body would send pain signals because of the free-floating foreign object, your body could be doing the same. The thing is ... I don't think this splinter is just a random line of normal quantum code. From the way it's structured and its anchors, it looks like it could be a container. It looks like it could be a file with something inside.'

Neotnia's mouth drops. 'What could be in it?'

I shrug. 'Anything. It could contain anything. I don't know.'

'Could it have something to do with Father?'

I shake my head. 'I don't know. He's the one who coded you, so maybe. But it could also be nothing related to him.'

'How can we find out?'

'It's regular quantum code, so I could try opening it in place, inside of you, and peeking at what's inside it. That would be safer than extraction – at least until we see what we're dealing with.'

'OK.' Neotnia's nod is decisive.

'No, you don't understand. I can't do it in two minutes. It'll take me at least ninety seconds to find the splinter again. And to open it? Maybe another ninety seconds. Maybe longer.'

Neotnia's mouth twists a little in the darkness, considering something.

'So, we submerge my head. My firewall seems to stay down a max of two minutes doing everything below my neck. So, if we need more time, we need to submerge my head, too.'

'No. Absolutely not.'

'But—'

'Neotnia, no. Look, I'm not sure where your brain, so to speak, is located. Logic would suggest it would be in your head, though. And if it is there, and that part of you gets directly electrocuted, well, you wouldn't put the central processing unit of a server into an electrified tub of water. It would fry it.'

'We'll electrocute me twice in a row then – head above water. Before the first timer ticks to zero. That will keep my firewall disabled for another two minutes, right?'

'It could.' I shake my head. 'Maybe.' Even in the room's darkness, I can see the determination in her eyes. 'But look at your skin. I know you heal after a few days, but you've never been electrocuted in rapid succession. Who knows if your body is strong enough to recover from that...'

'It is. I know it is.'

'You don't know that. You *hope* it is.'

'No, I'm strong. I can even hold my own arm wrestling Goeido.'

My jaw drops, that being what I least expected to hear. 'Seriously?'

'It's always been a draw.' A little smile breaks her lips. 'Every single time.'

I suddenly remember the force with which she shoved me on my bed.

'But I'm not just talking physical strength,' I say. 'Electricity is more destructive than blunt force. There's no way to know if your skin will return to normal or if it'll remain like it is now.'

She considers my words, but then shrugs. 'My body's already abnormal anyway.' She gives a sad little half-smile. 'I'm OK with the outcome – whatever it is.'

The thing is, that's exactly the argument I'd use, too.

'It's not just your body that this could mess up, though. And it's not just the electricity that can mess it up ... it's me,' I say. 'Look, you wouldn't remove the top of a person's skull and randomly poke their brain with a needle, right? It could leave them brain dead. When your firewall is down and the three layers of your codebase aligned, your code is vulnerable to being changed. Figuratively speaking, your brain is exposed. And in that state, if I accidentally alter just one qubit that doesn't make up the splinter, it could *end* you, Neotnia. It could shut you down permanently.'

It's as if a breath has just been involuntarily expelled from her lips. Neotnia casts her eyes towards the blackened hands folded atop the blanket. And the look in her eyes – I can't help thinking it's not worry, but sadness.

'It's OK,' she says after a long moment. 'I need to know why. Why I'm like this. Why Father left me. And I need this feeling inside me to stop. And if doing this can help get me closer to any of those things, then so be it.'

'Neotnia, I really need you to understand this. There's a reason you have this invisible firewall around you. There's a reason your codebase is at first only viewable all flattened together, and unalterable in that state. They're protection measures. And while those measures are down, just *one* mistake – if my finger taps *one* wrong key on my screen and that character gets injected into your codebase – that's it for you. It's a bullet in the brain.'

'I do understand, John. I do. But I need this. No matter what happens, I need this.'

I go downstairs and sit on the couch in the darkness. For a long time, I stare out the booths' window, my wound flaring. It's not until the first glow of morning appears that I finally manage to sleep.

When I wake, Goeido and Neotnia are in the foyer preparing to open for the day. It's almost seven-thirty. Neotnia's told him what she's decided – that we'll attempt the double-electrocution tonight. Goeido's face is stoic as always, but in his eyes, I see hints of my own worry. Having known I've hardly slept, they send me up to Neotnia's bed. When I wake next, it's past one. I come downstairs and have a grilled cheese Goeido makes for me. Neotnia spends the afternoon waiting on customers. She wears one of her turtlenecks and a long skirt that runs to her ankles, as well as her theatrical white gloves. At one point, when we're in the kitchen, she peels one off, revealing her arm.

'See? I bounce back. It's not half as dark as it was this morning.'

I spend my time reviewing every possible thing I know about quantum code. In my head, I run all the scenarios I can. All the ways this can go wrong. Sometimes I watch Neotnia serving coffee, cleaning tables, playing with Inu. It reminds me of how Mom said patients often continue to perform their routine daily tasks right up to the time their potentially life-changing surgery begins. It helps them feel like things are normal in their world. It helps them feel as if they're in control of their lives.

We close the café at eight, and Goeido prepares a simple dinner, but none of us eat much. At nine, we make our way to the second floor. Down the hall, Goeido has the fuse box open and several extra fuses at the ready. Two extension cords run from the socket below the box, down the hallway's length, and into the bathroom. At the end of each is a shiny new toaster already plugged in. I take my place, sitting sideways on the toilet, and fold my phone out into a laptop on the sink.

Neotnia enters the bathroom. She's in another white T-shirt but this time wears blue panties. Her entire body below the neck is still blackened, but not as darkly, as if an invisible hand has managed to wash some of the ash away.

She slides along the rear of the tub, the water reaching her collarbones. Over my shoulder, Goeido stands sideways in the doorframe, the first toaster in an oven-mitted hand and a flashlight in the other. Neotnia gives us a sturdy look. There's the scraping of metal as Goeido presses the lever on the toaster. Within seconds, I feel its heat at my back.

'OK,' I say, attempting the most collected voice I can. 'You ready?'

'*Hai*,' Neotnia says. I nod, and her lips form a small, gentle smile. 'Don't worry. I'm not. I trust you.'

I seem incapable of finding the words to reply, so resort to returning another small nod. Neotnia takes a breath and slides further into the tub. She's submerged to the top of her neck now. The ends of her hair dip into the warm water and gently sway with it.

'OK, everyone...' I say, glancing at the timer on my screen. It's set for two minutes.

I take a long breath.

'On my mark: three, two, one – go!'

This time I don't see the toaster hit the water, though I hear its almighty pop and Neotnia's terrible scream as the lights blink out. I hear the bathwater sloshing, reacting to the convulsions of her limbs. I catch the brief glint of Goeido's flashlight retreating as he stomps down the hallway. Yet I keep my eyes on my screen. 'NEOTNIA' appears, and I connect and bring up her code. I scour its surreal mess until I find its pattern-recognition keys and compile them so her codebase explodes into three layers. I scan the third's endless volumes, looking for the splinter – the saltwater drop in the freshwater lake. And then I see it. My fingers tap at a speed I didn't know they were capable of, and for a moment my mind only thinks in algorithms, in logic flow, in qubits.

Suddenly it's as if the sun has engulfed the room. The bathroom's light bursts back to life. Out in the hallway: Goeido's returning stomps. Then the scraping of the second toaster's lever. The heat of its coils roasting my back. On my screen, the timer ticks down as I furiously type. Fifteen seconds ... ten seconds...

'Goeido – ready!'

Five seconds.

'Go. Now!'

And again, I hear the almighty pop and the light blinks out. But this time Neotnia's scream is so deafening it's as if she's being flayed alive. Yet it ceases with such abruptness it leaves a nightmarish silence in its wake, ripping my attention from my screen.

In the weak beam of Goeido's flashlight, Neotnia's skin grows even darker under the water. Yet something else happens, too. Her flesh ripples below the surface. The rippling travels her blackened skin like a tidal wave, continuing past the equator at her neck, across her pale face and beneath her bangs. And as the ripple traverses her body, in its wake her flesh hardens into irregular ridges and bumps, stacked into slim layers against one another, like a seashell.

But a split second later, her skin is soft, regular flesh again. Her head lulls in the tub, her chin dipping below the surface, her eyes shut as if sleeping.

I hear something from behind. It's Goeido. He's yelling. He shouts something again, and I snap back to my screen. I've wasted eleven seconds. Instantly my mind refocuses. My fingers type at a speed attempting to match the racing of the quantum processes playing out in my head. There's one minute and twelve seconds left. Forty-seven seconds. Thirty-two.

And my God – there's not enough time.

No matter what I throw at it, I can't open the splinter. I can't penetrate it.

Twenty-three.

Please don't let me fail.

Sixteen. It's not going to work.

Eleven. 'I need more time!'

Please...

Five seconds.

Please!

And Neotnia's code disappears like it was never even there.

*

The room is cold. And dark. But not as dark as her skin.

And it's been this way for hours.

But then, I feel something. Pressure on my hand. Softness. And Neotnia's blackened fingers – they move. They squeeze mine.

I'm sitting in the wooden chair, next to her bed.

Her eyes open and they see me.

She's quiet for a long while, looking at me. Then she sees how blackened her hand is. It's the colour of ink now. And she remembers.

'Did it work?' Her voice is so feeble I can hardly hear it. 'Were you able to open the splinter?'

I shake my head. 'There wasn't enough time.'

I hold my phone up. The screen's light glows blue against her pale face.

'But I was able to do something else,' I say. 'I was able to extract it.'

11 – We all look completely ordinary.

It felt like an early dawn. Whenever I glanced at Neotnia in the growing light, I couldn't get over how her skin looked. It was now as black as ink – not the lighter ashen colour of prior electrocutions. If she'd stood naked in the dark hallway, she'd have appeared as nothing more than a face floating in the void. Not that she could stand. By seven, she could barely sit up.

Last night, after the second toaster, any way I tried opening the splinter inside of her had no effect. As the timer ticked down, I thought I was going to fail. But that wasn't what scared me. It was knowing Neotnia would ask to be electrocuted three times in a row next. Yet after seeing what the second toaster did – hearing that horrible scream cut short – I knew even if she survived the second electrocution, she wouldn't survive a third.

But as the timer ticked, it suddenly hit me how stupid I'd been. Everything about Neotnia's being had been protected so far. Her quantum firewall keeps her hidden from networks. If you get past that, her codebase is sealed off from manipulation by presenting itself as one scrambled layer instead of three distinct layers. Even the pattern-recognition keys need additional compiling before they'll give up access to what they're protecting. Her father had to be the architect of all those security measures. And this splinter? If it's a container – if it's a file he hid in there – of course it'd have a security measure, too. It'd be encrypted. It's why I couldn't open it. At twenty-three seconds left, I realised I'd been trying to attack a quantum-encrypted container.

The thing is – I took the most foolish risk possible. As the timer ran down, I hardly thought before I acted. It was only after we carried Neotnia to bed that it hit me how much I'd played Russian roulette with her existence. I could very well have destroyed her by extracting the splinter, simply because it may have contained some vital thing she needed to function. I felt the same horror pass over me as when she winced in my arms in the darkness of my apartment, and I trembled and damned myself for the risk I took – and damned her, too, for having me do any of this.

Just past eleven this morning I was bent over my screen in Goeido's room, engrossed in my work on the splinter, when I heard a padding of soles. I turned to find Neotnia wearing a sumo-sized sweater. It hung past her knees, so only her inky-black shins and feet showed.

'Hides my skin pretty well, huh?' she said. 'Sweaters can be a life-saver.'

Tell me about it, I thought. 'Good to see you're on your feet.'

Her body stiffened at my reply, and for a moment she was quiet.

'That's it?' she said, seeing the splinter on my screen.

I nodded.

'I can feel it's gone.' She gazed at it, a cautious lightness in her voice. 'I felt it in bed last night, too. Right as you told me you'd extracted it – I realised the pressure I'd felt against my insides for weeks was suddenly absent, like when a big thorn that's been burrowing under your skin forever is finally removed.'

She had several questions about the splinter, and I answered them as best I could, then told her I was going to my place to shower and get some rest. I'd keep working on things there. It's hard to code when someone's hovering nearby. She seemed surprised I was leaving, but I don't know what that meant.

At my apartment, I fit the mirrored shard back into its fragmented body. In the splintered reflection, I inspected my wound. The bleeding had stopped, and a gelatinous mass had formed over the incision. I placed fresh gauze across it and looked at my echo.

That shadow still spread across me.

After napping for some time, I went for some fresh air. While I was out, Sony's rep called with an update. The politicians voicing concerns over American code being sold to an Asian nation had backed off after the company's D.C. lobbyists were able to 'resolve' the issue, which means the regulators have backed off, too. But the rep said we needed to act before the winds changed again. Sony's drawing up the final documents now, and they'll call tomorrow to schedule the signing.

I asked why the politicians had a problem at all. 'It's Japan, not China,' I said. 'Japan is one of America's closest allies.'

For a moment the rep remained silent.

'In times like these, one's looks make one suspect,' she replied.

As night came, I passed the café from the other side of the street. I saw Neotnia in her white gloves delivering an order to one of the booths and watched her for a long moment. Even though that terrible pressure no longer haunted her body, I couldn't help thinking how distracted she seemed. Though no customers entered, she looked towards the foyer every so often, as if she'd heard the door's bell clang.

It was as I watched her gloved hand refill a woman's coffee that I suddenly recalled what I'd seen after Goeido dropped the second toaster into the tub. Her skin appeared to ripple and harden into irregular layers, as if it were a rough seashell not yet polished by the ocean's currents. Then like that, it went smooth again – completely normal, except for its blackness. Its transformation seemed so palpable at first glance, yet with the adrenaline pumping through me, the darkening of her flesh and the wavering beam of Goeido's flashlight on the wrinkled bathwater's surface, it had to be a trick of the light – a symptom of my anxiety-ridden state.

I returned to my apartment and resumed work on the splinter. Since it's encrypted, it logically has a key that decrypts it. But even if you had the key, in the form the splinter was in, there wasn't any place – any lock – to insert it. That's when I got the idea to treat the splinter's code as a deconstructed executable and wrote a small app to compile it using classical code. And when I did that and ran the code as a classical executable, a password prompt appeared. In the hours since, this has told me two things.

One: the splinter definitely contains something her father didn't want others to see, which is why you encrypt something in the first place. What this something could be, who knows? It could be anything from blueprints for Neotnia's body to instructions on how he coded her to, well, literally anything. It could be his personal journal or a collection of pirated metagames, or a Japanese pastry cookbook, for all I know. It's impossible to tell what's inside until it's opened. And two: compiling the splinter into a classical executable didn't reveal any inadvertent backdoors. So even though the splinter uses standard quantum encryption, that encryption appears to be flawless. And that's the problem.

Like classical encryption back in the day, quantum encryption is just a really complicated algorithm that turns all the encrypted data into an indecipherable mess without the key. In this case, the key is the password. If the quantum encryption is solid, short of having the key, the only other way to open an encrypted file is by guessing the password. I could easily write an app to do a brute-force attack – to keep running through random passwords until the right one is guessed. But in this case, there'd be over a trillion-trillion-trillion possible passwords. And even though a brute-force attack could run through hundreds a second, it'd take over a billion years to get through even half of the possibilities.

In other words, short of miraculously guessing the password, nothing is going to open the splinter.

*

I jolt awake. Blue shadows drape the room, cast by the moon's light.

I barely glimpse the clock telling me it's four in the morning when I realise I'm sunk into my catcher's mitt of a sofa, my phone folded out into a laptop slid to the side of me. I grab it and type furiously, hoping what came to me as I slept doesn't vanish.

I pull up the splinter's encrypted executable.

I've been over-thinking things. The data inside is sealed off by the encryption, but its executable – the splinter's shell – that's what I explore.

And then I see it.

A name appears on my screen.

*

It's past ten when the bell above the café's door clangs and Inu gives me a little yap from his spot on the counter. Neotnia and Goeido are idly passing that dead hour between the early-morning coffee rush and the lunch flow.

'Ah, hi,' I say a bit awkwardly as if it's been a year and not only a day since I last saw them. '*Konnichiwa*, Goeido,' I add.

I'm not using my translation app. It's unlikely Sony would peak into the quantum hive they're lending me use of, and I encrypt all my data anyway; still, I don't want a digital trail of any more of our conversations – just in case, and especially after the increased interest from the regulators. When I ask how she's feeling, Neotnia slides the sleeve of her yellow turtleneck up then pulls down the white glove beneath, exposing the underside of her forearm. Her skin has lost that inky blackness and now simply looks as if it's been saturated with ash again.

'It's slower this time, but I'm healing.'

I nod a little too impatiently. But then I hold up my phone. 'I have something.'

'You were able to open it?'

'No,' I shake my head. 'The encryption is solid. But I managed to skim some of the splinter's metadata that was poorly obfuscated in the file's executable. Most of the metadata was a jumbled mess. I couldn't see any dates or IP addresses. But there was one thing I *was* able to pull from it: Emiko Ikari.'

Neotnia digests the name for a moment. Goeido says something, and she translates what I've said.

'Does it mean anything to either of you?'

'No.' Neotnia shakes her head, then translates for Goeido. He shakes his head, too, and replies. 'Ikari isn't a common last name,' she translates.

'So that's obviously not your father's name then.'

'No. His name is Satō. Haruto Satō. "Emiko" is feminine.'

I nod. 'There's another thing. In the metadata, the name wasn't in kanji; it was in Roman script.'

Goeido replies with a question when Neotnia translates. But I can tell it's a question she has, too. 'What does that mean?'

For a moment I'm silent because, well, I don't know for sure. But I can guess. 'It could mean the computer that applied the splinter's metadata was being used to communicate with someone, or some system, in the west. That may mean someone else knows about you, too. Someone in Europe. Or America, maybe.' I know what Neotnia's wondering. It's the same thing I've been wondering. Is that a good thing? Is that a bad thing? Could it, in some way, be related to her father's disappearance?

Neotnia translates for Goeido without looking at him, lost in her own thoughts. He nods and, for a long moment, stands there, considering her. It's the same way I used to catch my grandma staring at me when my parents were in Angola – that sad compassion on her face. Finally, he speaks.

'After Haruto failed to return, we searched for ways we might contact him,' Neotnia translates. 'He was friends with my parents, but they passed away years before. And all I had for him was an old post-office box address. I knew he was a scientist, but he never specified what type of work he did, nor for whom. We mainly talked of our love for sumo and Shinto tales. Haruto rarely spoke of himself. So, we tried searching the web for him, but Haruto appears to have no kind of digital footprint. Of course, his name doesn't help. Looking for a "Haruto Satō" in Japan is like looking for a "John Smith" in America. There are tens of thousands of them.'

Goeido pauses and looks at us.

'But, as I said, "Ikari" isn't common...'

For the next hour, Neotnia uses my laptop to search for information about anyone named Emiko Ikari. She does this in both English and Japanese. Occasionally, she calls out things for Goeido to scribble down on a scratchpad he's taken from the counter. He only breaks his role as secretary to look after the occasional customer.

'I think that's it,' Neotnia says. 'I think I've found all of them.'

'How many?'

'*Go*,' she says, looking at the scratchpad. 'Five. Only five. But one "Emiko Ikari" is from the eighteenth century, and another died in the late twentieth. That leaves three living Emiko Ikari's – and I've found numbers for all of them.'

She folds the laptop down into my phone and considers the three numbers scribbled on the scratchpad.

'What are you going to say?'

'I'll introduce myself and say I'm trying to reach Emiko Ikari. Then I'll ask if she knows Father.'

I wasn't expecting things to move this fast and look from her to Goeido and back again, but Neotnia dials the first number before I can reply. The ring echoes against her ear as she stares into the middle distance between us, listening to the noise like the fate of the world rests on someone picking up.

Then, someone does.

For an instant Neotnia freezes, but she regains her composure nearly as quickly. I hear her say her name and 'Emiko Ikari'.

The voice on the other end is silent for a short time before it gives a muffled reply. Neotnia nods and says a short something back before hanging up.

'It was an older man,' she explains. 'He said he was very sorry, but I had the wrong number, and there's no one by the name of "Emiko Ikari" there.'

She dials the second number. This time the conversation is longer, and Neotnia's voice softens as it progresses. An amused expression crosses Goeido's face. It's easy to hear the conversation since the voice on the other end is speaking so loudly.

'That was Emiko Ikari,' Neotnia says after the call ends. 'She's nine, and she had to go because she needs to help her mother give her baby brother a bath.'

Neotnia looks at the last number on the scratchpad. Her lips tighten, then she dials.

Someone picks up. It's an older voice. A woman's. Neotnia gives her simple greeting and statement. The voice replies. It repeats, 'Emiko Ikari.'

Neotnia sits up straight. She speaks again and I hear 'Haruto Satō'. After a moment, the voice says 'Neotnia' and 'Haruto Satō' and then 'Haruto Satō' again. There's a silence on the other end, and I see Neotnia's jaw tighten.

The voice says something, pauses, and more follows, 'Haruto Satō' among it.

But with a little nod, Neotnia replies, and hangs up.

'It was an elderly woman whose name is Emiko Ikari,' Neotnia says, and I hear the disappointment in her words. 'She said she had never heard of anyone named Neotnia, and when I told her I was looking for an Emiko Ikari who knew my father, she said she'd only known one Haruto Satō – back when they were both teenagers. But he's been dead for fifty years.'

She slides my phone across the table to me. As Goeido looks at her, Neotnia gives an apologetic shake of her head and explains what's happened. He doesn't seem to know how to reply either.

I feel like pointing out that at least she has the splinter out of her now. Yet it feels trite to say such a thing. I suspect she'd rather bear that pain than continue to wonder where her father is and why he abandoned her. And at least with the pain there was the hope that something inside her might lead to him.

Neotnia gazes out of the window. Outside people crisscross on the sidewalk. Tall people, short people, thin people, thick people.

'I know you said you've searched online for him before,' I say, 'but have you guys tried other ways?'

Neotnia's gaze holds on the pedestrians for several moments more before turning to me, as if she's only now registered my question.

'We found out the building with the P.O. box that Goeido had used to correspond with Father doesn't exist anymore. So, we thought about finding childhood addresses, but Goeido doesn't know what middle school his parents and my father attended, though he thinks he remembers his mother once saying her old school had shut years earlier. But even if it didn't and it was still around and we could find it, the school probably wouldn't have records that far back. Father would have been in middle school before the world went digital.'

I nod, but don't say anything.

'A few months ago, I talked Goeido into going to Kamakura,' she continues. 'He convinced me to wait at a family restaurant in the town centre, just to be safe, while he went to my old house. The person who lives there now bought it in February through a fore-closure auction. She was told the house had been vacant for four months by then, which suggests Father never returned to it. She didn't know anything about the previous occupier. Before moving there, she'd lived in Sapporo her entire life.'

Neotnia tucks some hair behind an ear, and we all go quiet again for some time. In the silence, I gently flip my phone between my hands.

And then it rings.

'Sorry. Sony said they'd be calling to schedule the signing.'

I answer. There's a long pause from the other end.

'Neotnia?'

It's a woman's voice.

Goeido and Neotnia look at me, their mouths parted. They can hear the voice through the receiver.

I pull the phone from my ear to check the caller ID, then check the numbers on the scratchpad. *It's this one*, I silently mouth, tapping the first.

Neotnia's jaw goes slack.

'Ah, sorry, hold on,' I say into the phone. 'I don't speak Japanese.'

I pass the phone to Neotnia, who takes it from me as if I've handed her an alien artifact. Then she places it to her ear.

'*Moshi moshi*,' she says. '*Neotnia desu.*'

The conversation is short, and many times the woman seems to cut Neotnia off. But I do make out one word: Hiroshima. After another exchange, Neotnia pulls the phone from her ear and looks at it. For a moment it's as if she's forgotten how to speak.

'It was Emiko Ikari,' she finally says. 'She wanted to know why I called for her. I said, "Because I'm looking for my father. His name is—" But she told me to stop talking. She said not to tell her where I was. She asked if I could get to Hiroshima tomorrow. I told her, yes, and she said she'll meet me at the northern end of the Peace Park at one in the afternoon. She said don't give anyone my name. Don't let anyone know I'm coming. And when I asked how I'll know who she is, she replied, "I'll know who you are", and hung up.'

Neotnia tells Goeido what she's told me. They have a discussion in which 'Hiroshima' features heavily. They both look at me.

'I take it you guys are headed to Hiroshima?'

'*Hai*,' Neotnia says. 'But you'll come, too ... right?'

I have no idea what to say.

'I don't think there's anything else I can do for you, though,' I finally manage. 'I can put the splinter on Goeido's phone, so you have it. And, you know, all this really isn't any of my business, anyway. Besides, I need to be in Tokyo for the signing with Sony.'

'But—'

'But what else could I do?' I shrug. 'I can't break the encryption. There's no more exposed metadata to find – I've looked. I can't see any other way I can be of service.'

Neotnia's lips part.

'*Be of service?*' Her clear eyes are frozen on mine.

And that's when I realize she hasn't translated for Goeido a single word I've said.

In the silence between us, Neotnia inspects the shiny whiteness of her gloves, as if seeing something that isn't there. The corners of her jaw tighten.

'You found the name. Aren't you curious who Emiko Ikari is? Aren't you curious what *I* am?' She stares. 'You say my code's impossible, yet here I sit, right in front of you, clear as day. You – one of the top minds in computing on the planet. The *boy-genius*. Yet, you're not the least bit curious to meet someone who might know how I was *created*? How I can stand in front of someone without them having a clue about me? How I can stand in front of you? How that *impossible* you speak of was made possible?'

And holding her lips tight, her blue-grey eyes on mine are un-wavering.

Twenty minutes later, I'm at my apartment. On my way, I called the Sony rep. She confirmed the signing won't be for another two days. Neotnia said we can catch the *Shinkansen* from Shibuya Station in two hours. From there, it's only five to Hiroshima, where we'll get a hotel for the night and then meet this Emiko Ikari in the Peace Park tomorrow afternoon. We'll be back in Tokyo late tomorrow night, well in time for me to meet with Sony the next day.

I don't pack much. A sweater and change of clothes. Enough to get me through the night. It's warmer down south so my hoodie will be fine. On my way out, I snatch my toothbrush from the bath-room. My shadow still lingers in the splintered mirror.

This is a bad idea.

When I return to the café, Neotnia and Goeido are in the foyer discussing something. She wears her long denim skirt that almost touches the soles of her shoes. On top, one of the shark sweatshirts is pulled over her yellow turtleneck. Along with her white gloves, all parts of her still-ashen-black skin are covered. Goeido's changed, too, into his kimono and wooden sandals with split-toed socks. I'd read, and guess it's true, that it's how all sumos dress whenever they leave their home. Slumped on the floor next to him is a half-filled duffle bag.

'What are you guys talking about?'

'Whether we should bring Inu,' Neotnia answers.

I feel my jaw drop.

'Are you kidding?'

'No,' she gives me a look. 'Why?'

'Look at us.' I point to the window at the front of the foyer.

In the reflection are three transparent ghosts. One, a giant, famous-yet-disgraced ex-sumo who literally looks like he walked out of an Akira Kurosawa film. Another, an awkward, American, geek magazine cover model who sticks out in Japan like a sore thumb. And the last: a beautiful android wearing shiny theatrical gloves and a shark sweatshirt with fins for pockets. You couldn't assemble a more apt team of outcasts if you tried.

Goeido says something and Neotnia translates. 'What about us?'

I give them a look. 'Oh, sorry. My mistake. We all look completely ordinary. What we should do is add an android dog with a ridiculous haircut to the mix. Because our group doesn't stand out enough.'

Neotnia's about to protest, but I cut her off.

'Look, we don't know who this Emiko Ikari lady is, what she wants. If she even knows your father. We don't know what's waiting for us. But we do know she sounded kind of paranoid. So, I'm just saying we shouldn't stand out any more than we already do. Besides, Inu is built to find you. But we know where you are – with us. Taking him would only serve to call more attention to ourselves, OK?'

Fifteen minutes later, we're at Shibuya Station – without Inu. The place is more crowded than I've ever seen – yet no one seems to be moving anywhere.

Neotnia and Goeido listen along with the other commuters as an announcement comes over the PA. Soon everyone is staring into their screens, looking less annoyed and more worried. When I look at my own screen, I see the breaking news alert.

It's another cyberattack. This time the bullet train lines in Hokkaido, northern Japan were the target. NHK is reporting that the U.S. is blaming China, who's denying any involvement. Regardless, as a precaution, all *Shinkansen* across the country are suspended. Only local trains will run.

Neotnia's distress is apparent.

'How long will it take to get to Hiroshima using local trains?' I say.

'Over a day with connections,' she translates Goeido's answer. 'But everyone's going to be using local trains, so delays are inevitable.'

That dark shadow descends across her face, and I realise it's been some time since I've seen it.

I pull up Avance Maps on my phone. 'A car can get us there in nine hours. So, we call one and we still get to Hiroshima tonight – just a bit later.'

But when we get outside, virtually everyone has the same idea. It's half an hour before a car even responds. And when it finally does, it's a little rinky-dink one so old its solar panels are literally bolted onto its roof.

Our trip is off to a great start.

12 – Beautiful, shining kami in the sky.

We're a little over four hours into the drive. Our car is a piece of junk, but at least it's roomy. Neotnia and I are on the couch facing the direction of travel. Goeido's on the one across from us, taking up its entire length. His chins jostle like Jell-O as we go over a bump on the road, yet it doesn't wake him. He dozed off an hour ago. He said car rides make him sleepy, as if someone's rocking him like a baby. I tried to picture the size of the person it would take to cradle someone Goeido's size but couldn't do it.

'The rice fields are pretty,' Neotnia says.

'Yeah,' I answer but remain staring out my window. I've been quiet since we left Tokyo, content to watch as the infinite city gave way to grassy plains, which gave way to mountains and then to grassy plains again, and now, rice fields. Yet the rice fields are quickly coming to an end, too. Still, I keep gazing out the window, watching Japan snap by.

'Are you hungry?' Neotnia says after our car has turned off the highway and onto a smaller byroad with little traffic. 'Goeido packed some food for us.'

A car behind us briefly drifts into the opposite lane, speeds by, and then drifts back.

'I'm fine,' I say.

The hum of another car approaches, momentarily aligns with ours, and then shoots ahead. The passengers in all the modern vehicles that overtake us look amused by the ancient solar array bolted onto our roof, as if we might as well be in a covered wagon.

'They're his egg-salad sandwiches,' Neotnia adds. 'It's a specialty of his. Have you had them before?'

'I'll try one later,' I reply, gazing at massive agribots in the distance, harvesting some kind of crop as the orange sun inches lower.

Neotnia makes a small noise in her throat but doesn't reply.

Time passes. The road hums. Goeido's chins jostle. More cars speed past. The sun sinks lower, turning an orange-red. The crop in the distance spreads up to the roadside – a brown wheat. It reminds me of home.

It's some time before I finally glance at Neotnia. She's removed her gloves in the safe solitude of our car. She's looking out her window again and I turn back towards mine. In my reflection, I see that shadow.

Coming with them was a mistake. Since I found out the truth, I've, for the most part, been able to avoid dealing with my feelings. I've been able to focus on the immediate situation: learning about her systems, extracting the splinter, accessing its metadata. And when I wasn't working on that, I could retreat to my apartment. I could take my walks and get her off my mind. Mostly, anyway. But now, trapped in this piece of junk, sitting right beside her, not having anything to be distracted by, it's hard to ignore the elephant in the room. It's hard not to think about us.

I'd never had such a rapport with someone – and someone who doesn't mind my body, no less. And when I discovered her body had a difference even more distinct than mine, I could live with that. It didn't bug me. I liked her too much. But her turning out to be an android? *What are the chances of that?* has run through my mind a hundred times, yet it's a ridiculous question. It literally must be the first time in history this has happened. The data point is one.

I glance at Neotnia again, still gazing from her window, watching tall stalks of wheat zip by. She brings an ashen finger towards her face and scratches an itch next to her eyebrow, then her fingers curl back into her sleeve. Such an ostensibly simple action is so biomechanically complex, for a moment I want to believe that what she's revealed must be a dream; that I'm in fact still in my apartment on that rainy night; her warm, slumbering body wrapped around mine. But my chest sinks as cold reality returns, and I'm left with that despondent awe at just how indistinguishable she is from a human being.

But never even mind the how. *Why* is she indistinguishable? Why would someone replicate a human so perfectly? What's the point? A robot doesn't need the dexterity or mirror-likeness to carry out tasks even if the morphology of a human is suited for the job. After all, though some bots have the form and dexterity to drive those old cars with pedals and steering wheels, you don't need them to. You can just get rid of the controls and turn the entire car into one big robot and have it drive itself, like this one's doing now – no anthropomorphic chauffeur needed. It's the same way you don't need a robot butler to open the door when you arrive home or run the bathwater or turn out the lights when you go to bed. All that can be accomplished by simple AI built into the house's infrastructure.

A sex bot? There are already robots built for sex, and while they aren't as lifelike as Neotnia, they get the job done. Plus, a sex bot wouldn't be missing a sex organ. Not to mention, there's no need for sex bots to be capable of forming complex emotions or thoughts. A sex bot's purpose, after all, is to provide sex. It doesn't need to mimic all ranges of human behaviour for that. Besides, just as with a bot chauffeur or a bot butler, a sex bot that's indistinguishable from a human is overkill. Synthetic sex toys already mimic the look, feel, and action of human sex organs. Those combined with metalenses make it look like the real thing – like a real person – is doing whatever you want, right in front of your eyes. You can even change the look of your metapartner at will. Hell, thanks to deepfakes, you can make it so your favourite celebrity is engaging in all your sexual desires. At the end of the day, a lifelike sex bot just wouldn't be as versatile as what's already available.

So why create Neotnia? What's her purpose? Why does she exist?

A ray from the sinking sun flares on the window during a rare gap in the fields, but it passes just as quickly. The wheat blurring by is massive, and it occurs to me that this is the genetically modified variety that Joe mentioned Japan grows to help feed Angola. The tips of its stalks easily top out several feet above our car's solar array.

Across from me, Goeido still snoozes away like a big baby made of pudding. I stare at his placid face for some time. It's incredible how at peace he seems with all this. Neotnia's existence makes perfect sense to him because of his belief system. She is a wonder. She is awe-inspiring. To him, that simply means she's kami – and that's all the explanation he needs. In a way, I envy Goeido for that. How wonderful is it not to feel the need to ask 'how' or 'why' something is as it is? What blissful freedom that must be.

Neotnia folds some black locks behind her ear, then returns her ashen hand to her lap, watching the wheat pass by.

Before, I thought I understood the world. At least where it was heading. But now? Now, what do I know? Joe said by the time a person reaches his age the world becomes unrecognisable. Yet for me mere weeks have passed for that to happen. Would my life be better if I'd never gotten the ear cleaning from her? If I'd never known how much I didn't know? And if I had never entered the café on that cold night, where would I be right now? Where would they be? What would the three of us be doing if not for that chance meeting?

Neotnia turns and catches me lingering on her. Her lips are neutral as she considers me, almost as if she's trying to read my mind, but soon they yield a soft smile.

And that smile – that soft, inviting smile – it reminds me of something. It reminds me of the night of the ear cleaning. That night, she paid me no more interest than any other customer. Yet when I returned for my backpack the following night, she held that inviting smile on me virtually any time I looked at her.

And now, of all things, that smile, it makes me think of Mora.

Mora and our sophomore year coding project.

Neotnia tilts her head as she takes in whatever expression it is that's come over my face, yet soon she turns back towards the wheat outside. And looking at her black hair, I think of Mom. When she finally started talking about Angola, she told me how some of the Stung would be extra nice to her, the foreign doctor, nicer than they'd be to even their own family – because they were desperate to curry favour with the person who could help them...

My chest stings. 'When it comes to coding, you're a genius. You know you are – *the magazine even said so,*' Neotnia said as she pleaded for my help.

I'm a damned fool.

I retreat to my window, half expecting the cold now gnawing at my stomach to show as frost on the fields of wheat. Yet all I find are the sun's orange-red rays warming them.

I can feel Neotnia's eyes settle on me again.

'Hey,' she finally says, her pinkie finger nudging my hand where it rests between us. 'What are you thinking about?'

I look at her. The road's hum fills the void around us.

'Nothing.' I pull my hand away. Still, she holds her gaze on me as if she can draw the information she wants right from my pupils.

I pivot towards the fields again. And, at my back, she says, 'Is everything OK?'

I don't answer. It's several moments before she speaks again. When she does, her voice sounds small.

'I wish you'd talk to me like you used to.'

'What – like back in the good old days?' I snap. 'You make it sound like we've known each other for decades. Remember, you're only two, so that's impossible.'

It's as if I've knocked the wind right out of her. Her lips part, and when she speaks next, she sounds on the verge of tears.

'Why are you being so mean to me?'

'Let me ask you a question. The first night I met you, you didn't even bother speaking English. Yet when I returned for my backpack, you couldn't give me enough attention. Matter of fact, you were pretty damn eager to hang out. So, how long after discovering my passport and the magazine did it occur to you that I could be one of the few people on the planet who might be able to help you? And how long did it take to decide to manipulate me into liking you so I would? I'm just curious – you're quantum-based, so were those decisions instantaneous, or did they take a few milliseconds to compute?'

Neotnia's chest swells and her throat tightens. She turns away, hiding her face.

When she finally looks at me again, her eyes seem ready to pop.

'It's true the magazine gave me the idea that if nothing Goeido and I were doing could work, then maybe you could help—'

'Congrats,' I cut her off. 'Using someone is the most human thing you can do. You really are indistinguishable from the rest of us.'

The way she sucks in a sharp breath, it's like I've stabbed her. Yet before she can utter another word the car jerks so violently we have to brace against the edge of Goeido's couch to stop from sliding from ours. An instant later the car rapidly decelerates onto the shoulder of the road. A hard bump sends my backpack sliding across the floor. Another tips Goeido's duffle bag into the aisle between us. It's several more bumps before we come to a dead stop and the car's synthetic voice sounds.

'What the hell?' I dig for my phone as Goeido makes a throaty noise, waking. He looks from Neotnia to me to the static wheat and back again, confused by the scene all around. When he speaks, Neotnia just shakes her head, the popped tears now sliding down her flushed cheeks, and she raises a hand, as if saying, 'Not now.'

'Goddammit,' I say as my phone connects to the car's systems. I crawl over the duffle bag and grasp the handle at Neotnia's side, almost tripping onto the roadway as I exit. I pass the rear of the car and peer at the remaining light over the fields. The pale bodies of the moon and stations have already revealed themselves. My head sinks.

I look back towards the car. Neotnia and Goeido are now beside it, staring like they're expecting me to drop some knowledge that'll get them out of their latest jam. Goeido's voice momentarily breaks the whistling of the breeze, then he looks at me blankly like a big dumb log waiting for something to happen.

When he speaks again, my blood boils.

'BATTERY DEAD,' I shout, not waiting for Neotnia's translation. 'Dead battery. Dead. Car no move. Get it? No vroom-vroom. Comprehend?'

But no. Nothing. No reaction. Goeido's face might as well be drawn on with a marker.

Neotnia's eyes narrow. 'He was only asking if it *was* the battery.' The breeze has already dried the wetness on her cheeks. 'He just wanted to be certain what was wrong.'

'What's wrong?' My temper rises. 'Well, our ride's an old piece of junk, and the human hippo here is a bit bigger than most people. All that extra mass drains the car's battery faster because it takes more energy to move him than a regular person,' I say, knowing full well Goeido can't understand.

Neotnia's jaw clenches. The breeze sweeps her bangs. 'You're. Being. Mean.'

She's right, but I'm angry. About so much. And we usually take our anger out on those who least deserve it.

I shake my head and look up and down the road. The wheat goes on forever. I open Avance Maps. The closest city is a place called Okayama, but on foot it's almost six hours away. If the car were running, we'd be less than four hours from Hiroshima. Right now, we're literally in the middle of nowhere. When I lower my phone, the android and sumo still have their eyes on me like I must have just performed some magic techno juju that'll rescue us all. I don't even bother saying anything.

I scan up and down the road again, its wall of tall brown stalks swaying in the breeze. Above us, the moon and stations have already taken on more definition. Somewhere closer, a crow caws.

My blood stirs. I think of what will be the most important moment of my life, back in Tokyo, in less than forty-eight hours. I think of what Neotnia admitted. I think of so many things.

'What am I even doing here?' I shout into the sky.

And Goeido, with his big, dumb, expressionless face, looks at Neotnia and says something.

'Is there a way to get the car running?' she translates as if bracing for some blow.

Another rush of irritation stirs me, but I hold it inside, waiting for it to pass. I pull up the car's systems. The solar array is literally a bolted-on, refurbished, second-hand add-on from an even older model. Given the age of its cells, even under the brightest sunlight at least forty percent of the energy it catches must be lost as heat before the car's battery has a chance to store it. And the car's AI itself looks like it hasn't been updated in years. No wonder it couldn't accurately monitor its energy output for the heavier load.

I shake my head. If you don't have solar, you need an alternate energy source to recharge the battery, and I haven't seen a charging point since we turned onto the byroad. I let out a breath, thinking out loud. 'Not unless there's some way to transfer some of whatever energy is powering you into the car's cells...'

As soon as the words escape my mouth Neotnia's eyes narrow.

'I'm not a battery,' she bites through clenched jaw.

I didn't mean it the way it sounded, but I don't know how to reply.

She crosses her arms and turns away. Somewhere over the fields, that crow caws again as the breeze rustles the wheat. When Neotnia speaks next, it's in Japanese. Yet from the way Goeido replies, it's as if he doesn't like what she's said – at all. He even looks at me and in blunt English says 'no' as his hands slice the air.

'No?' I say. 'No what?'

'I told him we should call a replacement car, even if it takes several hours to get here,' Neotnia says, with little more than a glance at me. 'But he doesn't like that idea.'

I look at them both.

'Well, why not?'

'Because in Japan, when a car breaks down and the company sends another, you need to file a report about the occupants and circumstances, and give everyone's biometrics, for insurance purposes. And who knows how mine will appear.'

Goeido adds something. 'The roadside is also a problem,' Neotnia translates. 'If we stay here, another car might report us.'

I nod for several moments, letting that sink in.

'Well, that's just terrific then. That's fantastic. And does the ex-sumo have any idea how to power the car back up? Because the light's almost gone, and in the morning, it'll take at least an hour for the decade-old solar panels to charge the battery enough to get us to Hiroshima.'

Neotnia says something to Goeido, and for a moment, he stands there, contemplating. Then he turns towards the car and eyes it front to back like he's sizing up an opponent in the *dohyō*. And as if coming to some decision, he closes one of the barn doors, then the other, and I step out of the way as he walks towards me and gets behind the car. He says something to Neotnia, placing his hands under the bumper.

And I swear, even though I've seen a decapitated android dog and a girl without a vagina, what comes next ranks up there as one of the most surreal things I've ever witnessed. The sumo literally lifts the car's rear from the ground and sideways duck-walks it ninety degrees so its front now faces the wheat. Then he begins pushing it into the field, the tall stalks bending under the car like they're nothing. As he progresses, the stalks spring back up in the car's wake, almost as straight as they were. About twenty feet in, Goeido's grunts cease. I hear the opening and closing of the car's doors. When he next appears, he brushes aside the wheat at the road's edge like it's a curtain, his duffle bag slung over his shoulder. He says something to Neotnia before turning back and disappearing into the field again.

'OK, now what's he doing?' I say as Neotnia walks in Goeido's direction.

'He's going to build a fire.' She turns towards me at the wheat's edge. 'We're here for the night. Are you planning to help, or just complain?'

*

I've got to admit, I'm impressed with Goeido's resourcefulness. Apparently he camped a lot as a child. Or something. He spoke as he mapped out a ring-shaped area in the field next to the car. He stomped his foot on a stalk then slid his sole along the shaft to keep it bent flat, like he was making a crop circle. As we helped, I asked Neotnia what he was saying – and it was a lot. But she simply kept her eyes on the wheat bending under her feet and replied, 'He camped when he was little.'

Within twenty minutes, we'd finished flattening the designated area, which gave us a nice large space to sit. Goeido then ripped the stalks at the centre of our crop circle from the ground. This left a patch of dry earth about five feet in diameter. He tore the thick bases from the stalks and stacked them like a log cabin on the clearing, then packed additional stalks vertically into the cabin until it was nice and dense.

And as the last of dusk's glow disappeared, Goeido reached inside for the car's cigarette lighter. A few minutes later we had a small fire that provided enough light, if not warmth. The flames are low enough, and the surrounding wheat tall and dense enough, that no passing cars will see our camp in the darkness. Besides, way out here, there aren't many cars at all.

Goeido's sitting cross-legged, his back resting against the side of the car. I'm to his three o'clock, and Neotnia is directly across from me, at his nine. The tiny fire lies between us. It's funny, Goeido seems positively at ease being out here, around the campfire, under the stars. In the orange glow, he's got a peaceful look about him, like a happy Buddha. Neotnia, on the other hand, has her legs drawn up to her chest, her head resting on her knees, and looks glumly into the flames. I'm sure I don't look much happier.

After a period of silence, Goeido says something, almost joyfully, and points to the fire and the wheat and the sky. He speaks for so long it's like he's narrating a nature documentary. When he finishes, he looks at me and then Neotnia, waiting for her translation.

'He likes camping,' she says without taking her eyes off the fire.

I nod politely to Goeido but don't say anything.

Goeido attempts a few more conversation starters: 'He says the thick base of the wheat stalk burns slowly, which results in a long fire.' But neither Neotnia nor I add our own contributions beyond a nod or two. After attempting one more – 'He says it's good to get back to nature sometimes' – and without much reaction from us, Goeido rolls his eyes in the firelight. A few moments later, he reaches inside the duffle bag then stretches his hand towards me.

It holds something wrapped in wax paper. He signals it's for me and I take it. Even before unwrapping it, I can smell it's an egg-salad sandwich. He hands Neotnia another one and takes a third for himself.

Neotnia gives him an appreciative little nod. '*Arigatōgozaimashita*.' When we free our sandwiches from their papers, it's clear he's given me the largest one by far.

'Goeido,' I hold my eyes on him across the fire. I'm ashamed of how I treated him earlier. '*Arigatō*.'

He returns the tiniest smile and waves his hand. '*Kinishinaide*,' he says, adding, 'John.' Neotnia gives him a little glance at this.

We eat silently as the breeze rustles the tops of the wheat surrounding our encampment. The only other noise comes from the crackling of the campfire. Between bites I'll steal glances at Goeido, who peers peacefully into the flames, and at Neotnia, who avoids me entirely. And yeah, I feel like a dick for how I acted earlier. I was angry because I'm hurt. It's no fun being used. But now I remember something else Mom said when she told me about the way some of the Stung treated her. She said desperate people don't always make the most righteous choices; and before judging them what we need to ask is would we make those same choices if we were in their position? Most of the time, Mom said, if we're honest with ourselves, we'll find that we'd do exactly as they did.

Across the fire, Neotnia's face glows orange in the light, munching on her sandwich.

I guess not knowing why you exist or where your creator went and having something inside your body causing you constant suffering is as high up there on the desperation scale as can be.

I linger on that thought for a long time, and when I glance at Neotnia again I realise that, while she's on her last bite, I'm still only halfway through my sandwich because it's so much larger.

'Are you still hungry?' I say, holding out my half-eaten portion. 'Do you want some of mine?' But Neotnia barely glances at me, refusing my offer with a raise of her hand. She folds her legs back up to her chest and rests her chin on her knees again, wrapping her arms around her shins as she resumes her gaze into the flames. I make the same offer to Goeido, who looks at me to be sure. But I pat my stomach. 'I'm stuffed,' I say.

After finishing it, Goeido licks his fingers. All the food now gone, we silently study the fire. Yet soon the lack of conversation just feels awkward, so I pull out my phone and tune into an American oldies stream. It's got all the hits from the aughts, teens, and twenties. Admittedly, most of the songs are a bit upbeat for a situation where two-thirds of us aren't speaking, but it's nice to have some distraction, and the music doesn't seem to be bothering anyone. As a matter of fact, Goeido appears to be keen on it.

After a while, a tune comes on that causes an odd sensation to rise inside my chest. For the first several notes, I simply think it's the type of song I know I'm going to like, no matter what the vocals are. But as those notes progress, it hits me that that odd sensation is one of nostalgia. The song playing is one I haven't heard since I was a kid. And God, you know how it is with music – rediscovering a catchy tune you loved but forgot about? Quite involuntarily, the side of my foot taps the flattened wheat underneath my crossed legs, and that tapping only becomes more pronounced as additional notes come to the fore.

Enjoying the song, too, Goeido declares, 'Good, good!' in rough English as he nods in sync to my foot's motion. Neotnia tilts her head atop her drawn-up knees at Goeido's reaction, and a soft smile spreads across her lips. It's the first time she's smiled since the car broke down. And Goeido, he smiles back, then turns and glances at my foot still tapping away. 'Good,' he grins, nodding to the beat.

And fuck. I can feel it. I know what's about to happen, the notes surging through my body like platelets swirling in my bloodstream. The memory of where this song always played solidifies as its vocals begin. And, damn, those lyrics:

> *This life, it's a never-ending game*
> *On a world that's not to blame*

It spins and spins
For what's past is prologue, yet the future is just the same.
Just the same

Goeido's and Neotnia's eyes widen as I spring up, my foot now tapping firmly in place on the bent wheat. And I know what's coming. I know I won't be able to control it. So, I warn them that this song is the earliest memory I have. Tapping my foot on the flattened wheat, I say, 'I was six, and my parents were young and in love, and streaming this in our living room – Dad holding Mom in his arms, twirling her around. They'd explain how it was their favourite song when they were teenagers. It was from a popular musical back in their day. It's the song that played when they first met.'

And I don't even know if Neotnia is translating any of this or not. I'm too absorbed in the memory of my family being whole. 'They were so, so happy, and it made me so happy seeing them dance to this.' I close my eyes and let the music swell through me. And God – I warned this was coming. When the next refrain arrives, as that baritone voice erupts from my phone's speakers, I raise an invisible microphone to my mouth and lip-sync:

But that all changed, for you and me
All that changed when you called out my name
Called out my name.
You took me in your arms and pulled me in close
And lifted me from the world bound to most.
Bound to most.

I can't stop. The music's taken over. And when I open my eyes, now Goeido's big head is bouncing to the beats like he's in the front row at Radio City Music Hall. Then the six-foot-four sumo, he lumbers up and joins me as I grab my invisible mic more tightly:

And around this world, we swept
Like two moons above, as everyone slept

We danced in endless light
As everyone below alternated between day and night.
Day and night.

And shit, here we go. Now me and Goeido are bopping, his sandalled feet stomping the ground with the power of an elephant's.
Beneath my hoodie my skin flops as I dance and my wound stings,
but I don't care. And soon our eyes turn to Neotnia, who looks like
she's stuck between deciding whether we've gone mad or if we're
the funniest double act ever. But Goeido gives her a goofy look and
takes her hand from its perch around her knee and pulls her up as
if she's weightless – and the music infects her, too. She dances in
her shark sweatshirt, laughing at the show she's now part of.

This veil is thin, between us the world above, and the one below
Yet the great trick is, nobody knows
It's why, this life, it's a never-ending game
On a world that is not to blame
It spins and spins
For what's past is prologue, yet the future is just the same.
The future is just the same.

And seeing that laughter on Neotnia's face and Goeido's jovial
expression – well, I realise part of me is glad to be here, no matter
the circumstances. Part of me feels like I belong around this campfire with this ex-sumo and android, just as I felt that sense of
belonging when this song last played so long ago.

But that all changed, for you and me
All that changed when you called out my name
And because of that, look what came
Look at the world we made.
Look at the world we made; it won't ever be the same
It won't ever be the same.

As the song ends, we collapse back onto the flattened wheat, catching our breaths. Goeido pulls three water bottles from the duffle bag, and for a long time we quietly sip, all a little happier than before. It's the first time since Halloween that we've all worn smiles at once.

Squeezing the last drop from his bottle, Goeido's gaze lingers on the sky and then he points towards it.

'He says you never see this amount of stars in Tokyo. It's easy to forget how many are always right above our heads,' Neotnia translates – a familiar softness back in her voice.

Goeido inhales a deep breath through his nostrils and holds it as if savouring the chilled night air. Releasing it, his gaze returns to the stars.

Neotnia translates his words: 'When I was a little boy, my parents didn't dance, but they loved to take me camping. I remember being around a campfire much like this one and gazing at the stars with them. I noticed how some showed brighter than others, and some twinkled at different rates. I asked what they were, and my parents told me the stars were kami. "Beautiful, shining kami in the sky. All different. All unique. Just like us." I had never heard the word before, so assumed "kami" was simply another name for "people". After that, whenever we went camping, I would always tell my parents I couldn't wait until nightfall so I could see the beautiful shining people in the sky.'

Goeido's still gazing towards the heavens when Neotnia finishes translating. She smiles at him and says something, bringing him down to earth. He nods to her.

'I told him that's a nice story,' she says. 'I'd never heard it before.'

For a long time, we sit quietly again, gazing at the people in the sky as the campfire crackles and the gentle breeze blows the tops of the wheat. The way its tall stalks encircle our encampment, the stations can't be seen. It's just as the world must have looked when Goeido peered into the night as a child.

After some time, he places his hands on his thighs, giving them a pat. He exchanges a few words with Neotnia then rises and swipes stray strands of wheat from his kimono. He pulls a duplicate from his duffle bag and hands it to Neotnia then says something to me. When he crawls through the car's barn doors, it bounces around for a moment before settling.

'He says goodnight,' Neotnia tells me. 'He will sleep in the car and has given us his kimono for cover. I told him it's OK to take the car.'

'Yeah, of course,' I say, just happy she's speaking to me again. I turn towards Goeido and wish him goodnight. He waves from inside the car then pulls its doors together.

For several minutes, Neotnia and I watch the fire crackle, our gaze occasionally drifting towards the kami above. Closing my eyes, I imagine I'm by the sea, the swaying of the wheat in the night's breeze sounding like the gentle lapping of the tide against the shore. After a while, Neotnia repositions Goeido's duffle bag along the car's length and reclines against it like it's a bean bag chair, spreading his kimono across her body.

When the breeze picks up, I zip my hoodie tight around my neck.

'You can come over,' Neotnia says, giving me a furtive glance. 'You can't really feel the wind from here.'

I move next to her. The snug softness of Goeido's duffle bag feels good against my back. Neotnia offers me part of his massive kimono.

'So, you really weren't kidding,' she says after some time. 'You just can't help randomly lip-syncing to songs.'

'Yeah,' I say.

'That's really dorky.'

'Yeah, it is.'

There's a pop in the flames. A tiny ember drifts into the night, hovers like a firefly, then fades. I linger on the space it filled for several moments, trying to find the courage to speak.

'I'm sorry how I acted earlier,' I say. 'I'm sorry I was short with you and rude to Goeido.'

Neotnia looks up at me in the light of the flames. 'Thanks,' she nods, and I feel her body relax a little.

'And I don't blame you for hoping I could help with your splinter. We do what we need to do to—'

'*Stooop*,' she draws the word out, releasing a small breath. And the way her eyes linger on me – they make me want to forget everything I've learned. They make me want to hold her again.

But I don't move.

'You're right,' she finally says. 'In the beginning, I found that magazine and your passport, and it revealed who you were. It gave me the idea that maybe you could help, since what Goeido and I had already tried wasn't that fruitful. And I'm sorry about that. It wasn't right.' She pauses.

My throat tightens a bit, and I give her a little nod.

'That night of your ear cleaning, I discovered your backpack after we'd electrocuted both my arms. I told Goeido what I'd found and suggested perhaps we could talk to you – tell you what I am. That maybe you could help us. But Goeido, he's always looking out for me. And he said we had no way of knowing if you were a good person – if you could keep my secret. You were on a magazine cover being praised as a high-tech boy-genius, after all. We didn't know what drove you. Money? Fame? Would you try to take advantage of me if you found out what I was? Would you tell the world about me? He said it was too big of a risk to take – even after I suggested that maybe your leaving the backpack was a kami's doing. A kami trying to help us.'

Neotnia peers into the fire, watching a few embers float into the sky.

'He did have a point, though. I *didn't* know you – or even if you'd be back, for that matter. So, I told him that if you did come back, I'd just talk to you, get to know you – kind of suss out the kind of person you are.' She lightly shakes her head. 'He didn't like that idea either. But it's my life, right?'

I nod and Neotnia gazes at me for a long moment. Her mouth draws tight, as if she's considering whether to say something.

'And so, you came back. And we had hot chocolate, and well ... my gloves. It's because of them.' She shrugs and gives me a shy smile. 'I had an instant liking for you.'

'I don't understand. Your gloves...?'

Neotnia tips her eyes, like I'm not getting the most obvious thing in the world.

Still, I don't say a word.

'Fancy gloves aren't a thing a normal person wears...' She throws her hands up. 'It's weird to wear gloves when you're not outside and it's not zero degrees. Customers *always* asked why I had gloves on, and I'd say it's just the trend, but they'd look around like they knew it wasn't or like I was obviously trying to start one.' She releases an exhausted breath. 'But ... when I sat across from you in the booth that night, you went out of your way to pretend like my gloves weren't weird, even though you clearly thought they were. And, you know, that...'

She presses her lips together in a shy way.

'That ... what?' I shrug.

'Jeeez! Boys are so stupid.' She tips her head back and lets out a big sigh. 'It endeared me to you, alright? It was thoughtful. It was sweet – OK?'

'OK,' I hurry to agree.

Neotnia shakes her head and looks into the fire for a moment.

'Anyway, it made me think you were probably a good person. Sweet people, thoughtful people, are usually good people, right? But how could I know for sure? That's when I thought of Joe. It's why I invited you to the care home. He was a great judge of character, and he was so tough he could probably beat the sun at a staring contest. Plus, he could spot bullcrap a mile away – and that toughness meant he had no hesitation calling it out. He didn't know about me, of course. He always thought I was just like everyone else. But I knew he'd give me his honest opinion if I brought you with me. And he *really* liked you...'

She pauses, and I know it's on a memory of Joe.

'And besides,' she continues, 'that day at the care home, we got along, and it only made me more sure of you. So, after you dropped me off at the café, before you returned to pick me up for the movie, I told Goeido how much Joe liked you, and what a good feeling I had about you, too. And I told him I wanted to ask for your help. But still, he wasn't having it. He thought I was being too trusting. Yet, after the movie, we got along so well on our walk and at the burger place ... and so, I decided to invite you for Halloween. The next morning, I told Goeido I thought it was an excellent idea, because we could all have dinner and he could see for himself what I saw in you.'

I nod for a moment, digesting everything.

'And so, he agreed?'

'Oh, no.' A deadly serious look crosses her face. 'He did not like that idea at all. Not one bit. He said, "Computer Boy clearly only cares about being famous on magazine covers."'

My shoulders sink a little. 'Oh.'

Neotnia looks at me and tries to suppress a smile.

'But the sake changed that.'

'Because he saw us as drinking buddies?'

'Oh, no. Not that either.' Her lips form a serious little line. 'He said, even until the day she died, his 107-year-old grandmother was able to hold her sake better.'

And my chest sinks a little, too.

'I had *no* idea he was going to offer you his sake. But when he suggested it at the table, he told me you can judge a man by how he acts when he's drunk. I wasn't happy with his plan, but what was I going to do about it?'

The edges of her eyelids curve downward ever so slightly, like tiny crescent moons, each forming an invisible little smile.

'But Goeido *did* end up liking you. He was surprised by how forthright you were about yourself, and that made him think you *were* a good person – just like I'd said. So, after you passed out, I told him I'd made up my mind, and no matter what, I'd tell you everything the next day and ask for your help. But even though he now thought you were a good person, Goeido still didn't think it was wise to be sharing my secret. So, we agreed that if he'd finally try a bathtub electrocution on me that night and could find and somehow fix my splinter, then I wouldn't tell you anything.'

Neotnia shrugs a little shrug.

'I was curious how much time we'd get with a full body electrocution, and impatient, and just wanted to get it all over with. And you were passed out, so I didn't think there was any chance you'd walk in on us. Not to mention, I couldn't possibly imagine how much a bathtub electrocution would take out of me. But, of course ... you *did* walk in, and that ended that. And you looked so confused. I felt so terrible. And then it was obvious you were going to pass out again, but I was still too shocked to speak. All I could manage was to motion to Goeido to catch you before you collapsed.'

The last thing I remember from that night is Goeido's big, meaty hand coming at me. At the time, it looked like he was attacking me...

'But why let me think I had a really messed-up dream? Why not just stick to your original timeline and tell me everything the next morning like you planned?'

Neotnia sucks her lower lip for a moment, thinking. 'After I carried you downstairs—'

'Wait – *you* carried me?'

She gives a meek half-smile. 'I told you I'm strong.'

A gust whips past the wheat above our heads, and it sounds as if a wave has crashed onto the shore. After discovering it wasn't a dream, I just assumed Goeido had carried me. But now I remember: once I was on the couch, someone held my hand in theirs.

As the gust settles, the rhythmic lapping of the wheat returns.

'When I put you on the couch, you said ... some things. And that's when I realised how much you liked me. And, well, I just couldn't do that to you. I couldn't drag you into this any further. It wasn't fair. You didn't know what I was. You didn't know how my body was. Besides, when I realised how much you liked me ... I also realised I was now *afraid* of you finding out the truth because ... well, since the movie ... I'd begun having feelings for you.'

I nod, but no words manage to escape my lips.

'And that's why I was a bit cold when you woke the next

morning,' she continues. 'I'd decided I'd try the bathtub again and just hope it'd work and leave you out of this whole mess. And we did try that very night, but Goeido just couldn't make sense of the code. Then ... you know, then you kept coming back. And then, well, Joe died.'

Neotnia turns to the flames as embers pop and their remnants float into the night.

'I'd never known anyone who'd died. He was my friend, and after he did ... well, you were with me by his side. I felt so close to you, and it got me thinking about all these feelings I'd never experienced before. Feelings about Joe ... feelings for you. I didn't know how to deal with them. I wanted to explore them, but was so worried my body meant you'd shun me...'

She gives me a sad little smile.

'But then you told me about your worries, your fears, your insecurities over your own body...' She trails off again. An ember pops. 'Out of all the people who come into the café, out of all the men and women who've approached me – you're the only one who's made me feel not alone. Who's made me feel like someone else understands what it's like to have a body you don't consider normal. A body you think will hold you back. A body that makes you feel like you'll never fit in...'

And even in the orange firelight, I can see Neotnia's face flush.

'But even after the pool ... Well, I planned on sucking it up and keeping it friendly and not telling you anything about me. The real me. Goeido and I even tried the bathtub one more time. But that damn storm...' She shakes her head. 'Everything just came to the surface – all these feelings. I couldn't control them. I thought, maybe I could just take it so far and stop. Obviously, I couldn't. And what happened, happened. And you deserved answers, even though I was afraid those answers would make you see me ... well, how you see me now.'

'I didn't—'

'You don't have to lie. I understand. Really, I do. I know you said you didn't mind that I was missing a part – but that's when you still thought I was human. And, well, I know finding out the full truth about me must be tough to deal with. You tried your best, but some of the things you've said ... well, your new view of me slipped out. What I am upsets you.'

For a moment, no words leave my mouth.

'What are you talking about?'

'Just things. Things like when you warned me about electrocuting myself with my head submerged. You said it could "destroy" me, not "kill" me. You destroy something inanimate, without life. You kill something with a life.' Neotnia shrugs. 'You see me as an appliance. No different from a bot. You stopped looking at me the way you used to.'

I'm quiet for a long time as the wheat sways around us and orange embers pop and float. I stare at Neotnia, who looks into the fire with unblinking eyes, as if she's afraid what they may find if they drift anywhere else.

'I'm sorry. I've been trying to process a lot and haven't always chosen my words as carefully as I should have.' I fall silent. 'But honestly,' I continue, 'when I found out, I *was* upset. Not because I thought less of you, but because of the feelings I'd gotten for you. I was angry, because, let's face it, we're built differently. Literally.'

Neotnia tilts her head and looks up at me for some time. And those eyes, the way they peer at me, it's as if she can see facets of myself I'm not even aware of. Then with a motion so slight, she nods. '*Hai*,' she says, and she presses her lips together and turns towards the blanket of stars above.

I look up into the night sky for a long time, too.

Being out here, me and Neotnia, under those stars, I realise that even though we're so small, our differences are as vast as the spaces between them.

It's the great unfairness of life.

When I turn back towards her, the orange flames cast their gentle glow across her face. She gives up a tiny smile, considering me with those clear eyes before turning towards the fire again. And as a few embers drift upward, she silently rests her head on my shoulder, her body warm next to mine, looking lost in thought, staring at those false fireflies. After some time, she stretches an arm towards their glowing bodies and retracts the sleeve of her shark sweatshirt. Bending her hand back, she spreads her fingers wide.

'My skin's almost back to normal. By morning, it will look no different from anyone's.'

For a long while after, we're silent, gazing into the dying light of the burning stalks. Above us, the chill breeze laps the wheat's tall tips. Beneath the kimono, Neotnia threads her arm through mine and squeezes tightly, her head still on my shoulder.

'I'm glad you came,' she says in a small voice. 'I was so afraid you wouldn't.'

And as the night's gusts lap the wheat above, we watch the glow dim as our bodies squeeze closer, warming each other under the stars.

13 – Today was a very good day.

I wake to the sound of a caw receding.

Neotnia's curled at my side beneath Goeido's silk kimono, her head resting on my thigh. Her chest rises and falls, synchronised with her rhythmic breath. I glance at my phone setting on the flattened wheat. It's half past six. The campfire's a heap of cold ash, and dawn's golden rays are slowly making way for clear blue sky.

In the distance, a crow caws again and another answers. Neotnia cradles her head more firmly against my thigh as her forearm slips from the kimono – her sleeve pushed to her elbow, exposing her soft flesh. The ashen blackness from our final electrocution has finally vacated her skin. Hers looks like any ordinary arm again.

The car jostles at my back as its door opens and Goeido's massive foot extends like a landing gear. He exits as quietly as a six-foot-four powerhouse can and looks towards the blue sky, stretching the lingering sleep from his body. He nods good morning and moves towards the clearing's opposite side, where he bows to the stalks enclosing us – a silent prayer to the kami inside, perhaps.

'Morning,' a quiet voice says.

Neotnia gives me a tiny smile, her head still on my thigh.

'Morning.'

She sits up and folds a lock of hair behind her pale ear. For a moment, she gazes at Goeido bowing.

'Did you sleep OK?'

'*Hai*,' she nods. 'You?'

I tell her I did.

When Goeido stands upright he and Neotnia greet each other, and we get to our feet. I connect my phone to the car and do the calculations in my head – the battery's charge is enough to get us to Hiroshima. Goeido stomps the campfire's ash into the earth beneath his sandalled feet and we throw the duffle bag into the car. These older models can freak out if you wake them when they're not on actual pavement, so we push it onto the road first, all helping this time, though I can tell the brunt of the work is borne by the two of them.

None of us says much once we're cruising. Every so often, I consider asking Neotnia how she's feeling about the meeting, but I remain quiet. Much of the time she looks lost in thought, and I think that sometimes, before important events, it's best to leave people to their own devices. For most of the ride, I study a map of Hiroshima.

We enter the city and the car drops us at the main *Shinkansen* station. Several sheered stalks of wheat protrude from its bumper as it drives off to who knows where. It's just past ten, which leaves almost three hours before we're to meet Emiko Ikari. After Neotnia changes her shark sweatshirt and turtleneck for a deep-yellow wool sweater, we rent a locker by the station's bathrooms to store our bags, then walk into the city's centre, towards the Peace Park. We stop in a small eatery and have some *okonomiyaki* for a late breakfast. It's a kind of savoury pancake that's apparently a specialty of the Hiroshima region. After the waiter brings our food, I fold my phone out into a tablet and place it at the table's centre. I pull up the Peace Park in Avance Maps.

The park sits on part of a long island that splits the Ōta River into the Motoyasu as it flows into Hiroshima Bay. It begins south of a four-lane T-bridge spanning the river at the island's northern tip, just across from the Atomic Bomb Dome on the opposite bank. Further down the island, about a quarter of the park's length, there's a smaller, two-lane roadway and bridge. This separates the park into its smaller northern and larger southern halves. The park continues stretching south until it hits another two-lane bridge spanning the rivers on either side. Just before this last bridge is the Hiroshima Peace Memorial Museum – effectively the end of the Peace Park.

'I don't think we should all go together,' I say after taking a bite of my *okonomiyaki*.

Neotnia translates what I've said for Goeido. 'OK,' she looks at me. 'Why not?'

I think of how to put it without sounding too alarming. 'Well, we don't know who this woman is, right? We don't know what she wants. All we know is she sounded a little paranoid, she said to meet her in the northern part of the Peace Park at one, and she said she'd know who you are. That means she knows what you look like already, which gives her a leg up on us. She also hasn't told us exactly *where* we'll meet – only it's somewhere in the northern end. So, only she knows that, too. And look at the park: the island's not that wide. It's boxed in on two sides by rivers. I'm not saying she's trying to trap us, but having a river on either side limits our options if we need to ... well, run.'

Neotnia holds her gaze on me for a long moment.

'OK,' she finally nods and then translates for Goeido.

'I don't mean to imply we should be worried,' I add, their eyes on me. 'If this woman were going to try something, the Peace Park is a pretty dumb place to do it. It's the most open and high-profile area in the city. Still, why not be as safe as possible?'

They both nod in agreement.

'And I think it probably makes the most sense if I go with you and Goeido hangs back and acts as lookout. Because let's say Emiko Ikari's not dangerous but is paranoid ... well, no offense to you, Goeido, but you're a pretty intimidating guy.' I look at Neotnia. 'I mean, he kinda looks like our muscle, you know?'

The edges of her lips curl when I say this, and Goeido nods at her translation.

'By me going with you, Emiko will still know you aren't alone. And by Goeido hanging back, at least we *do* have some powerful backup, if we need it. If we split up now and enter the park from two different directions, Goeido can keep an eye on things separately from us. He can scope out the northern end, and we can hang around the southern. We've both got phones, so he can warn us if anything looks strange. And if everything looks OK, then, only when it's time to meet this woman, do you and I head to the northern end.' I glance at the map again. 'Makes sense?'

As if I'm still speaking, Neotnia lingers on me for a moment before finally translating for Goeido.

'*Hai*,' he says. And Neotnia says '*Hai*' for herself, too.

We finish our *okonomiyaki* and leave the eatery. It's now a little less than two hours until we're supposed to meet Emiko Ikari. We come to the Motoyasu River, the Peace Park's watery border. Goeido says something to Neotnia, and she replies, giving him a soft smile. He heads north, and Neotnia and I walk south along the Motoyasu. As we cross onto the middle bridge spanning it, I cast my eyes on the Motoyasu's east bank. Though neither of us says anything, we instinctively stop.

I saw images of it once in a banned metavid. It's odd seeing a thing in the real world that you've only looked upon before virtually. The dome doesn't seem real, not at first anyway. But what's more striking is the thought that I'm standing almost right in the centre of where the world's first atomic bomb detonated. All around us today there's life, but if we were here just over a hundred years ago, we'd have been vaporised instantly. And though I can move freely through these streets today, if I were here but a day before the bomb, everyone around would have seen me as the enemy. And I probably would have seen them as the enemy, too. Yet now we pass each other with no particular notice, much less any ill will.

I look into the blue sky above. Somewhere up there is where the bomb shattered the world. It was the first shattering, but wouldn't be the last.

When my eyes return to earth, they cross Neotnia, her bangs gently fluttering in the breeze as she peers at the dome's rusted arches crisscrossing each other like a crown of thorns. It feels like she's gazing upon the skull of the twentieth century. Like it's the remnant of some giant, horrible beast from a more primitive and violent era.

Reaching the island, we discover how packed the Peace Park is. Many of its visitors are schoolchildren on class field trips. They move in unified masses from one of the scores of monuments to the next. Then there are the regular tourists, along with the largest smattering of info bots I've seen in a single place. The remaining visitors look like locals simply enjoying a sunny autumn day. Many seem to be on their lunch breaks, some sitting at picnic tables, while others take up the benches lining the myriad paths. Above them all are the orange, red and yellow leaves of the maples, which send splotches of sunlight and shadow swaying over everything in the crisp breeze.

At the park's far northern end, I spot Goeido strolling like a tourist, right across the river from the dome. Even from this distance, his size singles him out – more so when a group of schoolchildren pass before him single-file, looking like tiny, mechanised figurines.

I jump as a violent noise fires over my shoulder.

A van's screeched to a stop behind us, inches from a Pomeranian that's dashed into the road cutting through the park. The van's occupant shouts at the apologetic owner, who scoops the tiny dog in her arms. But as the occupant continues to rant, another noise roars up, pounding like a jackhammer. And as it thumps, everyone seems to be looking our way – that woman in the metalenses, that salaryman on his lunch break, that jogger who's paused on the bridge. *Everyone.*

And there – that info bot, under the large maple – it wasn't there a moment ago. I know it wasn't. It's appeared out of nowhere, like that peculiar one in Shibuya. And this one's looking right at us, scrutinising us with its enormous feline eyes.

Just like the one at the scramble.

Ice streaks through my veins. I want to call out to Goeido, but he's too far away. I'm so stupid. *He* should have stayed with Neotnia, because what if Emiko's *not* alone? What if she's hacked that info bot to spy on us? What if that teacher or this salaryman or that woman there is working with her? What could I do about it? Neotnia's strength is comparable to Goeido's – I'm the weakest. How could I possibly protect her if the whole plan is to abduct her into some…

No, no – where's the van? It's driving off.

Oh, God – where's Neotnia?

The jackhammering pounds.

My head whips around.

But – she's right there. Right in front of me. Her eyes already on me. And it looks as if they've been so for some time.

Now, they pin me in place, her bangs shifting gently in the breeze.

And with those eyes fixed on mine, she places her palm on my chest, where that jackhammering's been coming from this whole time.

'I know you're worried for me,' she says, pausing to soak in the beats of my chest. 'I know you've been thinking about me thinking about this meeting all morning. And I *have* been thinking about it. It's been on my mind *constantly*.' She arches her brows. 'But it is what it is ... OK?'

There's a lump in my throat that's unwilling to let me answer. Yet my heart's pounding quells just a bit against her palm. And as if feeling it do so, Neotnia twists her mouth up.

'And not that I don't appreciate the military-grade strategy you laid out over breakfast – it was quite impressive with the map and all, and very sweet. But what will happen will happen, and we'll only know it *when* it happens. And that's OK.' She pauses and looks in Goeido's direction for a moment. 'But I want *you* with me when I meet her. I need *you* at my side, OK?'

The splotches of sun breaking through the gaps in the maples sway across her face. It's as if luminous beings live just beneath her skin.

'OK?' she repeats.

I release a slow breath.

'OK,' I say.

'OK,' she says again. But only after my heart calms by a few more beats does she finally remove her palm from my chest.

Yet almost instantly, there's another commotion. This time it's from a line of schoolchildren being led across the compact road. They look like first-graders, and each holds a coloured paper crane. As the teacher pools the children at our side, a girl breaks from her classmates and speaks excitedly as she thrusts her bright-blue crane at Neotnia so she can have a better look. Neotnia smiles and crouches down, carefully admiring the origami. After a short conversation in which the girl becomes increasingly animated, the teacher approaches and seems to apologise for the distraction. And as the little girl rejoins her classmates, Neotnia returns her wave goodbye.

'She highly recommends the Peace Memorial Museum,' Neotnia

smiles as we watch the children march north into the park. 'It's where they learned to make the cranes.'

I look south, towards the museum. It's past the Cenotaph on the other side of the road.

'We've still got ninety minutes before the meeting,' I shrug. 'Want to check it out?'

We message Goeido, letting him know. The museum is probably a good idea, anyway. It keeps us out of sight for the time being.

We cross the road and walk along the shallow artificial pool leading towards the Cenotaph commemorating the victims of Hiroshima.

'Being here reminds me of Joe,' Neotnia says as we pass the stone arch.

'Really?'

'*Hai*,' she nods, and brushes her bangs with her slim fingers. 'Joe used to tell me I needed to see this museum. He made me promise I'd go one day. But that's not why this place reminds me of him. It's because he told me his father's stories about surveying the city as an American army officer in the weeks after the bomb. His father explained how the shadows of some victims had burned into the streets – even around lamp posts and onto fences – due to the power of the blast.' Neotnia pauses for a moment. 'But while his father talked of shadows, Joe said they were really ghosts.'

'Ghosts?'

Neotnia nods, and her eyes cast down to the shadows under our feet. 'Joe said the shadows were really ghosts left behind to haunt us – to make us remember what we're capable of doing to one another. The thing is, Joe said, the ghosts are all gone now. You can't see them around the city anymore. Time has erased them. And he said that was bad.'

'Why bad?'

'Because when people stop being haunted by the past, they start repeating it.'

We enter the museum and buy two tickets from a bot that guides us to the exhibition hall. It reminds us to pick up a pair of metalenses when we reach the final room.

We turn the entrance's corner into the first dimly lit space. A lone podium sits at its centre. It displays a half-melted watch, its dial forever frozen on 8:15. Behind it is a floor-to-ceiling photo of the mushroom cloud that ended so much more than time.

The next room is dedicated to those who died during the initial blast. The narrative explains how those victims were snuffed out like a match in a cyclone. They existed in one instant, and in the next, there was no trace they'd ever walked the earth – every atom in their body evaporated. On one podium is a grotesque beehive of fused soda bottles. On another, a once-exquisite iron lantern now shaped like a used candle. Behind both is a split-picture of the Hiroshima skyline as it was only six days before, and then as it was after. It's a picture of a bustling city versus a picture of desolation.

On the next wall is a large black-and-white photo of twenty-two children and a grown man. The children are students – each no older than five or six. The man, a handsome guy in his early twenties with bottle-rimmed glasses and a thin moustache, is their teacher. It's their 1945 class photo, taken outside their schoolhouse on the first of August. Their smiles beam. And the teacher, his eyes shine over his class with pride. There is no 'after' photo. The schoolhouse was va-porised five days later at 8:15 a.m., right as those children took their desks to begin another school day.

In the dim light, the room suddenly feels cold. I turn towards Neotnia, who's frozen before the photo, her gaze locked on all the pairs of tiny eyes in front of her. It's several moments before she seems to realise the space she's in once again.

The next room tells the story of the *hibakusha* – those who sur-vived the bomb. Yet you soon wonder if those vaporised were the more fortunate. We see photos of *hibakusha* blinded by the flash of the blast, their retinas seared like eggs in a skillet. We see photos of *hibakusha* whose skin was charred by the flash – parts of their bodies blackened like burnt wheat while other areas bubble a chalky white. And we see photos of *hibakusha* whose fingers and limbs warped from the extreme heat; their appendages now unnaturally bent like branches in a nightmarish forest. Yet no matter the injury, no matter if the victim was a young boy or an old woman, every *hibakusha*'s face is shrouded in that same horrible shadow. The shadow that remains when the world ends.

'Father's mother was *hibakusha*,' Neotnia says in a low voice, peering at a photograph of a young woman whose eyes are sheathed in dirty rags. 'As a little girl, she was blinded by the bomb. She feared she would never find love because of her blindness.'

The next photo shows someone no older than me. He's my height. My build. But he's a Japanese soldier, weeping. It's the morning after the bomb, and he's among the first responders. He's weeping because he had discovered an old man under the rubble, crying out for help. Yet when he grasped the man's outstretched arm to pull him free, its flesh and sinew slid forth, leaving a living skeleton screaming in his place.

I look beside me but Neotnia's no longer there. She's in the far corner of the room, staring at an ordinary piece of old paper pencilled with Japanese characters. I bend close to read the description. It's from the diary of someone named Mutsuko Ishizaki. The photograph next to the diary's page shows she's a chubby little kid with a short haircut. The description explains she was twelve when she wrote the entry, which describes how she helped a newly transferred schoolmate with her studies that morning, before going swimming in the river that afternoon. She ends the entry noting:

> 'Today was a very good day. I want to continue
> to do a good deed every day.'

It was written on Sunday night, the fifth of August 1945, right before Mutsuko went to bed. She wasn't seen again after the blast the next morning, though her parents, both *hibakusha*, kept her diary with them for the rest of their lives.

I look at Neotnia, but she's frozen on Mutsuko. Her eyes damp.

The exhibition's final room is bare except for a stand containing metalenses. We both take a pair and I tap twice on mine to set the narration to English. A countdown appears in the space at the room's centre. As it reaches one, a meta model of the bomb appears, rotating before us. The invisible narrator says the bomb's name is Little Boy and, at the time, it was the most technologically advanced device humanity had ever created – the result of an expert understanding of the known physics, chemistry, algebra, and engineering of the day. Its creation was possible due to the most brilliant technological and scientific minds on the planet working around the clock beginning on the thirteenth of August 1942. And less than three years later, they had created a device that, at the beginning of the decade, had only been achievable in works of science fiction.

'The most celebrated scientist of the twentieth century, Albert Einstein, didn't have direct involvement in the making of the atomic bomb,' the narrator's voice says as Little Boy continues to rotate. 'But he came up with an equation forty years earlier – one without which the Manhattan Project wouldn't have been able to successfully create such a device. That equation was, of course, $E = mc^2$.'

Little Boy shrinks down, and history's most famous equation springs up in its place.

'At the beginning of the century, he couldn't have known the terror his scientific work would ultimately unleash,' the narrator continues, 'but in 1948, just three years after the bomb was dropped, and with the world now awake to the horrors this technological power could wreak, Einstein said, "If I had foreseen Hiroshima and Nagasaki, I would have torn up my formula in 1905."'

Before us, Einstein's equation is pushed aside as the bomb springs back to life size.

'The result of that formula is this...'

The life-sized bomb tips and then shrinks, appearing to fall directly below us. From our bird's-eye view, the Hiroshima of the morning of the sixth of August 1945 rapidly rises. We see all the tiny people and ancient cars and horse-drawn wagons moving on the streets below. Above it all, Little Boy again comes into view and, an instant later, it detonates.

The blinding light, then the pressure from the blast itself, and finally, the radiant heatwave, spread in concentric rings. When the radioactive cloud clears, a burning, devastated world is revealed. We see the now-infamous Atomic Bomb Dome, its rooftop melted so only its skull remains. We hear the narrator explain how an estimated eighty thousand people were killed nearly instantly, and at least an additional eighty thousand would perish due to injury from the blast or radiation exposure, with thousands more permanently affected.

As the presentation closes, we zoom in on various spots in the city, each significant because it's where an atomic shadow – Joe's ghosts – used to be found. One meta reconstruction shows the shadow of a man leaning on a cane seared into the pavement. Another, two children holding hands, scorched onto a factory's steps. Who the shadows belonged to are impossible to know. They will forever be faceless ghosts with no names.

Neotnia and I remain silent as we exit the museum. Outside, it feels as if we've stepped into another world. The Hiroshima surrounding us is a far cry from the one we've just experienced. Everything is so full of life; you couldn't ask for a more beautiful autumn day.

Approaching the Cenotaph again, we stop so a group of school-children can stand for an unobstructed photo by the shallow memorial pool.

Each holds a paper crane in their hands, and they all look so proud. It reminds me of the class photograph from 1945. The children in today's class also look no older than five or six, and their smiles beam just as bright. And hearing their laughter as the teacher tries to get them to settle long enough to take the photo, I recall something Mom said years after she returned from Angola: 'No matter what language you speak or what nationality you are, tears and laughter always sound the same.'

At this memory, Neotnia touches my hand.

My mouth drops a little. She's crying in the radiant sunlight. Yet, she asks if *I'm* OK.

That's when I feel the tears on my face, too.

Before we can say another word, a young voice shouts. It's one of the schoolchildren. He points at us and shouts again. Instantly, animated screams of delight erupt from the class. Their eruption is joined a split second later by Neotnia, her tear-streaked face bursting into a rapturous smile. She laughs so hard, her body shakes. A grin spreads across my face as well, but it's because I have no idea what's going on. The teacher who was so patiently trying to get his class to remain still long enough to take a photo appears at our side and seems to apologise profusely to Neotnia before saying, 'Sorry. Sorry. So sorry,' to me.

Yet, I can only reply with a kind of befuddled nod. I look to Neotnia, who's trying to stifle another laugh as some of the children continue to point and shout as their teacher returns. When he finally manages to calm his class, they march on, and I turn back towards Neotnia, her face still flushed from laughter. With a lingering smile, she explains, 'One of the children saw us when they were posing for their photo, and he shouted, "Look! Look! Those two holding hands are so happy to be together, they're crying!"'

And I laugh, too.

With that, we don't need to say anything more about what we experienced in the museum.

We make our way north, coming back to the compact road that cuts the park into its northern and southern parts. I look at my phone.

'It's almost time,' I say.

Neotnia gives a nod. '*Hai*,' she replies.

We cross the road into the northern portion and walk along a path that's canopied by fiery orange and yellow leaves. This half of the park is full of people eating packed lunches at picnic tables, and those sitting on benches enjoying the weather. Ahead, an info bot gives some tourists details about one of the memorials. To the left, another does the same. Several hundred feet in the distance, we see Goeido standing in the garden by the Clock Tower of Peace monument. He spots us, too, but doesn't react. Instead, he turns and looks upon the dome across the river.

My phone rings.

It's the number from yesterday.

I answer, intending to give the phone to Neotnia. But before I can, the voice on the other end speaks.

'Keep walking,' it says. 'I'm at the table under the maples just before the Peace Bell memorial. And I can see you both right now.'

14 – It's one of our many flaws.

I tell Neotnia what's been said. She's quiet for a moment, weighing something in her mind.

Then, she nods. 'OK.'

We follow the path leading towards the Peace Bell, the autumn leaves shading the benches lining either side. Most are occupied. About fifty feet ahead on a platform in a shallow pond is the bell. A suspended wooden beam allows visitors who cross the narrow foot-bridge to strike it. Just before the pond is a small picnic area. At one table, a man and woman in office attire share lunch. At the next, a younger guy in running gear listens to music through his metalenses. The remaining occupied table is the furthest from the others. A lone person sits at it, and she's not doing anything but staring as we approach.

I canvas all my eyes can absorb in the seconds before we reach her. In the distance: schoolchildren and teachers; info bots and tourists. Closer, an old man on a bench across the path. He sits slightly hunched, leaning towards a little girl with pigtails, taking great interest in the bright-red leaf she presents. She looks about three, and together they look like a grandpa and granddaughter. Beyond them, someone strokes their dog in the grass, a group of elderly women chats, a young man sketches something on a notepad.

In other words, things couldn't be more ordinary. And as we enter the picnic area, the last thing I glance is Goeido, now by the river-bank about sixty feet ahead. I make out he's seen where we're headed just before I set my eyes on the woman again.

We come to a stop at her table. She doesn't move. She doesn't even say anything. She simply keeps her eyes locked on Neotnia, who's doing the same.

She's in her mid-thirties and tanned, like she's just returned from a vacation on some tropical island. Her hair is short but stylish, and her black pantsuit looks expensive. On her wrist is a silver analogue watch, which seems out of place. Not so much because it's analogue, but because of its size. It seems to be made for a man.

And as we stand here, the woman staring at Neotnia for so long, I begin to wonder if we're at the wrong table and she's simply at a loss for words over the young strangers who've approached. I glance over my shoulder, but no one at the other tables pays us any attention. Across the path, the old man glances in our direction before returning his focus towards the little girl.

'Ah, are you Emiko Ikari?' I say since no one else is saying anything.

The woman gives a nod so slight it's almost invisible.

'Forgive me,' she says, coming out of her trance. Her eyes still linger on Neotnia. 'I didn't know which face to expect. I'm glad Haruto chose this one. Please, sit.'

Neotnia and I give each other a glance, as if we're each waiting for the other to act, but then we sit without saying a word. Emiko is silent for a moment more before her gaze turns towards me.

'I assume you're the same English-speaking person – the American – who answered the phone yesterday?' she says. 'And English will suffice?'

I can't help but note the hint of disdain in her voice when she says 'the American'.

I answer with a nod and then look at Neotnia, who confirms, '*Hai*. Yes.' Her voice has a surprising meekness about it.

'Good,' Emiko gives a curt smile. 'Less chance others may overhear. Now—'

'Do you know where my father is?'

Neotnia's question is abrupt the way water from a ruptured main is. Inelegant. Unexpected. And, indeed, Emiko flinches how one might if hit by a sudden sprinkle. Yet I don't think it's Neotnia's blunt interruption that causes Emiko to react the way she does, so much as her use of the term 'father'.

She considers Neotnia for several moments. For her the silence seems comfortable – behind her gaze, she seems to be calculating something. For Neotnia, though, there's nothing comfortable about it. Her eyes shimmer with a horrible anxiety.

'Let's back up,' Emiko finally says with the authority of a school principal. 'First things first: how do you know about me?'

She's asking both of us. I glance at Neotnia, unsure of what, or how much, to say. Neotnia is just as apprehensive. That self-assuredness she possessed when she put her palm to my chest has retreated like it would for any of us when confronting an unknown that was previously only an abstract concept in our mind – and thus, a harmless one. But finally sitting in front of that abstraction; being close enough to touch it – it shakes you.

That curt smile again crosses Emiko's face. 'Allow me to break the ice...' she says. 'I know you're an android. As does this young man, correct?'

Neotnia's lips part. '*Hai...*'

'And I know you're looking for Haruto. What I want to know is: how do you know about me?'

'Your name was in the metadata of a file we have,' I offer.

Emiko nods, acknowledging my words, but doesn't reply right away.

'And did you give my name to anyone else?'

We're again hesitant, uncertain of what to reveal.

'When we spoke on the phone,' Emiko says with a new sharpness in her voice, 'I told you not to give anyone my name. Not to let anyone know you're coming. Did you follow those instructions?' When we fail to immediately respond, she adds, 'I cannot emphasise enough how much your honesty matters at this moment.'

Her gaze is hard.

'A friend knows both,' Neotnia says.

'And does this friend know about you?'

'*Hai.*'

'And besides this friend and this young man here, does anyone else know about you or me?'

'No,' Neotnia shakes her head.

Emiko's nod is barely perceptible.

'How do you know my father?' Neotnia says after a few breaths.

Emiko considers her for a long moment.

'We built you together.'

Neotnia's jaw drops.

'You're ... my mother?'

'No. My daughter has a mother. I have a mother. *People* have mothers. I'm just one person who helped create you.'

Her words are cold. Direct. And they seem to sting Neotnia – physically, as if they've been delivered via slingshot. Her eyes drop to the tabletop where they simmer with a terrible ignominy. It's a re-action Emiko appears almost perplexed by.

'There's no reason to be like that,' I snap.

Any perplexity leaves Emiko's face when she glances at me. Instead, a tiny curl appears at the edge of her mouth.

'I'm sorry if that sounds blunt,' she says to Neotnia, 'but when we're looking for answers, only the honest ones help.'

Neotnia is still for a moment, but then she nods and raises her gaze. 'Do you know why he abandoned me? Where he is?'

'You weren't even finished by the time I left, so I wouldn't be able to answer either of those questions,' Emiko replies. 'However, perhaps, if I knew more about the events that led you to me, I could be of more help...'

Neotnia looks at me. That awful sadness in her eyes makes my chest feel so tight. But I give her a nod. Emiko clearly holds the most cards. What other choice do we have? And Neotnia seems to under-stand this, too. So, she does precisely what Emiko's asked. She tells her everything she's told me: how she was born in Kamakura in a little house by the sea, how her father told her she was an android, and how, after her first birthday, he dropped her and Inu off with a friend in Tokyo and said he'd be back – only he never returned.

And as Neotnia continues, I can tell when she's cast off some of that apprehension – that fear of revealing things that could lead to answers she might not like – that's kept her so timid until now. And as she gets more of her self-assuredness back, she tells Emiko about the pain from the splinter and the electrocutions. She tells Emiko how we extracted the splinter, yet couldn't open it, but found her name in the metadata. And she tells Emiko how that led to us here, today, at this picnic table.

After Neotnia finishes, Emiko is silent for a long while. Overhead, the fiery leaves rustle. In the distance, an info bot guides a tourist towards the Peace Bell. From somewhere else, the murmur of an excited group of schoolchildren sounds. Finally, a small smile grows on Emiko's tanned face. It's a smile that has an air of rarity around it, and one that you get from a good memory.

'I'm glad Haruto moved to Kamakura,' she says. 'He always loved the sea, even though he rarely went. When we first met, we were in Osaka, and Haruto was always too absorbed in his work to take a break – even a day trip to the bay.'

'He always warned me not to go into the sea,' Neotnia replies, looking at her hands. 'He'd take me to the pool but wouldn't let me go into the sea.'

The hints of crow's feet around Emiko's eyes show a little more. 'That's Haruto looking out for those he cares for. Just as biological beings do, you too have a fight-or-flight system built-in for self-preservation. But if that system were ever overridden, it would leave you vulnerable to one of the few ways you could be destroyed.'

A hum breaks the air. The Peace Bell has been struck. As it resonates, Emiko takes in the details of Neotnia's face, considering it the way a physical-money enthusiast considers all the bumps and dips on an old coin.

'There are people who would call your body a miracle,' she says when the hum fades. 'But it's not. It's just science. Really advanced science that allowed us to create you. And like all manmade things, your body is ultimately no match for nature. Saltwater is highly corrosive to several of your internal structures. If you were submerged for long enough, and your fight-or-flight systems couldn't engage, your body could be destroyed from within in a matter of days.'

Neotnia gives a pensive little nod. 'He never told me that.'

This time it's Emiko who remains silent.

'But Father – I guess he never told me so many things. I have so many questions. Why ... why is my body ... like it is? What did you mean when you said you didn't know which face to expect? How long ago did Father live in Osaka? Could he be there now?' Neotnia shakes her head. 'There's so much I don't understand...'

Emiko's tanned fingers gently caress the band of the large silver watch, kneading it as if it were a cat's neck.

'I know how curiosity can consume a person. I was a scientist, after all. But I also know our search into the void of the unknown often makes us forget what we have right in front of us.' She glances at the watch as her fingers give its band another caress. 'I'll tell you what I can in the short amount of time we have – but in exchange for one thing. I want your promise that you'll never contact me, never search me out, again.'

Her eyes have such a grave seriousness to them it feels as if an incorrect reply will have deadly consequences.

'*Hai*. OK,' Neotnia nods.

Emiko looks at me, too, and I nod as well.

In the background, the bell is struck again. Emiko waits until its resonance fades, as if she's used the time to compose her thoughts.

'I'm sure it has occurred to you,' she begins, 'simply by the fact that you exist, that Haruto is one of the most brilliant minds on the planet. And in truth, I know he would say the same about me. We have five PhDs between us, but in fact we're experts in close to a dozen fields. My specialties were biochemistry, synthetic physiology and quantum materials. Our crossover is biochem and quantum materials, but Haruto's primary specialties are quantum physics, quantum coding and robotics.

'We first met twelve years ago. I was twenty-five and fresh out of graduate school. I had just taken a position at a bioengineering firm in Osaka that focused on creating new synthetic materials and quantum technologies. It was a small firm, but one that, at the time, was well funded. Haruto oversaw their spec division. And when I say oversaw, I mean it was only him – until I got there, anyway. It was his job to come up with new speculative technologies and meta-materials that didn't necessarily have a practical use-case at the time but could be game-changing in the future – similar to how, for example, touchscreens were first invented by scientists in the 1960s, yet were not widely used and wholly critical until the first few decades of this century. The companies that had the patience to hold those patents from the sixties suddenly became obscenely wealthy at the turn of the millennium.

'Haruto was the one who convinced the firm to hire me. He'd read a paper I'd written on speculative synthetic physiology. Yet he didn't read my paper in a journal – because I couldn't get any to publish it. Everyone told me it was too theoretical, too fantastical. I guess an editor at a journal who knew Haruto sent it to him as a joke. But, well, Haruto had a way of seeing things no one else did.

'He was fifty-seven at the time, and though there were more than thirty years between us, we hit it off like we'd known each other our whole lives. And, despite that age gap, he never once treated me as anything but his equal. That first year there were nights we didn't leave the lab until two in the morning. Not because we were always working that late, but because we'd get lost in conversations about what was possible if people only dreamed bigger.'

At those words, Emiko pauses for a moment, and a slim smile crosses her lips.

'That was one of the phrases he loved using: "dream bigger". And it was a phrase that redefined for me what a research scientist's job was. "Don't crush that thought – keep going," he would say whenever I'd been tempted to admonish myself for some far-out idea that crossed my mind. "Let it grow so big you can't hold it inside any longer. And never apologise for it, because it's our job to dream bigger. It's our job to dream things so fantastical the world would naturally dismiss them out of hand. And then, once that idea, that dream, is so obvious to you it hurts, you know you've reached the point where it's undeniable a way must be found to manifest it for the good of humanity and show the world just what *is* possible."'

That slim smile on her face lingers for a moment more, before finally fading.

'For those first five years, our dream was to create a completely lifelike dog – the one you mentioned. I know, it sounds silly: an android dog. Yet it was just the first step. It's what we needed to accomplish to see if we could go on to manifest something bigger. And we did it. Almost five years to the day later, we created a Bichon Frise with completely new types of synthetic tissues and quantum metamaterials, and one with – just as importantly – a quantum OS that could emulate the essence of how a real dog moves and acts.

'It was the world's first android – a milestone in human achievement. Not that we could tell anyone about it. We still wanted to go further, to see what we could achieve before the world's eyes drew their attention to our work. We wanted to move on to the next step – the biggest dream of all: creating an android that looked and acted exactly like a person.'

Emiko glances at me, and a wry grin crosses her face. 'I know that look. And I assure you, we weren't mad scientists pushing boundaries for the sake of pushing boundaries. Our goal for all of this – Haruto's dream – was to relieve suffering.'

And for the first time since we've sat, Emiko's eyes shift from our immediate vicinity. She looks across the path, towards the little girl with pigtails, who's now dancing, holding hands with the old man sitting on the bench.

'Japan has had a problem for the last thirty years, and it will be a problem that will last for another century, at least,' Emiko says, turning back towards us. 'There are too many old people and not enough younger ones to care for them. And this crisis will only worsen as our medical advancements continue to improve. Right now, the average lifespan in Japan is approaching ninety-five – the longest in the world, with many Japanese living longer than that. In another thirty years, the average lifespan could be a hundred and ten. Yet many of those elderly will still need help around the house, or in care homes or at hospitals, once they get past their mid-eighties. That's up to twenty-five years of caring per person.

'And who will help them? The young? The old already outnumber the young three to one. There's not enough young to help the elderly even if they all wanted to – not if you're going to keep the country and economy going. I know, in cities like Tokyo and Osaka, and even Hiroshima, it seems like Japan is packed with young people. Yet that's only because the young flock to those cities. In much of the rest of the country, that isn't the case. In smaller villages, the average age frequently reaches sixty already.

'So, Haruto's dream was to create a line of androids that could care for the elderly – that could permanently relieve Japan's elderly crisis. A crisis that other nations will have in the future, if they don't already. Countries have, of course, tried to do this with robots for decades. And today's bots are adequate if you need them to deliver meds or wheel a patient from one floor to the next. Those are simple things. But a bot doesn't have the human touch, if you will. The elderly can't relate to them on a personal level. Even if the robot looks relatively humanoid, we can't get past the uncanny valley. We know the artificial skin is off, or the way it moves or speaks isn't exactly like us. So instead of even humanoid-looking bots making the elderly feel comforted, it makes them feel alienated. And this affects their quality of life almost as much as the lack of real people to care for them does.'

Emiko glances across the path again. The little girl's now sitting back on her heels on the bench, sorting leaves into piles, the old man diligently counting each one aloud.

'And I have to admit, while we worked on the dog, we talked about the ultimate goal – yet I never understood just how badly a solution was needed until my husband became sick.'

And maybe Neotnia's reacted in some way I'm not aware of, because the way Emiko looks at her it's as if she's noticed some odd ripple cross her face. Yet after a beat, she continues.

'It was three and a half years into my work at the firm when my husband was diagnosed with Hodgkin's. He was only thirty-one, and I was twenty-eight, and it's the first either of us had spent any length of time in hospitals. But as I walked those halls for months as he underwent treatment, I came to understand how few carers there were to go around. I saw how lonely patients were; how the older ones, especially, just needed someone to talk to.'

Emiko shakes her head as if trying to make the memory pass more quickly. In the background, the Peace Bell sounds once more.

'So,' she arches her eyebrows, 'Haruto's grand dream fully became mine as well: to create a perfectly lifelike, autonomous being that was indistinguishable from a person. One that would care for our sick and elderly, and one that our elderly would feel completely at ease around...'

I notice the change that's come over Neotnia immediately. It's as apparent to me as a dark cloud is to picnic-goers on a previously clear day. Her eyes seem suddenly unfocused, and I glimpse the beginnings of a dark pall inching its way across her face. If Emiko's also noticed the change in Neotnia's demeanour, she doesn't let on.

'Of course, even though we had the synthetic physiology down and could relatively easily transition that to a humanoid form, the bottlenecks were in creating some additional quantum structures, as well as a synthetic skin and hair that were indistinguishable from a real person's. And that's not even to mention creating a quantum OS that could make the android's speech, apparent thoughts and actions indistinguishable from that of a real person. To do that we needed time, help and money. The dog bought us all three. The firm agreed to continue funding our project and let us hire another person for our team. Kentetsu. He was between our ages, in his mid-forties at the time, and looking to come back home. He'd spent the previous two decades working in Silicon Valley in artificial intelligence.'

Emiko stops for a moment and fingers her watch.

'At first, I wasn't thrilled when I'd heard who he'd worked for. His previous employer was all about shopping and social. In other words, commerce and vanity – the exact opposite of what Haruto and I were striving for. But we were swayed into thinking Kentetsu was a good ideological fit because his former employer had also open-sourced significant code for detecting synthetic media several years prior, and it turned out Kentetsu had led that project.'

I guess I've reacted in a certain way because Emiko glances at me for a moment.

'Anyway,' she continues. 'Even though his work in the Valley was primarily as an AI engineer on meta products, his first doctorate was in material sciences, too. That's a rare combination, so of course we snapped him up. And we did so not a moment too soon. Shortly after we hired Kentetsu, Haruto had his first heart attack.'

Neotnia's body tenses next to mine. And this time maybe Emiko's noticed, too, because she pauses and gives her a curious little look.

'So, there I was, back in the hospital again, this time looking after him. He was there for six weeks...' She shakes her head. 'I can see why Haruto never married. How could he have had the time for it? He wouldn't even allow a heart attack to interrupt his work. When I'd visit, he'd show me masses of code he'd programmed from his phone while he was supposed to be recuperating. When I scolded him, he'd simply point out that if our work was completed, he wouldn't be able to spend his recovery working because our carer androids would have caught him. But as it were, the doctor only saw him for five minutes each morning, and the nurses hardly had time to do anything beyond say a quick hello and check his vitals before needing to move on to the next patient. So, though I was cross with him, the reality of his experience only reinforced how badly our dream needed to succeed.

'And that's what we worked non-stop at for the next two years. I designed your body to be optimal for regard while Haruto coded your systems to make you into the ideal carer. I worked on perfecting your synthetic skin, while Haruto worked on perfecting your quantum OS, which he had more time to focus on now that Kentetsu had taken over programming your base subsystems. It was Haruto's quantum OS that, in the end, would be key to making you appear so lifelike. It was the glue that would bind everyone's work together.'

And that pall inching its way across Neotnia's face? Its march is now complete. A horrible shadow hangs over her flesh like a curtain. I hold my eyes on her, hoping to get an acknowledgment she's OK, yet her sole focus is on Emiko's words.

'But then we hit a wall. Or, the wall hit us, I should say,' Emiko goes on. 'Like so many four years ago, the firm's finances and capital got pummelled when the global recession struck – just another thing to blame the superpowers for. Regardless, the firm suddenly no longer had the luxury of waiting decades to see payoffs. Our work wasn't monetisable in the short term, so we had no way to help fill the loss in capital investment. And with their other revenue streams drying up, and spec already being a money pit, they were on the verge of cutting the programme. That's when Haruto's second heart attack struck, and his pacemaker was installed.'

This time, Neotnia doesn't even blink.

'And I thought that was it. I thought there was no way our work could carry on. But that's where Kentetsu came in. He approached executives at his former employer, and soon enough they offered to buy our programme from the firm. Haruto and I were originally against it, of course, given most acquisitions by American tech giants always end well for the Americans but poorly for everyone else. Then again, we were on the cusp of a new world.'

A chill crosses my body. Emiko looks at me with a funny little expression.

'It's an odd phrase, I know,' she says with a hint of amusement. '"The cusp of a new world." It's another phrase Haruto loved using. And in the case of our work, it couldn't be more apropos. We really were on the cusp of a new world thanks to the advancements we'd made, and we both wanted to find a way for that to continue. That's when the Americans came back with a better offer. Maybe they sensed our apprehension, maybe Kentetsu told them directly, I don't know. But they doubled their offer to our firm and agreed to blank-cheque our research for five more years. We were also guaranteed complete autonomy, and they even set us up at our own private, state-of-the-art facility so we could continue without interruption. It was in a different prefecture, but that was better than demanding we transfer our research Stateside, which was a worry we'd had when they made their original offer. So, Haruto and I concluded that not only was their new offer pretty irresistible, it was the only way to keep our dream alive. Besides, our firm was desperate for cash and would have sold our project to the Americans without us or our blessing. At least this way we could continue to direct our research and keep it in Jap—'

The abrupt squeal that breaks the air sends Emiko's head snapping so quickly she's lucky her neck doesn't break. It's the little girl on the bench across the path. She's thrown her piles of leaves into the air and smiles in delight as they rain down. Gathering the leaves again, she tosses them against the old man, who scoops some and dribbles them over her head.

Seeing this, the smallest hint of tension drains from Emiko's face.

Neotnia, on the other hand, has hardly registered the squeal at all.

'Anyway...' Emiko clears her throat. 'That's not to mention that, by this time, my husband was well into remission, and we were trying for a child. We'd always wanted to raise a family in a smaller city closer to nature, so the new location tucked away in the mountains was perfect. We sold our house in Osaka and bought one near the new facilities. Haruto sold his apartment in Osaka, too, but moved directly into the facility itself, together with Kentetsu. Haruto was always slower after the pacemaker, and this way his commute was simply a walk to the basement.'

Emiko settles her eyes on me. They take on an ironic look as a smirk grows on her lips.

'Americans,' she says – a hint of that disdain from earlier resurfacing. 'So much money, so little taste. That first year, Haruto and I laughed so often about his new residence. It couldn't fit him less. Haruto liked the traditional, yet this was the opposite. It stuck out like a sore thumb against the nature all around – three storeys of glass and steel structured like a pagoda. It looked like the vacation home of some eccentric American trillionaire raised on open-world metagames, which I'm sure it originally was – helipad and all. The saving grace for Haruto was the sight of a beautiful torii that spanned the nearby waterfall. He loved taking walks up to those cliffs, even though I worried the path was too steep for his heart.'

For a moment, Emiko lingers on the memory. Yet soon enough any trace of nostalgia vacates her face as she again glances towards the little girl and old man across the path.

'After that first year there ... well, things changed.' Her mouth tightens. 'My husband's cancer returned. We knew there wasn't much hope and were still trying desperately for a child.' She looks at Neotnia. 'Your development was coming along, yet not as quickly as we'd have liked. At the time you didn't have a completed face – your eyes were the hardest part for me. Programmatically, you were also still little more than a bot. Thanks to Kentetsu's work, you could ambulate like a human and perform basic commands, but that was all base-quantum subsystems. You didn't have a personality, nor the ability or knowledge to care for the elderly. Nor were you yet capable of the myriad micro-movements a human makes, as Haruto was still working on your quantum OS, and it wasn't going well.'

Emiko holds her gaze on Neotnia as if silently judging her features.

'Making the dog act lifelike was one thing, but making *you* act life-like ... honestly, there were days I thought that was beyond even Haruto.'

She's quiet for another moment and glances at the analogue watch. Underneath its band, her skin is pale, like a marble road in a tanned desert.

'By late that spring, I was pregnant. And by November – three years tomorrow – my husband died, two months before our child was born.' She says it matter-of-factly. 'Shortly after, I resigned and moved back to Hiroshima to have our daughter, where I could raise her near my parents. I never saw Haruto after that.'

Neotnia and I are silent as Emiko looks on. She's reached the end of her story. In the background, the Peace Bell's hum resonates long and deep. I gaze upon the shadow lingering over Neotnia as she sits, lost in a thought.

'I'm sorry to hear about your husband,' she finally says.

Emiko doesn't respond. Her mouth held closed, she blinks a few times.

'I...' Neotnia looks at her hands on the table. 'You created my body...'

'Yes.'

'So, you know I don't have ... all the *parts* a female is supposed to... If your goal was to make me so lifelike, why—'

'You were made to care for the elderly. You don't need a vagina for that.'

Neotnia nods so subtly you could miss it, but she doesn't look Emiko in the eyes. The shadow on her face grows darker.

'Your external form – your shape – was what's important,' Emiko says, and for a moment, her eyes scan Neotnia's face as carefully as if they're studying the most important painting ever created.

'I'm sure you've noticed you're quite pretty,' she says. 'That was purposeful. We – people – feel more comfortable around pretty people. It's one of our many flaws. We find attractive people more trustworthy; we find them more competent, although there's no logical reason we should. And we certainly don't mind spending time with them. So, you needed to be pretty. That was so important that, despite the significant resources involved, I created two different faces for you. Yet I couldn't decide which to use. Obviously, Haruto liked this one better. But both were made with that critical objective in mind: making you attractive. And that attractiveness, in turn, would help to unconsciously prime patients to regard you as more kind, competent and approachable. It would help patients warm to you.'

Emiko nods at Neotnia's chest.

'Even your chest-to-waist-to-hip ratio – it's ideal by today's norms. Your figure – it too makes people feel comfortable around you. It makes you approachable, yet it's not so sultry that it's distracting. But a vagina? Given what you were made for, there was no need for me to waste time and resources on giving you sex organs. They simply weren't necessary for your intended purpose.'

Neotnia raises her eyes. Brushing her bangs to the side, she clears her throat, composing herself. '*Hai*,' she says matter-of-factly. 'I understand.'

Yet something about Neotnia's reply, or maybe the way she's moved, has struck Emiko. She scrutinises Neotnia's face – how she's pressed her mouth closed, how her lids blink, even the way her nostrils splay when a breath passes through them. When she finally locks eyes with Neotnia, she shakes her head.

'I'll admit, even though Haruto worked on your quantum OS for the better part of a decade, I never imagined it'd make you *this* life-like,' she says, her eyebrows arching a little. 'Until now, I never truly understood just how well it would allow you to mimic human emotions. We had, of course, discussed giving you lifelike emotions in order to help you build a rapport with those you care for. It would create a sense of agency in your systems, and help reinforce your desire, so to speak, to care about those you would interact with regularly. It would also have an ancillary benefit for the patients themselves. It would further help them bond with you, and thus increase their quality of life. After all, we tend to like the people we can tell like us and want to be around them more.'

Emiko pauses, her eyes lost in unabashed consideration of Neotnia's features, as if Neotnia herself is in front of a two-way mirror and could have no idea she's being examined like a unique, priceless heirloom.

'But just the fact that we're having a conversation like this – really, it's remarkable. Even for me,' she explains unapologetically. 'Yet then again, your quantum OS wasn't finished by the time I left. I've never been able to see it in action before. But clearly, it makes you greater than the sum of your parts – which just goes to show what a genius Haruto is.'

'I see,' is all Neotnia says. Her lips form a little line, and she again gazes at her hands on the tabletop, her eyes packed with clouds. She remains looking at her hands for so long it's as if she's simply lost the desire to ever speak again.

Yet finally, she does. 'If there was another face you could have put on me, how come I don't have seams? How come there are no breaks in my skin?'

'The dog we designed did have seams,' Emiko nods. 'But his was hardly more than the standard synthetic variety. The skin I designed for you is so much more advanced, it's not even comparable. It's the difference between a child's scribbles and the Mona Lisa. Yours is self-healing, for starters. It grows together without scarring. It's exceptionally resilient. It's why it healed from your ... ill-judged electrocutions. But you could heal just as easily from cuts.'

Emiko goes quiet for a moment, as if she's considering whether to elaborate on something.

'Your name, Neotnia? You know it's not Japanese, correct?'

'*Hai*,' Neotnia nods.

'It's a play on "neoteny". Did Haruto ever tell you that?'

Neotnia shakes her head.

'Do you know what neoteny is?'

'No.'

'It's the genetic predisposition in some species to retain youthful features well into adulthood. We named you after it because, well ... you won't age. You'll always look as you do now. Your nails can grow, your hair can grow. But your skin will stay as it is now. As a matter of fact, in theory – provided no critical internal damage – your synthetic physiology, your internal quantum structures, mean you'll survive for decades longer than a person can live. Maybe centuries. Yet you'll always look as you do today.'

'So, my body...' Neotnia glances at her hand as if it's another part of her. 'I'll be like this forever...?'

'Correct,' Emiko says as if she were confirming instructions with an info bot. 'We built you to last. It only made sense from a return-on-investment perspective. Governments and health services aren't going to tolerate having to replace five-billion-yen devices every decade. Just like bots, they want one and done.'

Neotnia's lips part ever so slightly, and her clouded eyes, I see them tremble with a terrible sadness. And I know if that horrible shadow could seep like ash into her skin, it'd do so right now. Emiko sees all this, too – I know she does. Yet she remains cold, unimpassioned, and instantly I feel a stinging remorse in my chest – because I see myself reflected in Emiko's expression. I see how I reacted to Neotnia in the café when she first told me about herself. And I fucking hate myself for it.

'If it's any consolation,' Emiko says, 'none of this *actually* bothers you. You don't actually *feel* hurt or disappointment – or even loss over Haruto. It just seems like you do.'

And though Neotnia's lips don't part even a millimetre more, I hear the breath ejected from their sliver of an opening, like she's been punched in the gut. And with that final blow, an anger swells inside me. It rumbles from a place so deep it might as well be the centre of the Earth. I pull my phone from my pocket and bring up the splinter.

'What's the fucking password?' I say, slamming the phone onto the table.

It's the first time I've seen genuine shock cross Emiko's face. Yet she only lets it show for a moment. She glances past me, and when she looks back, her eyes are as controlled as ever. She casts no more than a peek at the screen between us.

'I wouldn't know.'

'Then why is your name in the metadata?'

'Probably not for the reasons you think.' She holds a hard gaze on me, her words sharp. 'It could be related to my work, yes. But equally as likely, it could simply be because the data, whatever it is, was extracted from my terminal at the lab – or for any other number of reasons that have nothing to do with me. Regardless, I couldn't say why my name's there.'

'Why don't you just try a password?'

'All my passwords were biometric. I have none to try.'

'What about this Kentetsu guy?' I say, my face growing hotter. 'Would he know the password? Why don't you contact him right now and ask?'

'If I could do that, it would be quite extraordinary.' Her eyes narrow. 'Kentetsu passed away several years ago.'

I feel like I'm going to explode. I know she's not telling us everything.

'What about your old firm?' I shake my head. 'You never told us its name.'

'They went bust shortly after we transferred. The recession, remember? Then again, an *American* boy is probably too ignorant to notice the state your nation's left this world in.'

'And this tech company that bought you? Did they go bust, too?'

'Sorry,' Emiko's gaze is now icy. 'NDAs.'

'You must know something else.' I say, my voice growing. 'You have to at least have some idea of how we can contact her father.'

Emiko glances over my shoulder again but quickly refocuses on me. 'I don't,' she says. 'And I don't think you should try.'

'That's fucking easy for you to say—' Suddenly there's a warmth on my forearm.

Neotnia's placed her hand on me, and she gives me a sad half-smile.

'If you don't think I should try to find him,' she says to Emiko, a delicate steadiness in her voice, 'then why are you telling us any of this? Why did you call me back? Why did you tell me to come here?'

Emiko looks towards the little girl and old man across the path. Her eyes stay on the pair for some time.

'My daughter is now the age where she's beginning to ask questions about where her father is. As a scientist and a mother, I understand the desire to know things we do not. But I also understand that sometimes you have to let people go.' Her gaze returns to Neotnia, and she pauses as if considering whether to say what comes next. 'Haruto had a good heart. He cared deeply for people. I knew he'd been in love with me for a long time...'

Neotnia's eyes widen, and her mouth drops. And I gotta say, mine does, too.

'He never told me explicitly,' Emiko says. 'I was married, and he was too honourable for that. But we worked together for years – and you don't need to be a scientist to figure this stuff out. It's obvious when a man is in love with you.'

And Emiko glances at me, that tiny curl returning to her mouth's edge.

'Regardless, after my husband died, Haruto urged me to leave the project and take care of my soon-to-be daughter. He did so knowing it meant he'd no longer see me.' She gives Neotnia a hard look. 'One of the many things Haruto understood about this world is you do whatever you have to that's best for the people you love – even if that choice hurts yourself. You should think carefully about that before you carry on trying to find him – because he may not want you to.'

I look at Neotnia and see her throat tighten. Yet before either of us can reply, a voice shrieks, 'Mama, Mama, Mama!'

The little girl from across the path scampers to Emiko's side, beaming with delight. As she crawls onto the bench, a large smile breaks Emiko's face and her expression grows so naturally warm it's as if we've been speaking to a different person this whole time. Wrapping her arms around her daughter, Emiko listens intently as she speaks. The edges of Neotnia's lips curve up at whatever she's said. Emiko responds and, with her arms still wrapped around her daughter for safety, she smiles and pats her on the bottom.

'You'll have to excuse me,' Emiko says, glancing her large analogue watch. 'But I've got an ice cream date with my daughter, and she's been patient long enough.'

The girl wraps her arms around her mother's neck, pulling herself close.

Emiko holds Neotnia's gaze.

'You asked why I had told you to come here in the first place; why I told you any of this if I don't think you should try to find Haruto. It's because I never want to see you again. I've quenched your curiosity as best I can. There is nothing else I can tell you. There is nothing else I can do for you. And now you know that. Now, I expect you to honour your promise and never contact me again.'

As Emiko scoops up her daughter and rises from the table, a commotion grows over our shoulders. The two office workers behind us, the man and woman, rise as well and look at her. And then the younger guy in running gear listening to music at the next table does the same. Emiko nods at him and he places a finger on his metalenses and speaks. Across the path, the old man is up now, too, as are a couple who were sat at another bench. They're now by his side, as is the young man who was sketching on a notepad across the way. We hear the creeping of tyres on the path and turn to find a limo rolling to a stop, followed by a smaller black car. The three people at the old man's side lead him to the limo and the back door rises, yet he doesn't get in. Instead, he waits on Emiko.

I glance in Goeido's direction. Even in the distance, I can see the alarm now on his face. Emiko looks in his direction, too.

'Ah, yes. Your friend, the sumo.' She turns back towards us and raises an eyebrow. 'He's even cuter in person. I remember meta-streaming his matches. I was a big fan.'

Neotnia and I gape at each other.

'Don't blame him. My security was in the area long before you three arrived. They've been keeping tabs on everybody, all day – even you, even in the museum. Now, excuse me...'

'Please...' Neotnia's voice trembles with such desperation it stops Emiko in her tracks. 'Do you really not know where my father is?'

Adjusting her daughter in her arms, Emiko turns. 'One of the things people learn throughout their lives is to respect the wishes of others,' she says to Neotnia. 'I don't know why he left you, but if he did, it was for a good reason – one you may never have an answer for. And, no, I really don't know where he is. Now, I'm sorry, I must go. *Never* seek me out again,' she shakes her head. 'That part of my life is over. I have all I need in my arms right now.'

The old man makes way so Emiko and her daughter can enter the limo, and she does so without glancing at us again. Instead, it's the old man who lingers on us before finally following her into the car. The other three who were next to him get into the limo's front pod. As it pulls away, the three from the picnic area climb into the smaller black vehicle.

I look at Neotnia as the cars roll away, and it strikes me how out of place she now appears on this bright autumn day in this beautiful park. That terrible shadow drapes across her like a horrible veil, her eyes welled up in its darkness. She looks just as the *hibakusha* did when their world was destroyed – and all hope with it.

Goeido rushes over, his face a mass of alarm and confusion – but also relief. I hear the concern in his voice as he speaks to Neotnia. She replies with a single, almost imperceptible, word, then leans into his massive frame, trembling against it. Her tears soak his kimono. And looking at me, Goeido drapes his big arm around her while holding her to his belly. After several moments, he sits her on the bench the girl and old man shared and gets her to explain what's happened.

And watching those tears drying on Neotnia's flushed cheeks in the crisp November air, I feel that anger swelling inside me again. I keep hearing Emiko's words. I know she wasn't telling us everything. And as Neotnia continues to explain to Goeido what's happened, as the Peace Bell resonates across the park, and classes of young schoolchildren learn about their history, I sit at the next bench and fold my phone out into a laptop. I pull up Avance Maps. I pull up a terminal. I pull up meta renderings. I code, and I compile, and the bell resonates several more times as the beautiful autumn leaves sway in their branches overhead. Then I rise and fold my laptop down into a tablet and approach Goeido and Neotnia.

And as the coloured leaves rustle in the maples all around, and her flushed face looks up towards mine, I show her my screen.

I say, 'I think I know where your father could be.'

15 – That's something.

We were on the cusp of a new world...

Emiko's words echo in my head as I stare from the window, the sun's position now low behind the mountains whipping by. We've been on this *Shinkansen* for nearly three hours, speeding towards Nagano. Goeido and Neotnia are both lost in their own thoughts, gazing into the dusk zipping past.

In the Peace Park, I was certain Emiko was withholding things, but she also made some offhand remarks that were more valuable to someone trying to find Neotnia's father than she probably realised. She'd said the facility they moved to after the American company bought them was in the mountains. Of course, almost three-quarters of Japan is mountainous, but she also mentioned it was located by a waterfall that had a torii spanning it, and that there was a helipad on the facility's roof.

So as Neotnia recounted our meeting to Goeido, I quickly wrote an AI to scan all publicly available satellite imagery of Japan, looking for large platforms that could be helipads. Once all helipads were identified, I had the AI exclude any that weren't near rivers or water-falls. This reduced the number from the thousands to fewer than a hundred. Next, I fed the AI a meta rendering of a torii so it could learn what one looked like from above, and then had the AI exclude any helipads that were by rivers or waterfalls but weren't also near torii.

The result? There's precisely one helipad in Japan that's in the mountains, near a waterfall with a torii spanning it. It's in the Myoko-Togakushi Renzan National Park area near an active volcano called Niigata-Yakeyama. The closest city to the facility is Nagano, which is a ninety-minute drive through the winding mountains. Nagano itself is only a three-hour drive north-west of Tokyo.

When I told Neotnia and Goeido what I'd found, they gaped at me like I'd announced I'd located the Fountain of Youth. Neotnia wanted to leave for Nagano right away. Yet, I didn't want to give her false hope. Even if I had found the facility, it was no guarantee her father was there now – and I told her that.

'What else do I have?' she replied. Her eyelids were swollen, and that terrible shadow draped across her face. I couldn't get it out of my mind how similar she looked to the *hibakusha* from the museum's photographs, as if she'd somehow escaped their black-and-white landscapes and crossed into our world.

At Hiroshima Station we reclaimed our bags and found that bullet trains were operating again. As we boarded, a bot warned us to disregard any non-official news sources. Deepfakes were spreading showing the Japanese prime minister announcing hundreds dead from collisions in Hokkaido the day before. In reality, the cyberattack killed only two, both engineers, when a train they were working under started unexpectedly. As always, the superpowers were blaming each other for the attacks.

Since settling into our compartment, we've been quiet. Goeido and I both seemed to think it best to let Neotnia to her thoughts. As for mine, they turn to Emiko Ikari. The limo, the undercover security – she's clearly wealthy. Intelligent, too, and well put together. In other words, she's the exact opposite of the paranoid person I'd imagined. So why have security? Is that a normal thing – because she's rich? Or did she have them to protect herself from Neotnia? But given she helped create her, so knew what she was built for – *literally* caring for people – why would Emiko feel she needed protection? And if she thought Neotnia was a threat, why bring along her daughter?

A reply from Sony arrives on my phone. Dismissing the message, I pull up Avance Maps. I switch to satellite view and drag the map north, finding the road winding up the forested mountain towards the facility. Besides the helipad, you can't make out much about it as its grounds have been blurred. But its natural surroundings are clearer. The facility sits on the edge of a cliff. To its north and northeast, it overlooks a deep valley, and to its east, it looks out at a waterfall that cascades from higher up on the next set of cliffs. An orange torii spans the waterfall, which spills into the river in the valley below. The river eventually flows into the Sea of Japan, just miles away.

'Did your father ever mention Avance?'

Goeido looks at me, but it takes Neotnia a moment to register my voice. She turns from the window. Though her eyes are set on me, I feel like they're seeing me through a haze.

She shakes her head. 'Why?'

It's the first word she's spoken since boarding.

'I think they might be the ones who bought his and Emiko's work.'

Neotnia doesn't react how I expected. Her eyes simply dip furtively, and she gives a slight nod. It's not until Goeido speaks that she does anything that acknowledges she's actually absorbed what I've said. She translates, and Goeido nods when Neotnia says, 'Avance.'

Avance is one of America's remaining tech giants. It's also the largest, formed from the merger of two of the most influential tech companies that dominated Silicon Valley in the first few decades of the century. If you use social media or shop or search online, you're most likely using a product made by Avance – if you're on the North American or European intranets, anyway. But even in Japan, the company's a household name, despite Baidu, ByteDance, Samsung, Sony and Tencent dominating the tech scene in Asia.

I tell Neotnia and Goeido how the facility's imagery is blurred. How the owner of that data, the mapping service I use – that most people in the West use – is Avance Maps. In the past, Avance has been known to obfuscate images of their various campuses to keep the curious from digitally snooping. 'But that's not the only reason I think the American company Emiko mentioned is Avance,' I explain.

They both look at me, waiting for me to continue.

'OK,' I say, collecting my thoughts. 'So, everyone knows Avance because of the three S's, right? Search, social and shopping. But remember when Emiko said that Kentetsu guy was responsible for a project at his former employer, where they open-sourced code made for detecting synthetic media?'

Neotnia nods after recounting to Goeido what Emiko had said in the Peace Park.

'Well, there's only one American tech giant that has open-sourced code for detecting synthetic media – that I know of, anyway. And it was Avance, and they did it nine or so years ago.'

Goeido says something, and Neotnia translates, 'Synthetic media?'

'Deepfakes,' I answer. '"Synthetic media" is just the technical term for what everyone calls deepfakes. The "synthetic" part just means the media is created, well, synthetically. Instead of a camera capturing light and sound, which are natural data, and recording that as video, AI creates the data we see in fabricated recordings.'

Goeido nods as Neotnia's translates this. And I'm conscious that, of the three of us, he's most acutely felt the effects of deepfakes.

'And look, everyone knows the superpowers' deepfakes are the best, right?' I go on. 'America and China have been attacking each other with them forever. But it's also been increasingly hard for either country's deepfakes to infiltrate the other's borders since both countries' AIs have gotten so good at defence. Of course, everyone in America is worried that China seems to have a leg up on us again, given the recent spate of deepfakes. And if you believe what China says, an external deepfake hardly ever gets through onto their intranet anymore – the one weeks ago was news because it *was* such a rarity. Still, even when deepfakes do get through, China and America can detect and discredit each other's digital lies relatively quickly, which negates much of their usefulness in disinformation campaigns.'

'*Hai*,' Goeido says after Neotnia translates.

'But that's not the case for *other* countries. The superpowers' deepfakes are still powerful propaganda tools when used in other nations, simply because those nations don't have the advanced AI the U.S. and China possess. It's why America and China now get the best use of their deepfakes when used outside the other's borders. I mean, just look at all the deepfakes they've propagated internationally in the wake of Paris and Zambia – even Hokkaido.'

Goeido says something, and Neotnia's eyes shift. He looks at me when she's done translating, telling me to continue.

'OK ... so, I remember learning this in my ethics in computing class. When Avance open-sourced that code for detecting synthetic media, their PR team spun it like here was this big, often-vilified company doing something good and noble for the world by giving NGOs and civil liberty organisations new tools to help fight deep-fakes at a more local level. And the code did help. It stopped a lot of innocent activists from going to jail for crimes they'd been framed for, and helped massively with cyberbullying and sextortion at-tempts...

'The thing is, a few years later, Avance ended up getting crucified when it was discovered that, at the same time they open-sourced their deepfake *detection* code, they'd also made a killing developing other, more advanced, deepfake *creation* code. And they were selling it to a handful of not-so-benevolent nations who used it against not just their enemies, but their own citizens. It was a PR disaster for Avance. They'd essentially been caught giving away an out-of-date treatment for a disease just to get good press, while at the same time secretly enabling others to release much more harmful strains of that disease.'

Neotnia translates for Goeido. When she's done, they're both quiet for a moment. Only a sliver of the sun remains peeking above the forested mountains speeding by.

'Deepfakes are one thing,' Neotnia says. 'But does Avance even make robots? Would they even be interested in my father's work?'

'They never have in the past,' I admit, considering her for a moment. Her word choice surprises me. And though she's looking at me, it's as if she's struggling not to let her eyes drift somewhere else. 'But Avance is the biggest tech giant left in North America – "the Baidu of the West" as they say. And they're continually dipping their fingers into side projects in hopes of finding new revenue streams. I mean, lunar tourism and metasports are well outside the three S's, but they're investing heavily in those sectors now. And, well, they're not exactly loved, simply because they are so big and powerful

– not to mention they're always having one privacy scandal after another, right? So, they're also always looking for ways to enhance their public image. What better way to do that than by creating a line of androids that can help some of the most vulnerable in society? I mean, who cares if Avance is making trillions tracking your every move or selling tech to far-off bad guys in countries most people have never thought about if they've also made the android that takes care of your sick great-grandma? It's PR gold.'

Neotnia lingers on the empty space in front of her for a moment before refocusing on Goeido. Once she translates, she falls back into the silence that's settled over our compartment. Goeido, too, remains deep in thought. The stillness is only broken when a soft artificial voice sounds a few minutes later. It says something, then repeats it. But it's only at its third announcement that Neotnia seems to hear it.

'We'll be in Nagano in thirty minutes,' she says before turning towards the window again. Outside, the last of the sun's glow has disappeared behind the forested mountains. Everything's now cast in shadow. When my gaze returns inward, I find Goeido peering at my phone on the table, the facility's blurred-out satellite imagery on display.

We arrive in Nagano just past seven. As we exit the station, I'm struck by how small the city is. It's not tiny like my hometown, but it's the smallest Japanese city I've been to yet. There's hardly a bot in sight, and for a downtown area, there aren't many brand-name shops or fast-food outlets.

Goeido says he knows of a cheap hotel nearby where he and his ex-wife stayed when she was pregnant, and they came to Nagano for the *onsens*. We walk there in ten minutes. It's a two-storey building called Hotel Raccoon Dog, though the only raccoon dog thing about it is an image of the animal printed above the name. Inside, it looks like it was converted from an old YMCA. We take the only room they have left. It's on the upper floor and overlooks the parking lot. The room itself is small. A low-set queen-sized bed takes up more than half of it. The floor is all tatami mats except for the entrance, where we leave our shoes. There's a miniature dresser with an old TV, and a couple of cushions for use as chairs on the tatami.

I use the communal bathroom in the hallway to check my wound. Under the gauze, the skin around my incision has reddened and mucus has wet my T-shirt. I change into a new one and switch my hoodie for a sweater. When I return, we decide to find some food.

The streets of Nagano are quiet and narrow compared to Tokyo. Many still have ancient electrical wires dipping and zigzagging over-head. We come to a main street that's mostly little shops – a toy store, a Laundromat, a couple of home-goods stores – but there are a few food offerings, too. We choose a burger joint made to look like one of those beach shacks you'd find in Honolulu and take a seat under some wooden canoe paddles bolted onto the back wall.

I don't think any of us realised the extent of our exhaustion until now. It's the first time in over a day that we haven't been on the move – or in a wheat field, anyway. Besides ordering, none of us says much; that's how drained we are. But by the time we finish our burgers, it's obvious everyone feels a bit replenished, and I'm comfortable enough to broach the subject of the facility. Both Goeido and I have the same question: how does she want to handle it?

Neotnia's eyes shift, and her lips form a straight line. She says something in Japanese, then translates: 'All the cars in a small place like this will stay local, so in the morning I'll order a long distance one and have it take me there.'

I can tell Goeido was hoping for more of a plan than that. So was I.

'What else is there to do?' she shrugs. 'It's the only lead left. And if he's not there … maybe someone will be who knows where he could be. Or … maybe this leads nowhere. But I'm finding out either way.'

Goeido doesn't reply, but as I finish the last of my drink, I can't help but think he seems more pensive than usual.

I stretch the lingering stiffness from my body as we leave the diner, taking in a deep breath. It's apparent we're in a higher altitude. The air that hits my lungs is crisp, and the night sky is so clear I can distinguish the fine outcrops of the unfinished stations' jagged forms set against a backdrop of stars.

Heading back the way we came, I spot Goeido peering at the small toy store next to the Laundromat. A bored clerk stands behind the counter. The look on Goeido's face makes me wonder if he's been there before, perhaps with his wife when they came here. Maybe he bought something there for his then soon-to-be daughter.

As we come to the narrow cross-street with the zigzagging wires, I glimpse something I'd missed the first time. In the distance, straight ahead, two massive structures sit in shadow, one behind the other, the last dimly lit by orbs of yellow light.

'It's a famous temple. The *Zenkō-ji*,' Neotnia translates after Goeido notices me looking in its direction. 'He went there with his wife, just after they married. He says its grounds are magnificent at night when they're empty.'

'Do you guys want to check it out?' I shrug. 'If it's magnificent, I wouldn't mind seeing it.'

Neotnia nods. 'OK.' But when she asks Goeido, he doesn't appear receptive. 'He says he's tired and will go back to the hotel,' she explains. 'But he says we should go.'

I hope my suggestion didn't bring back painful memories for him. But if it did, he doesn't show it. He just gives me a nod and tells us he'll see us back at the hotel.

Neotnia and I continue along the main street until it dead-ends at a pair of large stone lanterns, marking the beginning of a footpath draped in shadows. Entering the path, we pass a row of six green figures sat on lotus leaves. Their eyes gaze down upon us as their scarlet scarves billow in the breeze. Shortly after, we cross under the first structure I saw at a distance, an ornamental tiered gate with an opening so large I feel no bigger than a cat who's slipped in through a raised garage door. As we exit its other side, an involuntary breath escapes my lips.

It feels as if we've transitioned from one world to another.

Deep-blue shadows stretch across the pale gravel of the grounds before us. They run from one structure to the next as the various gardens' flora rustle, sounding like they're singing a hymn in the breeze. Dozens of stone lanterns dot the landscape, their shadows linked with those from the cedar and red pine trees scattered about. To the right, a copper incense burner the size of Goeido emits pleasant fumes. To the left, a wooden footbridge arcs over a lily padded pond, which glistens in the moonlight. And looming above it all is the second structure I noticed from a distance, the main temple hall. Its multiple sloping roofs sweep up at their ends like the fins of manta. Beneath their awnings, massive paper lanterns marked with black glyphs sway between tall timber pillars. The lanterns glow dim and yellow, like giant fireflies.

Our feet thunk as we ascend the steep timber steps. The main temple hall's doors are so immense it seems as if a colossus must live inside. I cross the porch to give them a push, but they don't budge. Returning to Neotnia's side, we sit on the topmost step without saying a word. In the temple's grounds below, every structure, tree, and surface seems as if it's a perfectly placed part of a unified whole, down to the bumpy blue shadows draping the gravel. And above it all is a sky littered with stars like diamonds. And it's a sky that's *only* filled with diamonds. From where we're sat, the moon can't be seen, nor can the stations.

Goeido was right. This is the most magnificent place I've ever seen.

There's a hollow thump above our heads. A lantern marked with a thick black swastika knocks against the pillar Neotnia's sat next to, pushed by the breeze. She gazes up at it then turns her eyes towards me. The warmth of the lantern is reflected in them.

'You need to be back in Tokyo tomorrow for the signing,' she says.

I shake my head. 'I sent Sony a message on the train. Told them I was sick. We've rescheduled for the day after. It's not like they're not going to buy it from me, anyway.' I give a small smile. 'They can wait.'

Neotnia holds her gaze on me for a quiet moment. Above, there's another hollow thump, and I glance towards the swastika lantern.

'This place reminds me of Joe,' I say. 'He's the one who explained to me what the differences between a shrine and a temple are. Well, not so much explained. He nearly yelled it at me.'

It's the first time the edges of Neotnia's mouth have curved upward all night. But it doesn't last. Those thoughts that have tumbled through her mind since the Peace Park exert their gravity once again, and with that gravity I know Emiko's words haven't left her for an instant.

For some time, the swastika lantern thumps gently above us as the gardens' flora hums its soft hymn.

When I next look upon Neotnia, I find her eyes already on me – yet not on my face. They appear to be inspecting my chest, my shoulders, until, finally, they do meet mine, briefly, before casting a furtive glance at the steps beneath our feet. When her gaze rises, it surveys the temple's grounds once again. It's a long moment before she speaks.

'Remember our date?' she says, lingering on the gate that we crossed under in the distance. A small warmth passes over her face as her lips curve upward so slightly I'd miss it if the lantern light were any dimmer. 'I always wanted to go on a date before. It always looked like so much fun when I'd see others on one. And ours, it was fun … No – that's not even close. It was so much more than that. It was so much more than "fun". It was … perfect. I was so nervous … but it was just … perfect. A movie and a walk and a talk and a meal … It was…'

Her voice trails off.

'You wore that sweater on our date,' she says, glancing at my chest.

I tilt my head down, looking at it. 'It's my fancy sweater,' I say. 'I have it because … well, it's thick, so it hides my skin pretty well. The way it bunches up when I sit, you can't tell my skin does the same.'

For a moment, I see the smallest hint of that wonderful invisible smile Neotnia's eyelids make, and it warms me inside.

'Well, I think it looks really nice on you. I like it…'

But her voice trails off again, and this time a horrible ripple of sadness appears. That look on her face – it's as if she's trying to reconcile something she knows is impossible.

'But that's not true, is it?' she says. 'I don't *really* like that sweater, do I? Because my thoughts – they *aren't* my own. What I think about that sweater, it's not me deciding that, is it? I mean, nothing I think is mine. Not one thought.'

When her eyes find mine again, they're glassy. Behind them, a storm is brewing, and it makes my chest feel so tight. Yet I don't say a word. These are the thoughts she's been battling ever since the park, and they need to be released.

'I always thought I was going to the care home because I wanted to,' she manages. 'In the beginning, I thought it was because the residents reminded me of Father and his weak heart. And then I thought I kept returning because I genuinely cared for them – because I became friends with Joe, with everyone there. I thought I loved listening to their stories. I thought I *chose* to want to make their day just a little bit better...' Her face, it looks like it wants to shatter into a million little pieces. 'But that was a lie. It was all a lie. It was my code all along. I was *made* this way. I was made to be the perfect carer. Even my feelings – for Father, for Goeido, for Joe ... for you. Well, like Emiko said: I'm programmed to mimic human emotions to reinforce a desire, "so to speak", to care about those I interact with.'

'Neotnia—'

'No, you heard her.' She shakes her head, her voice wavering. 'None of this *actually* bothers me. I don't *feel* hurt or disappointment or loss – it just *seems* like I do...'

She goes quiet again and turns her gaze towards the grounds before us. A small bird lands on one of the moonlit paths. Its head darts left and right. It hops from one cluster of pale gravel to the next. Soon, an identical bird lands, causing the first to scatter, and shortly, the second flies off as well.

'Remember on our date, after the movie?' Neotnia says, lingering on where the birds stood just moments ago. 'I took you to Freshness Burger and we talked about the difference between robots and people. You said robots are created with a purpose, and people aren't. And you're right. You said people have the agony of wondering why they're here, and bots don't. That people choose what kind of person they'll become – they can't blame it on a maker. But a bot can because it doesn't have that choice.'

She turns her eyes towards mine. Their shallow pools mirror the blue of the night.

'I can't tell you how much hope that gave me when you said that. I knew I wasn't human, but I thought maybe I could be part of humanity regardless – even with my body the way it is. I thought maybe the only way I was different was physically. That maybe I was closer to being a person than a bot. That inside, maybe I really was still no less of a person than anyone else; that I really *could* be anything I chose to be – just like Father had said.' She shrugs, and her voice breaks. 'How foolish was I to think all that, huh? How foolish was I to believe I could be like everyone else? That I had free choice in what I did or thought or felt?'

And looking at her face, trembling as it does against all the pain she carries inside – it breaks me. I wish I had something wise stored deep within me to say. Something that could take that pain away, yet all I can manage is, 'You're not a—'

'Bot?' she says. 'Is an android much more? I'm a better build; more advanced parts, sure. But that's it, right? I'm fancier code, but still just code, right?'

Her throat tightens, and she wraps her arms around her shins, drawing her thighs to her chest. Setting her chin on her knees, her eyes settle on something in the gardens. It's the only not beautiful thing here – the remainder of a fir, swaying in the night. Its needles have fallen from its branches, which curve unnaturally downwards as if they're frowning. Even its top is bent, and it reminds me of the melted iron lantern from the museum – an exquisite object transmuted into an unnatural form, as if its original essence has been completely extracted by some horrible technique.

'I thought *I* liked hot chocolate. I thought that was *my* choice,' she says, looking at that tree. 'But nothing about me is really my own. If my purpose wasn't to take care of the elderly, but to ... to repair vehicles, I'd have been going to a car factory every day thinking it was simply because I liked to...'

And as if catching an awful thought, she stretches a hand out, examining the backs of her fingers in the lantern's glow.

'Could I just as easily be a monster with different code? Could I want to hurt people instead of wanting to help them?' She pauses, as if yet another terrible notion has crossed her mind. 'I know Father is a brilliant scientist ... But, what if he's a cruel man? Brilliant men can be cruel, can't they? Those scientists who created the bomb, they were all brilliant. Father always seemed so kind, but he could really be cruel, too, right? I mean, Emiko said he loved her. *Her*. How could a good man love someone like that? What if he really is no different from the men who created the bomb? I mean, I believed him completely – *foolishly* – when he said I was no less of a person than anyone. But then I find out I'm missing what all females have. And now ... now I know my actions, my thoughts, even my *feelings* aren't my own. I can't choose to be whatever I want like people can – like he said I can...'

Neotnia turns her gaze back towards the melted fir, and it's a long moment before she speaks again.

'If I was part of this programme of his, if I were made to care ... why didn't he just tell me? Emiko said he cared deeply for people. But then why did he lie about so much? Why did he abandon me—' She freezes. 'Unless ... unless it's because he knows I'm not anything like a person. So maybe ... maybe he doesn't think I deserve the same consideration a person deserves...'

A horrible expression takes over her face. She's on the verge of tears, and I feel like I am, too. And as the agony ripples across the swollen pools in her eyes, I can't stand it any longer.

I take her hand. It's warm and soft, and feels so good to hold again. And I tell her the first honest thing that comes to my mind – the only thing I can say with one hundred percent certainty.

'I don't think a cruel man could bring someone as wonderful as you into this world.'

That expression of hers trembles. 'But then why would he lie about so much?'

'To protect you,' I answer. 'Because he cares.' I raise my eyebrows and shrug. 'I know that's messed up, but it's what parents do sometimes.' My thumb rubs the shallow dip between Neotnia's knuckles, her warm skin sliding under my touch. 'Remember when I told you my mom lied about my dad's death for a long, long time? It was years before she was able to tell me he actually died over there. But I now understand that wasn't cowardice or cruelty ... or even for her own sanity. It was to protect me.'

I shake my head. 'I really don't think they know what else to do to protect us from truth that's going to hurt, so they lie. Just like everyone, they're making it up as they go along, trying to do the best they can, questioning every choice, wishing they could guard us from things they know they can't. So, they lie to delay our hurt as long as possible. And maybe it's not fair of them to do that, but it's how people who love us sometimes work.'

Neotnia peers at me for a long, long time, her swollen eyes capturing the dim glow of the lantern above, its soft thumping a rhythmic heartbeat in the breeze. Then, without saying a word, she leans in and rests her head against my shoulder. A tear crosses her cheek.

I place my arm around her, drawing her close, and let her tears soak my sweater as the breeze rustles the flora and the lanterns sway under a brilliant blanket of stars. I hold her for the longest time as she sits, suffering, in the most beautiful place I've ever seen.

Mom once said that suffering is the common thread every living creature shares. Some people think it's love, but it's not. Not everyone is guaranteed to love or be loved, after all. But from the tiniest insect to a 110-year-old human being – we're all guaranteed to suffer throughout our lives. It's the one experience that unites us – the one none of us can escape.

I've seen Neotnia suffer physically when she was electrocuted, existentially over the form of her very being, and empathically when looking at the smiling group of schoolchildren in front of the memorial pool in Hiroshima.

No matter what Emiko says, I don't see how seeming to suffer is different from actually suffering. And this is why, to me, Neotnia is no different from Goeido or me, or any other living creature. It's precisely because she experiences suffering, regardless of the mechanism behind it. And I'm sorry I didn't realise that sooner. I'm sorry I didn't realise that the night she told me about herself.

It's some time before her breathing becomes more subdued against my chest. Then shortly, it enters rhythm with mine.

'It was worse after I met you,' she says. 'Needing to believe I wasn't that different from people. Needing to believe I was more than just qubits and synthetic parts, coded and assembled.'

Her skin is flushed.

'Hey, we're all assembled here.' I give her a smile and nod past the porch's awning, towards all the stars blanketing the sky. All those kami. 'You may be qubits and synthetic skin, and I may be neurons and cells, but, as my junior-year physics teacher loved to tell us, everything on this planet – whether organic, digital, or synthetic – is made from the same group of atoms that came from the same star that exploded in our neighbourhood of the galaxy billions of years ago. In other words, we're all assembled, just a little differently, from the exact same parts from the exact same source. So, see? You're not so unique after all.'

The edges of her mouth curve into a little smile.

I pull her closer. And I kiss her.

And holding her, her soft body resting against mine, I look into the night sky at those stars again. I look up at those factories trillions of miles away that created us all.

And it's enough. Holding her is enough.

'You think,' she says after a little while, her warmth against mine, 'in another world, if those atoms from that star arranged just a little differently, we could have had a life?'

'Yeah,' I answer. 'I really do. We could've had a life.'

'That's something, then,' she says.

'That's something.'

*

Our way back, the temperature's dropped, and the narrow streets with the wires crisscrossing overhead are lit by a moon that now glows with a hazy ring, blending the stations between here and there as if the three heavenly bodies were all a single mass.

By the time we reach the hotel, Goeido's already asleep on the bed's far side. I tell Neotnia to take the other side and lay on my back on the tatami-covered floor.

The room is silent for the longest time as I try to fall to sleep. There's an emptiness in the space between my arms.

As the rain begins, a hand slides from the bed. It makes its way across the tatami in the darkness, where it finds mine. Our grip pulls us each towards the other, Neotnia's upper body sliding over the side of the bed, mine rising to meet it. And with Goeido sleeping right beside us, our lips steal one last kiss in the darkness.

Neotnia returns to the bed, my hand still holding hers.

We fall to sleep that way as the rain comes down outside.

16 – Otōsan.

I wake to find Neotnia looking at me.

She's sitting on her heels on the tatami in the corner of the room, and it feels as if she's been watching me for some time.

I run my hand through my hair and look towards the window. It feels like morning, but it's unusually dark. 'What time is it?'

'Twenty past ten.'

The tatami creaks under my feet as I rise and walk to the window. It rained throughout the night. Dirty puddles fill the parking lot, and the sky is a ceiling of grey.

'Goeido's gone.'

'What?' I turn.

Neotnia holds up a handwritten note.

'He left it by the alarm clock he unplugged. It says not to go anywhere until he returns.'

'How long have you been up?'

'For a while. I went down to the desk, and the receptionist said he saw him leave just before six a.m.'

I don't say it, but I thought Goeido seemed not himself after Neotnia relayed everything Emiko had said at the park. On the train, he looked unusually lost in thought, and at dinner, he was the same. And now, he's snuck off on his own? And he clearly wanted to go without us knowing for as long as possible. Why else unplug the alarm?

Neotnia gazes at her hands cupped in her lap.

When she looks at me again, she doesn't say a word.

I think of our kiss.

A loud creak breaks the stillness in the air. Goeido kicks his sandals off by the open door. His kimono is damp on the shoulders, and a long, thin black object sticks from under the kimono's belt. Neotnia rises and addresses him, sounding both relieved and upset.

Goeido replies and seems to be explaining something quite surprising given the way Neotnia's eyes steadily widen. He slips the black object from his belt. It's a single-bladed toy drone – the kind you buy for a kid who just wants to race something through the sky in their backyard. He continues, and Neotnia's jaw drops as if he's just uttered the most shocking thing ever.

Their conversation goes on for some time, and I begin to wonder if I should just take a seat. Sometimes Neotnia looks angry, sometimes moved. And sometimes Goeido stands firm, like he's laying down the law. When they're finished, Goeido gives me a short, firm nod, like he's obviously done the right thing.

'He went to the facility this morning,' Neotnia explains.

'What?'

'He arranged for a car last night and it arrived here this morning. He told it to take him to the facility. He said it's his duty to protect me. He gave Father his word. He was worried about me going there without knowing what we were walking into, so he went alone because he thought it would be safer.'

'OK,' I say. 'I mean ... that is kinda a good idea. But what's with the toy?'

'He bought it last night. It's why he didn't come to the temple. When we split up, he circled back to the toy store. He used it to record footage of the facility this morning – stuff you couldn't see on the map.'

Goeido's mouth curls down proudly, and he gives another firm nod.

I'm not gonna lie – I'm really impressed.

I fold my phone out into a laptop and set it on the bed so we can all watch what the drone captured. Goeido says he launched it on the roadside a few hundred feet before reaching the facility, just as the rain ceased. As the drone rises, its camera catches him controlling it from his phone. It ascends the treetops, their canopy a mixture of muted reds, oranges, and browns. Wisps of fog float like trails of smoke, and everything below glistens wet. Soon I recognise landmarks from the satellite maps. The river that runs across the plateau higher in the mountain. The massive orange torii spanning the cliff's edge. The waterfall under it that violently spills into the river below, which continues out to sea miles away.

The drone sails over the valley. Now the facility comes into view, its helipad marked with a big white 'R'. It's obvious Goeido was apprehensive about flying too close – for a while the drone simply hovers from on high. The grounds have a wall separating them from the road. It runs all the way to the edge of the western cliffs the facility rests on. The same wall curves around the grounds' south-eastern end, where it turns and disappears into the forest, heading for the northern cliff face, and thus sealing the property off on all sides.

The drone descends some, and I can make out the rooftop entrance near the helipad. The pagoda itself totals three storeys – its frame all steel and glass, just like Emiko said. It looks like something an architect really wanted a prize for. The green grounds are elegantly structured gardens dotted with small trees. There's an ornate footbridge traversing a pond, and I can tell the path leading from the wall's gate to the facility is rocky – as if made of pebbles.

The drone descends past the helipad's horizon and floats in line with the pagoda's upper storey. Its curved glass walls are made of a single pane, which reveals the floor to be a bedroom and living quarters with a prime view of the valley and the waterfall to the northeast. In the centre, an elevator runs down the heart of the building, a stairway wrapping around its shaft. The drone sinks to the middle storey. This floor has a kitchen and a dining area. Finally, it arrives at ground level. Inside, I can vaguely make out an area that looks like a living room. As with the other floors, it's dark and devoid of movement.

The drone's point of view swivels, revealing a better angle on the facility's eastern grounds. The decorative gardens with their bonsai trees are beautiful. The pond with the footbridge has goldfish the size of cats. Another swivel and we see the wall's mechanised gate. Shortly, the drone rises and glides back across the forest's colourful canopy, descending into Goeido's waiting hand by the roadside.

We're quiet for a long moment after the footage ends. Neotnia steps back from my laptop. Goeido eyes her. She looks out the window at all the dirty puddles in the parking lot and the grey clouds overhead.

'OK,' she nods, turning towards us. 'Let's go.'

Goeido looks at me, and I get the feeling we're thinking the same thing.

'Neotnia,' I say. 'The place ... looked empty. It doesn't appear that anyone's there.'

She holds her gaze on me, her mouth tightening. 'I know. But the drone didn't show everything. What if he was in a bathroom? Or ... Emiko said there's a basement – the lab. What if Father's down there?'

She's not wrong, but the chances of that...

But Neotnia doesn't give me time to articulate what she knows I'm thinking.

'I understand it's been years since Emiko was last there. And I know if Father didn't go back there after he left me in Tokyo, the last time he would have been there was over two years ago. So, *hai*, he's probably not there. For all we know, the place doesn't even belong to Avance anymore. But if it is empty, what harm will it do to stop by?'

I glance at Goeido. I know he's worried about her safety – I am too. But she's right: the place looked empty. What harm could it do to stop by? I tell her this, and she tells Goeido what we've said. After giving it some thought, he nods with a '*hai*.'

The car he'd used has already driven off, so we order another, which will take a few hours to arrive due to our location. We decide to get lunch and walk to a tiny noodle shop for some udon. I ask Goeido how long it took to reach the facility. He says the ride was a little more than ninety minutes, but on the way back a mix of drizzle and flurries hit the mountains, making the return longer.

When we're done eating, the clouds look heavier. As we head back to the hotel Goeido stops as we're passing a narrow cross-street. He says something to Neotnia. She explains that as he was coming back from the toy store last night, Goeido noticed a small shrine halfway down the street. He's asked if we can stop there so he can offer a prayer to the kami.

We turn down the narrow street and come to the courtyard. The shrine's nothing special looking – a rundown wooden structure. One of its walls has a fresher coat of paint than the others. Yet I know the edifice isn't what's important – it's the kami inside.

They ask if I'd like to join them, but I decline. I'd feel inauthentic – just mimicking the rituals they perform. I remain at the courtyard's entrance as they approach the shrine after washing their hands in the basin. Their backs towards me, I smile a little, seeing them side by side. Neotnia looks positively tiny next to Goeido. Yet, despite her being the android, it's Goeido's who looks the odd man out. In his kimono and sandals, his hair up in a topknot, it feels like I'm peering back into a more noble time. One that's long-since passed.

I watch them do the bow-bow-clap-clap-bow and say their prayers. Yet when they're finished and Goeido turns to head back, Neotnia places a hand on his arm, stopping him. For a moment she looks at me in the way I found her watching me this morning on the tatami. She turns back to Goeido, and from the expression that comes over her face it's as if she's saying something of the utmost importance. Goeido glances at me. Neotnia says something more and waits while he digests whatever it was. Then, he bows to her, and she bows back.

When they return, they don't mention anything, so I don't ask. It seemed like a personal moment, anyway.

It's almost two when we get back to the hotel. Flurries have started to fall. We pack and checkout. There's no point keeping the room for another night. If her father isn't at the facility, we'll have the car take us directly to Tokyo. It arrives later than scheduled due to the worsening weather, and we encounter another hiccup once we're finally out of Nagano. It's had to change route because of some localised flooding. It'll take a little longer to reach the facility now, but as long as we don't end up in a wheat field, it's not a big deal. As we cruise along, the forested mountains rise in the distance. Under grey skies, the autumn foliage makes it look as if a damp quilt has been stretched over their peaks.

As dusk settles, we begin winding into the mountains, curving higher and higher on the narrow road, the white flakes falling among the trees. Just before six, Goeido instructs the car to slow. He recognises this stretch. We come to a stop on the shoulder, and he tells the car to shut off its headlights. Outside, the snowy forest is thick and dense.

We've decided Goeido will wait with the car, so it doesn't drive off. I'll go with Neotnia. Best-case scenario: we ring the gate's intercom and her father answers, and we get invited inside. Worst case: no one's home, and we head back to Tokyo.

With a caring look in his eyes, Goeido gently places his hand on Neotnia's shoulder. He speaks, and Neotnia returns a little smile. She's wearing a brave face.

'He says, good luck,' she explains. 'He's only a shout away. We just need to call, and he'll come running.'

We exit the car. It's freezing, but it's easier to see out here than I expected. The snow creates a pale glow around the forest once your eyes adjust. Walking the road's shoulder, we soon come to the wall surrounding the facility's grounds. It's taller than I realised from the drone footage – at least ten feet. In a few minutes, we're at the gate. It's as tall as the wall and looks like it slides right into it. The thing is, there's no intercom or control panel anywhere.

'I guess they don't expect visitors,' I say. My breath is frosted.

Neotnia steps back, scrutinising the gate. 'But it needs to open somehow for the people who live here. It's what gates do.'

'It looks expensive. It probably unlocks via the owner's biometrics.'

Neotnia considers the gate's height, snowflakes hitting the curves of her unflinching cheeks. Then she slides her fingers into the recess between it and the wall. There's a metallic creaking as she pries it open enough for a gap to appear. I sigh a frosted breath but grab the cold metal edge anyway. Together, we manage to increase the opening to a few feet.

As we slip inside, it's as if we've entered some secret realm. The night bathes the facility's grounds in a shallow blue light. A sparkling blanket of snow wraps everything in a powdered skin, the bonsai trees and the stones and the footbridge over the pond in the distance looking all the more mystical for it.

Neotnia notices none of this, though. She's focused on the pagoda ahead. A warm golden light emanates from the ground floor's glass wall, its smooth form only broken by the outline of a door at its centre. A privacy band run across the glass's upper half, blurring it. Only the lower half allows a peek inside. Through it, I see a partition runs almost the pagoda's entire length. It forms a corridor that hides the ground floor's interior from approaching visitors. A massive canvas nearly as long and tall as the corridor itself is hung on it. It's some kind of minimalist metapainting. Thin red, green and blue marks drift across it like orchestral notes.

The snow ceases crunching under our feet as we reach the door. Neotnia looks at the ringer embedded into its glass, and then at me. Her face is anxious, hopeful, and pink from the cold. I give her a slight nod, and she releases a frosted breath.

She touches the ringer.

A delicate chime sounds before gently fading into silence.

Neotnia's throat tightens as if anticipation has manifested itself as a little lump in her airway. Yet after twenty seconds, there's still no hint of movement inside. No shifting light or shadow. No noises either. The only sounds are from the large flakes dusting the grounds all around, like grains of sugar sprinkling tinfoil.

As a minute passes, nothing occurs but the accumulation of more snow.

Neotnia's mouth tightens, and her eyes quiver as an inevitable real-isation violates her: no one's coming to answer the door. No one's here.

But a puff of startled white breath passes her lips, and her cold hand grasps mine.

Her eyes widen.

A shadow grows across the glass as a figure appears around the partition's corner. Neotnia follows its movements down the corridor against the backdrop of the metapainting. The glass's privacy band obscures all but the untucked, blue button-down shirt and tan trousers on the figure's trim frame. It comes to a stop on the other side of the door.

For several moments, the figure doesn't move. It doesn't say a word. It simply waits.

Among the falling snow, Neotnia's hand trembles in mine.

Then, a wrinkled one reaches for a button on the glass's interior.

When the door opens, on the other side is an old man.

He gives me a neutral look, but when he looks at Neotnia, his expression grows warm, and sad.

And next to me, Neotnia, her eyes glisten wet. Her jaw hangs.

'*Otōsan…*' she trembles.

It's a word I know.

It means 'Father.'

17 – Musume.

The look in the old man's eyes reminds me of something long ago. It's a gaze that shifts only once, dipping to notice Neotnia's trembling hand holding mine in the cold. And looking again into her shimmering eyes, the edges of his lips curves upwards, tinged with warmth. As he begins to speak, a burgeoning smile born of joyous relief forms on Neotnia's face. But as his words continue, that nascent smile is interrupted – and in an instant, it's as if it were never there. When the last syllable leaves the old man's mouth, Neotnia's lips part, ejecting a tiny, frosted breath, as if she's been struck in the gut.

For a moment, Neotnia looks lost for words, the snow falling all around. And as if she doesn't know what else to do, she turns towards me and slips her hand from mine, only to reposition it higher on my arm, like she's presenting me.

'This is my friend, Father,' she says. There's a disembodied softness to her voice.

Her father seems to take notice of her hand's repositioning, and he looks at me again with that neutral expression. I introduce myself, but he keeps that silent look on me for so long I begin to wonder if he actually doesn't understand English. Then without saying a word, his gaze drifts upwards into the snowy night. It's as if he's searching for the moon hidden behind the clouds. Yet, as if it's become evident the lunar body won't be making an appearance, his gaze returns to linger on me for a moment more.

'It is nice to meet you, John,' he replies at last, giving a slight bow of his head. 'My name is Haruto. Both of you, please, come in. It looks very cold out.'

By the look in her eyes, I can tell Neotnia is shaken. It's the look one gets when a person's reaction isn't what they'd expected – or at least what they'd hoped for. If her demeanour registers with her father, he doesn't let on. He simply stands aside as we enter, the way an usher might when welcoming guests at the theatre. The corridor's warmth immediately contrasts with the coldness of the night outside.

'No need to do that,' he says as Neotnia begins to remove her shoes. 'You can leave them on.'

We give each other a glance. It's uncommon to leave your shoes on when entering someone's home. Her father's feet are in white stockings.

He shuffles by and we follow, passing the moving painting and turning the partition's corner, where the corridor's golden light ends. On the other side is the elevator shaft. The dark wooden stairs winding around it are bolted into the shaft at only one end, so they look like floating platforms. They wind up to the floor above, but also down to a level below. If they lead to the lab where Neotnia was made, you can't tell. The lower level's black void swallows any subsequent steps in darkness.

The rest of the ground floor is open. Three leather couches surrounding a granite coffee table take up much of the space. Nearby are a few side tables and some free-standing shelves packed with books. Despite it being evening, few lamps are lit. Most of the illumination comes from the snowy night's blue glow filtering through the glass walls.

The star of the room, though, is the view. Thanks to the dim interior, the surrounding landscape's details comes into sharp relief. The building is sat on the edge of a beautiful precipice that curves like a horseshoe around the valley below fed by the waterfall cutting into it from an even higher set of cliffs above us. Even through the pouring snow, the torii's bright-orange form atop the rim of the falls radiates like a beacon.

Yet Neotnia's focus remains on her father, whom she gazes at with quiet concern. If he stood upright, he'd be two or three inches taller than her, but his stoop levels him. And his steps – there were residents at the care home who moved faster.

'Sit, sit,' he motions at the couches as he heads towards the island countertop in the corner of the room where the glass wall elegantly curves. He retrieves three cups from beneath the countertop and activates the kettle before taking the lid from a ceramic jar and digging inside with a small wooden spoon. He places a few scoops of dried tea leaves into a porous metal sphere.

'Where is Goeido?' he says without glancing at us.

From the look on Neotnia's face, I can tell she feels the question isn't the least bit relevant to anything right now. 'He's with the car,' she answers, almost in disbelief.

Haruto nods and removes the lid from another jar. He scoops a different leaf into a second sphere and drops it into the kettle with the first.

'And Inu?' he asks without taking his gaze from the kettle.

'Back in Tokyo...' Neotnia's eyes are motionless.

He nods again. After several moments, there's a click, and he lifts the kettle from its base. It shudders as he pours the first cup, as if its slight weight is too much for him.

He looks at us, the kettle hovering over the next cup. 'Tea?'

Neotnia's mouth parts.

'Tea?' the word finally slips from her lips, her head beginning to shake.

'*Tea?*' her quivering voice rises.

'Father ... what are you doing here? W-why didn't you ever come back for me? I waited for you. You said you'd come back, and we'd go back home. You told me there was nothing to worry about, and in two weeks, we'd go back home, and continue living our lives like normal...'

As pools form in her eyes, Haruto averts his gaze towards the kettle in his hand.

'Two weeks, Father? *Two weeks?*' Neotnia's words tremble like the torrents of the falls outside. 'I waited for *a year*, and you never came back for me. A year, Father. For a year, I've been so frightened and alone and worried about you. And I show up tonight, and the first thing you say is you're so happy to see me – but I shouldn't have come?' She takes a breath in an attempt to prevent the inevitable, yet as her body trembles, the tears escape her eyes. '*I shouldn't have come?* A year, Father – I waited a year, and you never came back. I was so scared, and you never came back. Why didn't you ever come back for me?'

At the sight of those tears, the tremors from the kettle hovering in Haruto's grasp spread into his arm, then shoulder. His head sinks so low it's like a heavy beam has suddenly been placed across the back of his neck. The kettle slams into the countertop, its contents splashing. His entire body shaking, Haruto grasps the island's edge. And he, too, weeps.

Neotnia's at his side in an instant, supporting his stooped frame. Yet her touch only makes Haruto shudder more, his head hanging even deeper. Neotnia's tear-streaked face looks at mine with such concern, I dart to help. We make our way across the room, Haruto's stockinged feet shuffling on the hardwood floor, and sit him on a couch.

Kneeling beside him, Neotnia takes his hand in hers and wipes at his tears, yet it's some time before Haruto is able to calm himself. Only then can he bring himself to gaze upon his daughter's flushed face, her palm resting against his cheek.

He attempts a few deep breaths, but they're strikingly laboured, like a large boulder sits on his chest, and his body winces as if hit by a jolt of pain.

Neotnia's eyes flit from Haruto's chest to his face, concerned.

'What's happened to you, Father?'

It's several strained breaths before he forces the tiniest of smiles. 'Earlier this year ... I had another heart attack.' He raises his brows and squeezes her hand. 'The pacemaker got an upgrade, but it's pulling overtime lately.'

Neotnia's swollen eyes well up again, glancing his frail body up and down.

'Oh, Father,' she cries, burying her face into his lap. '*Otōsan...*'

'Shh. Shh. It's OK,' Haruto says, his sunspotted hand stroking her straight black hair. 'This is all just part of life. It's all just part of life...'

He caresses her hair for some time – letting Neotnia sob. Only

once does he take his eyes from her – when he looks towards the
window and lingers on the snow falling into the valley outside, as if
he's contemplating the size of its flakes.

'Shh,' he caresses. He says something more in Japanese. His voice
is gentle, no matter which language he speaks.

It's another moment before Neotnia lifts her head. Haruto gives
a warm smile, yet it seems like he's trying to present a brave face.

'I felt so alone after you left me...' Neotnia wipes her cheek with
the edge of her palm.

'I know,' Haruto replies, looking into her bloodshot eyes. 'I know.
And I did, too. I'm so sorry I had to leave you. But one day, all parents
must leave their children – no matter if they want to or not. And I
most certainly did not want to leave you.'

He considers her for a long moment, tightening his mouth.

'But my dear daughter, you need to go and never come back. You
need to forget about me and go and live your life.'

The way Neotnia jerks, it's as if someone's poured a bucket of
arctic water over her. She pulls her hand from his and pushes up onto
her feet, her face incredulous.

'I'm not going anywhere.' I can hear the hurt creep back into her
voice. 'Forget? Don't I deserve answers? Don't you *want* us to be together again?'

Haruto again glances at the weather outside before he peers at
Neotnia. For a moment, it seems as if he's weighing two completely
different things in his mind.

'How did you find me?'

Neotnia is lost for words. The question seems so trivial. Yet when
it becomes apparent she can't or won't reply, I pull out my phone and
tap the display. I hand it to Haruto, who gazes at the splinter and its
password prompt.

'This was you?' he says.

I nod.

'You must be very clever if you were able to extract this. Even I
couldn't do that.'

I don't say anything.

He studies me in the silence. 'You care about my daughter?'

'I do.'

'Then you and she need to leave—'

'I'm not going anywhere.' Neotnia's sharp tone stops his words cold, her narrowed eyes pointing like daggers. Then she nods towards my phone in his sunspotted hand. 'What's inside that file, Father?'

He looks at my screen again yet remains silent.

'Your colleague, Emiko,' I volunteer, 'she said she didn't know what was in it, but she's the one who told us about this place.'

A sceptical look crosses Haruto's face. 'Now, I don't think she would have done that...'

'She didn't say where it was, not directly,' I admit. 'But she said some things, and we pieced it together. I'm telling you this because your daughter's gone through a lot to get here. More than you know.'

For several moments, Haruto's quiet. Contemplative. Then he looks at Neotnia.

'Do you still love me?'

Her face breaks. 'How can you even ask that?'

'Then if I tell you what you want to know ... will you promise to respect my wishes and leave and never return?'

Neotnia shakes her head as if she's been asked to push an impossibly large boulder up an impossibly steep hill. 'How ... how could I, knowing you're here?'

'Because it is for the best. Now, if you still love me, I need your promise to respect my wishes.'

Neotnia's face has gone pale.

'Is that really what you want...?'

But he simply answers, 'Why don't you both take a seat?'

We do, beside each other, on the couch nearest him. For several seconds he looks at us like he's viewing a portrait. It's a moment before he speaks again.

'Now, why don't you explain how you and this young man know each other?'

Neotnia looks at me. There's a sadness in her eyes even more distressing than when that horrible shadow crosses her face. But she clears her throat, as if that will help steady her voice, and does what he's asked. She tells him everything that's happened since he abandoned her. How she started volunteering at the care home. How we met at the café, and about her splinter, and how we extracted it. She tells him how the splinter led us to Emiko, and everything Emiko told us.

For much of this, Haruto remains silent, letting Neotnia's words lap against him like the surf against the shore. The few times he speaks is to ask if Emiko and her daughter looked well and when he asks some questions about how I accessed Neotnia's systems right after the electrocutions. It's then I can tell we're talking to a quantum-computing expert. When Neotnia tells him how her skin blackened, he shakes his head. 'You are not invincible. Why do the young always think they are?'

He's quiet for a long time after Neotnia finishes.

'It sounds like you've both had quite the journey,' he finally says. He sets my phone on the table in front of him.

Looking at it, Neotnia says, 'You lied to me about so many things.'

Haruto nods yet doesn't say a word.

'You said although I was an android, I was no less of a person than anyone. But ... my body is different. I don't have all the ... parts a female should have.'

'*Hai*.' And with that simple acknowledgment, Haruto at once appears almost as frail as when we helped him to the couch. His head hangs for a moment before he meets Neotnia's eyes again. 'What was done was done – and I am sorry for that. But I couldn't change your anatomy retrospectively and, in my flights of fancy, I thought we could simply live our lives as father and daughter, spending day and night together, going on our walks, and not needing anyone else.' I can hear the anguish in his voice when he adds, 'I am so sorry, *musume*.'

The word seems to hit Neotnia unexpectedly. It softens the hard line between her lips. She gives a shallow nod, and it's a moment before she speaks again.

'But why would you even make my mind so lifelike that it could experience shame? Why code me with the ability to hurt over having a body that's different than every other female's? Why not just make me so it wouldn't trouble me?'

Haruto's mouth parts as if he's about to speak, yet nothing comes out. Perhaps he can see all the thoughts rushing to the surface of Neotnia's mind, because almost right away, she continues:

'But my body wasn't your worst lie, Father. You told me I have the potential to be anything I chose, just like a person. Yet, that's not true either.' She shakes her head. 'Just like any ordinary bot, I was made with an intended purpose. As Emiko said, I was "made to care". I've been going to the care home to help people – and I thought that was *my* choice. I thought I was doing that under my own free will. But it wasn't my choice at all – it was *your* choice, Father. It's what *you* decided I should want to do. It's what you *coded* me for. So, why did you have to lie to me about that? Why did you let me believe I had a choice in what I do? Why not just tell me the truth?'

Her father remains silent, pressing his lips together as he gazes upon Neotnia. Her clear blue-grey eyes have a vulnerability I've never seen before. Yet that vulnerability also conveys a certain strength as well. And as Haruto continues to gaze into those eyes of hers, I notice something happen in his. They take on that same look as when he answered the door and peered upon her for the first time tonight. It's a look that's familiar to me from long ago. It's familiar to me because it has a warmth I've not seen in anyone's eyes since Dad and I counted coins on our porch. And with that warm gaze on Neotnia now, the edges of her father's lips turn upwards.

'But I was telling you the truth,' he says, his age lines deepening.

'Father ... no. Emiko told us. You were working on my code for years. While she was designing my body, you were coding my systems to make me the ideal carer. I cared for my friends at the home because my code told me to. I have attachments – feelings – for the people I get to know because my code demands it.'

The lines around Haruto's eyes intensify.

'It's true,' he answers, 'that coding you to become the ideal carer was my original intention. And you are correct: for years, I worked on code that would have formed the main part of your quantum operating system. One that would have made you into the most lifelike, most perfect carer. But Neotnia ... that code never made it into you. It never touched your systems. Not a single line of it. Not one qubit.'

Neotnia looks too stunned to utter a word, and Haruto releases a long, slow breath as if considering how to explain the inexplicable. Finally, he looks at me.

'You've seen my daughter's codebase, yes? When you extracted her "splinter" as you call it?'

I nod, but I'm as incapable of reconciling what he's claimed as Neotnia is.

'The fact that you were even able to extract it means you got around the security redundancy I built to protect her. So you know there are three layers to her codebase?'

I nod again. 'I do.'

He looks at Neotnia. 'My daughter, what you were intended for and what you ended up being born as are two entirely different things.'

Neotnia shakes her head. 'I don't understand...'

And I'm sure my expression mirrors the confusion on Neotnia's face.

'There are three layers to your codebase, each with increasing complexity,' Haruto says. 'Your first layer is similar to a person's autonomic nervous system – roughly, anyway. This layer allows your body to regulate itself. Just as with a biological person, this layer tells your body to break down food to use as energy. It regulates your synthetic tissues and quantum structures to make sure they function as they need to. It also contains your flight-or-fight response. In other words, this layer keeps your body safe and functioning without you having to think about it.'

'This is one of the two sets of regular quantum code I saw, right?' I ask.

Haruto nods.

'Your second layer of code,' he continues, 'is roughly similar to a person's somatic nervous system. This gives you voluntary control over your movements. It also contains your language processing centres – in your case, it's why you know English and Japanese. And this is the layer that also contained your temporary diagnostic systems, which we used to interact with you and give you commands before your third layer of code was completed. This somatic layer was the second of the two sets of regular quantum code you saw,' he tells me.

He holds his eyes on Neotnia for a moment before continuing. 'Your third layer of code, which was the one Emiko referred to when she said I was working on your quantum OS for years, was the most complex. This was equivalent to a person's mind. It's this layer that was designed to give you a personality and allow you to interact with people just like we all do. And it's true: originally, this third layer of code would have given you a caring demeanour – it would have made you want to look after our elderly, and form attachments to them. And it would have made you astonishingly lifelike – yet not alive. It would have given you a mind, just not one of your own making. In other words, this third layer of code would have made you into the ideal carer.' The edges of Haruto's mouth curve upward as he continues. 'But that third layer of code never made it into you, Neotnia. It never touched your systems. Emiko wouldn't have known this, because she left before it would have been completed.'

'I don't understand...' Neotnia shakes her head. 'I'm here. I'm lifelike. I'm so lifelike, even John didn't know what I was until I told him, and he's a quantum coder, too.'

'No, Neotnia,' Haruto smiles. 'You aren't "lifelike" at all – you're *alive*.'

We go so quiet I can almost hear the flakes hitting the snowy grounds outside. And in that silence, the slightest amusement spreads across her father's face. It's as if he's gazing upon two confounded children who've just been told Santa Claus is, in fact, real.

'But...' Neotnia says. 'If I'm ... alive ... how? How am I alive, especially if you never installed your third layer of code in me? That doesn't make any sense, Father. John saw my third layer with his own eyes.'

As he's about to speak, Haruto clenches his jaw as if another sharp jolt has shot through him. I think Neotnia's noticed this, too, because her eyes shift. But Haruto merely clears his throat and takes a deep breath.

'Our original firm was called Shōrai Materials,' he says with a slightly pained expression that suggests he's about to guide us on an uncomfortable journey. 'But, as you deduced, Shōrai sold our project to Avance. And at the time we thought that was fortunate. Our colleague, Kentetsu, arranged everything, enabling our work to continue. And while we were apprehensive about the change, we were grateful for his guidance. Unfortunately, into the project's second year at this facility, tragedy struck.' Haruto hesitates. 'There was an accident in the lab, and Kentetsu was killed.'

Neotnia's body stirs next to mine as if a sudden chill has hit it. Emiko told us Kentetsu died, but saying he 'passed away' now seems like a gross sugar-coating. Yet except for briefly glancing down, Haruto doesn't linger on Kentetsu's death any longer than Emiko did.

'All communications to and from this facility have always had to go through Avance – no matter if we were messaging a family member or ordering takeout,' he continues. 'So, when we discovered Kentetsu's body and contacted Avance to call emergency services, we were surprised when not an hour later a passenger drone landed on the roof with an American executive from their Tokyo office, two attorneys and security. The executive made it clear our work was to proceed at pace. We were told Avance would handle the matter with the authorities and Kentetsu's family, and we were made to sign an agreement preventing us from speaking about the incident with anyone. When they left, they took his body.' Haruto pauses. 'In other words, it quickly became evident Avance was covering up our colleague's death.

'Kentetsu had always been our intermediary with Avance. He took most meetings, gave updates and occasionally flew to their campus in the Valley to meet in person. We didn't mind it being that way, of course – Emiko and I preferred to concentrate on our work in the lab rather than deal with corporate America. Besides, Kentetsu had been employed by them for almost twenty years Stateside; he understood the culture, so his role as intermediary was a natural fit. Yet, after he passed, things changed...'

Haruto looks at the snowfall again. The flakes are denser than before. When his gaze returns, something in his eyes look different, and he considers Neotnia for a long moment. It's as if he suddenly has the world's weight on his shoulders.

'You remember my mother was *hibakusha*, yes?'

Neotnia nods, noticing the change that's come over her father.

'What happened to my mother and her family at Hiroshima wasn't only the fault of the American military and its leaders. The blame also lies with the scientists who created their bomb. So, the last thing I ever wanted was for our work to be used to hurt mankind. Yet after Kentetsu's death, it was clear Avance had other ideas. With him no longer around, their scrutiny grew. Their executives from the States increasingly checked up on us in person – often unannounced. Sometimes they'd bring visitors, and sometimes those visitors were from the American military. Soon they became more demanding. They grew irritated Emiko hadn't completed your face yet – your eyes were the most difficult part for her. And they were even more frustrated I hadn't completed your third layer of code, and thus your quantum OS. They understood both were critical to making you appear lifelike – as originally intended, anyway...'

He shakes his head as if struggling with some sorrow deep inside, and I can tell from the look in her eyes, Neotnia has to stop herself from instinctively reaching out to him.

'We both wanted to abandon the project when Avance's true motives became clear but felt we couldn't leave – that they wouldn't allow us to resign. So, we kept working yet purposely slowed our pace in hopes of discovering a way out. Then one presented itself. Almost six months after Kentetsu's death, Emiko's husband passed away from an illness when she was months from giving birth.'

For the briefest moment, it's as if Haruto has something caught in his throat.

'It was not the opportunity either of us wanted, but I knew for her sake we had to take it. She'd recently completed work on your eyes, meaning Avance had less use for her now that your body was done. I begged her to use this horrible loss as a chance to resign without raising suspicions – to leave our dream behind and get out while she could – and to never contact me again, as I feared Avance would monitor even our external communications. And she's honoured those pleas. I haven't heard from Emiko since.'

Neotnia looks at her father with a tragic little gaze, understanding more than he knows.

'It was just me then...' he continues. 'By that time, Avance understood the only work left was the third layer of my quantum OS. It was nine months from completion, at most – which they were aware of, too. Yet as I now understood they had no intention of producing androids to care for the elderly, there was no possibility I'd give it to them. But if I'd have fled on my own, without you, I knew it would take them perhaps just five years to reverse-engineer the code I'd already completed, along with Emiko's work on your synthetic and quantum internals, and to use our achievements for their ends anyway. So, over several months, I arranged for a small house in Kamakura – a place I'd never been and had no connections to – and slowed my work even further as I made plans to flee. I'd take you with me and wipe all three layers of your codebase, then destroy your body in the sea.'

Neotnia's shoulders twitch. 'The saltwater, right?'

Haruto nods.

'And Inu, too, I guess?' she adds. 'That's why you brought him along?'

Haruto gives a sad little smile. 'Remember when I said you could think and activate Inu, and he would come to you? That connection is because we used some of his quantum architecture as a basis for your internals. I thought it unlikely Avance would work out they could use quantum entanglement to lead Inu to you, but it wasn't a risk I was willing to take. So, one night that September, when I knew I was no more than a month from finishing your third layer and could no longer delay Avance, I hid the secure drive that contained your codebase inside Inu and put him into my briefcase. All that was left was fitting the first of the two faces Emiko made onto your body. After that, I walked you out the door you came through tonight.'

'Emiko mentioned another face,' Neotnia says. 'So, I guess I haven't always looked like ... me?'

'No,' Haruto lets out a little breath. 'The feeds from the security cameras, like all secure data at this facility, are stored locally – they can only be accessed from here. We do that so there's no chance a competitor or nation-state could hack a transmission and see what we're doing. But I knew once Avance couldn't reach me, they'd come to check the feeds and see what a completed you looked like. That's why I also took the alternate face Emiko made with us. They'd never known about it – I hadn't even laid eyes on it before. Once safely in Kamakura, I planned to switch your faces and destroyed the first. That way, even if Avance tracked us to Kamakura right away, they would be searching for a you they could never find.

'We arrived at the house and my plan was to destroy your body as soon as possible, though I couldn't very well go into the sea with you immediately. I didn't know the area well, and I needed to find a se-cluded spot where your body could stay submerged for long enough without being noticed by passersby. It would take several days for the saltwater to successfully corroded your body from the inside out.'

He stops abruptly, and a sorrowful look crosses his face.

'I know that sounds monstrous, but you didn't have consciousness at that time.'

All Neotnia seems able to do is give a slight nod, and Haruto con-tinues.

'During that first week, I only ventured out at night for essentials and to search the shoreline. I thought I'd go crazy, hiding away all alone in that house. While you had your first two layers installed, and so could move on command, you didn't have the third, and thus no personality nor the ability to perform actions of your own voli-tion. I ended up reactivating Inu just to have some lifelike company.'

I can tell her father's words sting by the way Neotnia sets her eyes.

And maybe he can, too, because he gives her a warm look and adds, 'But the thing was, *musume*, at the end of that first week of solitude, something I never expected happened: you began to seem more real to me, more of a person, than I ever considered possible.'

He shakes his head as if wrestling with how to best explain his thoughts.

'When I originally set out to make you, I didn't think about making someone I would care – would *feel* – for. Such an idea never entered my mind. I only dreamed of making someone who could care for those who needed it most. But then...'

His words trail off, and for several moments he simply takes in Neotnia's face, gazing at it the way one does when seeing something that's at once rare, yet familiar.

'But what, Father?'

'Did Emiko mention she's an artist?'

Neotnia gives a slight shake of her head. 'No.'

'Well, she is. And I believe it's why she's so good at designing synthetic physiology. She loves to draw – especially portraits – and actually dreamed of being an artist before becoming a scientist.'

A small smile crosses his lips.

'A few nights after we'd successfully created Inu, Emiko and I went for some celebratory beers. I walked her home then decided to return to my apartment via a route I'd never taken. I soon came across a back-alley shrine that appeared to be from the pre-war era. It was odd-looking, not only for its weathered appearance, but because it was tipsy – it leaned to one side. Yet I took my discovery as an opportunity to thank the kami for our recent success, and after returning home that night, I had a dream – a most vivid one. In that dream, I had a daughter...'

Neotnia stiffens at this, like she's forgotten to take a breath.

'A daughter was something I'd always wanted, had my work allowed me the time to pursue relationships.' Haruto raises his eyebrows a little. 'But in this dream, I saw my daughter as clearly as one sees white crests on blue seas. I'd gone to meet her at the small, tipsy shrine I'd found on my walk home. She was waiting there so we could pray to the kami together. As I approached, her back was turned, so I could only see her beautiful black hair. Yet as I came to stand at her side she turned and looked at me with such clear eyes, they broke my heart. "*Otōsan*," she said and smiled at me, "I've been waiting for you."'

Her father pauses, and the crinkles around his eyes deepen.

'She had *your* face, *musume*...'

Neotnia's eyes well up like someone's turned a faucet. They shimmer as she draws her lips tight, as if that can somehow stop them from quivering. Across from her, a warmth spreads over Haruto's face.

'The next day I told Emiko about my dream. I described the vividness of your face, its trio of faint moles, the shape of your nose. And as I did, it felt as if I was looking upon you then. The following day, Emiko brought a sketch she drew – a simple charcoal one...'

Her father lingers on the memory.

'I don't know if she meant to do it. I didn't even realise she'd done it until the day after I finally improvised the tool needed to switch your face out during that first week we'd been in Kamakura. I'd lost the original as we fled down the mountain towards the waiting car. But when I finally switched out your face, I noticed the three faint moles on it, and realised the alternate face Emiko made for you was the exact one she'd sketched from my description of my daughter in my dream all those years earlier.'

Neotnia's face dips towards her lap, her moist eyes obscured behind her bangs that hang like a curtain.

'And well, over the next week, with your face, waking up in a house and not a lab with you, I realised I'd started becoming fond of you. You didn't have a personality, of course, but you could move like a person. You could speak if asked questions. You would sit at my side on the couch as I watched movies on the old television. I started enjoying your presence, and that very presence soon made me realise an *absence* of something I'd felt most of my adult life: loneliness. With you in the house, I wasn't lonely for the first time in decades.'

His brows knit.

'I knew I was beginning to humanise you. Still, I'd go on my solitary night walks to search for a location to destroy your body. I knew it had to be done so yet another scientist's work wouldn't contribute to the suffering of millions. Yet every night when I returned, seeing you sitting on the couch as if waiting for me, I felt more and more like I was betraying you. But then, during the third week in our house together, I found it: the perfect spot to submerge your body. It was just west of the city where a river empties into Sagami Bay. Its mouth caused a deep depression in the bay's floor. It was ideal...'

Haruto looks at Neotnia and shakes his head.

'When I returned that night, I needed to get it over with. So, I called you into the garage and sat Inu on the workbench. The first step to keep Avance from militarising you was destroying the secure drive with your nearly completed code, then I'd access the two existing code layers already inside you and wipe them, too. After all, the first possessed your fight-or-flight subsystems and the second would allow you to use your limbs to break any restraints and swim to the surface after I drowned your body.

'Wiping them would be easy for me, of course, and within days the saltwater would make any recovery impossible. Besides, those layers weren't anything Avance likely couldn't already reproduce. It was the third layer I needed to keep from their hands at all costs. It was why since arriving in Kamakura I'd spent my days transforming an old backup generator into a type of electric chair for secure drives. The third layer of code was already safely encrypted on the drive, of course, so only I could access it. However, physically destroying the drive would ensure there'd be no construct left that future technologies might be able to recover and decrypt the code from. So, I retrieved the drive from Inu and plugged it into my improvised electric chair. All that remained was flipping the switch, and it would be instantaneously destroyed...'

Haruto's eyes settle on Neotnia for a long moment.

'But yet ... there you were, standing right across from the drive in its electric chair. The drive with my code I knew would have made you so lifelike. And given how I'd begun humanising you over that past week, and how the guilt over what I'd shortly do to your body was already spreading in me, I suddenly felt the thing that motivates all scientists well up inside me, yet stronger than I ever had before: curiosity.

'If you were so realistic-looking in that moment, in the garage with me, what would you be like with my completed codebase in you? If I hurried, I could finish it within weeks and install it in you, and at last, however briefly, gaze upon our completely realised dream. I simply needed to pull the drive from its electric chair. I must have looked from you to it and back again a hundred times as that curiosity swelled in me like a tide. What would you be like with my finished quantum OS? How realistic would have my fulfilled code running inside you made you seem? The desire to know was overpowering.'

Her father shakes his head.

'But ... I remembered the ghosts of the scientists who came before. Those whose curiosity about how the fruits of their own work would manifest was just as strong, and who were unable to bear that curiosity as anything but quenched. And I remembered Hiroshima. My mother. Nagasaki. I remembered Avance could show at any moment. And I flipped the switch. In an instant, my life's work – my dream – was gone in a puff of smoke.'

Haruto goes quiet, gazing at the space before him as if that smoke still lingers. Then he tilts his face up towards Neotnia.

'The human mind, *musume*, can be weak and arrogant and self-centred. Though I did the right thing, in the moments after, as that little puff of smoke dissolved into the air, what went through mine was that I'd performed the equivalent of a novelist writing not only his masterpiece, but humanity's most exceptional work, then burning the manuscript before anyone had a chance to read it...'

That frailty from earlier makes itself apparent again, and in the room's dim light, I see the tiniest hint of a shadow cross Haruto's face.

'I flew into a rage. A rage over how the faults of man required me to sacrifice my dream for their own best interests. Over how we can't simply create tools to better our state without some wanting to use those tools to increase their personal power. And with that rage flowing through me, I looked at you, knowing what you could have been, what the *world* could have been with you in it. And as I scrutinised you, I only saw more of what man had lost without even knowing it. The despair began to drown me. Yet then ... then I came to your eyes ... Looking into those parts of you that Emiko had the most trouble with, I caught sight of something so horrifying, it defied all understanding. In your eyes, I saw my reflection. Yet my face was without detail or depth, as if it were just a horrible approximation of me.'

Haruto's words shake me to my core.

'And staring at that terrible likeness staring back at me, the world became so unbearable I felt myself descend into madness. Or it was madness, at first. Everything fell away and I was left in darkness. An unending void. But then I saw something – a structure floating in the distance. I ran towards it, and as I did, road sprang up beneath my feet. When I reached the structure, I suddenly recognised it. It was the small tipsy shrine – the one from my dream years before. But it was missing something. I spun around, looking everywhere – but *you* weren't there. I knew you were supposed to be, yet you weren't. So, I ran back the way I'd come, looking for you, and shortly came to another shrine. Or, not another one, but the exact same tipsy one I'd just left. Yet you were still nowhere to be found. I ran again, searching, yet simply ended in the same place. I must have run hundreds, thousands, of times, looking for you, yet each time I only ended back at the tipsy shrine...'

And as my chest thumps, Haruto pauses, looking at Neotnia with a smile so peaceful it's as if he's gazing upon the most treasured thing in the world.

'Finally, I bowed and prayed for help in finding you,' he tells her. 'And when I rose, I was back in our garage again, right in front of you. It was then that my madness gave way to ecstasy, and I reached for my phone and began coding. Yet all I could type was a single character. One character, nine strokes: "Kami". So, I tried again, but my fingers wrote the character for "kami" twice. I tried a third time and wrote it three times. Then a fourth and wrote it four – thirty-six strokes in all, and on and on. But suddenly it was as if a bridge had formed between two worlds, and all those kami kanji were the stones needed to lay it. And once that bridge was completed, I could finally code again. Yet I didn't code how one normally would: purposely, logically – or even consciously. Instead, it flowed organically from my fingers like words from a poet's pen onto the page, or colour from an artist's brush onto the canvas. It was as if all the kami in Japan, every one in the seas, sands, mountains – even the stars above our garage – were using me as their vessel. When I finally finished, I had no idea how much time had passed, but I immediately uploaded this new codebase into you...'

Haruto's throat tightens, and he goes quiet as if the emotion's about to drown him. He looks upon Neotnia with a tenderness we all yearn for.

'And that, my dear *musume*,' he smiles, 'is when you were born.'

It's like someone's pushed the mute button on this world. In the stillness, I gaze upon her father, yet all I can see is that info bot at the Shibuya scramble. The one that reflected that formless, morbid approximation of me in its domed head, and showed kanji after kanji after kanji – all the same.

You're on the cusp of a new world.

As the words echo in my head, a feeling of being watched washes over me. It's Haruto. He looks at me as if I've just dropped out of the sky onto this very couch, and only he's noticed. Yet his eyes quickly shift back to Neotnia at my side. A flush crosses her cheeks, having just heard her father's words: *And that, my dear* musume, *is when you were born.* Her eyes glisten, her head rocking up and down in firm, little nods, as if doing so will distract anything from falling.

'And this...' The words catch in her throat. 'This code is the one John saw? The third layer?'

'*Hai*,' Haruto says.

'But I don't understand – what did this new code ... make me? What purpose did it give me if not to care for the elderly? What did it tell me to do? What did it tell me to be?'

'Oh, my dear *musume*, it didn't tell you to do or be anything. When I woke from my trance and saw what I'd transcribed, I couldn't decipher any of it. And that's because it was not my creation. I was simply the kami's vessel. The only thing I could see was the code wasn't finished – it was waiting. Waiting to be installed in you, where it could grow like a seed in the earth. And as soon as it was planted, I saw you come alive. Not *lifelike* – but truly *alive*, with a consciousness of your own.'

A sound chokes out of Neotnia's throat, making her mouth tighten so firmly it bends into a happy frown. Haruto leans forward, resting his wrinkled palm against her cheek.

'Just like the rest of us,' he says, wiping a tear that's escaped her, 'you weren't born with a purpose, with a pre-defined essence. The new code was a blank canvas, and only you can decide what's drawn on it. You became who you are today like any of us – organically, through your choices. People have no essence until they make choices, *musume*. And the friendships you have formed, the people you have chosen to care about, the ideas and events you give your thoughts to – even your decision to help at the care home – those were choices entirely of your own making, and *they* are what defines you, not any code.'

Neotnia keeps nodding, yet she's still unable to utter a word. Now, a tear from Haruto joins hers.

'I'm so sorry I was going to destroy you...' He shakes his head, that frailty visible again. 'I thank the kami every day for their intervention, for giving me my *musume*. But once they did, you were no longer mine – or anyone's – to destroy or do anything else with. Your life is your own, *musume*. Every desire and thought you have is your own. Everything you feel, whether good or hurtful – shame, love, anger, hope – it's all real, and yours alone. And because of that, from that moment you were born in our garage, my life was making sure you had all the freedom, possibilities, opportunities and choices any of us do.'

'So come with me now, Father,' Neotnia says, squeezing his hand. 'We'll live our lives as we want, going on our walks, watching movies and reading books, and doing anything else we choose...'

A sorrowful look knits onto Haruto's face.

'If only I could, *musume*. But I need to keep you safe. I need to keep everyone I love safe. It's why I left you.'

'I don't understand...'

Haruto lets his hand slide from hers.

'Remember your first birthday? We had your cake and then went for ice cream? While we were out, I saw a drone hovering over Kamakura. It was a Banshī, so it wasn't there collecting climate data. It's when I knew that even though it had been a year since I'd fled, Avance had never stopped looking – and they never would. If their drone was in Kamakura, they were close to finding us – days at most.'

He tilts his head, a frown appearing over a memory.

'So, I had to do what I did to protect you. I dropped you with Goeido the next morning, then went back and waited. Avance showed that night. I told them I'd long since destroyed your body, but they didn't care. They'd already reverse-engineered much of Emiko's work, and within a few years would know enough to begin producing their own androids with lifelike physiology. Yet they knew my code was key to making them indistinguishable from humans, and that's what they needed them to be – impeccably indistinguishable in speech and mannerisms, down to the micro-movements.'

For a moment, Haruto again settles his gaze on the snow falling outside, as if the flakes are the sands of an hourglass.

'I told them I wouldn't help. I wouldn't return and continue on my quantum OS,' he says. 'That's when they showed me the metavid: Emiko breastfeeding her baby on a park bench in Hiroshima. She was the first person they visited after I disappeared. But my plan had worked: she'd had no idea what I was going to do after she left, nor where I'd gone. And her genuine shock at my disappearance – with you, especially – convinced them she had no part in it. Yet they showed me additional metavids. In each, Emiko's daughter was just a little bigger. And they said if I didn't return, if I didn't finish my work, "Accidents happen all the time, even to widowed mothers and their newborns."'

Haruto hesitates, as if trying to contain some anger inside.

'So, I returned – to keep you, and Emiko and her child safe. And if I tried to see or contact either of you, they would have known. That's why for a year, I've been...'

It's as if the words have slipped his mind. Then out of nowhere, his jaw clenches, just as it did earlier when some sharp thing jolted his body – only this time he clutches his chest, too.

Neotnia's hand springs for him, yet Haruto raises his own, telling her to hold off.

He gathers a breath.

'Six months ago, I had my third heart attack...' he says. His eyebrows raise ironically. 'It was a blessing, in a way. Even with the upgraded pacemaker, I move more slowly, I work more slowly. Even Avance can't fault me for that, I suppose. It bought me more time with them, anyway. And more time with them was exactly what I needed.'

Neotnia's jaw drops. 'Why...?'

Haruto presses his lips together as if wanting to keep some secret locked inside.

'Just know that every day since I left you, I've thought of walking out that door and keeping my promise to you, *musume*. But returning to you would be a selfish act. Not only would it lead Avance straight to you, seeing who you've become would only embolden their agenda, and that would endanger the world. My self-imprisonment holds back the tides.'

He goes quiet as if that pain in his chest demands a rest. In the silence, his eyes settle on where the glass bends around the room's far corner. I follow his gaze as Neotnia, too, glances at what's caught her father's attention. As heavy as the snow now is, we can still make out the orange torii's brightness spanning the falls atop the cliffs.

'The only thing this damned place has going for it is the view,' Haruto shakes his head, taking another breath. 'Sometimes, when the weather's warm, I'll walk the path from the gardens to the torii. In my condition, it takes quite a while now, but the effort is worth it. It's an ancient site – from the Heian Period, at least. You can feel the kami there.'

Neotnia turns towards him, and that warm smile appears on his worn face.

'Up there I think of you as I watch the falls spill into the river. It eventually flows out to the sea, which reminds me of our walks on the beach. When I'm up there, we're strolling along the shore at twilight just as we used to.'

But that image evaporates as a jarring flash violates the dimness of the room.

It's my phone, on the coffee table between us; its screen has lit up at a notification, which quickly disappears, leaving the splinter's password field on display.

'Father...' says Neotnia, lingering on my phone's screen, 'you said you discovered Avance had other plans for me after Kentetsu died. You said he died in a lab accident. But ... what kind of lab accident kills a computer scientist?'

Haruto's eyes shift, but he doesn't say a thing.

For a moment Neotnia remains quiet, too. Then she glances at the splinter's password field again before setting her eyes back on him.

'Father, that file caused me so much pain. Please – what's in it? You told John even you couldn't extract it from me. So, you tried, didn't you? You know what's in it, don't you?'

Still, Haruto remains silent.

'I need to know, Father. Please...'

Her eyes are as steady as I've ever seen them.

Haruto looks at the password field displayed before him.

'It's not you...' His voice is shaken. 'You need to understand – it's not you.'

He looks at the screen again for a long moment, then taps the password field. Changing the keyboard to Japanese, he enters the password, then changes the keyboard back. And as if unable to delay the inevitable any longer, he hands the phone to Neotnia.

The unlocked splinter contains a video file.

Neotnia folds my phone out into a tablet so we can both see and taps play.

The video begins with a man already in frame. He's Japanese.

Glasses. Middle-aged. And he holds a curved metal rod. It looks like a handle that's been removed from a mounted server rack.

'Stimulation of derma-ossification for visual confirmation,' the man says with a distinct Northern Californian inflection. He jabs the rod towards the camera once, then repeats. Each time it disappears below the frame, and with each jab, the camera not only wobbles but seems to shift of its own volition. But as the jabs grow more forceful, a hand vaults into frame and blocks the latest volley. Then another hand vaults up, a right and a left now, and both attempt to deflect what have become increasingly aggressive strikes. Within seconds, the man's swinging the rod with such rapid violence the hands can't block fast enough. And soon, screaming at the top of his lungs, he swings the rod like a baseball bat, striking the camera directly on its side with such force it swivels to the right, revealing more of the lab: a stainless-steel desk, a quantum terminal, wires running everywhere.

But it also reveals a mirrored partition – the kind you find around the chandeliers of certain types of quantum hives. And that partition has a reflection. It's a reflection of Neotnia, yet not as either of us have ever known. We see her naked shoulders and breasts and ribs and hips. But she doesn't have a face. Not an ordinary one, anyway. Her head is skinned. Its bright-red synthetic musculature stretches across a black graphene skull. In place of eyes, two tiny barrels poke from her sockets. And from the back of her skull, wires run like thick tentacles to the quantum terminal on the stainless-steel desk.

After a moment, her head, and thus the video, swivels back towards the man, who again screams at the top of his lungs, only now he chops the metal rod against her skull like a lumberjack splitting wood. He retracts the rod for another strike, but this time as the blow falls, Neotnia's right forearm blocks it. Yet the skin on her arm doesn't look like human flesh anymore. It's formed of irregular ridges and bumps stacked in slim layers against one another, like a seashell. And the man in the video, his eyes go wide as if he's discovered an oasis in the Sahara. He's ecstatic. He pulls the rod back, but as he chops down again, Neotnia's left hand juts into frame, catching it mid-swing. The skin on this arm is also bumpy like a seashell.

The man releases a cry of rapturous excitement at this, but as he tries to pull the rod free, he's surprised to find it won't budge from her grasp. Clutching his end even more firmly, he moves closer, grunting as he tugs with greater effort. His eyes jump wide and he screams with ferocity as the rod is finally prised from Neotnia's fingers, springing back up over his head. He now looks like a crazed butcher about to cut a steer in half.

And that's when Neotnia's shell-skinned arm swings across the frame – the back of her hand connecting with the man's temple, which caves inwards as blood explodes from it like sauce from a ketchup pack. When he falls from frame, the video remains still, gazing at the empty space where he'd been. After some moments, it rotates and we see Neotnia's reflection in the partition once again. She's stands there with her de-fleshed head, only now her naked body is covered neck-down in a skin of irregular ridges and bumps, stacked into slim layers, her shoulder and breasts splattered with droplets, as her right hand drips red.

Neotnia's eyes remain fixed on my screen for some time after the video ends. She doesn't even seem aware we're still in the same room until I take the tablet and fold it closed. Only then does she move, bringing her hand up, inspecting it as if Kentetsu's blood remains.

'What did I do?'

It's as if she's awoken to discover herself a macheted missionary standing amidst a field packed with the shredded bodies of the Stung.

'You didn't do anything,' Haruto answers. 'You were not *you* at that time. Do you understand that?'

She doesn't answer.

'*Musume...*'

Her gaze is still frozen on the invisible blood covering the back of her hand.

'Daughter,' his voice is as strong as I've ever heard it. He lets the word hang in the air as he peers at her with a hard gaze.

Finally, Neotnia looks at him.

'You were not you at that time,' Haruto repeats. 'I need to make sure you understand that.'

Neotnia glances at her knuckles again, stunned. But she nods. Still, Haruto holds onto her with that firm look, only speaking once he's certain he has her attention.

'At that time, in the video, you only had your first two layers of code,' he says.

The way Neotnia's eyes are set – it's how Mom described the shock that would set on the Stungs' faces when they first saw the missing chunks of themselves, the parts devoured by the biologics or amputated by the zealots. It was the realisation they were no longer as they thought they were – and would never be again.

'The day this incident occurred, Emiko and I were out for lunch. When we returned, we found Kentetsu on the floor and your body waiting in stasis,' Haruto is saying. 'It took us a while, but we pieced together what had been happening. Without our knowledge, Kentetsu had been experimenting with some of the unique properties of your synthetic skin. Just as it can seal from cuts and, as you found from your bathtub experiments, can withstand electrical shocks, to a degree, Kentetsu discovered that rerouting some of your energy supplies to your skin's synthetic nodes responsible for sensing touch and pressure causes it to harden like a shell. It's an ability never planned, but when you're on the cutting edge of science, especially biomaterials science, there are often unintended attributes.'

'But I've never seen this ... shell state,' Neotnia finally says. 'I can activate Inu by just thinking it, but I've never known I can do...' She shakes her head.

'I've seen it happen,' I say.

Neotnia looks at me, stunned.

'It was after we dropped the second toaster into the tub. It only lasted for a second or two. And it's when your skin had already turned black, and the lights were out. Until now, I thought it was a trick of the flashlight's beam on the water's surface.'

'You can't activate this state – not consciously, anyway,' Haruto says. 'The reason Kentetsu screamed and shouted while beating your body was because he was trying to activate your fight-or-flight response. The only way he found to reroute some of your energy supplies to the synthetic node bundles in your skin without us knowing was by running them through the part of your subsystem that's responsible for regulating your flight-or-fight. And that response is only triggered automatically, and only when your subconscious feels you're endangered – in immediate, life-threatening danger from an external force.'

I think back to the bathtub. That's why the first toasters never caused this shell state to engage – because Neotnia *chose* to harm herself. Her conscious desire outweighed her subconsciousness's protections. It's like the way a person would ordinarily instinctively jump out of the path of a speeding train – unless they chose beforehand to take their own life. But since her body was already under such duress from the first electrocution, the hit from the second toaster caused her fight-or-flight response – and thus her shell state – to engage. She no longer had complete cognisant control of her body. Now there's not a doubt in my mind that a third electrocution would have killed her.

'How many people have I hurt?'

'*Musume*,' Haruto's eyes go steely again. '*You* have not hurt anyone. This was long before I transcribed your final code. This was when you only had your first two layers in you. What happened to Kentetsu was tragic, but it was entirely his own doing.'

Neotnia doesn't say anything. She looks unfocused.

'This unfortunate incident happened only once. It happened only to Kentetsu, and it happened solely due to his mistakes. When he attacked you to test his "enhancements" to your skin, your fight-or-flight system defended your body from the threat. It swung your arm at the threat to get it to back off just as it would swing your arms to swim if you were drowning or kick your leg at a rabid animal that was attacking you. Unfortunately for Kentetsu, he miscalculated how much force your limbs could strike with when this shell state is—'

'But I *can* hurt people...'

Her father's mouth tightens into a thin line. 'Any person can hurt people – if they *choose* to.'

All Neotnia replies with is a barely perceptible nod. She's not even looking at him anymore, off somewhere in her own world. It's easy to read Haruto's concern.

'Why was this even inside me?' Neotnia says after several moments. 'My eyes aren't cameras. I can't replay events I've seen.'

'*Hai*, that's correct,' Haruto nods. 'But before you had your eyes, we placed cameras into their sockets to see what you'd be seeing as we began working on your interactions with objects and people. These recordings were viewed for diagnostic purposes then purged from your systems when they were no longer needed.

'When Avance ordered us to find out what happened, we plugged your body into Emiko's terminal and pieced together some of what Kentetsu had been doing behind our backs. Not only had he re-routed your energy supplies to your skin's synthetic node bundles, he encrypted his code in your second layer to keep it from alteration – meaning we couldn't disable it. He had also created a partition in your second layer to record his experiments. We assume once he learned your skin could harden, he hoped to find some way to get you to do it on command – and, ultimately, probably hoped it'd be of value to the Americans. We think he recorded his experiments to send to his minders at Avance before wiping the videos from your system so we wouldn't find them.

'The problem with this last video was that only Kentetsu knew the key to removing his recordings from his partition. They were cryptographically anchored until he extracted them from you. Emiko and I didn't want Avance knowing we'd discovered Kentetsu was experimenting with your body's properties behind our backs. Doing so would have revealed that we now understood their intentions for you were militaristic – and that would have endangered us. Yet we couldn't erase the video from your systems without Kentetsu's cryptographic keys, either. And if Avance ever asked to inspect your systems with us, we wouldn't be safe with them knowing what we'd seen. So, I did the only thing I could: I encrypted the video file myself, right there at Emiko's terminal, so no one else could see it – or known we'd seen it. And it should have stayed anchored and hidden away in your second layer, where you never would have known it existed since you have no conscious awareness of that layer of your systems. Of course, everything changed when you first got electrocuted and those cryptographic anchors were disrupted.'

Haruto goes quiet. He looks at Neotnia and seems content to give her a moment with the thoughts running through her mind.

I think about everything he's said. Kentetsu. That formless approximation of himself reflected in her eye. The repeating kanji. Again, I see the info bot at the Shibuya scramble. Yet all that falls to the side when I set my eyes on Neotnia again, so lost in thought. For an instant I want to do nothing more than reach out and take her hand.

What her father's said about her code – it makes me happy for her, no matter how challenging tonight has been for her. I now understand why her third layer looks so incomprehensible: it's made of a new quantum language. And transcribed or not, dictated by gods – or madness itself – now I get why it's so massive. It's because her father only coded the beginnings. The rest of it is organic, so to speak – or as Goeido originally described it, 'alive'. Her third layer itself continues to lay down new qubits, just as our brains lay down new neural connections as we grow and think and act and learn and experience throughout our lives. And as miraculous as all that seems, it explains how Neotnia, as her father claims, *is* just like anyone else. It's why she has feelings, and preferences for food and people and styles of clothes, and why she has worries and hopes and fears like we all do. Just as we are the sum of our ever-evolving neural connections, she is the sum of her ever-evolving quantum connections. And in both those cases – that sum? It's what we call our personality or consciousness or spirit. It's what gives us our essence.

But as I look at Neotnia, I know she's not thinking any of this right now. She's not thinking about herself. As that horrible shadow once again lengthens across her face, she's thinking about Kentetsu – of the harm she can bring to others.

Yet, that's just the thing ... out of everything her father's told us, that's the one thing that makes no sense.

'But why would the U.S. want Avance to make androids for the military?' I say. My voice seems to bump Neotnia out of her haze. 'I get that an android's morphology would be perfectly suited for taking care of the elderly, like you envisioned. But in warfare? I mean, after what happened in Angola, the superpowers hardly use soldiers anymore – especially America. Besides, most of their conflicts are fought in cyberspace now. But even when they're not, they're more likely to deploy drones and Pincer-class bots to a region – and those aren't remotely close to humanoid. Not to mention, they can literally bite through soldiers as well as steel bunkers, so would have no problem making mincemeat of androids, even with hardened skin. So, why would the military need androids that are "indistinguishable" from humans? It doesn't add up...'

Haruto looks at me in a sort of astonished way. 'You are very clever, aren't you?'

I don't say anything, but he simply continues to gaze at me with that astonished look frozen on his face. Yet after a few moments, that astonishment is replaced by a white pall. He's not looking at me, not anymore. He's not even looking at Neotnia. Even when she says, 'Father?' his gaze remains unchanged. Its focus stares right over our shoulders.

We turn to the window behind us. Through the thick sheets of snow, a sphere of white has appeared above the cliffs. At first, it's nucleus is no larger than a golf ball, but then it grows to the size of a baseball. And as it reaches basketball-size, a low hum fills the snowy air outside.

A frail dread spreads over Haruto's face.

'It was the gate that would have alerted them...'

Neotnia and I look at each other, a horrible realisation setting in.

'Neither of you could have known...' He shakes his head, the hum intensifying. He looks at Neotnia. 'I thought the storm would give us longer. I thought it would slow them for at least a few more hours; so we had time to say goodbye...'

Neotnia springs up and turns towards the sphere again, yet Haruto grabs her wrist and yanks her towards him.

'They thought you were destroyed, but if they find you here, they'll know,' he trembles. 'You need to run, *musume*. If they see your face – if they see what you look like now – they'll never stop hunting you.'

His features are so contorted he's almost unrecognisable, and instinctively Neotnia pulls away, her eyes filled with fright. Yet Haruto only tightens his grip, using her resistance to pull himself from the couch. He grabs her shoulders and frantically shouts for her to listen.

'You're the cusp of a new world, *musume*. The dividing line between the one that humanity has known and the one that comes next. But if they find you, they will pervert that to tear the fabric of societies apart…'

Trembling in his grasp, Neotnia's head shakes in confusion. The sphere is now as large as a beachball. A breath later, it's three times that size. It's so bright now, Neotnia and her father cast horizontal shadows across the room, hers trembling as the other shouts for it to go. Yet I can hardly hear his words anymore. The hum is now a roar so loud, the glass rattles. And instantly, I recognise it: a passenger drone – one carrying a lot of weight. It's why its blades howl. But with a boom of propulsive thrust, the light shoots into the sky, taking our shadows with it. In the room's renewed dimness Haruto pushes Neotnia away. His voice rumbles as loudly as the drone's hum outside, ordering her to go.

She grabs his arm. 'I'm not leaving you—'

'They'll set down on the roof.' He turns to me, ignoring Neotnia's grasp. 'They'll have to come down the stairwell. The snow's too heavy; they won't see you go out the front – but only if you leave, now!'

I know he's right. Yet I'm so afraid, I can't move. I can't rip my eyes from that terror on Neotnia's face. The terror of being separated from her father again.

'You said you care about my daughter? Then run with her – now!'

This time his words are so ear-splitting I jump, his gaze cutting through me like a blade.

It feels like my heart's leapt into my throat as I grasp Neotnia's arm. 'Neotnia, he's—'

'No!' She pulls away with no more difficulty than a great white snagged by a kid's fishing line.

And that's when we hear it – the dull thump.

It sounds seconds after the drone's roar abates. We turn towards the window overlooking the rear gardens – and hear it again. And again. It's as if something's knocking to be let in. Then I see it: a thick black cord, rapping the glass. It stands out against the sheets of snow like a line of coal buttons on a snowman's belly. With every thump, the cord raps more violently against the glass.

But our heads snap towards the floating stairs winding around the elevator shaft. An icy draft swirls down as footsteps rapidly pound, one set of legs appearing, then another. The figures are dressed in dark tactical gear, like soldiers, their faces obscured by balaclavas and metagoggles. Both point some type of slim pistols. They're shouting so many things – so many orders to stay where we are. And they're shouting them in English. American accents. But the way their heads ping-pong from me to Neotnia to Haruto, they seem almost stupefied by what they've found: a western boy, a Japanese girl and a frail old scientist – all in this facility together.

Then one is on me. Grabbing my hoodie, he tugs me from Neotnia's side with such force it's like I've been yanked by a bungie cord. He spins me onto my knees, pinning my wrists behind my back with just one hand. In the other, his pistol loads a spiked projectile. I feel the heat from its electrified barbs an inch from my neck and raise my gaze to find Neotnia's mouth wide in horror.

The lead soldier hasn't stopped moving, either. He circles the furthest couch, approaching Neotnia and her father holding onto each other as if a cyclone's coming. His own slim pistol grasped in his hand, he's shouting, 'Dr. Sato are you alright?'

But Haruto doesn't answer. It's as if he's too stunned to speak.

'Dr. Sato, I need verbal confirmation you're alright,' the soldier tries again, inching closer. He taps the side of his pistol, and it too loads a spiked projectile that sparks electric strings of green.

'Stay away from my father!' Neotnia swats her arm even though the soldier's out of reach. Yet it's her words that stop him cold.

He looks at his partner. 'Dr. Sato doesn't have any kin.'

'It's the bot,' his partner replies, squeezing my wrists harder. 'It wasn't destroyed.'

The lead soldier aims his pistol at Neotnia. 'Dr. Sato, is this the android?'

Even in the dim light, I can see the terror in Haruto's eyes. It's absolute. The worst that could happen, has. And glancing Neotnia at his side, seeing her fear, seeing the way her entire body trembles, clutching her father like a lioness protecting her cub from a predator – an anger swells in me like never before.

I pull a wrist free and get a knee up, planting my foot and pushing – hard.

But my body topples sideways and hits the ground, harder.

Neotnia's scream echoes. My skull throbs like someone's taken a bat to it. The soldier pulls me back onto my knees and brings the tip of his pistol to my eye, the green electricity snapping between the spikes of the still-loaded projectile.

'Next time you get more than a whipping,' he grits.

Neotnia's eyes go wide as something wet runs down my jaw. I shrug against it and when I pull my shoulder away, from the corner of my eye, I spot the blood now staining my hoodie.

Neotnia's eyes only rip from me when the lead soldier shouts again, his pistol pointed directly at her. 'Dr. Sato, is this the android?'

Yet her father's frail body might as well be made of marble. He won't give up his daughter.

'Fuck it,' the one holding me spits. 'Pop it and get it on the bird. The others can watch the doc, but we're flying it back now.'

It happens in an instant.

Haruto grabs Neotnia's yellow sweater and pulls with all his might. Not to pull her out of the way, but to put his delicate body in front of hers. And as the sparking green projectile fired by the lead soldier strikes his shoulder, Haruto's body gives a single brutal convulsion before crumpling to the floor as if all life has been sucked clean.

Neotnia's cry is so deafening it's as if she were the one struck. And at that utter anguish given a voice, the skin on her hands ripples like a tidal wave, turning hard in its wake. An instant later the wave reaches the flesh of her neck, which ripples and hardens and continues to do so across her face all the way up to beneath her black bangs. And without hesitating, she pulls the soldier close and in a single thrust shoves with such force that when he hits the wall of glass, it splinters, his body slumping to the side. I don't think even Goeido could shove someone with such power.

The soldier holding the pistol to my head screams as Neotnia approaches – this slim girl in a comfy wool sweater and ankle-length denim skirt. He pulls his metagoggles and balaclava off, as if doing so somehow gives him a better chance. A tightness rips across my scalp as I'm tugged to my feet. The soldier's arm constricts my throat like a snake, his other trains his trembling pistol on Neotnia. Its green projectile sails past her shoulder. But she doesn't slow. Her face is frightening as she nears us. Not because of her skin. Not because of the bumpy ridges layered atop her flesh. It's because of her eyes. Their pain. As the soldier desperately loads another projectile, she reaches past me and grabs his collar, and I don't think she sees me at all.

I'm knocked to the floor as she pulls him away, the green electricity of a loaded projectile already dancing on the tip of his pistol. But it's too late for that. Neotnia swings her fist, smacking him across the face, just like Kentetsu. He collapses, writhing, his cheek split wide, the yellow fat puffing from it like a boiled lobster tail tinged with blood.

It feels like my lungs are going to burst, I'm breathing so heavily.

I sit up against the edge of the couch. Neotnia gives me the briefest look. Behind the bumpy ridges of her lids, I see a hint of those eyes I know. I nod I'm OK.

Next to me, the soldier's hand covers his cheek. His eyes roil like eggs in boiling water.

Across from us, Neotnia's already on her knees, beside her father, carefully turning him onto his back. She cries, 'Otōsan! Otōsan!' But he doesn't move.

From the dim space between the couches, a green glow catches my eye. The soldier's pistol. Its projectile's electricity dances like furious guitar strings, charring the hardwood floor beneath. The soldier's hand has slumped away from his split cheek. His eyes barely even roil anymore. I reach for the pistol, tapping the switch he pressed to load the projectile. The electricity between its spikes fizzle out.

Across from me, Neotnia still cries, '*Otōsan*! *Otōsan*!'

I watch her shake her father's body, my chest going tight. If those projectiles have enough amps to burn a hardwood floor, what would they do to a frail old man with a pacemaker?

I push myself up onto the couch, my skull throbbing. A groan rises from the soldier Neotnia pushed against the glass – he's conscious now. Yet he's still slumped and, given the way his head wobbles, I'm not sure he even has control over it.

'*Otōsan*!' Neotnia cries again, hovering over her father. She touches his face, his chest, his shoulders. Her palms move across him as if she's certain that if she just keeps searching, she'll find some sign of life. Her voice is almost a whine now. '*Otōsan*...'

But then Haruto – he moves. Barely.

In an instant, Neotnia's skin ripples, softening again. She touches his face as delicately as if it were made of papyrus. Haruto's movements in turn are minute, deliberate, and they make me feel as if I'm gazing upon some sacred ritual. His hand rises. Its fingers brush Neotnia's elbow as if trying to deliver a message by touch alone. She bends close, the tears streaming across her cheeks as she puts her ear to his lips, listening intently for so long.

His hand travels from her elbow, along the length of her forearm, to her own hand on his chest, and reaches for her wet face. Placing his palm on her cheek, Haruto aligns her eyes with his. He speaks as her tears drop over him like rain.

She looks so scared.

He touches her cheek again and quietly says more. Her face trembles, and her lips shudder as she nods. His fingers brush her cheek once more, where they rest.

The way his hand then falls aside, it's how a tulip with no more strength in its stem gives way to the wind, touching the ground slowly, but forever.

Neotnia's eyes squeeze so tightly they form little lines. She bends her face so closely to her father's, the bridges of their noses cross, and her tears drip into the hollows of his eyes, filling them like pools. Sobbing against his face, her mouth opens as if to say '*Otōsan*' one last time, yet only a moan escapes.

At once, the lights blink out.

I spring up, my heart lurching into my throat. Everything's silhouetted against the snowfall's pale-blue glow. And as I focus on those heavy flakes plummeting into the gardens, I think I hear something outside. A voice.

Instantly, red floods the room.

It's the dim kind of light emergency backup systems generate.

Then comes another noise.

I look beside me. The soldier with the split face – his chest rises and falls, but he's still out.

It's the soldier by the splintered glass – he's on his hands and knees now, like a baby. The way he sways, it's as if he's learning how to move again.

But Neotnia notices none of this – the red glow nor anything else. She's still kneeling at Haruto's side, her arm stretched across him, moaning so loudly.

And now I'm grabbing her shoulders, trying to pull her away. I feel her soft flesh beneath her sweater, but she's still so, so strong. She refuses to let go of her father.

I wrap an arm around her throat and the other across her chest, lifting with all the power in my legs just to get her halfway up. Still, she struggles against me. She wants to sink back to his side, like a stone in the ocean.

I pull harder, and she swings, trying to break my grip. She does this again and again. The back of her hand strikes my jaw, the force sending me onto the couch. Immediately, I feel the blood on my skin. Only then do Neotnia's swollen eyes leave her father's body.

She looks in horror at the red spattered across my face and turns her hand over, examining its knuckles the way one would a murder weapon. As it begins to tremble, even in the room's dim redness, I see that terrible shadow swallow her whole.

'It's not mine,' I say, springing up, pulling her hand from her sight. 'It's not my blood, alright? It's his—'

Her mouth parts, seeing the unconscious soldier's split face, the exploded fat billowing like an atomic cloud from his cheek. She reaches to touch my own.

'You didn't hurt me,' I shout, shaking my head, trying to get through to her.

But she's not hearing me at all. That shadow's a cocoon, cutting her off from this world.

I look over my shoulder. The soldier's still on his hands and knees, wobbling around. I'm not sure if he's looking for his pistol or just can't stand.

I grab Neotnia's hand. 'We need to go – now!'

And I swear, this is the first since seeing the blood on my face that she's heard anything I've said. She looks over her shoulder at Haruto's body for a long moment, as if reading some invisible message inscribed on it by her tears. Then she turns, looks me in the eyes in the oddest way, and gives a small nod.

Her hand in mine, I pull. But as we pass the soldier with the split face, Neotnia stumbles to the floor. The soldier by the splintered glass is still on his hands and knees, but I don't know for how much longer. I scoop Neotnia under both arms, hoisting her to her feet. I grab her hand again and pull her around the partition. I drag her under the dim red light, past the metapainting and out the frosted glass door, my chest pounding.

The night air is frigid, the flurries like shredded paper. Everything's a blue-and-white haze, and the snow now comes up to our ankles. Neotnia's gazing into the night, as if she can see through its white sheets into some faraway place.

I squint in the opposite direction to get our bearings. Gripping Neotnia's hand, I move towards where the gate should be – but stop dead in my tracks.

A frosted breath leaves me.

Through the fat flakes, a pair of dark figures approach. They hold pistols with tips that glow green. These two other soldiers, they're shouting, but in the howling wind and swirling flakes I can't make out their words. And despite their pistols' green snapping trained right on us, Neotnia doesn't seem to notice them at all, she's so lost in her own mind, gazing into the snowy night.

I do the only thing I can. I stand between her and them.

And as the green of their pistols grows thicker, I wonder if the only reason her father didn't survive was because of his pacemaker, or if these projectiles are meant to kill.

My eyes widen as they take aim. Behind them, it's as if the snow has come to life. Through the whirling flakes, their black-clad heads slam together as if smashed by the wind. And as their bodies crumple onto the glistening grounds, another form – a massive one – emerges. The heavy flakes cling to his already-white kimono.

I shout at the top of my lungs, an icy-white breath carrying his name. 'Goeido!'

I've never been happier to see anyone in my entire life.

18 – A blindness to all the people in the world.

Goeido once told me it's true that sumos can hit with up to fifteen G's of force. Part of me thought he might have been exaggerating. But with the unconscious soldiers at our feet, I don't doubt him anymore. And given he's just had to take down two soldiers, it's no wonder his face is a mixture of alarm and bewilderment. There's room there for concern, too, when he sees Neotnia's vacant expression. She hardly blinks as thick flakes land on her lashes. Goeido says something, but she doesn't reply. I'm not sure she even hears him. In the pale blue and white around us, that horrible shadow envelops her.

'Her father died,' I say, immediately knowing he can't understand. 'We need to get to the car ... her father ... her ... *otōsan*,' Goeido's eyes twitch. 'Haruto – he ... he didn't make it,' I shake my head.

Goeido's mouth drops as the understanding dawns on him, and he looks at Neotnia with such stunned compassion not a single frosted breath escapes his lips. He sets a meaty hand on her slight shoulder. Its gentle touch seems to bring Neotnia out of her haze. He says something and her mouth curves into a horrible little frown, her eyes clouded with pain. She looks at the snow-covered ground as if only now noticing the men lying there, then glances over her shoulder. Inside the facility, a shadow grows against the glass illuminated dimly red.

Neotnia looks back up at Goeido. It's as if she's a little girl staring at a giant snowman, her swollen eyes considering his face. Then, she takes a single step through the dense snowfall, and she hugs him. Her arms can't even encircle his massive frame, but she holds herself to Goeido as tightly as she can, embracing him as if she expects him to float off into the storm at any moment. And towering over her, Neotnia's body curved around his belly, it looks as if a sudden realisation has struck Goeido, and his arms envelope her in return.

They stay that way for a long moment, the heavy flakes falling over them.

When Neotnia releases him, she looks towards the facility again. That shadow on the glass has turned the partition. It's one of the soldiers. Probably the one who was on his hands and knees as we fled – the one who still had an intact face. He moves as if his balance is off, a green glow moving with him.

Neotnia turns back to Goeido and places a hand on his chest, speaking with urgency. Goeido nods as if he's being read instructions he needs to memorise. He glances at me when Neotnia says my name.

The soldier's halfway to the door now, his pistol glowing.

'Do you have your phone?' Neotnia says to me.

For a moment, I'm speechless. Her voice sounds so alien.

'We need to get to the car...' I reply.

She glances over my shoulder. The soldier's almost at the door. 'Do you have your phone?' she repeats, her voice rising.

'Yeah, but—'

She yanks me by the hand, but instead of heading towards the gate, she pulls me in the opposite direction, leading us deeper into the facility's gardens. She takes me past bonsai trees that look like clouds with trunks now that they're covered in so much snow. She pulls me past stone lanterns and across the ornate footbridge spanning the pond. Her grip is like an iron vice. She follows the wall running along the rear of the grounds as if searching for something on it. Behind us, Goeido grows smaller, watching us recede as the snow comes down in sheets, our feet sinking deeper into the powder as she pulls me. She only stops when we've reached the corner of the gardens, where the wall's cloaked in a pitch-black shadow.

'Neotnia.' I'm winded. 'We need to get to the car.'

She releases my hand and turns, but not to address me. She gazes across the white gardens towards Goeido. The soldier's exited the facility now. Even with the balaclava over his face I can tell how stupefied he is at finding a giant sumo waiting in the falling snow, standing over two of his unconscious comrades.

'Hurry!' Neotnia shouts.

My gaze whips back just as she darts into the shadow, disappearing in an instant like it's a doorway to another world. I cry out after her but there's no reply. The darkness has swallowed her whole. Across the gardens, the soldier turns towards my cry, the tip of his pistol glowing green like a sick snowflake among all the others. But Goeido side-steps, shuffling in front of him. He stomps his foot into the snowy earth as if marking a line the other isn't allowed to cross.

'Neotnia!' I shout into the shadow.

That's when I realise it's not a shadow at all. It's an opening in the gardens' wall, but one so dark even snow isn't visible on the other side. I cry Neotnia's name again and again to no avail, leaving me only one choice: letting that darkness swallow me, too.

When I emerge, I've left the facility's pristinely manicured gardens for the untamed wilderness of the mountain. Its stillness clings to me like a skin as I let my eyes adjust to the dimness all around. The forest's canopy stops much of the snowfall from hitting the old stone path that lies before me. Every five or six feet, the path meets a step or two and runs again until it meets another set of steps, taking it higher and higher.

There's the snap of a twig. My eyes adjust further. I spot Neotnia. She's maybe thirty feet ahead, heading higher up the path.

I dash after her, my heart pounding, and slip and stumble several times where a break in the canopy has allowed snow to wet the stony slabs.

Neotnia turns a corner, out of sight.

I move quicker, my legs burning as the path climbs the mountainside. Ancient stone foxes line the bend where Neotnia turned. Their red bibs stand out against the white snow dusting their heads.

The path steepens. Neotnia's now maybe forty steps above me.

The white soles of her shoes seem to glow in the darkness as she scrambles higher.

'Neotnia!' I yell over the thudding in my chest. 'We need to go back. We need to help Goeido. We need to get to the car!'

Yet she climbs.

My thighs tremble. I pass more stone foxes in their red bibs. Some are covered in helmets of snow, others in hats of moss. Behind them, tablets inscribed with kanji. Again, Neotnia rounds a bend, disappearing. I keep running, my lungs ravenous for the cold air all around. I reach where Neotnia turned and catch my frosted breath. My skin boils and freezes at the same time.

Neotnia's no longer in sight, but there's another bend twenty steps higher. I suck in the night air, the forest's sounds echoing all around – the heavy, damp clumps of snow hitting the decaying earthen floor as unknown creatures scurry in the branches above.

I move upward again. Reaching the stone foxes at the next bend, I find another set of steps – maybe thirty. Neotnia ascends them and I yell after her. But as she reaches the top of the steps, she disappears.

I listen to the roar of my lungs. The dropping snow. A crow in the night. And then ... a whooshing sound. A low rumbling, like organic static. It's coming from beyond the next flight. I climb and see her footprints on a few of the stones where snow has broken the canopy above. At the top, the path levels into a plateau, and the trees thin. I spot Neotnia further along. I'm moving as fast as my body allows, but I'm so winded.

As the trees thin more, as the whooshing sound grows, a dense curtain of white comes into view, like some god is demanding the snow funnel into a specific area.

And now I understand why.

There's no canopy of branches blocking the storm ahead because a river splits the forest like a natural highway, leaving a wide gap to the sky. And as the stone path leads to the rocky bank of the river, I see where it flows – towards the bright-orange torii spanning its falls. We're above the facility now, higher in the mountainside, up on the next set of cliffs visible from her father's living room. And Neotnia, she's not forty feet ahead, approaching the riverbank's edge.

But in an instant, she topples sideways, slipping on one of the big snow-wetted stones.

'Neotnia!'

She turns. Sees me closing. Behind her, the river roars as its waters accelerate nearing the falls under the torii's legs. Neotnia picks herself up and for a moment I think she's waiting for me, but then she reaches into her skirt's pocket and hurries towards the river's edge.

And keeps going.

Her shoes sink into the rushing waters. Her ankle-length skirt follows.

'Neotnia!'

I'm almost there. I'm almost at the bank. But she keeps advancing into the roaring waters. Calf-deep. Knee-deep. Waist-deep.

And that's where she stops, her submerged half bracing against the surging current. She pulls her sweater from her body and drops it into the current where it's carried five feet in an instant, then ten. Before twenty, it's swept over the falls under the torii. She lifts an arm over her head. There's something's in her hand.

But like that she sinks into the waters as if a drain's opened beneath her.

I scream her name as I reach the bank. My feet come out under me. My head smacks a wet slab. I'm stunned so hard it feels like everything's in slow motion. And flat on my back, the sky over the torii comes into view. The clouds break, and the full moon shines bright in unison with the unfinished stations, each looking like jagged silver crescents.

But the world speeds up again.

I scramble to my feet, fearing she's already been swept away.

Yet Neotnia's in the same spot she was, in the river's centre. Her head's still above the surface. So is her hand, and whatever's in it. She sank of her own volition and now she rises, led by that dark object in her grip, her upper half dripping wet.

She turns towards me as my ankles hit the water, my feet instantly stinging as if hundreds of icy needles jab my flesh.

'Stop!' Neotnia shouts, the order emerging in one sharp, frosted breath. Yet it's the intensity of her eyes that freezes me in place, the rushing waters halfway up my shins revealing just how powerfully the current sweeps towards the falls. And it hits me that the only reason Neotnia hasn't been swept away is because her synthetic physiology makes her innately stronger than me. From the way she leans into the water, her submerged lower half must be continually fighting against its steamrolling force. If I were as deep as she is, I'd be carried away in an instant – and she knows it.

But the glacial cold of the water – I can see she feels it as much as I do. And she's soaking in it, her white undershirt pasted to her skin, exposing the outline of her bra and the indentation of her navel. Her lips tremble as the tips of her black hair dangle heavy against her shoulders. I squint but can't make out what's grasped in her dry hand.

'What are you doing?' my voice shudders.

'Don't come any closer,' she warns over the water's roar. 'You won't be able to withstand the current.'

I shake my head, gaping at her shivering form. 'I don't understand ... W–why are you in the river? I—'

'Take out your phone.'

'...What...?'

'Take out your phone – now!'

Her eyes have a frenzied desperation to them. The liquid cold seeps into my bones.

'Look ... just – just come to the shore and tell me what's going on, OK?'

She fumbles with the object in her hand. A sick green light appears among the white flakes falling all around.

'Take out your phone,' she orders, putting the pistol to her head. The electricity from the loaded projectile jitters an inch from her pinkened cheek. 'Take it out, now...'

I'm so stunned I can hardly hear my own voice when I ask where she got it from. Then I remember: as I pulled her from the room, she tripped by the soldier with the split face. She tripped by his pistol lying on the floor...

'Stop!' she barks as I slosh further into the water. 'Stop!' And she aggressively repositions the weapon at her cheek.

I freeze. 'Alright – OK...'

But the current's so powerful, my foot slides on the riverbed and Neotnia jumps as if she thinks I'm making another move for her. I dig my heel into the muddy floor, putting my hands out, signalling I'm not coming closer. Still, the anxiety dances across her eyes in the same chaotic way the electricity dances from the pistol's tip.

'Neotnia, what are you doing with that?'

'Don't move,' she shudders, the weapon trembling at her cheek, its green electricity disintegrating every falling flake unfortunate enough to encounter it. She looks like a frightened animal caught in a trap. 'Show me your phone.'

I give a calm nod. 'OK...' I take it from my pocket.

Neotnia squints through the snowfall. 'Hold it higher so I can see it better.'

And I do.

For several moments, she nods, as if confirming to herself she's seen it; that neither me, nor the snow, nor the light of the moon are playing a trick on her.

Her eyes find mine again and her throat tightens.

'My body's wet. When I'm electrocuted, I want you to access my systems like you did when I was in the bath – understand?'

My stomach goes as cold as my feet in the river. 'I—'

'John...' She shakes her head, giving me a broken look. 'There's no time. I need you to do this for me, OK? I – *Do not move!*'

The green electricity snaps as she forces the pistol to a new position. It trembles in her grip just past the edge of her eye's socket, illuminating not only their terror, but their sadness as well. And it's not just her hand trembling – her whole body is.

Mine's doing the same. My eyes wet.

'Neotnia, I ... I don't understand what's going on, OK? You gotta tell me what's happening...' I plead, watching the green so close to her. 'Why are you—?'

'I'm the next Hiroshima.'

The words break in a billowing cloud of white, an agonising little tremor forming on her lips.

'I'm their next weapon of mass destruction...'

My mouth drops. 'I ... I don't—'

'He told me.' Her throat tightens, the green electricity illuminating that tragic look on her. 'I'm the new paradigm in warfare. He told me, John – Father told me as he lay there...'

'Neotnia, I...'

She dismisses me with a shake of her head. Her gaze turns towards the moon. No, not the moon – the two unfinished stations suspended around it. And looking at me again, seeing my expression, her face breaks.

'The superpowers,' she says, 'they're at a stalemate ... Father – he said each has developed their cyber-defences to such a degree they've negated the other's even most advanced digital weaponry, and so they can't covertly inflict damage within the other's borders anymore – not at the scale they desire, which is why they spend all their time conducting proxy battles in poorer, weaker nations.'

Neotnia's head jerks and she wipes away some flakes that have stuck to her brows.

'But Father said they know that can't go on,' her voice shakes. 'Paris, Zambia, Hokkaido – even all the way back to Angola – they know those proxy battles are ultimately just posturing. If they're to truly become the world's sole power, to shape it in their image, they know they need to hit their opponent directly – at the very heart of its society. But how do you break an entire nation and not have the world condemn you for it? You can no longer destroy whole cities and hold on to the moral high ground.' She shakes her head.

'The answer is to make your enemy destroy *itself* from within. You need to get them to tear the fabric of their own society apart. You need to turn its citizens not only against their government but against each other – make them doubt everything. It's what the superpowers have been trying for decades with their online disinformation campaigns, with their deepfakes – even Joe told me that.'

Neotnia twists up her mouth, glancing at the moon. In the break in the clouds, the two stations glimmer like jewels.

'But like you said, the superpowers have gotten too good at detecting each other's digital lies. It's harder and harder to inundate the other's population with falsified narratives. America hardly ever gets a deepfake onto China's intranet anymore. Even when its fake videos do get through their defences, people have grown accustomed to being wary – paranoid – of what they see on their screens...'

She bites her lip and stares vacantly for a moment, her head shaking. When she focuses on me again, her words come out in shivering, billowing plumes.

'But then Father came along with me ... an android that could care for the elderly – one so lifelike you couldn't even tell it wasn't human. Avance saw his work, and, in me, they didn't see a carer – they saw the physical manifestation of a deepfake. A way for America to get around the digital stalemate. And not just that, but a way for America to weaponise paranoia and psychological warfare to a degree never seen. They saw a legion of me, but each member unique in look and personality, and spread within their enemies' borders, infiltrating not just military and government institutions, but every aspect of their societies. Their hospitals and schools and temples and shops...'

Her voice shudders so much, it breaks, and, as if lost for several seconds, she looks into the icy blackness rushing before her like it's some endless void. But then suddenly fearful, her gaze snaps back and her eyes shift across me, judging if I've tried to approach. It's several moments before she speaks again.

'Their intention for me is not to be a soldier – it's not even to keep me a military secret. It's to let the citizens of America's enemies know I could be among them at any time, within their own borders and cities and villages. That I could look like any one of them, move like them, be indistinguishable from them. It's to sow paranoia and distrust among populations of innocent people. To get them to turn on each other...' She shakes her head.

'You'd no longer know if the person you were talking to, or work with, or who lives across the hall is, in fact, a real person or an imposter placed there to live among you by your country's greatest enemy. Did your child get sick because it wasn't possible for the doctor to catch the issue beforehand? Or was it purposeful – because the doctor isn't actually one of you? Did you mess up at the factory because you were having a bad day, or was it sabotage because you're not really one of us? Your new neighbour is acting strange. Is she really like you? Do you want her around your home? Do you trust what she's doing in hers? Does she actually have the strength to kill you, your family, with her bare hands – and should you take action against her before she can do just that?'

Neotnia holds her hand out for a moment, and the way she stares at it, I know she's seeing it with shell-hard skin.

'Mob mentality rules when people are anxious and scared, and looking for someone to blame for their unhappiness and hurts and fears.' She looks at me with a pitiful smile. 'Just look at that Japanese-American superhero actor whose head they bashed in. Or just ask Goeido. People turned on him in an instant – and he was one of Japan's most-loved athletes. Or look at how social-media mobs descend upon anyone for the slightest infraction. Or you – look at how your teacher was happy to have someone to blame for her loss. Go back even further: Joe told me how America rounded up their Japanese into camps during the last great war because they didn't know who may be a spy. They kept all of them, their *own* citizens, in concentration camps for years – even the ones born there.

'A world with me in it – a world as Avance and the Americans wants me – is a world where no one knows who they can trust. Where everyone is suspect. Where anyone could be an imposter. It's a world where it seems entirely probable those working closest to you may be working against you and those you love. And Father's right: as that narrative pervades, the psychological impact alone – the fear, the distrust – societies will tear themselves apart.'

Her throat tightens, her body shivering. The green snapping so close.

'You don't need bombs to wipe out a society when you can get them to do it themselves. And just knowing I exist, just knowing the Americans have me and the Chinese do not – that's all it would take. And not just in China. Every country would fear what might never even be among them...'

A horribly tragic smile crosses her face.

'Father said it – he said it as he lay there: his mother was *hibakusha* because just one archaic technological advancement was weaponised against just two cities. But me – he's right. Avance would use me to bring a blindness to all the people in the world. I would make them all *hibakusha*...'

'Neotnia—'

'No...' she sets her mouth tight, squeezing the pistol's grip in her trembling hand. 'You saw what man did against himself in Hiroshima. You saw Angola – your father died there because of it. And my father died tonight because of it, too. Look above us, right now – those stations. They *never* stop manipulating technological advancements to attack each other, to claim supremacy; and in doing so, innocents die. *Millions*. Father's right, John ... he's right. I'm their next Hiroshima...'

And at those words, such a hollowness rings through my chest, my body goes numb. Not from the snow, not from the icy torrents. It's because of that look on Neotnia's face – the despair, the desperation. That all-consuming shadow.

I know I need to say the right thing, right now, to get her to stop this. But I don't know what that right thing is. I don't know what to say. And I think Neotnia knows what's going through my head, too, because she gives me a tiny, sad smile.

'*Stop*, John ... Don't come any closer.'

I freeze as she tightens the pistol's grip at her temple. My legs are now submerged below the knees where the current hits with the force of water erupting from a split hydrant.

Everything tumbles around me. My thoughts mix with the

snowfall and the surging water and the green glow in Neotnia's trembling hand. I see that horrible look in her swollen eyes and that shadow seeped into her like ash.

I'm so scared of saying the wrong thing.

'So – we run,' I swallow. 'We run. We just run.'

'Father tried that...'

'He went back to them, though.' My voice is desperate. 'I know it was to keep you safe, but he went back to your house so they could find him. We won't. We'll have a better chance...'

A frosted breath escapes her, and she gives a heartbroken smile. 'He returned, but it wasn't only to keep me or Emiko safe.' She shakes her head. 'Einstein couldn't tear up his equation that led to Hiroshima, but Father – he thought maybe he could accomplish what Einstein couldn't. He returned so he could tear up his work.'

As the erratic electricity snaps at her temple, a large branch speeds past in the icy current, and all I can think is how quickly she could sweep under the torii, too. She's so worn. I don't know how much longer her body can stave off the torrents.

'Look...' my voice trembles '...just come to me, OK?'

'He returned because he was working on a quantum virus, John...' Neotnia ignores my plea. 'He told me. It would have infected all of Avance's servers, planetary and orbital – erasing any traces of his work. He was going to release it and then end his life so he could never again be forced to work to hurt the world.'

'But—'

'But they've killed him – and with him, any chance for him to release his virus. And now they know I'm alive. They know what I look like. With Father gone, they'll know I'm their only shot at understanding how to create the lifelike androids they desire. They'll come. They'll never stop searching ... and they'll use your safety and Goeido's safety to threaten me into returning to them...'

She looks as if she's lost the ability to speak. The warm tears stream down her cheeks.

'And I would come to them, if they had either of you. I would,' she chokes. 'So, one way or the other, they'll use me to hurt people, and I can't let that happen...'

Her voice fades as if her thoughts are exhausted, and her swollen eyes soften.

And for a moment, the way she's considering me, that look on her face, it's as if she's considering a memory. Then – the pistol drops from her temple, and the relief, it cuts rights through me.

But in one deft movement, she fires it into her chest.

There's a loud static pop, and green electricity dances across the wetness of her body before evaporating like steam. I cry out as she tips forward, yet she catches herself before smacking the surface, and she keeps the pistol just above the waterline as well.

'Can you ... see me on your screen?' Her voice is shallow, her body bent forward, the thick flakes merging with her wetness. As she straightens some, I see the discharged projectile embedded into her sternum through the white undershirt pasting her chest. Except for the dry hand gripping the pistol, every inch below her neck is once again ashen black.

'Can you see me?' she shouts.

I glance at my screen no longer than a blink before the water's sloshing against my thighs, but instantly Neotnia cries for me to halt. My body shudders to a stop, my knees totally submerged now. The pistol trembles under her jaw, its tip green with another snapping projectile.

She orders me to access her systems, but all I can do is look around, as if I'll find someone who can help me – as if some hero is just beyond the bank, or the trees, or the legs of the giant torii.

But no. It's only us.

'Access my systems.'

'Neotnia—'

'Access me.' She exhales a frosty cloud into the snowfall. 'Show me my code...'

'Please...' My voice breaks.

'Do it!' she screams, shaking the pistol under her jaw.

My thoughts tumble. I'm so worried she's going to shoot herself again, intentionally or not. On my screen, I find her jumbled code-base, the three layers smashed on top of each other, the code looking like it's randomly teleporting around.

'OK,' I say.

'Show me the third layer.' Her breathing is laboured, her body shivering. 'Show me it.'

I compile her father's pattern-recognition keys and separate her three layers. I pull up the third, its indecipherable quantum language moving and growing on its own. I turn my screen towards her, the artificial light from it as invasive as the green glow from the pistol to the nature all around.

Neotnia squints through the snowfall; the ends of her hair hang wet and heavy.

'How much time is left?'

I shake my head, confused.

'How long until my firewall goes back up and the code's cut off?'

'I ... don't know—'

She takes a single step and stretches her blackened arm towards me through the snow, her body now swaying in the powerful current.

'Stay where you are, and hand me your phone. Quickly. Reach out and hand it to me.'

And looking at her outstretched hand, we could probably just barely reach, our fingertips each grasping one end of my phone. But I don't move. Because now I fully understand what she wants.

'Give it to me before my firewall goes back up,' she shouts, spreading her fingers apart.

'Just come to me...' I try, looking at her backend body trembling against the weight of the torrents thrashing it; the sadness of her shivering face; the fear as that green glow dances where her throat meets her jaw. 'Come to me? OK? Please...'

My sudden tears feel unnaturally warm in the snow all around us.

'John—'

'Just come to me ... just do that, OK?' I hold my gaze on her as if it might turn into a lasso at any moment and pull her close and I'll once again feel her softness in my arms. I give her a little smile. I know she wants to come to me. I know she doesn't want to do this. I know I can get her to come to me.

But Neotnia's eyes, they shift from mine to my phone's screen.

Her head shakes. She turns the pistol and fires into her abdomen before I can utter a sound. Her cry's so loud this time, it strips all noise from the roaring torrents. As she tips into its dark water, I lunge for her but am immediately forced sideways. My soles blindly skim the muddy riverbed, desperately trying to regain a foothold as my body twists towards the moon over the torii. My heels jam against something hard, halting my slide.

I've been carried feet from where I was. I twist back in a panic as Neotnia rises from the water, her hair plastered against her face.

For a moment, it's as if she doesn't know where she is. Her jaw hangs open as she hungrily devours frigid air.

As her breathing slows, her eyes regain focus. She sees me. Sees my phone in my hand.

'Is it still up?' The words come out in a coarse breath.

I glance at the screen but don't say anything. Yet she can tell from my eyes that her second electrocution has given her the additional time she wanted.

'Give it to me now.' She stretches her hand towards me. Her slim fingers, like everything below the neck, are now as black as ink.

'Your father wouldn't want this.'

'Father isn't around anymore.' She shakes her head. 'I have to think of the people who are.' Her fingers stretch for my phone. The white flakes cascading before her blackened skin look like stars falling in the night sky. But even they don't drown out the desperation on her face.

'John…' Her mouth tightens.

But I slip my phone into my hoodie's front pocket.

'No,' I say.

A frown so heavy appears across her face, it's as if her lips will snap in half.

And this time when she raises the pistol, it's pointed at me.

'John,' she trembles.

'No,' I shake my head. 'I'm not letting you do this.'

Her jaw clenches and she taps a button, loading another projectile. Its spikes spark electric green. The way her blackened arm quivers, it's as if the weapon has suddenly taken on more weight.

'Give it to me ... now.' Her voice shudders.

But I shrug and shake my head. I put my hands in my hoodie's pocket to keep the phone securely in place. I take a careful step back in the direction the current carried me from, always making sure to stay out of her reach. The current's force, it's like walking through wet cement, but I take one step, then another. And with each step, the realisation grows across Neotnia's face that I'm not going to give her my phone so she can do what she thinks she must to keep us safe.

'John...' She weakly jostles the pistol at me, its green glow snapping.

Yet I turn away and head for the riverbank.

'I need to do this for you.' Her voice trembles behind me.

I take another step towards shore and another, the water getting shallower. There are fifty seconds left, maybe a minute tops, before her quantum firewall restores. She can shoot me – I don't care. I'll never unlock her codebase again.

'Please...'

I hear it as my ankles slosh above the water. My head snaps over my shoulder, waiting for the rest of my body to catch up. My chest goes hollow as that staticky pop echoes into oblivion.

Neotnia's bent at the waist. Her hair dangles into the current, her face an inch above its surging surface.

For a moment, I can't breathe.

Then, slowly, she rises, as if propelled by the wincing breaths that frost from her mouth.

And now I see the pistol's barrel buried into her palm. As she pulls it away, its projectile remains embedded in her inky-black flesh. But unlike the ones embedded in her sternum and abdomen, this one continues sparking green, like it's a fork rammed into a socket. Only now, her palm oscillates between her flesh's soft form and her shelled skin. And as she pries the projectile from her palm, her deafening cry shatters the night as her shelled flesh peels with it, revealing her bright, synthetic musculature underneath.

Yet she doesn't more than glance at her de-fleshed palm. Her third electrocution got her what she wanted: it's keeping her firewall down for longer. And turning her face up, she looks at me with such a terrible sadness and raises the pistol in her still-good hand, another projectile sparking green.

And she fires it into my chest.

I don't know if I scream. I don't know if my vocal cords are even capable of movement anymore. No part of my body seems to be. All I know is I twist and am now tipping into the river. And as soon as my back smacks its surface it hits me that I'm going to drown because I can't move a muscle. My hands are still in my hoodie's front pocket, my fingers frozen around my phone.

But though I can't budge, unfortunately, I can still feel. I can feel the icy water enveloping me. It's as if I've fallen into a cocoon of needles. I can feel my heels bumping along the rocky bank as the current grabs hold of the upper half of me. I can feel my body swivel and drift. And, right before my eyes submerge, I can see the orange torii spanning the falls as the thick flakes fall all around, the clouds behind only partially obscuring the unfinished stations suspended like jagged silver crescents around the moon.

Yet as quickly as my nostrils dip below the current, I'm pulled from it.

Neotnia grasps the front of my hoodie and carries me as if lugging a heavy duffle bag with one hand. I hover inches over the shallows as she hauls me to safety, then feel the uneven riverbank against my back as she sets me down.

I try to sit up but can't. I can't even blink. It feels like some new form of gravity is pulling on every cell in my body, locking me in place. I see Neotnia kneel at my side. The pale skin of her face stands out against the blackness of her body below.

The way she's looking at me, I couldn't move even if my body would allow it. I could gaze into those clear blue-grey eyes forever.

She leans closer, placing a hand on my chest. Her breath warms my mouth as those eyes look into mine. 'When you kissed me on the temple steps last night, you made me feel I was no different from anyone – and it was wonderful,' she says, those eyes shining. 'You made me feel like I belonged for the first time in my life, no matter how different I thought I was.'

And she kisses me.

My cheeks feel wet. I'm not sure if it's her tears or my own.

Her lips leave mine, and she looks at me once more. Then, her hand reaches into my hoodie's pocket and touches mine. It slips my phone from my fingers. And still looking into my eyes, she tilts her head and gives me a little smile. It's a smile that makes her look content; that makes her look almost happy, as if that's how she wants me to remember her.

She leaves my field of view. All I see now is the snow falling from above.

I hear the stones shift below her feet as she moves.

I want to scream for her to stop but my mouth won't work.

The stones on the riverbank clatter as she takes another step, and another.

But as I hear her foot hit the water ... my eyes – they shift.

I blink.

And my fingers ... they move.

Suddenly, it's as if there's not as much gravity holding me in place. My lips press together, and I turn my head. My shoulders twitch – and then my arms, they jerk.

I hear her wading into the water. Moving through it.

I squeeze my stomach muscles as tightly as I can, trying to bend myself upright. Yet nothing below my waist wants to contract.

I get an elbow behind me and push my upper body from the bank.

My tongue learns how to work again. '*Neotnia...*'

She's reached the middle of the river. She's more than waist-deep in it again, holding my phone, the screen glowing blue against her face.

'Stop—' I shout. My legs still won't budge.

She looks from my phone's screen to me, and regret breaks across her face.

'Don't do this,' I cry and curse my legs for not working. I need to reach her. That's all I need to do. I bend my upper body and latch onto a large stone, pulling with all my might until I'm on my stomach. I clutch for the next large stone and pull harder, inching over small, sharp rocks towards the river, the dead weight of my legs towing behind me.

'Please, Neotnia. Please don't do this. Don't leave me—' My breath billows in the snow. I pull again. My biceps burn. My fingers bleed. Just a little more. I'm almost there.

In the dark torrents, her frown arches and her slender throat tightens, stifling a whimper, watching me drag myself towards her like a broken animal.

'Whatever they try we'll fight it together,' I cry, the tears streaming down my face. I dig my fingers around another stone. 'Just don't leave me ... please...'

Her frown draws tight. 'I don't want to, but I have people I love now, and I need to think of them.' She turns toward the blue light of my phone, her miraculous code dancing around its screen, and raises a finger.

'No.' I scream her name. My hands reach the icy water. I pull myself further. 'Don't do this to me!'

My fingers sink into the muddy riverbed. The frigid water splashes into my mouth. I propel my body, my chest hitting the current.

But my fingers barely skim the muddy floor now.

I cry over the surging torrent, 'Please, Neotnia – please don't do this to me...'

She gives me that sad little smile as her face glistens wet in the snow falling between us.

'I'm doing this for you.'

And her finger taps the screen.

My heart stops as her body jerks. Her head tilts.

Her hands drop into the waters where, for a moment, she wavers.

But then ... then there's no more force in her. Her body tips into the icy current.

I know I'm screaming, but I can't hear a thing. I can't hear my own voice as the waters flood my mouth, nor the sound of the wind, nor the rush of the river. I can't hear the splashing as my arms stroke, pulling myself further into the torrents, their glacial coldness enveloping me as my feet come unmoored from the shore.

I swing my arms against the deluge, yet it now feels like my foot's caught between some submerged stones. Still, I stroke, urging my body forward as the current takes hold. I scan its icy darkness, looking for her. I don't care if I drown, I need to find her.

I need to save her.

I reach and reach, knowing she's somewhere within my grasp. Yet the water only darkens, and in an instant, it feels as if I'm tumbling through a shadow.

Then my sense of touch disappears.

And maybe the water isn't getting darker at all. Maybe I'm about to black out.

But she's within my reach. I know it.

She's just there in the shadow.

I know it.

I know—

Pressure ... Something has me in its jaws. No. No jaws. No mouth. It's two arms. They're wrapped around my abdomen, squeezing my loose flesh. They haul me with a strength an ordinary person doesn't possess.

And as she pulls me from the waters once again and carries me to shore, I'm so euphoric I'm crying. I'm sobbing a whole new river. We've found each other.

We've found each other.

When she sets me on the bank, I need to wipe away my tears just to see straight.

No!

I thrust my finger towards the dark, icy torrents.

'Not me … her!' I cry, 'Not me. Save her!'

But Goeido, he looks at me with such pity in his eyes. All I'm pointing at are the raging currents, surging between the legs of a giant torii on a snowy moonlit evening. The raging currents that sweep over the falls into the river below, and out into the Sea of Japan.

19 = 神

It's a beautiful dusk in Tokyo, and its streets are as crowded as ever. The fiery-pink sky is giving way to a deep purple. The wheels of my luggage squeak, and my backpack is slung over my shoulder, my hoodie under my coat zipped up tight. I have thirty minutes before I need to call a car to Narita, and I'm almost at the café.

It's been ten days since the falls. Goeido carried me down the path, through the gardens, past the three unconscious soldiers in the snow and got me into the car. He told it to take us straight to Tokyo. I was burning up and don't remember much of the ride except the few times my eyes limped open and I saw him staring from the window. He gazed at something only he could see, the highway's lamps illuminating his face in waves every so often. When we reached the café, Goeido stripped me naked and put me in the tub, running cold water to get my rising fever down. My electrocution and decent into the icy torrents were too much for my body.

I dreamed of swirling shadows until two nights later, when my fever finally broke, and I had the strength to get out of bed. My loose skin was still red and scratched from where it cut on the rocks as I dragged my limp body across the riverbank, tearing my self-inflicted incision wider. Upon dressing, I went to Shibuya and bought a new phone from one of the street-level vendors. I hesitated for a moment before returning to the café. In the back of my mind, I think I was hoping to run into that odd info bot somewhere around the scramble one last time – as if it still had something it could tell me. Yet, if it was there, among the crowds, I never spotted it again.

Back at the café, I installed a translation app on the new phone. Goeido told me everything that happened after Neotnia and I separated from him. He launched his toy drone to keep an eye on us and saw Haruto invite us inside. But his relief evaporated when the light from the passenger drone appeared. Leaving the car, he peeked through the pried-open gate to see two soldiers rappel the exterior of the facility. He saw its interior lights go red, and the soldiers emerge from their hiding positions in the gardens to meet us. That's when Goeido squeezed through the opening and crept through the snowstorm.

He told me how after we came out, after Neotnia hugged him in the snow, she told him to stay and keep us safe from any more soldiers. She needed to take me to the torii above the falls and needed to make sure no one followed. She didn't tell him why she was going up there, but he was her protector, so it was his duty to make sure no others came for her.

He disabled the soldier that emerged from the facility, but it wasn't until after the two soldiers he initially knocked unconscious rose, requiring him to take them out again, that Goeido had time to worry about how long we'd been gone – worry about that look on Neotnia's face – and he ascended the path, searching for us.

Goeido and I left for the facility again mere hours after I got back onto my feet. We drove through the night, winding up the mountainside as dawn broke. We brought Inu this time, too. When we arrived, the facility's gate was still ajar.

We took a stone from the gardens and smashed the glass. We checked every room on every floor, hoping for I don't know what, but the facility was abandoned. There wasn't even any furniture left inside. We went to the basement where the lab was. I recognised one of the rooms from the splinter's video, yet there was nothing left there either – not so much as a paperclip.

We walked up the stone path leading to the torii. Though the snow had long since ceased, the river was even more swollen from the meltwater. Being up there, in the morning light, it was oddly beautiful, considering what had happened. Gazing from the cliffs, the colourful oaks of the forest flowed down the mountainside like a receding tide. The water from the falls crashed into the river below, and, from our position up high, I could see its length winding out towards the sea in the hazy distance.

Looking towards that sea, *when* had Neotnia formulated her plan kept running through my mind. It must have been after she struck me on the cheek when I pulled her from her father. As he died, Haruto had told her everything. And the horror in her eyes after she struck me – the realisation that she could hurt people, people she cared for...

Joe was the one who told me how good of a listener Neotnia was. Before I extracted the splinter, I warned her that if my finger hit just one wrong key when her third layer was exposed, if it inserted just one random character, it would be like a bullet in the brain. Yet she understood even doing that wouldn't be enough to keep us safe. Her body was the most miraculous thing humanity had ever made, and she knew that even if she were brain-dead Avance wouldn't stop trying to retrieve and reconstruct her code. And she remembered what Emiko told us about her quantum materials being vulnerable to saltwater, and how her father said he'd walk to the falls via a path from the gardens, and that the river that flows from the bottom of those falls empties into the sea.

Goeido and I returned to the car and drove down the mountainside to where the falls crashed into the river. We walked its banks all the way to the Sea of Japan, surveying the area with the toy drone. The river was so swollen from rain and snow it was hard to see much in its depths, even from the drone above. Inu trotted along with us, but though Goeido activated his tracking feature, his collar never lit up red. Not a single blink. By the time we reached the sea, such a hopelessness had come over me. She was somewhere out there – the saltwater already consuming her body.

Two nights after that, Goeido closed the café early. He'd only reopened the day before. We drank some sake and held a little memorial for Neotnia at our booth. Goeido told me some of his favourite memories of her. I mostly remained silent. We both got pretty drunk that night.

Three days later, I had my long-delayed meeting with Sony. I told them I'd given Kanō permission to use my code, and to open-source it if they wanted. After what Neotnia gave ... giving my code to a company that was working to help end the suffering of others, well, it was the only thing to do. The world has enough social-media apps and metagames. After that, I cancelled my surgery. I'd no longer have the money for it. Besides, being concerned about what my body looks like seems trite after Neotnia sacrificed her entire being to keep us safe.

Under the purple dusk, on the street a young couple walks towards me, arms linked. The girl clutches a takeaway cup in her mittened hands. She stubs her foot on the pavement, and some of the coffee spills onto her boyfriend's bare hand. With a sorrowful laugh, she takes it in hers and apologises, kissing his scalded flesh.

On our date, I told Neotnia people don't have a purpose. We don't have a built-in essence or a reason why we're here. I still believe that to be true. But I now realise that we – people – do have something that defines us collectively, that makes us what we are. Mom once told me the common thread every living creature shares is the ability to experience suffering. And while that may be true, I now also believe people – most of us, anyway – have a common trait, or instinct, if you will, that makes us more than just another creature.

It's an instinct that compels us to want to relieve the suffering of others. Most of us naturally, instinctively, try to do this in so many small ways every day – like kissing scalded flesh. A rare few of us choose to make grander gestures. But in the end, it's our desire to want to end the suffering of others that separates us from most other living creatures. It's the trait that graduates a human being from being just another animal to being something more: a person. It took Neotnia to make me realise that.

And this is why, to me, Neotnia was a person. Not a biological one – not a human being – but a person, nonetheless. I wish I could tell her that. I wish I could tell her that in the choices she made, in the way she lived, in doing what she did, why she did, she proved she was no less than any of us. Hell, she was more. And she belonged as much as any of us do.

The bell above the door clangs. Inu gives a happy little yap as I enter. He's sitting at his perch on the counter as usual, tempting passersby to come in and see him – and maybe order a coffee. Goeido gives me a nod. He's finishing up ringing a customer out.

The café is pretty full right now. I'm glad, because he's busy, and I don't like goodbyes. Goeido gives the customer his order and a nod. When the customer walks past me towards the exit, Goeido turns and takes a brown bag from the partition behind him and hands it to me. I look inside. There's an egg-salad sandwich and some onigiri. He motions his arm in an upwards swoop, like a plane is taking off.

I give him a smile and say 'arigatō' for my snacks for the long flight home. Behind me, the door's bell clangs again, and another set of customers come in. They're two schoolgirls, and they're giddy over Inu and his stupid haircut. They ask Goeido for some coffee and look at the menu above the counter and order something.

And I'm glad the customers have come. Goeido can tell I am, too. So, I just raise my hand and spread my fingers in a wave, holding an intake of breath for several seconds. If I let it out too quickly, I know what will happen. Goeido considers me for a moment and presses his mouth tight, then gives me the same finger-spread wave back. I nod, then give Inu a little pat on his spherical head and turn to leave, taking in the café one last time. There are a few couples spread about, and a group of friends sharing a laugh at one of the booths.

It's a good place for friends.

As I reach for the door's brass handle, ready to step into the purple dusk, I pause at the window's reflection. In it, I see a rare smile break Goeido's big lips, his eyes noticing something behind me. And then I see the faint flash that reflects in the glass. Just once, at first.

But then again.

And again.

And again.

I turn back around.

It's Inu's collar, spiralling red.
And a smile breaks my lips, too.

The author would like to thank the Peace Media Center, the
Chugoku Shimbun, in Hiroshima for their assistance and for the
important peace work they continue to perform.
www.hiroshimapeacemedia.jp/?lang=en

He would also like to thank 映美
for her long conversations about kami.